Tessa Wilson is a ps̶ [text obscured]
was born and brought [text obscured]
of the Fens. He attend̶ [text obscured]
and his love of East Anglia – its landscape, people and
history – has always been central to his life and work.
He submitted his first novel, MASTER OF
MORHOLM, for publication at the age of twenty-
three, at which time he was a student on the University
of East Anglia MA Course in Creative Writing, under
Malcolm Bradbury and Angela Carter. His MA
submission was part of the novel which was later
published in 1989 as TREADING ON SHADOWS.
His six most recent historical sagas, A GREEN HILL
FAR AWAY, HEARTSEASE ('a beautifully written
novel' *Fife Free Press*), HESTER VERNEY ('a lovely
book' Reay Tannahill), ROSES IN DECEMBER ('a
spellbinding summer read' *Peterborough Evening
Telegraph*), JOHN TWOPENNY ('filled to bursting
with memorable characters' *Peterborough Evening
Telegraph*) and THE STRAWBERRY SKY are all
available from Headline, as are his five crime thrillers,
PURGATORY, CLOSE TO YOU, FREEZING
POINT, I SPY . . . and CRUEL TO BE KIND. He was
shortlisted for *The Sunday Times* Young Writer of the
Year Award for 1992. He and his partner Mary-Anne
live in Peterborough with two cats.

# The Poppy Path

Tessa Wilson

**HEADLINE**

First published in 1997
by HEADLINE BOOK PUBLISHING

First published in paperback in 1998
by HEADLINE BOOK PUBLISHING

10  9  8  7  6  5  4  3  2  1

ISBN 0 7472 4946 6

Typeset by CBS, Felixstowe, Suffolk

Printed and bound in Great Britain by
Clays Ltd, St Ives plc

HEADLINE BOOK PUBLISHING
A division of Hodder Headline PLC
338 Euston Road
London NW1 3BH

For Kathleen Johnson

# ONE

'Is a bear bigger than a lion, Miss Jordan?'

'I don't know. I would have thought so. But I suppose it depends what sort of bear it is.'

'I like brown bears best. Do you think they'll have brown bears?'

'Probably. Now let's hear your finger exercises.'

Six days a week Rose Jordan worked at Madame Carette's music shop on the corner of Shipden High Street. She served at the counter where they sold sheet music and gramophone records and rosin, and she waited on those customers who came in to look at musical instruments – usually one of the highly polished pianos that took up most of the floor space of the shop, but sometimes a violin or one of the intricate, silvery accordions that were displayed in the window between the portrait busts of Handel and Bach who, like a pair of bewigged gossips, forever looked out across the market square.

In the afternoons and on Saturday mornings she gave piano lessons in a music room upstairs, separated from Madame Carette's private apartments by a bead curtain through which would filter, sometimes, the smell of that lady's herby cooking and the squawking of her grey parrot.

Most of Rose's pupils were children and with most of them she got along very well; but the little girl called Olivia, who was eight years old and wore her hair in stiff black pigtails that gave her a look of oriental gravity, was something of a favourite of hers.

1

'Very good, Olivia. I can tell you've been practising. Now your scales, please.'

'I always practise when I come home from school. Daddy says it goes right through his head sometimes and when am I going to learn to play a tune? Do you think there'll be a camel?'

'Oh, I should think so.'

'With humps?'

'Well, it wouldn't be much of a camel without humps. Now, your scales, please.'

Olivia had been coming for piano lessons every Saturday since the end of last year. Rose had learnt to tell the difference between a pupil who mastered lessons because it made life with demanding parents easier and one who, like Olivia, had a genuine facility and flair for music. All the little girl lacked was concentration. Her lively mind was easily distracted from the task in hand, especially when, as today, she had an exciting prospect in view. Her parents had promised her a trip to the zoo and the thought of it kept bubbling up.

'Miss Jordan,' once again the pigtails swung round and the big eyes met Rose's in solemn excitement, 'how did the animals get to the zoo in the first place? Say an elephant – that would live miles and miles away in another country, wouldn't it?'

'Yes – they must bring them by ship, I suppose.'

'But then when the ship gets to the place where ships stop – you know . . .'

'A dock?'

'Yes, then what? How would they get the elephant from the dock to the zoo?'

'Well now. It would have to go either by road or by rail. But I must say I've never *seen* an elephant travelling like that. And you could hardly miss it, could you? If you had an elephant sharing your railway carriage.' Olivia giggled and Rose, beginning to laugh too, went on, 'And think how confusing it would be if the porter offered to carry his trunk. "Certainly not. I have always carried my own trunk, thank you very much. What? Put it in the luggage van? How dare you!"'

2

The little girl leant against her, laughing, just in the way Elizabeth did when Rose told her stories before bedtime, embellishing them as she went along and putting on different voices. Rose felt touched and pleased, and then admonished herself. She was meant to be teaching Olivia piano: that was what her parents paid for.

As if echoing this thought, the little girl sat up and said, 'Mummy said I wasn't to keep talking on about it.'

'Well, it's natural that you're excited. But now I think we should have your arpeggios.'

The girl applied herself to the keyboard. The faint frown of concentration on her smooth brow, the way her lower lip jutted forward, again reminded Rose of Elizabeth. She found herself picturing the two little girls playing together, hunting for shells and starfish along the pebble beach below the sea wall, or running along the sands at the foot of the western cliffs. For a moment she could hear their voices calling to each other and the bright free sound of their laughter in the open air.

Olivia's eyes sought hers.

'Miss Jordan?'

'Yes . . . yes, that was very good. Remember to keep your wrists lifted, like this. Then you won't get that stiffness in your fingers.'

'My friend Margaret got her fingers trapped in the door! She screamed and screamed. It made her mummy have her nerves.' The girl leant towards Rose in candid confessional. 'Margaret hasn't got a daddy.'

Reaching out to reset the metronome, Rose paused. 'Hasn't she?' She found she could not quite meet the large eyes that were fixed so luminously on her.

'He didn't come back from the war.'

'. . . That's very sad.'

'He got a medal after he got killed,' Olivia said. 'I don't see the point of that, do you?'

'No,' Rose said, 'I don't see the point of that.' She looked

3

at the clock on the mantelshelf. 'Now I think there's just time to try that little piece of Bach before your mother comes.'

The little girl's mother, Mrs Betts, was a large frothy woman who always wore furs and whose voice could presently be heard in the shop below, assuring Madame Carette in cheerful, penetrating tones that she knew her way up. When she swept into the music room it was with an effect as if several people had come in.

Rose stood up.

'Well, my darling, have you been good? Probably not,' Mrs Betts boomed, caressing the pigtails with a kid-gloved hand. 'Miss Jordan, I dare say you've heard precious little music today and a great deal about zoo animals. Never mind. They do get so taken with an idea at that age, don't they? I only wish, my dear, that I could be that enthusiastic about *anything* nowadays.'

Fleshy and healthy and voluptuous, Mrs Betts laughed while Olivia clung affectionately to her fur-swathed arm.

'Olivia's coming along very well,' Rose said. 'Even with the elephants and camels.'

'She does seem to have a gift for it, doesn't she? Heaven knows where she gets it from. I can't play a note and Mr Betts is absolutely tone-deaf. Just between the two of us he's a fearful grump about the music and doesn't see the use of it. But that's men, isn't it? We adore them of course but they're frightfully lacking in imagination sometimes. Quite at the opposite extreme from these young ones who I'm afraid can have too much of it. We bought Olivia a Mother Goose with Rackham's wonderful pictures but the poor child had nightmares from looking at them.'

Olivia confirmed this with a blush and a rueful look.

'It's all very well to dismiss these night terrors,' Mrs Betts said, 'but I remember suffering from them terribly as a child.'

'And it's not much use saying there are no such things as ghosts and goblins, because you picture them so vividly when you're small that there might as well be,' Rose said.

'Exactly. And it's not as if the world isn't a frightening place. After all, twenty or even ten years ago who would have believed that there would be airships in the skies over dear old England jolly well dropping bombs on us? But it happened. All over now, thankfully. We must make sure these little ones never have to go through a time like that again. Luckily I'm an optimist, aren't you?'

'I think it's the only way to live.'

'That's because you've got a woman's sense. Of course one can't wholly shield children from beastly things even though one wants to. This is the dilemma. One wants them to grow up strong and unafraid but to do that they must take the knocks. I don't mind telling you how I blenched when we had to take Olivia to a dentist. There was an infection of the gum and the man had to dig deep and the poor child fairly yelled, didn't you, darling? And every cry absolutely went through me. But what is one to do?'

'You can't sit in the dentist's chair for them,' Rose said, 'no matter how much you want to.'

'This is precisely it. And then there are the childhood illnesses. The poor mites have to spend so much time covered in spots and swathed in flannel and really the whole thing seems most unfair. It's as well to get them over with early but of course one can hardly explain that without it seeming dreadfully cold comfort. Thankfully Olivia's already had the measles and the chickenpox, so the worst is behind her, but I'm still rather a fusspot and send for the doctor at the first sign, which I dare say he thoroughly despises me for.'

'Oh, I understand,' Rose said eagerly, 'I'm the same with my little girl. And of course when they're very small they can't really tell you how ill they feel, so it's best to be on the safe side and let the doctor think what he likes.'

'I'm sorry, my dear,' Mrs Betts said, head back, only her mouth smiling. 'I don't quite follow. Your little girl . . .?'

'Yes,' Rose said. 'Her name's Elizabeth.'

For a second the change was not apparent. Mrs Betts'

posture of smiling attention did not alter: she merely said, 'Oh?' And then she stopped whatever it was she had been about to say. It was as if the words were literally snatched from her mouth, leaving nothing but a long, slow, audible breath. Her left hand was pressed to the fur stole at her bosom and it tapped there twice, plump and peremptory, as she said, 'Oh,' again and looked at Rose's left hand and then at Rose's face.

'Oh,' Mrs Betts said again, this time on a note of utter finality.

Then she took hold of Olivia's hand and walked smartly out of the room.

Rose remained where she was, breathing a little hard, one hand resting on the lid of the piano. As she stood there some detached and dispassionate part of herself analysed the precise form that Mrs Betts' reaction had taken, and came to the conclusion that she had not exactly looked indignant, or angry, or embarrassed or disdainful. She had looked rather as if she had accidentally seen something discreditable, like the commission of a crime or a man relieving himself against a tree, and had chosen to pretend that she had seen nothing.

Yes, that was it. A new one, at any rate.

Downstairs in the shop Rose could hear Mrs Betts' strong voice, mingled with the more muted tones of Madame Carette. She tidied the music room and stirred the fire that the tardy spring still made a necessity, postponing going downstairs not so much out of fear of her employer as to give herself time.

Time to calm down and collect herself; time to wonder how it was that she had been betrayed into such incaution. For four years she had schooled herself against impulsive revelation; she had taken caution into the marrow of her bones. Rose felt disappointed in herself as much as in Mrs Betts. Quite simply, she should have known better.

But it was one thing to be cautious, and another to be frigidly reserved. There had seemed to be a great openness

6

and sympathy about the big fur-swathed lady, and Rose could not help but respond in kind. And when the limits of that sympathy had been so curtly revealed, Rose had still felt a momentary shock. Even after four years' experience, it could still come as a shock to find a person's opinion of you wholly reversed by that simple piece of information.

It was not true to say that she didn't mind for herself. She minded a great deal. She didn't long for the good opinion of someone like Mrs Betts; given what had just happened, it wasn't worth having. But she minded being judged and she minded being condemned to a shame that she did not feel.

Most of all, though, she minded for Elizabeth's sake. When Rose had made her decision to bring up her child here in Shipden, she had known there would be snubs. She did not accept the morality behind them but she accepted that they were inevitable. And she could put up with them: she had done so before and would again.

But the thought of Elizabeth being looked at as she herself had just been looked at . . . that was something else again. And this encounter with Mrs Betts, precisely because it had begun with what should have been an innocent conversation about children, raised more sharply than ever the question of Elizabeth's future that had been nagging at Rose of late.

While Elizabeth was very small, things were simpler. It was the mother, Rose, who came in for the unpleasantness; it was possible to protect the child almost completely. But Elizabeth was growing. And as Mrs Betts herself had said, you couldn't shield children for ever. The world had a stake in them.

Downstairs the voices ceased and the shop door banged.

Rose's heartbeat quickened as it occurred to her that protecting her child from the sneers of the world was not, after all, the most immediate of her concerns just now.

Her job was.

Without work, she couldn't even support Elizabeth.

It seemed likely, from the tone of the voices downstairs, that Mrs Betts had complained to Madame Carette. It was possible, indeed, that she had withdrawn her custom altogether. It had happened before, twice, though never in quite these circumstances: a new pupil's lessons had been cancelled at the last moment, another had abruptly stopped coming; and there had been no doubt in either case what was behind the sudden change. There were many worse employers than Madame Carette, but she was a fretful lady, understandably anxious as a foreigner in a small town to preserve her good name, and her patience was far from limitless.

Rose turned cold with misgiving as she thought of Elizabeth and what that momentary lapse might mean for them both.

'Rose! Rose, come here!'

Madame Carette was calling up the stairs to her, sharply.

# TWO

'It is not fair, Rose. It is not fair that I am worried like this.'

Madame Carette had come to England in 1914 as a refugee from the war in Belgium. Her husband, a professional musician, had stayed behind and died fighting at Ypres. His bloodstained battledress had been sent to her in a brown paper parcel. The sale of such property as she had been able to salvage had enabled her to start the music shop in Shipden and there she chose to remain after the war ended. 'Go home?' she had said once to Rose. 'What for? The Boche took everything away. They finished it. God punish them and their children.' This outburst of bitterness in her was rare: the Madame Carette whom Rose knew and had worked for these past two years was a sentimental, greedy, prosy lady, her nature diffused and enveloping rather like the voluminous print shawls and scarves she wore. In the overheated rooms above the shop, crowded with fringes and beads and Tiffany lamps, she kept a cat as well as the grey parrot. The two were at eternal enmity and every time the cat tried to get the bird she was as hurt and disappointed as if it had never happened before. At forty she had grown plump but retained a skin of waxen fairness, and with her abundant piled-up hair and almond eyes and grand, jet-garlanded bosom there was a matronly sort of sensuality about her. It was most exceptional in a place like Shipden and it was perhaps this touch of the alien, this hint of the outcast, that had made her look favourably on Rose at a time when most of Shipden kept a disdainful distance.

But Madame Carette did not like trouble. She liked comfort

and sweet things and mild gossip; and anything that threatened her enjoyment of these things made her fractious.

'It is too much. No, really, it is too much. My nerves are not strong, I shall . . . I don't know what will happen to me.' Half-pathetic, half-waspish, Madame Carette paced between the gleaming pianos, her ringed fingers nervously pressed to her cheeks, her jet necklaces, and the pince-nez that she wore on a chain, swinging and rattling in her agitation. 'When I am spoken to in that way in my own shop, what is there – what am I to do? It is too much. I cannot suffer in this way.'

Rose came forward. 'Madame Carette – please tell me what happened.'

'That woman. She says I have misled her. It is not fair I should be blamed,' Madame Carette said, patting her breast with a venomous look; then, her tone altering a little, 'Though she's lying – I never misled her. And if you are Miss Jordan and have a child, what then? You can still teach the piano. I don't understand people – after all that has happened, all that terrible war, and still this . . . Well, no matter. The little girl will not be back. No more lessons. Not respectable, the mother says. Not respectable.'

At the pitch of her anxiety, Rose found room for a fleeting regret that she would see no more of Olivia.

'I'm very sorry,' Rose said. 'Quite by chance I mentioned that I had a daughter too, and . . . that was the end of it.'

'Perhaps not the end. Who knows? The woman must have friends – what will she say about my shop? No, no, it's no good – I cannot be upset like this.' Madame Carette turned from her. 'We shall have to part, Rose. It's the only way.'

'Madame Carette – please . . .' Rose tried not to show it, but she was thrown almost into panic. There was so little work to be had in Shipden – at least until the holiday season began – and the strain it would place on Aunt Dolly . . .

'I'm sorry, Rose.' Madame Carette waved a fluttery hand and would not look at her. 'I cannot be troubled like this. I know it's not your fault, but people – people have these ideas about a woman like you and they will not change them. I don't agree with them, but what can I do?'

Madame Carette's voice quavered. She was habitually tearful and would cry as readily at happy things as at sad ones, savouring the emotions like sweets. And for an instant Rose found herself about to put her hand out and touch Madame Carette's arm and appeal, in the most blatant way, to her incorrigible sentimentality. It might well work; and if it meant, from a strict point of view, that she was manipulating the lady's weakness, the circumstances surely justified it.

But Rose did see it from a strict point of view. This was perhaps her own weakness: she was stern about truth. Getting Madame Carette to change her mind simply by drowning the whole question in tears seemed to her untruthful in a way she could not countenance. It was pretending.

So she did not reach out for her employer's arm: nor did she reach out for the lady's all too vulnerable capacity for feeling. She only said, 'I'm very sorry, Madame Carette. Could I carry on here until I find another job? If not a month, then at least a fortnight.'

'I don't know what to do,' Madame Carette said vaguely, going to the window and peering out. 'It's so hard that I should be alone like this. I don't know. All I know is that it cannot go on this way. I'm sorry, Rose—'

All at once her cottage-loaf head bobbed excitedly. She ducked low, trying at once to see and not to be seen between the busts and the accordions and the music stands, her necklaces swinging and rattling.

'Rose! Look! The new doctor. He's parking his car near the church. Quick – you will see him.'

In the excitement of curiosity Madame Carette seemed wholly to forget what they had been talking about. It was hardly likely that Rose could dismiss it so quickly, and she stood in bemused surprise for several moments too long.

'Quick – he's getting out of his car. There – ah, *chut*, you missed him.' Madame Carette sighed and patted her bosom,

11

eyes alight with inquisitiveness. 'He has a bearing – a true bearing. They say he is from London. Old Dr Vickery speaks very highly of him. Rose, you were so slow! You could have seen him!'

There was a general interest in this newcomer, who had come to the town a month or so ago to take over the retiring Dr Vickery's practice. As far as Rose knew she had yet to set eyes on him, but she was only mildly curious to do so – and certainly at this moment the matter of the new doctor could hardly have been less urgent.

'Madame Carette—'

'Yes, quite a bearing. I wish you had seen him. He went into Gunnell's Haberdashery.' Madame Carette's fluting accent made this sound like a sophisticated establishment, with a select clientele of boulevardiers, rather than the dismal grotto where customers groped about, bumping their hips against the counters, because Mr Gunnell was too mean to light the gas. 'Well,' Madame Carette went on, 'there is the car anyway. You can see the car.'

There were still not many cars in Shipden in 1920, but the sight was familiar enough for Rose to see that the car had been parked rather badly. One wheel was up on the kerb and the rear stuck out at an angle so that old Mr Coxon, the bellringer, wobbling along the High Street on his bicycle as he had done so often that he no longer looked at the road, very nearly ran into it.

Again Rose tried to bring her employer back to the point. 'Madame Carette, please, I need to know—'

'Now what can he be buying there? I wonder. Perhaps shoelaces. Or a hatband. Or collar-studs, perhaps.' Again her liquid tones gave these articles a certain glamour and poetry. 'Unless it's an emergency. Someone sick. Of course, a doctor, what am I thinking of? Oh, *mon dieu*, what a terrible thing. Perhaps it's Mrs Gunnell—'

'Did the doctor seem to be in a hurry?'

'Well – not really. No.'

'Then I'm sure everything's all right.'

'Of course. How silly . . . You calm me down, Rose. Always you calm me down.' She turned her pretty, misty eyes on Rose. 'I don't know what I've been saying. I cannot bear upset and yet I don't want to lose you . . . Let us carry on as we are, yes?'

'I do want to stay – very much. But if what happened today happens again . . .?'

'Oh, let's forget about it. Let's worry about that when the time comes,' Madame Carette said. She waved the question away with a flick of her wrist, and returned her attention to the view of the square from the window.

'Well, thank you, Madame Carette,' Rose said.

There was relief, enormous relief. Yet still she felt the question had not truly been settled. In her heart she felt that this was at best a postponement; and it was part of that rather stern regard for truth that Rose hated uncertainty.

She was prevented from saying anything more just then by the jingle of the shop doorbell.

'Afternoon, ladies. Just thought I'd step in and say how do.'

Mr Seymour Gaze used these exact words every time he came into the shop, which was two or three times a week. And always too he would enter with a sort of tentative sidling motion, as if the music shop were filled with whirling and perhaps dangerous activity, like a sawmill; pausing just inside the door with a placating smile and nervous wipings of his hands across the white front of his apron before advancing further.

'Mr Gaze, did you see? The new doctor. There's his car,' Madame Carette said, keeping her station at the window.

'A Talbot, I believe,' Mr Gaze said. 'Very natty.'

He had come all the way in now, and stood with his hands tucked into the waistband of his apron and his mild eyes amiably roaming around the shop but always, at last, alighting on Madame Carette. Mr Gaze kept the barbershop next door.

13

He was a fleshy man of forty-odd with jet-black hair parted so cleanly and severely down the middle of his head that the parting resembled a stripe. It gave him the look of a badger, and there was something badger-like too in the way he kept his head down and enquired after Rose's and Madame Carette's health in a snuffly, cakey voice.

They said they were both well; and Mr Gaze said at once with a pouncing readiness, 'You look it too. You look it, I should say. Blooming, in fact – that's what I'd call it.'

'But of course,' Madame Carette said with a tinkling laugh, 'a *Rose* should be blooming.'

'Absolutely,' Mr Gaze said, dipping his badger-like head in Rose's direction. 'A blooming Rose. I don't just mean Rose though – I mean the other rose as well. The one who ain't called Rose.' Scarlet-cheeked, he kept his eyes fixed on Madame Carette while he laboured his way through these compliments. His admiration of her was of long standing, and expressed itself in a cheeky banter that was also terribly bashful. Whenever she did look at him, he seemed to quiver at the knees. But it was doubtful whether she noticed this. She was as oblivious as he was devoted.

'Come to think of it,' he said, 'I don't reckon I've heard your first name, Madame C. That's a rum thing, isn't it? – what with you and me knowing each other all this time. I wonder what it could be now. Something . . .' he gave his characteristic quiver as Madame Carette briefly turned her dreamy eyes to him before looking out at the square again, 'something with a bit o' refinement, I reckon.'

'Well, you must know it begins with M,' Madame Carette said absently, 'because that is written on the shop door.'

'Is it now? Well, so it is. Only I'd always took that M to mean Madame, as it happens.'

'No, no. In French M only stands for Monsieur.'

'Does it now? Well, I went wrong there. I was pretty wide of the mark there.' Mr Gaze winked at Rose, puffing humorously and working himself up to a new compliment.

'Nobody could ever mistake you for a monsieur, that's for sure. Anybody who'd mistake you for a monsieur—'

'My name is Marie,' Madame Carette said.

'I knew that'd be something like that. That fits you like a glove, that do.' Flame-faced, Mr Gaze seemed to feel he had gone too far, and said hastily, 'So how's trade?'

Trade was good: trade was picking up everywhere. Rationing was over and people were enthusiastically turning to the good things of life again after the years of grim necessity. There was a passion for music, and not only the music that Madame Carette had known in her youth and that had been played by the late Monsieur Carette. Even in provincial Shipden there was a demand for the new kinds of dance music from America. Madame Carette did not much like this, but she had to please her customers.

'And you, Mr Gaze?' She moved reluctantly away from the window. 'Do you thrive?'

'Well, the photography side's picking up,' Mr Gaze said cautiously. Behind his barber saloon he kept a photographic studio. These odd conjunctions were not uncommon in Shipden, where even the undertaker also ran an ice-making service in the summer months. 'I'm booked for half a dozen weddens between now and May. Weddens are all the rage again, seem'ly.'

His eye accidentally alighted on Rose as he said this; and he looked wildly away as if about to flee.

'I was married in May,' Madame Carette sighed, her encrusted bosom heaving. 'I was so happy. I hope they will all be happy.'

'Well, there's one wedden I've been booked for three times over. They keep fixing a date and then crying off. So that don't look too hot,' Mr Gaze said thoughtfully.

'With me and Philippe there was never any doubt,' Madame Carette said, seating herself on a piano stool and raptly gazing at her left hand. 'I was so lucky. It can only happen once.'

Mr Gaze looked glumly down at her elegantly lowered head

and jingled the change in his pockets.

'Ah well,' he said, 'I'd better get back to the shop. See wha' that boy of mine's about.' A regretful bachelor, Mr Gaze employed a nephew as an apprentice. 'He'll turn out all righ' at the hairdressing, I reckon, but when that come to money he's a donkey. Never known the like of it. Can't give change to save his soul. They can't be teaching 'em their sums righ' at school nowadays is all I can think.' As if to make up for his earlier embarrassment, he bestowed a meek smile on Rose and said, 'I dare say that little chicken of yours'll be starting school soon, eh?'

'Yes, it'll – it'll soon be that time. She's looking forward to it, I think.'

'Grow so fast, don't they?' Mr Gaze said. Loneliness had made him kind. 'She'll be bright, I'll bet. Take after her mother.'

Rose thought of her own mother, shortly before she had died, opening her eyes and with startling suddenness hissing from the bed the words, '*Fool. Stupid, stupid fool.*'

'It is a sad world,' Madame Carette mourned to herself, still caressing the ring on her left hand. 'Children are a ray of light in this sad world. They give you hope for the future.'

Mr Gaze looked unhappily at her: Rose sensed two different sorts of loneliness that could not touch each other.

'Well, I must love you and leave you,' Mr Gaze said; and then, seeming to find that remark outstandingly unfortunate, made a sort of hurried scuttle for the door.

It was only after he had gone that Madame Carette came out of her abstraction. She lifted her head and for consolation popped into her mouth one of the Parma violet cachous of which she was fond and which left their purple fragrance everywhere she went.

'Oh – did Mr Gaze go away?'

'He went back to his shop,' Rose said.

'I was in a dream,' Madame Carette said, getting up and going to the window. Looking out, she gave a squeal of disappointment.

'What's wrong?'

'The car is gone,' she announced tragically. 'The new doctor's car – he must have gone while Mr Gaze was here. Now you won't see him!'

'Well, never mind,' Rose said, 'I'm sure to see him sooner or later.' This was certainly true. In a small town like Shipden everyone came under public scrutiny – no one knew that better than Rose.

'We missed him,' Madame Carette said, thin-lipped, 'and all because of that man'; and Rose felt that poor Mr Gaze, if he had ever had any chance at all, had quite unwittingly just ruined it.

# THREE

She still had her job: that was the main thing. She had to remind herself of this when she left the music shop and set out for home at one o'clock that day, because she found her mind quite as sore and oppressed as if the worst had happened.

It was that experience with Mrs Betts, of course: the nasty taste of it still lingered. And its consequences too; for notwithstanding Madame Carette's change of heart, Rose knew that from now on she was very much on probation. Next time the scales might very well tip the other way.

Next time. It was utterly unrealistic to suppose that there would not be a next time. That was the way of it in a small rumour-ridden town like Shipden: your past was public property.

Crossing the square in front of the vast flint church, Rose realized what was weighing most heavily on her heart. It was Mr Gaze's simple casual remark about her daughter starting school. That crystallized the dilemma she faced – or rather, that faced her and would no longer be dismissed or denied.

Elizabeth would be mixing with other children and strange adults. If she did not understand just now what it meant to be the child of an unmarried mother, she would soon be made to understand. The sentimental tolerance of Madame Carette, the clumsy kindness of Mr Gaze were the exceptions in a world ruled by the likes of Mrs Betts.

Olivia's little friend had no daddy – but that was because he had been killed in the war. There were many like her just now: children who at the mention of the word 'father' could

19

only point to a photograph of a man in uniform. The ubiquitous war widow was often a mother too.

Here was an irony. Elizabeth was emerging into a world in which being fatherless was far from uncommon. And she was going to learn that she was fatherless in the wrong way. The lesson, judging by Rose's own experience in the past four years, would not be gently administered.

If anything, the loss of all those poor dead heroes in Flanders and France sharpened attitudes, made the stigma worse. Rose recalled last year attending a public meeting in the town hall. It was to discuss plans for a war memorial to Shipden's fallen. A pretty young woman in mourning had given her a look of burning hatred and then spat near Rose's shoe.

And yet . . . In this very situation there was a promise – a possibility. Walking down the High Street where every brick and stone was familiar to her, Rose for the first time allowed herself to confront that possibility. Always before she had set her face against it; now she looked at it squarely.

Go away: leave Shipden with Elizabeth, and begin again somewhere else, where she was not known, under another name.

A married name.

A dress ring on her left hand, perhaps a mourning band on her hat, and the transformation would be complete.

There were practical difficulties involved in this scheme – there would have to be work waiting for her at the place she moved to, first of all – but for the moment she was concerned simply with the idea. She was testing it on herself, like a medicine or a poison.

She drew a succession of swift mental sketches. Signing her name as Mrs Jordan; explaining to Elizabeth's schoolteacher that Mr Jordan was killed in the war; commiserating with another war widow on the loss of her husband over tea and a cake whilst Elizabeth and a faceless other child played together on the floor or in the yard or on the lawn of some other place . . .

20

Poisonous, indeed. She would be, in the most literal sense, living a lie. And a dogged, downright refusal to lie was part of her. It had caused her grief, but it had also been her redemption over the past four years. To adopt the poisonous plan might well make life easier, but it would entail losing something too. Call it pride, self-respect, independence – whatever it was that had kept her free of that word *shame*.

She had never let that word in. She had never let it express her or apply to her position in the slightest. It was what had baffled people; even her mother. 'No shame!' Probably if she were to slink away now and hide behind a conventional identity, people would be grimly satisfied – shame catching up with her at last. But it wasn't what people thought of her that was important to Rose but what she thought of herself.

Which was all very well; but she didn't just have herself to consider. There was Elizabeth. If sacrificing her principles meant giving Elizabeth an easier life, then how could she even hesitate? What did a lie matter, beside the wellbeing of her child?

Lost in thought, wrestling with her heart's stubborn assertion that it did matter, Rose turned from the High Street into Pound Street and felt herself briefly pressed against a tall obstruction.

'Sorry—'

'Not at all—'

Something like that was said; she was so preoccupied that she didn't know who said what. Nor did she even look up at the man's face. All that registered on her mind were his shoes. They were handsewn Oxfords of two-tone leather – not particularly fancy; but there was something dapper about them, and something dapper too about the way their wearer sidestepped nimbly to give her room, almost as if he had broken into a momentary dance.

The impression was brief, but vivid while it lasted. And before her other thoughts returned to displace it, Rose had a strong presentiment that the stranger was the new doctor whom Madame Carette had been so eager for her to see; and hardly knowing why, she stopped and turned back to look.

But there was no sign of him: he must have already turned into the High Street.

And that was how it came about that, the first time she saw him, she didn't really see him at all.

Rose's late mother would not have been surprised at this. She often used to say, accusingly, that Rose went around with her eyes closed. This was true, in so far as she never saw many of the things her mother saw or even guessed their existence. There was a whole repertoire of looks, for example, that she did not understand but which had been plain to her mother. 'Such a look she gave me!' Mrs Jordan would say, or, 'The look on his face!' or, 'He didn't say it – but I could tell by the look he gave her,' in tones somewhere between scandal and satisfaction. Her daughter's failure to notice these things was disappointing, but then so was much about her.

In saying that Rose went about with her eyes closed, however, her mother had come close to a certain physical truth. Rose Jordan's eyes were noticeably heavy-lidded, and shaded by long thick eyelashes. This together with her habit of rapt thoughtfulness gave her a slightly sleepy, unstirred look; and meant that a person meeting her for a short time might not have been able to say afterwards what colour her eyes were.

In fact they were a very dark brown: dark with a concentrated intensity which, when she did lift her heavily fringed eyelids and look straight at you, gave them the piercing quality more usually credited to eyes of pale blue. And it was then that you saw that there was nothing sleepy about her at all.

There was a certain deceptiveness about her stature too. She had the look of being taller than she really was because of her habit of standing very straight, with her shoulders thrown back; and perhaps too because of her bone structure. She was long-legged and long-fingered with slender, pronounced wristbones. Again there was deceptiveness in this apparent delicacy, because she was a physically strong woman, impervious to cold and wet, and capable of walking the five miles from Shipden to Saxburgh, its neighbour on the flinty North Norfolk coast, without quickening her breath. Her hair was brown – but that was a little deceptive too, because in full sunlight you saw red tints glinting in the thick wiry depths of it. And while she looked no more than her twenty-five years, there was an apparent self-possession about her movements and about her deep, unhurried voice that suggested a woman five or even six years older.

It was ironic that there should be this deceptiveness about Rose's appearance, in view of her almost painful honesty and truthfulness. As she walked home that Saturday afternoon and tried to imagine herself living a lie she flinched from the picture almost as if she were planning a murder.

But the events of today had demonstrated to her that a decision would have to be made: one way or another, she was coming to a turning-point.

I'll ask Aunt Dolly about it, she thought suddenly, with an effect on her spirit as of a shadow lifting. I'll ask Aunt Dolly what she thinks. And at that thought, and the thought of seeing Elizabeth again, she began to hurry her steps.

They took her down to the end of Pound Street, a place of modest terracotta-faced shops interrupted by narrow flint-clad houses with steps up to neat green doors and here and there a glimpse into surprising little whitewashed yards, like Dutch paintings, where cats outstared each other from the tops of water butts, and flowers bloomed with solitary brilliance in wooden tubs and planters. They took her past a triangular public house called the Three Horseshoes and into a narrower street, quiet and shadowed, where the few shops had a faded and retiring look and many of the drab newish terraces advertised *Vacancies* in their bay windows and where enamelled signs bearing names like Sea-spray and

Fontainebleau swung grumbling in the breeze above fanlights of coloured glass, dingy from the smoke of the railway station near at hand.

This was Princess Street, and near the very end of it Rose and Elizabeth lived with Aunt Dolly in her squeezed slice of terrace, with a boarding house on one side, and on the other a maker of funerary monuments who bore the inappropriately jolly name of Jos. Tickell. Though Aunt Dolly's place had no shop window and no sign or brass plate, the front door led into a sort of premises. She did dressmaking and mending, and this was her workroom. At the best of times it was untidy, with skirts and sleeves and bodices hanging from the picture rails, the tables heaped with buckram and chiffon and georgette, and the floor covered with scrawled paper patterns; but today when Rose opened the door it looked as if it had been hit by a whirlwind.

'A mouse! Mummy, there was a mouse and we had to catch it!'

Elizabeth flung her arms round Rose's waist and excitedly danced her in.

'Hello, dear,' said Aunt Dolly, who was hastily gathering up armfuls of the scattered fabrics. 'Just a bit of brouhaha, that's all.'

'The mouse came out of a dress and went all over and we had to throw everything up and get it.' Breathless, Elizabeth widened her eyes to vast dimensions to express the drama of the episode.

'Tiny thing,' Aunt Dolly snorted. 'Hardly there. Why God made a creature so small I can't think. Makes no sense to me.' As usual when flustered, she affected grumpiness, hurrying clumsily about and breathing stertorously through her nose.

'What happened to it?' Rose said.

'Well, I caught it and put it outside, of course,' Aunt Dolly said. 'Let the poor thing have its chance. Is it raining, dear? I didn't think so. It never does when you want it to.'

'Why did you want it to, Dolly?' Rose said, helping her clear up.

'To wash the air, of course,' Aunt Dolly snorted. 'I'll do this, dear. I know where everything goes, you see. You can begin dinner if you like.' Half-visible behind great festoons of material, Dolly flapped her away.

Behind the workroom was a little room that was officially known as Aunt Dolly's parlour, though it was where all three of them spent the evenings; and behind that the kitchen and scullery. Rose took her daughter in here and began to make dinner for them whilst Elizabeth chattered, alternately sitting on a bentwood chair and leaving it with a quick slither to fetch something from her own little room upstairs and show it to her mother with much eager explanation.

The house was cramped, a little shabby, and spoke throughout of a constant struggle to make ends meet. The telltale signs were not untidiness and dirt: rather it was the profusion of antimacassars, the careful placing of meagre pieces of furniture to cover a threadbare patch of rug or discoloured area of whitewash, the inviolable neatness of a pair of thin drapes that could never be closed because they would not meet in the middle, that revealed how limited their resources were. Wealth, it occurred to Rose, was being able to move something freely without leaving a gaping hole.

It occurred to her but did not trouble her. She thought of this as a good home and a kind one – kinder indeed than her parental home, certainly after her father had died and she had been left alone with her mother. Even when there was such an upheaval as today – and Aunt Dolly, who could be heard snorting and stamping about even here, was not generally a restful personality – the house still took her into its arms as only a home could.

How much of this was due to the presence of Elizabeth in it she did not know. Certainly whenever she saw Elizabeth after being away for only a short time, and whenever Elizabeth put her small hand into hers, Rose felt nothing less than literally blessed. The mere sight of her daughter conferred a benediction. These were Rose's feelings, and they struck down so deep in the heart of her that nothing else in life had quite the same reality; there were lesser truths, but her love for her daughter was the one great truth that overshadowed all others.

That the bringer of this sense of blessedness was not a saint or angel but a very human child who could be nerve-tearing in her talkativeness, who sometimes fibbed and sometimes sulked and who plainly had her share of Rose's own stubbornness when she believed herself in the right, only added to the miracle in Rose's eyes.

Peeling potatoes at the sink, Rose was visited by a memory of her mother standing in just such an attitude as this, putting flowers into a vase with sharp primping fingers, and saying to Rose out of the back of her head, 'You'll curse it one day, you know. One day you'll look at the child and curse it.'

It didn't matter whether you believed in ghosts or not, Rose thought. You could still be haunted by a person after they were gone.

'Where will that mouse go, Mummy?'

'I don't know. It might go next door to Mr Tickell's.'

'It's not very nice there.'

'That's true.' Having put the potatoes on to boil, Rose dried her hands and came to sit beside her daughter. 'Well, he might go down to the front and stay in a hotel. The Grand or the Metropolitan. Or he might catch a train and go over to Yarmouth.'

Remembering the elephant on the train, remembering Olivia and Mrs Betts, Rose's laughter had something of pain in it. She looked at her daughter – just a few years younger than Olivia – and noted the differences and, more strikingly, the similarities: Elizabeth too was very dark, though her face was rounder and more comfortable, and her hair would have had that same wiry stiffness if its thick unruly bob had been coaxed into pigtails; even the carefree, bubbling note of her laughter was the same.

26

Yet Mrs Betts, with her raised eyebrows and her plump tapping hand and her expressionless, damning 'Oh', would have seen only difference: all the difference in the world.

Rose squeezed the little girl tightly.

'Mummy,' Elizabeth said, taking the hug as a matter of course, 'you got a letter. Shall I fetch it?'

It was from her friend Millie Watlyn. Rose read it with Elizabeth looking over her shoulder. She had already begun teaching her to read and there were several words she could recognize, even in Millie's haphazard handwriting.

The news from Millie was the usual tale of hope deferred but unvanquished. The boarding house at Saxburgh, intended as a temporary expedient until Frank Watlyn, Millie's husband, should realize his prospects, was still their chief source of income – their only source of income, Rose suspected, reading between the lines: Frank had had a golden opportunity but had just missed out to a fly-by-night jerry-builder from Norwich. 'They'll regret that,' Millie wrote, loyal as ever. 'They don't know a good man when they see one.' Now Frank had another project in view – and this one was the chance of a lifetime. Rose remembered the phrase: Millie and Frank had married on the strength of just such a chance. She hoped this one was different.

Millie concluded by inviting Rose and Elizabeth over to Saxburgh to stay next weekend.

'Would you like to go and see Auntie Millie next Saturday?' Rose said to Elizabeth, going to the meat safe above the drainer and taking out the three small chops. The end of rationing had not made a great deal of difference to their housekeeping.

'Yes please. Mummy, how old is Auntie Millie?'

'She's twenty-five, I think. The same as me.'

'Auntie Dolly's old, isn't she?'

'Well. Not that old. But Auntie Millie isn't your real auntie. We call her that because she's nice and she's our friend, like an auntie.'

'Auntie Dolly's my real auntie, isn't she?'

'Yes. Well, she's your great-auntie. That's the same, only older.' Rose glanced at Elizabeth's frown of concentration. At times like this she marvelled that she herself had ever got to grips with such complexities: being a child was like being continually coached for a testing examination.

'Is Uncle Frank my real uncle?'

'No. But he's nice, isn't he?'

'Yes,' Elizabeth said absently, chewing a strand of hair. 'Have I got a real uncle?'

'No.'

'Is that because I haven't got a daddy?'

Rose was saved from having to answer that one by Aunt Dolly, who came noisily in bearing aloft, like a banner, a half-finished frock in voluminous yellow voile.

'I forgot to tell you! Look at this! Guess who I'm making *this* up for. You'll never twig. It's the absolute penultimate.' Dolly hugged the frock to her and spoke with husky relish, eyes wicked and peeping. 'Only Mrs Snell. Can you imagine it? Like a great yellow haystack, I should say. But what can a person do? She would pick it. I just had to bite my tongue.' She began to laugh her whooping laugh, her big untidy bosom quivering under the frothy material. 'I hope it wasn't written all over my face!'

Mrs Snell was the bank manager's wife, and had a fair claim to the throne of queen of Shipden society; she was not petite. While it was not strictly true that there was no malice in Aunt Dolly's laughter, there was a certain innocence in it too. It was her one mild weapon against the patronage of ladies such as Mrs Snell, who used much sharper instruments on each other, and would scarcely have considered that their dressmaker might have an opinion on them at all.

Still chuckling, Aunt Dolly carried the material back to her workroom. 'Well, that's about enough of that for today,' she boomed, coming back and closing the workroom door behind her. 'Mrs Snell was full of this new doctor, by the way. Talked of nothing else. Young, apparently, and unmarried. One can

28

only assume that people are planning on marrying him off already. But I thought the Snell girl was already engaged to some chap from Wells-next-the-Sea.'

'She was,' Rose said, setting the chops to fry. 'She married him last month.'

'Of course, of course she did.' Dolly stomped into the kitchen and peered into the pan of potatoes. Steam wreathed her big jowly face with its hint of silvery moustache, making her look like a jovial witch, and again there was a glint of mischief as she turned to wink at Rose and said, 'Well, unless Mrs Snell is hoping to set her cap at him herself. Perhaps that's what that yellow creation's all about. Poor man!'

'Dolly, you're terrible.'

'A bit naughty,' Dolly said, chortling and flattered. 'A bit naughty, that's all I am. How was your day, dear? Wasn't it your favourite pupil today?'

'That's right.' Home, Elizabeth, Dolly had partly dispelled the anxieties of the morning; but still the troubling question remained, gnawing at her deep within.

Rose knew that it was not going to go away, but at the same time her heart rebelled against the knowledge. By the standards of Mrs Betts or Mrs Snell this home she had found and this life she had made were, no doubt, beneath contempt – or rather, they were exactly what she deserved. The cheap meals at the oilcloth-covered table, the quiet evenings punctuated by the sound of Mrs Tickell practising oozy funeral hymns on the harmonium through the thin party wall, the scraping together of money when they needed a new gasmantle or an extra sack of coal in winter: it was all, doubtless, highly unsatisfactory, the merest getting by, and even someone sympathetic to her predicament might have shaken their head and pronounced it no way to live.

And yet Rose valued it; and she felt a fierce defiance at the thought of giving it up simply in deference to a public opinion that she had never respected anyhow. It was here, since the death of her mother two years ago, that Rose had brought up her daughter, and here she believed the child had had as happy and secure and contented a life as it was possible to have. It might not be a conventional household: Rose brought in the lion's share of what money there was, and Elizabeth spent a lot of time with Dolly at home, and male presence was limited to the calls of the milkman with the cans on the handles of his bicycle and the monosyllabic greetings of Mr Tickell across the back yard fence. But Rose knew what a conventional household was like, and she did not believe it to be endowed with any special virtues – at least, not unless it had warmth and love and ease within it.

She had those here. Or, more importantly, Elizabeth had them. Rose had grown so used to subsuming her own wellbeing in that of her child that she could not separate the two. It would have taken an actual effort to bring from her unconscious to her conscious mind the knowledge of her own loneliness, for example, and even then she might have rejected it as mere weak complaining. She was accustomed to stamping hard on anything weak in herself. It was only through strength, determined strength, that she had Elizabeth at all.

And here again was her dilemma. All she wanted was what was best for Elizabeth. Did that mean taking her away from this odd, happy and fundamentally honest life? And was that the strong course, or the weak one?

Once again, as Elizabeth laid the table with her customary pause for thought over which side to lay the forks and Dolly made mustard with as much rattling energy as if she were mixing cement, Rose said to herself: I must ask Dolly about it.

Rose put her question that evening.

She had spent the afternoon with Elizabeth, going on a long walk by the cliff paths and then descending to the beach to the west of the town. This was the area not greatly frequented by visitors to the resort, and they saw no one but a solitary horsewoman who passed with extraordinary silence and grace through a bridle track that crossed their footpath, up amongst the mint-green spring ferns of the clifftop. Down on the beach, where a barefoot Elizabeth walked tightrope-style along a timber groyne with a daring that pleased Rose even as she admonished her, theirs were the only footprints in the spongy ginger-coloured sand. The only signs of life were the gulls in the cold blue sky, mounting with arched wings to a height and then plummeting with a shriek down an invisible slope of air; and out at sea a single ship on the cusp of the horizon, so still it might have been a painting on glass.

When the holiday season began the solitude of the spot would be broken, but not by much; and even in Shipden itself the season did not bring a boisterous invasion such as came each year to Great Yarmouth, round the coast. Shipden still retained the gentility so much prized by the Victorians who had turned it from a little fishing town into a fashionable watering place. With the railway had come the pier and the Royal Golf Links and the Winter Gardens and the great hotels that stood like elaborate but slightly stern châteaux along the promenade with its profusion of curly ironwork; but the Midland millworkers who came by charabanc and trainload to Skegness and Hunstanton and Yarmouth in search of spit-rock and blackfaced minstrels did not come to Shipden, or if they did they went away disappointed. It was a formal, sedate, plushly upholstered sort of holidaymaking that went on at Shipden.

There was, however, change in the wind. The Great War had interrupted the town's tranquil existence in a decisive manner. Sea defences had entangled it, several of its grand hotels had been requisitioned by the armed forces, and many of its smaller establishments had folded during those dark and thrifty four years. Peace had brought a boom and last summer the visitors had come in eager flocks, but things were not quite the same. To the dismay of the town's elders and self-appointed betters, a fried-fish shop and an ice-cream parlour had appeared in the quaint narrow streets; and these traditionalists noted with the same disapproval that many of the illustrious names who regularly took suites at the Metropolitan and the Grand were missing. In their place came rich unknowns to ascend in the hydraulic lifts and tread the sand-thick carpets of the verbena-scented lounges – 'Lloyd George knighthoods', it was said, men who had made money from the war instead of decently inheriting it. And though the great hotels seemed to be flourishing as before, flourishing too was an entirely different species – the family hotel with its stucco facing and timber veranda and its guests who thanked the frilly-aproned maid every time she came near them. Proud and exclusive as Shipden was, it was waking up from the long troubled sleep of war to take a reluctant peep at a new world.

But whether it was a world that would suddenly choose to be tolerant of the likes of Rose and Elizabeth was doubtful. And that was part of the question Rose put to Aunt Dolly that evening, after Elizabeth had been put to bed in a blissful ozone-drugged sleep.

'Dolly,' Rose said, 'I didn't want to mention it while Elizabeth was here. But I had some trouble at work today.'

Dolly jerked her head up. The evenings were still cold enough for a fire, and sitting by it had made her drowsy – though brandy had probably also had something to do with this. That Dolly tippled was a secret well known to Rose – and Dolly probably knew that she knew – but they maintained an easy fiction that Dolly was as dry as a Salvationist. Rose saw no harm in it. Dolly kept her bottle hidden in her sewing-machine case and applied herself to it when she was alone. Its effect was to make her cheeks red and her laugh looser and, curiously, it divested her of some of that often shattering physical clumsiness that afflicted her when she was sober.

'What sort of trouble, dear?'

'Well – I nearly lost my job. No, no – it's all right now,' Rose said, as Dolly gave a puff of agitation. 'That is, it's all right *for* now. I'm just afraid that what happened today might happen again. I've been thinking about it so much and – well,

I wanted to ask you what you thought,' she concluded, and told Dolly the story of Olivia and Mrs Betts, the fat tapping hand, and the fretful wrath of Madame Carette that had been so narrowly averted by so fortuitous an accident as a glimpse of the new doctor.

To many people in the town the idea of asking Dolly Jordan what she thought would have been absurd. Shipden society, from the Rotary Club-dining, fête-opening likes of Mrs Snell to the corseted matrons who gossiped at whist drives and sewing circles and referred to their one part-time slavey as 'the staff', had long ago weighed Dolly Jordan in the scales and found her wanting. She was a spinster who did not, as spinsters should, busy herself with good works or the Church. She did not know how to dress or, worse, did not care, and her grizzled hair often resembled a last year's crow's nest. She was lumpy and garrulous as an unsophisticated schoolgirl and sometimes, during the season, she could be seen down on the sands laughing at Punch and Judy with trippers' children or publicly slurping ices in a deckchair, her skirts hiked up above her big lisle-shiny knees.

Also she had no sense of things. When Rose and Elizabeth came to live with her, at Dolly's invitation, no one was surprised. 'Of course,' they said, 'Dolly Jordan wouldn't care. That's her all over.' Indeed nothing could have better emphasized the completeness of Rose's fall than the fact that she had ended up sharing a cramped set of rooms with Dolly Jordan.

In fact forty-five years ago Dolly Jordan had been a beauty. She had been devoted to poetry and had written verses herself. Her parents had admired them; she had been their darling, and men too had been rapturously drawn to her. And then they had drawn away. Dolly always said exactly what she thought and the men, at first pronouncing this to be ripping and jolly, soon found it anything but. They liked a girl to be a lady, meaning she should not talk too much or spontaneously wish to climb up a tree. Intelligent enough to have changed if she had wanted, Dolly chose instead to go on alone, growing a shell of eccentricity and turning to dressmaking when her tiny inheritance ran out. Her closest relationship had been with her brother, Rose's father, who spoke of her as a woman of character, whilst sadly aware that it was precisely that combination that people did not like.

Rose loved Aunt Dolly with an unsentimental love. The old lady could be difficult in ways that old ladies were not traditionally meant to be. She had foul moods that she called, in her schoolgirlish way, 'getting cross'; and when she had made too many trips to the sewing-machine case she would cook herself chaotic snacks of toasted cheese and withdraw into curmudgeonly, crumb-strewn silence.

But she was supremely, transparently truthful. She paid lip service to no proprieties; she had no axe to grind. Somehow, in spite of all that a genteel upbringing in the English provinces could do, Dolly had omitted to learn hypocrisy.

'But my dear,' Dolly said when Rose had finished, vigorously scratching her big calves, 'you always knew this sort of thing would happen. That's the way people are – the sillies. You've always borne up against it before.'

'Yes. And I'm still willing to. But it's Elizabeth. I'll have to think about sending her to school in the autumn. She's been . . . sheltered here. But that can't go on much longer. Once she starts mixing with other children – and I do so want her to do that – then there'll be questions. You know what children are like. She'll begin to realize that she's different.'

'She will always be different,' Dolly said emphatically, 'because she is a beautiful child, an exceptional child.'

'Well,' Rose said, warmed and touched by these words, but not wanting to be deflected from what she had to say, 'I hope so. But a lot of people, most people, won't see it that way. All they'll see is her birth.'

'Ah.'

'Other children will want to know about her daddy. And then the parents of the children, the schoolteachers . . .

34

Elizabeth's going to find out that she's meant to be ashamed of herself.'

Dolly snorted and twitched her shoulders. 'I was going to say that grown-up people surely wouldn't be cruel to an innocent child on that account. But of course they would. They're capable of any nonsense, as long as it means they don't have to think for themselves.' Dolly suppressed a belch. 'I do see, dear. I see exactly what you mean. But you must have known this was coming too.'

'Yes. I suppose I did. Though when she was only a baby it was easy to shut it out of my mind, somehow. As long as she was healthy and safe. But this – this is something I can't protect her from. At least, not here.'

'What do you mean, dear?'

'Everyone knows us here. Shipden's such a small place and you can't hide or pretend.'

Dolly sat upright and gave her a piercing look. 'Rose, my dear, I never thought you were the hiding or pretending sort.'

'No,' Rose said, made a little uneasy by her aunt's gaze, 'I – I tried not to be. And I still don't want to be, not really. But I wondered today whether it might not be better, for Elizabeth's sake, if we went away somewhere else, where we weren't known, and started afresh.'

'You'd still be the same people.'

'In a way. But in a way we wouldn't, not if I went under a married name. I could simply . . . pass myself off as a war widow, and everything – everything would be different.'

Somehow she had expected the mere voicing of this idea to make it real and solid. Instead Rose found that speaking the words out loud only showed her how unconvincing they were. *Simply*, she said; but no word could have been more inappropriate to the violent tangle of feelings within her.

Dolly's stillness, and her beady gaze, suggested that she at least was not fooled. But she seemed to draw back from the brink of what she had been going to say. Instead she shrugged and said, 'It's up to you, of course. I'll miss you, but I'll manage, so you needn't trouble about that.'

Rose had troubled about it, of course, from the moment she had seriously addressed the idea. Telling herself that Aunt Dolly would be better off without the disruption and responsibility of both herself and a growing girl in the house made no difference: it would still be a dreadful wrench.

'I should hate to go away,' she said. 'I wouldn't do it at all if it wasn't for Elizabeth. But just suppose it happens again – what happened today – and I lost my job. There isn't much work in Shipden. We'd be such a burden to you.' The pain and confusion of thinking these things had made her plaintive: hearing the note in her voice, Rose pulled herself up smartly. She hated that sort of thing. 'I don't mean that would happen. I was careless today and I won't be again. I just mean that I – I haven't been thinking of the future and I ought to.'

Dolly leant forward to stir the fire, her elbows mannishly propped on her sturdy knees.

'When your mother died,' she said, 'I invited you to come and live here because I felt it was what your father would have wanted. Of course one can't be sure, but your father and I felt the same about a great many things. And as he was no longer with us when you had Elizabeth I felt that it was up to me to think for him, as it were. I don't go so far as to say he would have been happy. I can't say that I was happy when I heard. What I thought was: poor child, what a lot of grief she'll have. And I believe your father would have thought the same if he'd been around to know. *But* he would have been proud too. He was always proud of you and I don't think that would have changed one jot. Your poor mother, of course, had different ideas about these things, but that couldn't be helped.'

It was noticeable that Dolly always spoke with the utmost respect of Rose's mother – who would never have returned the compliment and sometimes used to produce cruelly accurate impressions of what she saw as Dolly's indignities, the urgent leg-scratchings, and blowings, and the thumping collisions with the sharp edges of furniture.

'And so in a way I wanted to be what your father would have been to you and Elizabeth if he had been alive. My good gosh, what a jolly funny father-figure *I* make!' Dolly said with sudden hearty humour, glancing down at her ponderous bosom. As she smiled, revealing white teeth that were curiously startling in their perfection, there was a glint of the beauty she had been, a glimpse of buried youth and distant hope. 'Your father believed that people should be true to themselves. He always taught you to think for yourself. And you did. He would have been proud of you for that alone.'

Rose thought of her father, an intensely serious man of Franciscan gentleness who had sometimes seemed a little too thin-skinned for the world. A schoolmaster, he had been deeply hurt, with a wounded sort of bewilderment, when he had found a favourite pupil pilfering from his desk. His manners had been impeccable in an old-fashioned way yet stiffened by awkwardness, the result of his almost fanatical regard for truth: he found it difficult, simply on an ethical level, to say he was delighted to see someone when he was not. It was he who had taught Rose music and in his love for this too there was something a little other-worldly. 'There, Rose – that was written two hundred years ago,' she recalled him saying after playing over a piece of Bach, 'and in two hundred years' time people will still be listening to it.'

He could not see that life itself is a compromise and that people are mixed or they are nothing. But he was not at all dictatorial and Rose had deeply loved him; had felt indeed, after his death when she was seventeen, that a change had entered the world, important and irreversible as a change in climate.

The scrupulous passion for truth and the disdain of pretence had passed down to her. Yet she had not acted as she had done these past four years with any sense that she was doing as her father would have wanted. Indeed, if she had pictured her father's shade looking down at her, it was with an expression of pained, reserved disapproval on his face.

The thought that he might instead be proud of her was new.

'Well, you've always thought for yourself up till now, at any rate,' Dolly said. 'But perhaps there does come a time when you have to give in.'

Rose had to smile at Dolly's look of sly innocence.

'I don't want to give in,' she said. 'Dear God, I don't. Not when we've come so far. And if I thought that I could be there myself to protect Elizabeth from every snub and every hurtful remark—'

'Why, has there been anyone to protect you these past years?'

'. . . No.'

'Did you want anyone to?'

'No. But I'm an adult.'

Dolly waved a hand. 'Children are stronger than we think.'

Rose felt faintly irritated at this. 'But it doesn't mean I liked it. Or that I'd want anyone else to go through it.'

Dolly patted down her indigestion, faintly smiling at the fire. 'Mm,' she said.

Rose suffered another wave of irritation and then, with a sort of mental sidestep, realized that her irritation was not with Dolly but with herself. She looked at the part she was playing and did not like it: you could ask someone's advice on the pretext that you valued their judgement and that they would find this flattering, but too often it could be a way of shifting responsibility. And if the decision turned out to be wrong, you had someone to blame.

Not a very nice way to behave. Decidedly nasty, in fact. But before she could say something in apology Dolly turned her vaguely smiling gaze on her and said, 'You'd tell Elizabeth the truth eventually, I suppose? If you went off and lived as Mrs So-and-so the war widow.'

Rose thought, and had to resist an impulse to wipe the palms of her hands.

'Yes. I would have to tell her as soon as she was old enough to understand it,' she said, and it was as if someone else had spoken for her, with utter emphasis and authority.

'And you'd have to tell her why, of course,' Dolly said, yawning and settling her head back as if to doze. 'Why you pretended. Otherwise she might think you did it because you were ashamed of her.'

In the silence that followed the fire spat and crackled and then rolled a live fragment of coal out on to the rug right at Rose's feet, as if challenging her to pick it up.

# FOUR

Rose returned to work on Monday no nearer to a decision, and this in itself was perplexing to her and gave her a feeling of not being entirely herself.

Always before she had been decisive. She thought deeply about things, but when it came to the point of making up her mind Rose was absolute. In the same way she tended not to indulge in regrets. This was simply what was most comfortable to her. She remembered as a child going down to the beach with a friend – this was unknown to her mother, who would have been horrified – and how the two of them had stood on the breakwater, in petticoat and drawers, looking down into a cold grey autumn tide. Suddenly Rose had jumped in. It had taken a long time to induce her friend to join her and when at last she did she was full of gasping amazement at Rose's daring. But the fact was she found that easier than the shivering, agonizing hesitation. She jumped to escape the fear.

And now she was in just such a limbo, confused, torn all ways. It had been her habit to reduce things to essences – thus, as long as she had work, it didn't matter if the work was dull; as long as she was basically healthy, she wouldn't worry about sleeplessness; as long as Elizabeth was happy, she was happy. But the ingredients of this situation wouldn't boil down, wouldn't distil.

Bereft of her usual certainty, she wondered about herself. Did she really know where she was going or what she wanted? Had she lost herself somewhere in these past years as one might mislay a familiar article – supposing it safely put away in a box somewhere only to find it hopelessly, inexplicably absent?

And then what happened on Wednesday offered her some clues. Quite by accident she found herself being reflected in two different mirrors; and though both were distorted, that in itself helped point her towards the true image.

That day brought, first of all, Angelica Harwood, as it had every Wednesday for the past six months: Angelica with her exquisite rose-water fragrance and her endless hats – in all this time Rose was sure she had never seen her in the same one twice – and her look of not having the faintest idea what she was doing in the world or how she had got there.

Angelica was not from Shipden. The town, for all its gentility, did not run to the likes of the Harwoods, who were so wealthy and distinguished that a title would somehow have lowered them, like a gaudy accessory. Occasional Ladies and Honourables descended to the town from their country places in the hilly, woody, secretive hinterland beyond the cliffs to grace a civic reception or lay a foundation stone, but no Harwoods ever sullied their hands in that way. Their Georgian mansion, deep in that inland world of coverts and spinneys and bridle paths through poppy-rich meadows, was more exclusive and inaccessible than any baronial castle: the country omnibus had to make a detour of several miles just to get round its park. If the Harwoods ever went anywhere, it was presumably only to other such private fiefdoms in Norfolk or Suffolk, or else to London and abroad, keeping their eyes averted all the way.

The exception was Angelica.

Why Angelica's people – as she referred to them – should have decided that she should take piano lessons at the age of nearly nineteen Rose could not say. She gathered, from halting conversations with her pupil, that Angelica had been ill a lot as a child, though she looked as strong and sleek as a thoroughbred now; and that the feeling was she needed a little final polish. She also gathered, by more intuitive means, that Angelica was regarded as a drip and a dunce, a dismal letdown, who must be brought up to something like scratch without too much expense. The Harwoods could probably have afforded Paderewski himself as a private tutor. Instead Angelica was sent alone into Shipden every Wednesday afternoon in a chauffeur-driven Bentley, there to struggle unavailingly with sharps and flats above Madame Carette's shop while the chauffeur lounged about the market square, smoking cigarettes, in a way that Rose somehow doubted he would do if it were any other member of that illustrious family he was waiting on.

For through the screens of Angelica's almost incredible shyness and inarticulacy Rose glimpsed figures who filled the girl with awe: parents and siblings and cousins who were everything she was not and in whose vast shadow she crept about, wondering how such godlike beings could ever have anything to do with her. It did not appear to Rose that the parents and siblings and cousins took much trouble to correct that impression either.

There was one in particular, a brother, who seemed absolutely to oppress Angelica with his magnificence.

'Clive says it's the fairies,' she would say, squeezing the words out with a painful breathless chuckle, after failing again to master the simplest five-finger exercise.

'Really? What about the fairies?' Often Rose had to coax words out of her, as with a tongue-tied child.

'Cursed me in the cradle,' Angelica said with the same chuckle, her eyes cast down. 'Gave me trotters instead of hands.'

Clive's remarks all seemed to be of this kind. Yet there was never a hint of resentment in Angelica's voice when she mentioned them. Clive was Olympian, beyond criticism: even to look at him was to risk blindness.

'I simply can't fathom those foreign words,' Angelica would say with muted hopelessness, looking at the markings on a music score.

'They're Italian. "Allegro" means quickly. "Adagio" is slowly. There are only a few of them – you'll soon pick them up.'

Angelica shook her head tightly. 'Not me. I'm a perfect clot with these things. Clive speaks Italian wonderfully well. Sometimes he calls me things in it. It's a tease. Like when he puts spiders in my teacup. He's frightfully funny. Everyone roars.' And she gave her clenched, distressful chuckle.

Rose thought Clive sounded like a nightmare. The whole clan did, in fact; and it was impossible not to sympathize with the girl whom awkwardness had relegated to a sort of chauffeur-driven, silk-and-kid-clad Cinderella.

The awkwardness, though, was extreme. It had taken six months for Angelica to attain this level of ease with the piano teacher whom she could have bought several times over with her loose change. There was nothing amiss with her figure, but she moved like a person who was afraid of her own body – as if at any moment it might let her down in some spectacular and violent way. Her shoulders were always round her ears and when she was not chewing her fingers she was twisting them in white-knuckled knots; and to get her to lift her groomed head and look you in the face was an achievement.

When she did, you saw a gentle, unaristocratic prettiness, and the most nakedly defenceless pair of china-blue eyes in the world. On the evidence of those eyes alone it was plain that bullying Angelica would be about as difficult as dominating a new-born kitten.

What did not bewilder her caused her mild alarm. She was alarmed by Madame Carette, who always pressed her inert hand fulsomely on her arriving and leaving. She was alarmed by the shrieks of Madame Carette's parrot and by the bland gaze of Madame Carette's cat and by the sound of penny whistles being tried out in the shop below. And in spite of Rose's best efforts, she seemed to be mildly alarmed by Rose too, even though the ice had melted sufficiently to allow those tense little spurts of conversation. Rose was getting virtually nowhere as far as teaching Angelica the rudiments of piano

44

was concerned – though her family appeared to take no interest in her progress anyhow – and she had supposed that much the same applied on the personal level. All she could say was that Angelica seemed to be slightly less afraid of her than of other people, to the extent of insisting in a blushing murmur that she call her Angelica and not Miss Harwood, 'because that's awfully – it's – you know.' Rose felt a sympathetic interest in the girl, but she supposed it no easier to get near to her than to get to the Harwoods' mansion through its acres of fenced and keeper-guarded park.

And then, that Wednesday, Angelica surprised her.

Angelica had been conveyed in solitary luxury to Madame Carette's as usual, and as usual had come to the music room as if meekly ascending to the guillotine, and as usual had sat stiffly down at the piano stool and stared at the keyboard as if it were a page of advanced algebra.

And then a violent tremble passed over her and, as if offering a dreadful confession, she blurted, 'I think Freddy Collymore is a pig,' before subsiding into hunched and burning silence.

Startled, Rose said, 'I'm afraid I don't know who Freddy Collymore is.'

'You're lucky. I do and I think he's a perfect pig.' She looked timidly into Rose's face. 'That's awful, isn't it? To say a thing like that.'

'I don't know. Not necessarily. Not if he *is* a perfect pig.'

Angelica did not smile. She just nodded solemnly and then said, 'They want me to be nice to him. I do try. I always try to be nice to people but I'm not very good at it. There's a knack, you know – Clive has it, people absolutely love him and he tells me I ought to learn and he's right of course but I – I can't get the hang of it. I'm so dreadfully dense.'

It was a long speech for Angelica. In spite of a feeling that she should perhaps not be hearing this, Rose could not help but respond to such a desperate sally of frankness.

'Who wants you to be nice to Freddy?'

'Oh, all of them. Clive especially. It was he who introduced

Freddy. He said, "Be nice to him, old girl," in this jolly way he has. And I feel awful because I'd do anything for Clive but – it's so very difficult.'

'What's Freddy like?'

'Quite old,' Angelica said, knotting her fingers. 'Nearly fifty. Of course there's nothing wrong with that, as Clive says, it's just when he acts in – in a rather young way. He's something rather grand in banking. His wife died last year which is awful for him but he's – he's full of life.'

'I see,' Rose said: and she did see.

'He has the most horrid wet lips,' Angelica whispered, with a last wretched agony of confession. 'But he can't help that, can he?'

'No,' Rose said, 'but it doesn't mean you have to like them.'

Angelica looked up at her with a visionary sort of surprise; but then turned her head and said, 'I think I must be a dreadful person.'

'Why? Because you don't like Freddy Collymore or his wet lips?'

'I let people down so. They want me to be nice to Freddy and it really isn't much to ask, as Clive said.'

'What about what you want?' Rose said.

Again she knew that it was hardly her place to talk in this way. It was probably best to stay out of it; and she didn't after all know the whole story. But she felt she had a pretty good idea. Angelica, so painfully artless and transparent, was no more capable of lying than flying. And her subservience to her family was so great that Freddy must have been repulsive indeed to have provoked her even to this flicker of resistance.

'I just want everything to be all right,' Angelica said, as if repeating a catechism. 'I want everyone to be happy and everything to be all right.'

Rose suspected she knew the answer to her next question, but she asked it anyway.

'Is there anyone you could talk to about this – a friend, perhaps; someone in your family . . .?'

Eyes wide, Angelica was shaking her head. 'Oh good heavens no. They would just think I was – no. Not at all.'

Rose felt the difficulty of her own position – but that was to think in the abstract, and Rose distrusted abstractions. The simple question was what you did when someone stretched out a hand to you, even half-consciously, as seemed to be the case with Angelica.

'Well,' she said, 'all I can say for sure is that if you don't like someone, you don't. I don't see that as any sort of failing. It's just the way it is. And you certainly can't make yourself like that person. Not even to please others.'

'Everyone else seems to like him.'

'Well, that's up to them. It's what you feel that matters.'

This notion was evidently striking to Angelica. She stopped twisting her fingers, and gazed thoughtfully at her fashion-plate reflection in the highly polished lid of the piano. Then she frowned.

'But I can't possibly be rude – you know, I simply can't – it wouldn't be right.'

'You don't have to be, necessarily. I don't think you would ever be a rude person anyway. But nobody should ever have to do anything they don't want to do.'

To her surprise and alarm, Rose saw a tear running down Angelica's cheek: a very Angelica tear, perfect and round and translucent like a well-cut jewel, but a tear nonetheless. There, Rose told herself, you shouldn't have said anything; you should have minded your own business.

'Oh, please don't,' she said helplessly, as more tears followed. She was really not very good with tears, even Elizabeth's childish ones. There was something so primitive about them, erupting through the civilized surface of the world. 'Please, don't upset yourself—'

'Oh, I'm not upset. Don't think that. I'm terribly sorry – I don't know what you must think of me. But I've never really – you know – spoken to anyone like this. It's a sort of – tremendous relief, you know.'

Blinking away the translucent tears, Angelica smiled at Rose, fully and openly. She looked human and alive and also rather beautiful: Rose could imagine all too well the response of Freddy of the wet lips.

'I'm so sorry to put all this on you,' Angelica went on, dabbing at her face with a lace handkerchief. 'I shall buckle down to the piano in a moment, really I will. You just seem to understand so. I mean I couldn't talk to Effie Brissingham, say. We had the same schooling and we chat at parties and so on but she's – well, she's a girl, you know, and so caught up in it all – very gay and simply too busy to think. But you – you seem so thoughtful and sensible.'

Rose said nothing; and could not even be sure, just then, what she felt at those words.

Angelica took her silence as an indication that she had rattled on too much; and in spite of Rose's protestations that it was not so, clammed up at once and began dutifully bashing away at her scales. Only when the lesson was over did she peep once more out of her shell and murmur, as she put on her gloves, 'I am sorry about earlier, Miss Jordan. I never meant to – you know.'

'I'm glad you did. It helps to get things off your chest sometimes. And it would be nice if you called me Rose, you know.'

'Oh – that's awfully – but I don't know if I could.' Angelica looked startled, even abashed. 'Still, you know, I – I shall remember what you said. I don't mean I shall be impolite to Freddy or anything. But I shall remember what you said.'

With a quick blundering warmth she shook Rose's hand.

From the music-room window Rose watched Angelica cross the square to the waiting Bentley. A rippling sun-shadow cast by the tall lime in the churchyard gave a curious momentary impression that she was walking on water.

She looked very young, Rose thought. Nineteen: yes, that was young – though there was only six years' difference between them.

48

Rose sat down at the piano and placed on the music stand an album of Schubert. Her hands softly began to play over the G major Impromptu that had been a favourite of her father's.

Even her amateur execution found the kernel of bitter-sweet longing at the heart of the music, and she stopped.

She looked at her own reflection in the piano lid, and thought of how Angelica saw it. An older woman. Even with no knowledge of Rose's past (and the attitude of her family to Angelica suggested that they would not care much even about that if it did come out) Angelica saw her as a woman whom experience had placed on a serene height from which, kindly and disinterested, she could look down with objective eyes.

Sensible.

Well, that was the last word that would have been applied to her in the past. But had she, almost unconsciously, remade herself in that image in the last few years? Had she come to regard her one passionate and in some ways catastrophic lapse as an ending – a spree of emotion that had bankrupted her for ever?

Call me Rose, she had said; and, 'I don't know if I could,' Angelica had said.

Was she the sort of person whom you simply didn't think of calling by their first name? Who heard Schubert with an appreciation of the ingenious harmonic modulations instead of melting at the beauty?

This was the first reflection of herself she was presented with that Wednesday. She rejected it, but it saddened her in some indefinable way.

The second reflection made her blazingly angry.

Angelica's lesson ended at three, and for the rest of the day Rose was in charge of the shop whilst Madame Carette went out to tune a piano. For these expeditions she took Albert with her, partly to carry her bag of tuning instruments and partly as a miniature chaperon. Albert was an undersized boy of fourteen who in addition to these duties polished the pianos and swept the shop and made deliveries on a bicycle that Madame Carette kept in the little yard at the rear, draping it with a Liberty shawl when it was not in use because she could not bear anything ugly. Every shop in Shipden delivered: often Albert would be away for two hours, delivering an album of sheet music or a single gramophone record to a villa five miles away at the top of the steep wooded slopes that encircled the town. Madame Carette addressed him as Al-bare and he seemed rather to like it: once Rose had even heard him style himself thus when answering the telephone in the shop. 'Hello,' he had said. 'This is Al-bare Stubbs speaking.'

Soon after Madame Carette had left a spring shower began to sizzle down with surprising vehemence and did not let up. The square emptied and Rose had just reconciled herself to the dullness of an afternoon with no customers when Leo Liddell came in.

'Phew, lucky I brought this out with me this morning,' he said, shaking an umbrella at the door. 'It's funny because the sky was as clear as anything then, not a cloud, but something just told me it would rain later. I saw several people look at me as if to say, "What on earth is he doing with that brolly?" They must have thought I was mad. Raving crackers, what? But I just had this feeling. And as it happens it was right. Ho ho.'

Leo Liddell continued to flap the umbrella at the door and congratulate himself on his foresight for some time. Meanwhile he kept stealing glances at Rose, behind the counter. The phrase was very apt when it was applied to Leo Liddell. When he looked at you it was as if he took something away from you.

'Madame not present?' he said, coming in at last, smoothing his hair.

Rose said no. 'She shouldn't be long, if you need to see her.'

'Oh no! I'm sure you'll be able to oblige. Fact is, I'm just on the lookout for some new material. We start the good old twice-weeklies at the Winter Gardens next week. No one wants to hear the same old tunes over and over, now do they? Another season approacheth. Cor blimey, time flies, don't it?'

He had this slick and facetious way of talking, with slangy snatches thrown in – as if, Rose thought, he were trying to be all things to all men all of the time. What people called a good mixer, she supposed. He was the leader of Shipden's resident orchestra, which was ubiquitous and grand during the season, and off season got by as a slimmed-down ensemble playing in hotel lounges and at village hops. Madame Carette did not like him and privately referred to him, with a devastating sense of his pretension, as 'the bandmaster'.

But lots of women did like him: he was handsome in a youthful, faintly Latin way and carried something of the theatrical confidence of the podium about with him. There had been frequent rumours of lady flautists ending the season broken-hearted, and of pretty widows who made their annual holiday at Shipden for reasons quite other than the ozone. His wife was rather older than he and was not seen much.

The shop took a great deal of sheet music, including numerous and endlessly varied arrangements right down to 'Scots wha hae' for piano and cornet. There were several parcels of it still unopened in the little stockroom at the back and Rose fetched them, opening them out on the counter and letting Liddell hunt through at leisure.

'Dear dear, not more "Roses of Picardy". I think people have had enough of the good old war tunes, don't you? They always get a sort of sentimental applause, but really everyone's trying to hide their yawns. Now here, that's more like it. American, of course – that touch of syncopation. That's the way the wind's blowing, but whether dear old Shipden will take to it's another matter. You know what I mean. Not the most forward-looking of places, is it?' He kept glancing covertly up at Rose as he spoke: seemingly an ingrained habit, a swift gauging of his audience's reaction – he would change the tune completely if it wasn't going down well. 'Bless it though. I wouldn't alter it for the world. That's rather a nice melody, isn't it?' He crooned a few bars, then gave an apologetic grin. 'Cripes. Never could sing to save me life. Well, I'll take those and see what the chaps think of them.'

Rose knew Leo Liddell well enough not to like him very much, or trust him very much, which with her came to the same thing. He was, naturally, a frequent patron of the music shop, and had established a casual friendliness with her on that basis. In fact he liked to hint that there was an unspoken understanding between them, a sort of us-and-them collusion. Rose merely ignored this, knowing that he would nod and wink to a girl working in a baker's shop in just the same way, as if they were the only people who understood the finer points of cake and pastry. He couldn't help himself, to be charitable about it.

'Would you like me to wrap these?' Rose said.

'Would you? Just a bit of good old brown paper and string to keep them together. Pianist's hands,' he said approvingly, watching her wrap the sheaves of music. 'I should say you were pretty well wasted here, wouldn't you?'

'I don't know about that – you haven't heard me play.'

He cocked his head enigmatically, then glanced back at the shop window, still rattling with rain. 'Good old English spring. Send it down, David. I hear the Prince Edward's opening its restaurant to the public. Did you hear that? Can't get by just on the guests. That's the way the wind's blowing again. Good idea, if you ask me. There's such a thing as being too damn exclusive. Anyhow I happen to know they've got a pretty good chef. Perhaps we could have a spot of supper there one night and find out what it's like.'

'Yes, why not?' she said absently.

And then she understood. The 'we' he was referring to was not him and his wife, or him and anybody else, as she had supposed.

He was watching her, both soulful and alert.

'Sorry,' she said with a little laugh, 'I didn't catch on. I thought you meant—'

'Never mind,' he said, answering her laugh in what might have been a charming way if it had not been designed as such, 'you know what I mean now, don't you? Just the two of us, spot of the old supper, catch up on old times. I think it would be pretty nice.'

What old times could he mean? For the moment she was simply startled at the absurdity of the whole thing.

'So. When could you manage it?' He had seized on her silence: and, like some enchanted tree in a fairy tale, he had moved without her seeing him right round to the end of the counter, trapping her behind it.

'That wouldn't be a good idea,' she said. There is often a moment, before situations turn nasty, when they seem about to turn ludicrous, and this was it – she was still holding his parcel of music and she briefly pictured herself clouting him across his brilliantined head with it.

'We'd be discreet, of course,' he said, edging closer. 'That's easy enough.'

'No, thank you.'

He shrugged, smiling. 'I don't see the difficulty. I may as well tell you that I'm pretty well a free agent – just one of those odd things – so don't worry about that.'

'Well, I'm a free agent too, and I'm freely saying no thank you.'

She had been right not to trust him. She saw a moment's indecision on his face, and then he renewed his smile and reached out and touched her.

His hand closed round the top of her arm, close to the shoulder. The thumb, close to her breast, moved a little, hinting.

'Come on, Rose, old girl—'

She pulled smartly away from him. The smile left his eyes, though not his mouth, as he saw the look on her face.

'My mistake,' he said shrugging. 'Sorry and all that. I just thought—'

'You thought wrong.'

His eyebrows went up. 'Mercy me. It's a bit late in the day for this snow-white stuff, isn't it, Rose? Horses for courses, you know. You're not exactly—'

'Don't say anything more.'

He took a step back, lips tight, his tongue exploring his mouth. 'Well. Profoundest apologies. I simply thought you'd be up for a bit of fun. *You* know. Horses for courses, as I say. I don't imagine you get a lot of fun nowadays.'

'You'd be surprised.'

He chuckled on his way out. 'Oh, I don't think I would, you know.'

That was the second reflection she saw that day. It hurt her. Even though the glass that showed her it was so foxed and grubby a one as Leo Liddell, even though she rejected it violently and completely, her pain and humiliation cut deep.

She lay awake that night, listening to the last spatterings of rain on the window and the deep distant sigh of the sea – the sounds so markedly distinct that it seemed scarcely possible they were both made by the same substance. The pain had worn off, but in its place she became aware of another sensation – one that must have been, like the sound of the sea, ever-present yet only noticed at times like these: an emptiness at the very core of her.

She prided herself on standing on her own two feet; on the fact that, if something were needed in her life, she would supply it. But this emptiness seemed beyond her power to fill.

# FIVE

'But can she *cook*, James?'

'I presume so.'

'Aha – you presume. You don't know.'

'Well, I don't suppose she would have applied for the post otherwise. I advertised for a general housekeeper, cooking included.'

'But did you *specify* the cooking in your advertisement?'

'Did I? I can't remember. I suppose I took it as read.'

'Aha,' Sylvia Vickery said again. 'Now this is where you go wrong, you see.' She laughed, looking knowing.

'Well, all I can say is she seems very satisfactory. I think I'm pretty lucky to get her.'

'That's funny you should say that. Now I knew someone who needed a housekeeper and took on a woman through an advertisement just like you have. And he used your exact words. He said he was lucky to get her. Those were his very words.'

As it seemed to be his cue, James said, 'And what happened?'

'Oh, she was a disaster. Absolute catastrophe. *She* couldn't cook to save her life. Mealtimes became purgatory. She very nearly poisoned him.'

James laughed.

'No, no.' Sylvia Vickery was insistent. 'Absolutely true. She served him fish that had been packed in ice and then cooked straight away. Now *you* know how inadvisable that is. He was extremely ill. I think if he hadn't had a very strong constitution to start with he would probably have died.'

'I think what Sylvia is trying to say,' old Dr Vickery said, 'is that we shall miss having you here to dine.'

'Oh no!' Sylvia pursued. 'I didn't mean that particularly, though of course we will. I just wanted to point out to James that you can never be sure. I knew someone who employed a chauffeur who it turned out didn't know how to drive a motorcar. In fact he was frightened of it. Wouldn't go near it. That just shows you. That's what I mean.'

'Well, James drives his own car,' Mrs Vickery said with comfortable inconsequence, 'so that's all right.'

'Oh yes, I know that, Mother. But it's the question of the housekeeper, you see. It's really quite important.'

'Penn was the name, did you say?' Dr Vickery said.

'Mrs Penn, yes,' James said. 'Has a cottage over at West Shipden, I think.'

'I remember. A widow, isn't she? Husband was a, let's see, a boatbuilder. Killed in the war. Sad business. I remember now.'

'Good heavens, you don't mean to say the woman's young?' Sylvia said. 'Really, James. I don't want to be a Jeremiah, but I see all sorts of difficulties ahead with *that*. And if there are children—'

'He lied about his age,' Dr Vickery said, cutting across his daughter in his dry lean way. 'I remember. Penn was getting on for fifty but he was determined to volunteer. He lied about his age and the army took him. And never gave him back. Sad business.'

'That's right,' James said. 'I should think Mrs Penn must be in her late forties. She has a grown-up son who went overseas, just before her husband was killed. Now the cottage is far too big for her and she needs a position.' He remembered the quiet, gauntly handsome woman whom he had interviewed last week, and the utterly stoical way in which she had spoken of her life, a life that had been swiftly overturned in ways that her worst fears could hardly have prefigured. He had offered

56

her the job without hesitation, and almost with a sense of personal unworthiness.

'Yes, but can she cook?' said Sylvia, rather loudly, as if feeling herself pushed a little out of the limelight. 'Don't forget, James, you've been used to eating with us, and we have a treasure in the kitchen.'

'James has his own life to lead,' Dr Vickery said. A fleshless, upright, immovable man of sixty-five, he made James think of crab apples, though whether because of the complexion and texture of his skin or his look of tasting something sour he could not say. There was a small element of the ecclesiastical about him too: one could imagine him, austere and dome-headed, acting the Grand Inquisitor with a weary knowledge of human frailty.

One saw this especially when he looked at his daughter, Sylvia. He seemed to regard her neutrally, without either indulgence or irritation. It was as if he had long ago made up his mind about her.

'Of course,' Sylvia said, 'of course James has his own life to lead. I do see that. But it's the quality of that life that concerns me. It can be very comfortless being a bachelor. Much more so than being a widow or a spinster or a widower.'

'All about the same, I would have thought,' Mrs Vickery said.

'Oh no! I don't think so, Mother. A bachelor has the worst of all worlds. Because he's not a natural homemaker as a woman is. And even a widower has had that home made for him, and just has to keep it up. So it is worse for a bachelor. It is, you know, when you think about it.'

'You've been very kind, helping me settle in,' James said. 'But I really mustn't keep taking advantage of your hospitality.' He was, certainly, appreciative of the way the Vickerys had taken him under their wing since he had moved to Shipden a month ago; but he was also looking forward to living on his own account here.

'And there's another thing,' Sylvia said. 'Not only a bachelor life, but a bachelor life in a place that's entirely new to you. You can't get much lonelier than *that*.'

'Well, I'm getting to know quite a few people already,' James said. 'Patients are beginning to come to me, though they're a little suspicious as yet. I am an unknown to them, after all.'

'Good heavens, I don't see why they should be suspicious,' Sylvia said. 'After all, it's Father's practice you're taking over and Father approved you and they trusted Father for thirty-odd years. So really it makes absolutely no sense for them to be suspicious when you think about it.'

'People get used to their doctor,' her father said. 'It's a wrench when they have to change to another.'

'I don't see that at all. It wouldn't trouble me. Because obviously the new doctor must be qualified and competent, or else he wouldn't be there at all. I wouldn't think twice about it if I found myself with a new doctor, I really wouldn't.' Sylvia took a gulp of her tea. It had gone cold and milk-skinned while she talked, but she didn't seem to notice. 'And besides, James, getting to know your *patients* is different from getting to know *people*.'

'My dear,' Dr Vickery said, 'you make James sound like a vet.'

'No, no,' Sylvia said, deciding after a moment to laugh, 'no, not at all, you know what I mean. Peering down throats isn't mixing socially.'

'James may not want to mix, my dear,' Mrs Vickery said.

'Oh, you don't have any choice in a place like Shipden. The main thing is to be sure you don't get taken up and absolutely *swallowed* up by the wrong people. You'll never get free if that happens. I knew someone who moved to Southwold and fell in with the most awful people when they first arrived and that was it: they were stuck with them.' Sylvia waved away an early bee that was making a drowsy circuit of the garden. James tried to suppress a mental picture of it blundering right into Sylvia's open mouth and Sylvia barely pausing to swallow it down before talking on. 'All I'm saying is, be careful of accepting any invitations. Submit them to us for screening first, because we know everyone and it will save you a lot of trouble in the long run.'

'Oh well, I dare say I shall be rather too busy for that anyhow,' James said.

'You'd be surprised,' Sylvia said. Again she looked knowing, and grimly satisfied with her own knowledge. She was a dark, straight-nosed, high-cheekboned woman of nearly thirty, with a touch of the Red Indian about her features and, James noticed, a very faint strabismus which gave her brown eyes an attractively unfocused look. It reminded him of old portraits of society beauties and he wondered if Gainsborough and the rest had deliberately painted the eyes that way as a trick of the trade. 'You'd be surprised how they get hold of you, James. Don't say you weren't warned.'

She used his name a lot. This was, he supposed, fair enough, as he had spent a good deal of time at the Vickerys' this past month. It was true that he did not know many other people in Shipden yet. Still, this did not greatly trouble him: he could manage pretty well without company. And grateful as he was for their kindness, he did not intend channelling his acquaintance through them, nor letting Sylvia gently and humorously boss him. Nor, though he respected Dr Vickery's experience and opinions, did he intend having the old man as a mentor. Dr James Blanchard was independent-minded and self-possessed, and notably stubborn.

People were surprised when they came up against this, because he did not look it. Being fair, slender, young-looking, and quick, with an unassuming pitched-back voice and a dapper taste in clothes, he gave the impression of a lightweight. A patient who had come to him yesterday had clearly felt this. An elderly boatman, gnarled and cryptic, he had delighted in emphasizing the mysterious nature of his ailments. 'Ah – thass what Dr Vick'ry thought at first. Didn't work, though. Not on me. This chest o' mine play up in ways you'd never guess. Yew'll have to eat another yard o' pudden before you understand the way my chest carry on, Doctor.'

But James was not troubled by this. He was confident in his abilities as a doctor, and he had cultivated his detachment. These were the requirements for the life he had set out for himself. He did not see the need for more, and he did not imagine that anything would happen to him which would render them redundant.

He had not, however, anticipated quite such a stir as his arrival had made, though he had known that Shipden was a small community and guessed that it was an inquisitive one. Bemused, he spotted people pointing at him in the street. One or two had even left cards at his house, which struck him as bizarrely Victorian.

'It's to be expected,' Dr Vickery said, a little later – as James was getting ready to leave he had invited him into his study, saying he had some medical periodicals to give him. 'You're more than just a newcomer. The doctor in modern societies is something like the old medieval priest – a public figure who also has intimate access to private lives. Quite a combination. I came in for something of the same treatment when I first came here thirty years ago. Not quite the same, of course; because I was already married.' He blew dust off a stack of papers. 'Which you, my friend, are not.'

'Not so unusual, surely?' James said.

'In these times, yes, I'm afraid. So many men taken by the war. It's curious to see how readily we plunge again into peace, having lost a good part of a whole generation. The societies of the ancient world would have found such a loss so devastating that they would have believed they had offended the gods, and made public penance. We go jazz-dancing instead.' Dry and unmoved, Dr Vickery riffled through the papers with a long simian thumb. 'Yes, I should like you to have these – you'll find some interesting articles here, when you have the time of course . . . We suffered no direct loss in our family. But Sylvia's fiancé, I'm afraid, was killed in France.'

'I didn't know – I'm so sorry.'

60

'In 1916. He was a lieutenant with the Norfolks. A good fellow. Not overintelligent, but solid. The engagement was a little hastily concluded, and I'd go so far as to say it might not have come to anything in peacetime. But still, the loss is felt.' Dr Vickery placed the stack of periodicals in James's hands. 'Anyhow, I'm glad you're fixed up with a housekeeper, James. You need order at home if you're to work well. Don't be a stranger to us, however. You know you're always welcome here.'

The Vickerys came out to wave him off as he drove away. The house stood in large gardens, in a quiet leafy close up at the high west end of the town: Dr Vickery had done well for himself. From a distance they made a strangely assorted picture: Dr Vickery like a long lean enigmatic mandarin; Mrs Vickery, a comfortable plump lady seemingly no more capable of separation from her husband than his shadow; and Sylvia, not at all comfortable, a piece of dark restlessness, waving as if it were an urgent matter and not an empty social formality.

He had come here alone and knowing no one, and there were signs that the Vickerys were ready to welcome him not just as a friend but as part of the family. But James had never known or missed a family in that sense. He was enough of a loner not to boast of being one.

At the junction of the close he waited for a horse-drawn coal dray to lumber past, and glanced at the medical journals on the seat beside him. Some were twenty years old, he noticed, and would be hopelessly out of date. There had been such progress in the past five years, war as ever giving a stimulus to medicine that peace seemed unable to provide. He pushed them aside. He was not dismissive, but he was not greatly interested in the past.

Driving on, he noticed a heavily shawled woman in a bathchair, being pushed by a lady-companion in full high-collared long-skirted Edwardian regalia. Amazing: invalids were still coming here for the air as they had done a hundred years ago, just as if the days of leeches and Peruvian bark and neck-or-nothing surgery had never died.

What a place I've come to, James thought, stimulated and amused; and he wondered with interest what he and Shipden would make of each other.

# SIX

Mille Watlyn looked not a day older than when she and Rose had both left Shipden High School for Girls.

At that time Millie Truelove (her maiden name, and apparently inappropriate) had been a bright, brisk and unsentimental girl who looked thoroughly ready for adulthood. She knew about clothes and the latest dances and how much it cost to run a household and precisely what you should put on a bedside table for an overnight guest (mineral water and biscuits, and have a slice of bread-and-butter sent up at the same time as the drawing of the hot water in the morning). She could talk to anyone and was quite without fear, even of Shipden's ruling caste of matrons, who for some reason took a delight in cowing young women fresh out of school – perhaps because they were not old, fat and chained to dull men. Beside her Rose had felt like an unworldly child.

'Oh, it was all show,' Millie said that Sunday morning, when they took a walk down to the shingle beach below the Arcadia Guest House, and talked over old times. 'I was absolutely falling to pieces inside most of the time. I think, anyhow. At that age, you don't quite know what's going on inside you or who you are or what you want, do you?'

'I suppose not,' Rose said. 'I wonder how old you have to be before you do know?'

'Hundred, probably. Or that age,' Millie said, nodding ahead at Elizabeth and her own little girl, Carrie, who with skirts tucked up in their drawers and straw hats on their heads were investigating a rock pool with forensic thoroughness. Spring warmth was in the air at last and in the sky, which was like beaten pearl, but there was still an iron look about the dark bay beyond the shingle, and the calm of the sea was betrayed by long muscular ripples.

'It's a nice age,' Rose agreed. 'Age of innocence.'

At twenty, to the eternal perplexity of her family, Millie had become engaged to Frank Watlyn. Her father, a clever sharp-nosed, acquisitive solicitor, had always spoken approvingly of Millie's having a good head on her shoulders suddenly whatever was going on in that head became a mystery to him. Why, in the name of all that was sensible, choose Frank Watlyn? He might have forbidden it if he had been less civilized and Millie less determined. As it was, he could only hope she would come to her senses, right up to the moment when he handed her to Frank Watlyn at the altar of Shipden church.

Frank Watlyn was getting on for forty. He made a sort of living as a speculative builder, and even his friends would have admitted that he did more speculating than building. At the time of the engagement, he had a scheme in view for covering the clifftops between Shipden and Saxburgh with cheap bungalow-style dwellings made from converted railway carriages and the old Victorian bathing machines that now reposed in lumber yards all along the coast. People would snap them up – as second homes, retirement homes, holiday homes. Or fishing lodges, or artists' studios, Millie had added, infected with her fiancé's enthusiasm.

But at the time there was a war on. The prospects for such a scheme were not immediately appealing. Even Frank Watlyn, a man who could persuade himself that the sun would not go down at night if he wanted to believe it, had to admit that. But peace would bring a boom; as soon as peace came, the scheme would take wing and soar. Both Millie and Frank had been so confident of this that they had married on the strength of it, whilst Millie's father stood by in bewilderment, as if wondering whether he might not wake up at any moment.

Two years after the armistice, the bathing machines and railway carriages were still in the lumber yards, and a few staked-out clifftop plots, overgrown, and mined by the lean sandy-footed rabbits that thrived along this coast, were all that remained of the scheme that had been going to make the fortune of Frank and Millie Watlyn.

Instead there was the Arcadia Guest House, at Saxburgh – a close neighbour of Shipden's that had stayed a little closer to its cobbly, pebbly, briny fishing-town origins, welcoming the railway and the trippers but eschewing the vast hotels and pier entertainments. The Arcadia, a roomy seafront villa with the usual turreted windows and elaborate loggia and secret, dismal plumbing, had never figured in Frank Watlyn's schemes. It had come his way because he had built it and the buyer had defaulted. It was a stopgap, no more; a living, until one of his many speculative ships came in.

In fact it was doing rather well: what Frank still regarded as a temporary expedient had provided the only secure groundwork for their marriage. Millie knew this but did not take a stand on it. She still entered into Frank's dreams, and Rose did not doubt that she would have given the Arcadia up in favour of a plan to build summerhouses for Eskimos: Millie's father probably knew it too, and the knowledge probably added to the dyspepsia that made him perpetually chew chalk tablets and gave him the look of a pained and nervous hawk.

What he could not fathom was that it was Frank's dreams that Millie loved him for. Being practical and hard-headed was only one side of her, and not necessarily a side that gave her fulfilment. When people said that Millie had changed since meeting Frank, it did not occur to them that she might enjoy the change, nor that a change could be an adding rather than a taking away.

'They do ask such odd things sometimes,' Millie said. 'Carrie heard someone say "raining cats and dogs" and wanted to know what it meant. It means pouring with rain, says I. Why? says Carrie. And do you know, I was stuck. What on earth *do* cats and dogs have to do with it? Carrie concluded that it was silly. Young minds can really be quite ruthless. You simply can't fob them off.'

Rose shielded her eyes against the sun, looking over at Elizabeth. She was a year older than Carrie, and was explaining something about shells to the smaller girl with all the wisdom of seniority.

'Elizabeth asks a lot of questions,' she said. 'I've usually found some sort of answer to them. So far.'

Millie gave her a glance of understanding, but said nothing. The friendship between them was a special one. Neither had done what was expected of her; neither had judged or reproached the other for what she had done. They had stayed true. It was possible that Rose had unwittingly played a part in reconciling Millie's family to her marriage to Frank Watlyn, simply by furnishing an example of how much worse things could have been.

But these considerations played no part in their friendship. It was affection that bound them together, and Rose felt a warm rush of that affection as she returned Millie's glance. No, Millie had not changed: fresh skin, pert nose dusted with freckles, candid eyes as bright and undeceptive as fully opened flowers. Only her hands showed the passage of time; unlike the proprietors of the Grand or the Metropolitan, the Watlyns had no army of staff to do the cleaning and cooking and laundry. At the height of the season, Rose knew, there was a sort of tightly controlled pandemonium behind the green baize doors of the Arcadia.

'How's Dolly?' Millie said.

'She's well, and busy. And enjoying a bit of peace and quiet this weekend, I should think.' Dolly would, Rose knew, be enjoying the opportunity to drink brandy and make midnight snacks to her heart's content. Having the place to herself now and then was a luxury which Dolly was too kind to make much of.

Contemplating this, Rose wondered again about her idea

of leaving the district to start afresh – but that was hard to think of just now, with her sunstruck eyes making out the glimmering bare legs of Elizabeth and Carrie in the rock pool, with the sea drawing rough rattling music from the shingle, with her friend walking beside her in the gentle, unpressed silence of companionship.

She had held out for days like these. It was in the hope and belief that there would be such days for the two of them that she had brought up Elizabeth without secrecy and on her own home ground, in spite of gossip and open hostility.

'I wonder if we could matchmake for Dolly,' Millie said. 'The Captain was telling me the other day that he was tired of the single life and asked me if I knew any ladies. What sort of ladies, says I. Ladies of *character*, says he.'

'Dolly's certainly that. I don't know if the Captain's quite her type, though.'

The Captain was an elderly gentleman who had made his permanent home at the Arcadia. Grimly, gauntly ancient, he wore chimneypot collars and jewelled tiepins and in summer could be seen making a tottering promenade of the seafront or training a telescope across the bay, his bald head a rich mahogany colour and an amber cigarette holder drooping from his grizzled jaws. Precisely which war he had been a captain in no one knew. He looked old enough to have been at Waterloo. Even Agincourt was a possibility.

'Well, perhaps not. I wonder why he's contemplating matrimony at this stage, though?' Millie said.

'Perhaps even at that age you don't quite know what you want in life. Or perhaps he's just lonely.'

'Is Dolly, do you suppose?'

'It's hard to tell. People always assume that spinsters are. Even the word's got that association. But I think Dolly likes the way she is. I certainly don't think she'd change for the sake of it.'

'Some people are all right on their own. They're whole. I'm not, I'm afraid. I would never have believed that before I met Frank. I was sure of myself, or pretended to be. But I was only half alive. That's rather a terrible thing when you think about it, isn't it? It's probably much better if you *can* be whole. But good and bad doesn't come into it. I remember trying to explain that to poor old Pop . . . I know, of course, what they say about Frank,' Millie said, lifting her candid face with a small smile. 'Hopeless good-for-nothing is one of the milder names he's been called, I think. As a matter of fact he isn't. As a matter of fact, he has a project in view that's going to make everyone eat their words and when it's under way we certainly shan't have to rely on the Arcadia any more. But even if he was . . . what they say he is, it wouldn't make any difference. If people don't understand that, they don't understand anything. Sorry. Preaching to the converted.'

'You're not preaching. So, would you give up the Arcadia altogether, do you suppose?'

'Well, I shouldn't mind keeping it going just for sort of sentimental reasons. But Frank, as you know, really doesn't like me having to do the work that's involved and I think he would insist. I don't mind it, but I've a feeling he'll absolutely make me put my feet up.'

Millie spoke staunchly, and her belief in what she said was so implicit that it was really impossible to call it self-deception. And what she said of Frank was true. He did look pained when he saw Millie ironing a heap of bedsheets. A fair, softly spoken man with a lined face and sad-dog eyes, he looked pained a lot of the time. He was a devoted father and a generous friend, even to the point of being generous with money he did not have. It was his quite sincere intention that Millie should never have to iron bedsheets again. With each year that passed he got more sincere about it.

But he loved her dearly; they were happy – any approach to judgement was blocked by this immovable fact. There was no doubt that Frank would shower Millie with gold, if he ever got the gold. Anyone who had suggested that a steady trickle of silver and copper might be more helpful in the long run would have condemned themselves as unromantic, in both Frank and Millie's eyes.

'Of course,' Millie said, 'Carrie's used to it here. Frank's started making her a doll's house, and I think she'll expect it to have a visitors' book and a breakfast gong in the lobby.' She laughed healthily.

Elizabeth and Carrie were sitting together on a rock at the edge of the pool now, dangling their feet in the water and carrying on a solemn conversation. Children, Rose had noticed, rarely if ever looked each other in the face at such times. They were not awkward about it: they just looked elsewhere. It was only adults who glued their eyes to each other's faces while they talked, perhaps because they mistrusted each other so much.

'Would you like to have more?' Rose said.

'I'd like to – Frank too. But I don't seem to be very productive. Some women seem to get pregnant just by seeing a pair of trousers on the bedpost, but not me.'

Rose's thoughts were actually elsewhere, but Millie took her silence as pertinent and turned red. 'Rose,' she said, 'that was rather awful of me.'

'No, it wasn't,' Rose said laughing. 'It was very true. It reminds me of when I was little and I had a new pair of shoes. Mother trusted me to go out in them alone because the weather was exceptionally dry – had been for weeks. Somehow I managed to find the only puddle in the whole town and step in it. I think of that sometimes when Elizabeth's naughty – when she seems to be doing exactly the thing I've warned her against. I try and remind myself that sometimes it's like that when you're a child: it's as if you've got the gypsy's curse on you.'

Millie seemed reassured by her laughter, and laughed too. Carrie and Elizabeth looked up at the sound, and their mothers waved to them.

'They get along awfully well,' Millie said. 'Like sisters.'

'Yes,' Rose said; and again groped sunblind at the impossible thought of leaving.

'Not that all sisters do, of course. Look at me and Clara.'

'You always seem quite friendly.'

'Well, that's precisely it. Just a cool friendliness as if there's nothing closer between us at all. Which I suppose there isn't. I don't understand her in the least. For heaven's sake, she *smiles* all the time.'

Clara Truelove, Millie's younger sister, was an impeccably pretty, impeccably feminine girl, the shining star of Saturday tennis parties and Sunday afternoon church parades, the demure princess of Shipden society. It was a role for which Millie had been prepared; and even though she had willingly abdicated, the touch of envy in her voice was forgivable.

'Her great topic at the moment is this new doctor you have at Shipden,' Millie went on. 'Well, no. It's Mother and Pop's great topic. Clara just smiles. Apparently he's thirty-two, good-looking, well set up, and unmarried. Have you seen him?'

'Yes. I mean, no,' Rose said with a sharp and peculiarly piquant memory of the dapper two-tone shoes.

Millie looked surprised but made no comment. 'Anyhow, I think they mean to make damn sure that he sees Clara. Poor man. A few months in Shipden and he'll be feeling like the greased pig at the fair.'

'Suppose he simply doesn't want to get married?'

'Oh, they'll wear him down until he does. It would be fun if he shocked them all, though, wouldn't it?'

'Yes. I hope he does.'

'Rose,' Millie slipped her arm through Rose's, 'I heard something and didn't know whether to tell you. You know how it is. There's such a lot of gossip, and one rather dreads joining in. But this is pretty well founded and . . . you might never get to hear of it but then again you might and if you thought that I knew all the time . . .'

Rose squeezed her arm. 'You can say anything to me, Millie. Or not say it. It wouldn't change anything.'

'Well. Here goes then. Mind you, this is something that probably doesn't matter to you either way—'

'Millie . . .'

'Sorry.' Millie took a deep breath and fixed her eyes on the lazy soaring of a seagull above them. 'Alec Taverner. He's back in Norfolk.'

Rose pressed Millie's arm again, absently. That name: it was strange to hear it spoken after so long. She had not even allowed it to sound in her head; had created a silence around it, a white space where the words should be.

'You know his stepmother went to keep a hotel at Lowestoft. Well, apparently he's been living there since February. Where he'd been living before that I don't know. But it seems he's looking to settle in Norfolk again. And with money. He had a grandmother on his mother's side, apparently. She died and left him everything.'

'I remember him mentioning her,' Rose said, or rather heard herself say. 'I think he was a favourite of hers.'

'It certainly seems so.' Millie was steadfastly refraining from looking at Rose's face for her reaction. 'Anyway that's what I heard. As I say, it may not be of interest to you either way. And Lowestoft's a fair distance, so it's not as if . . . I just thought . . .'

'It's a turn-up, isn't it?' Rose said with an effort. It felt as if a chill, inevitable as the tide, had crept over the too-calm day. She looked across at Elizabeth, who had shed her straw hat: her hair was blue-black in the sunlight. Unusual hair for a child.

'They used to say . . .' Millie stopped, biting her lip.

'Go on.'

Millie smiled apologetically. 'They used to say that if he fell in the river he would come up with a fish in his mouth.'

Rose laughed. Again the sound did not seem to come from her.

'Set up by his grandmother,' she said, beckoning Elizabeth to come to her. It would soon be time for them to go home. 'Well, of course, it would have to be a woman.'

71

# SEVEN

In the summer of 1915, the war that had been expected to last a matter of weeks had been going on for nearly a year.

To twenty-year-old Rose Jordan, it seemed to have been going on for ever.

Looking back, twenty-five-year-old Rose was stern with herself for having viewed that slaughterous cataclysm as a tiresome interruption of life. But someone less self-critical than Rose would have found it excusable. She was not alone: most of the girls she knew felt like that. The war was a long way away, even from Shipden where coastal defences looked out at the Hun-haunted North Sea and where black-bordered rectangles, like little graves of print, regularly announced to readers of the *Shipden and Saxburgh Post* that another of their sons had fallen in the field. Fallen: that word was very redolent of the time. It suggested something swift and clean and sportsmanlike. It was more like being out at cricket than getting shot to death or blown to bits.

But that was how they were in 1915. Bullish enthusiasm still reigned and it was that which caused the feeling of weariness and irritation in Rose and her contemporaries. Everything was war. Dances, clothes, excitement, laughter – these were not war, they were frivolous, to be put away for the duration. The Shipden season was muted, and its colour was khaki.

At that time Rose lived in a bay-fronted villa at the quiet rear of the town with her mother and a between-maid, or skivvy, whom Mrs Jordan hated because she was not three maids, a cook and a chauffeur. Rose's father had died a couple of years before the war – the final letdown, Mrs Jordan's expression seemed to say at the funeral, after a lifetime of disappointing her – and he had not left them a great deal to live on. Rose wanted to get a job to help out, but Mrs Jordan would not hear of this, preferring to lament acidly the fact that she had married a schoolmaster. Mr Jordan had been a very good schoolmaster; but to his widow that was a contradiction in terms. She sprang, remotely, from one of the county families who still kept their Norman grasp on the wooded acres inland from the town, and liked to give the impression that she had lowered herself by marrying him.

'I could have had anyone,' she would say sometimes, when she was low. 'There's no point in being falsely modest about it. I could have had anyone. But I chose your father.'

And Rose, though she said nothing, would wonder why. If it had been because of an overwhelming and irresistible love for him, Rose had never seen much evidence of it.

But she saw clearly enough that, in her mother's eyes, marriage was dreadfully important: too important a matter to be left to chance, to inclination, to happy accident. A woman must prepare herself for marriage as a nation prepared itself for war.

And so a job for Rose was out of the question. It was better that they live in the most pinched circumstances – even though these were an endless source of irritation to Mrs Jordan. 'I'm not used to this,' she would say with fastidious distaste as she darned a petticoat or sniffed at the boiled bacon that was their Sunday joint. 'This is not at all what I'm used to.' It was about this time that Rose suggested using the one undoubted talent she had, which was music. Her intensely musical father, a conductor of choirs in his spare time and a brilliant organist, had given her a thorough coaching: she had passed examinations and won prizes. It had all been undertaken through sheer love of music but she saw no reason why it should not be turned to good account too. At that time

Shipden was enjoying its first motion pictures, in a converted drill hall on Pound Street, and someone was badly wanted to play the piano accompaniment to the shows. Rose threw this suggestion out, thinking that, at a pinch, it might be seen rather as an artistic pursuit than a job. Her mother dismissed it with a shudder. It was not only a job but a public job – the worst of all worlds.

Very well, if her mother would not countenance her going out to work, then perhaps she might give music lessons at home to augment their income . . .? It was no use. Work was work – and work, Mrs Jordan mysteriously pronounced, spoilt a girl for marriage.

So Rose did nothing. She lived, with her mother, the life of a young lady, even though they lacked the resources to support such pretensions. Inevitably she was bored, though Rose was unsure, looking back, whether she had quite realized her own boredom. She was such a dreamer then – scarcely connected to reality at all, it seemed to her older self; and her narrow upbringing had taught her that this life was all there was. If she was frustrated, the frustrations took no definite form. The fences around her had been too high for her to glimpse anything beyond them. What lay on the other side was the province of her imagination only, and Rose's imagination was no less excitable and perilous than that of most sheltered, sensitive, and passionately innocent twenty-year-olds.

And so the coming of war only added another dimension to the boredom, and by 1915 had produced touches of austerity in their already straitened circumstances: even the bacon joints were smaller. As for Mrs Jordan's plan of campaign to get her daughter married – which had begun just before the war with frosty introductions at winter tea-dances and vigilantly chaperoned mixed tennis, and which had engaged Rose's emotions about as much as a game of chess – that had to be pretty well abandoned. So many eligible men were joining up, and the social chess game just wasn't the same. Already informality, which Mrs Jordan hated, was creeping in. There seemed nothing to do but wait for the war to be over.

And yet there was something in the air too. Beneath the dullness could be felt now and then the throbs of a quickened pulse. That strictly private way of life on which Mrs Jordan insisted – to the extent that she not only had all her groceries delivered to the back door but even sent in her order in a sealed envelope rather than have any direct communication with the shopkeeper – began to break down. The War Office had requisitioned the Metropolitan and several smaller buildings in the town, and an official came to the Jordans' house to assess their circumstances and how much room they had. Though nothing came of this except a fit of the vapours on Mrs Jordan's part, it was a sign of the times. Other callers came too – without prior invitation and not at the recognized calling times, to Mrs Jordan's dismay: ladies of the town who had found in the war an outlet for stifled energies. They had thrown themselves into every conceivable variety of voluntary work and were eager – insistently so – to pull other ladies in with them. They knitted socks for the Western front and gloves for the Eastern. They made up parcels of chocolate and condensed milk, of books and writing paper; they collected eggs for the soldiers and shoes for Belgium. They sported Red Cross armbands and practised bandaging each other; they manned tea urns and sandwich stalls at railway stations and hospitals. Some even belonged to a strange organization that patrolled billeting areas at night to prevent soldiers and young women doing immoral things with each other. And all of this, though it was work, was not work of the sort that Mrs Jordan deprecated. Indeed, it was bad form *not* to enter into it, which placed Mrs Jordan in something of a quandary. Her pretensions had never before required her to do anything more strenuous than dress up and eat cakes in tearooms. Suddenly the done thing needed effort.

So they were recruited. And as Shipden was a seaside resort with, in peacetime, many more musicians, entertainers and places of public amusement than an inland town of the same size, it was natural that the mounting of shows and concerts for wartime charities should play a large part in their activities. This was something Shipden could do for the war. And it was something that Rose, especially, was suited for.

'We must have you, my dear,' the various organizational ladies would insist, as they planned a patriotic pageant with music, a convalescent soldiers' glee club, a choral evening for Belgian refugees. 'My dear, we must call on your services again. There's Mrs Coxon but she bashes at the keyboard so. And we have a children's chorus and they respond to you so wonderfully.'

Rose was kept very busy. She thrived on the activity, and she relished the freedom. It was odd, perhaps, to discover freedom in charitable beanos with bustling provincial ladies – but this was to discount the extreme narrowness of her previous life. Before this, she seldom went anywhere alone. Such social life as she had been permitted had been dictated by her mother. Suddenly she was, in the resentful phrase of Mrs Jordan, who participated as little as she dared, a gadabout. One never knew where she was or what time she would be back. As for her health, Mrs Jordan didn't like to think: she would probably catch her death rehearsing in these draughty halls and whatnot. It was a habit of Mrs Jordan's to label anything she disapproved of as likely to make you ill. Even the idea of women going to university she condemned on the grounds that they would all catch colds from each other.

There was a terrible irony in this. But like most ironies it was only apparent after the event. And like most ironies it was possible to make too much of it. That what happened should have happened under the auspices of genteel busybodying was an irony; that her mother's chief fear was of Rose catching a nasty chill was an irony. But in looking back, Rose had never felt that some malignant and satirical fate was at work on life then. There was no need to impose such a melodramatic pattern on it. Naïvety met opportunism in the forcing house of wartime. It just happened.

Before her involvement with the Orpheus Follies she knew Alec Taverner only by sight. Though he was a native of Shipden, he belonged to that side of the town's life to which Mrs Jordan turned her exclusive cheek. His parents, both dead, had been in the hotel trade and the stepmother with whom he amicably lived had carried it on. She ran a hotel on the clifftop at West Shipden, a place which had a certain racy sophistication beside the stuffy palaces of the Grand and the Metropolitan. It served French food, cooked by Mrs Taverner herself, and there was a small ballroom in which, it was said, you could dance the turkey trot and the bunny hug. Sleek elderly men could be seen driving up to it in new motorcars with young and expensively coiffured ladies beside them.

Alec, whilst he lent a hand with the running of the hotel, chiefly interested himself in the town's entertainment business. At quite a young age he had assumed the role of impresario – a word the flamboyance of which suited him if not Shipden. Just before war broke out he had taken out a lease on the Pier Theatre and had founded the Orpheus Follies, a troupe made up of the best entertainers from the concert parties of Shipden and Saxburgh. He was at that time twenty-six or twenty-seven. Rose never did know his precise age.

In that summer of 1915 the Orpheus Follies were below strength. Several of the male performers had joined the forces. Alec himself had applied, but been found slightly underweight and told to come back when he had put on a few pounds. One of the departed members was the troop's pianist. Alec had been filling in for him – he could play a little, just as he could dance a little, sing a little, scene-paint a little, and act rather well – but the arrangement was not ideal. And then the charitable ladies descended on the Orpheus Follies. There were Territorial camps and hospitals and convalescent homes all over Norfolk that would welcome a visit from a concert party. Rose was part of the impromptu committee that called at the Pier Theatre to discuss this with Mr Taverner.

'Good heavens, look no further for a pianist, Mr Taverner. We have an absolute treasure when it comes to the musical side of things.'

That, Rose remembered, was Mrs Shillingford; who something like a year later crossed the street to avoid Rose, the first time she went outside with her new baby.

Alec Taverner responded readily to the charitable call. It would have been unfair and cynical to point out that the Follies were underemployed anyway, with the holiday crowds depleted by war. Alec was genuinely fired by the idea, as he was by most new ideas; and typically he took it a step further. He began at once to plan a charitable patriotic extravaganza to be given by the Follies at the Pier Theatre in August, to mark the first year of the war. (By now everyone had given up pretending it would soon be over.) His enthusiasm was genuine and infectious and the ladies were thrilled.

There was something different about Alec Taverner. Many people on that Anglian coast had the undiluted look of their ancestors who had stepped ashore from Saxon and Norse longboats: tall, fair, big-boned and solid, or stolid if you liked. Beside them Alec, dark, slight, olive-skinned, theatrical, quick in movement and speech, was like a Mediterranean cuckoo in a Nordic nest. He had an imp's smile and sometimes, when he was intent on something, the look of a monkey, charming and crafty. He got on famously with women of all ages, and had few male friends. He was something of a drinker and would sometimes appear at the theatre for rehearsal in the morning very pale and seedy, his hair a rat's nest, and dressed in the most casual and haphazard manner – flannels held up with a tie, an old blazer from the costume box, cricket boots; though these random outfits looked so well on him that they might as well have been carefully chosen. He knew more jokes than anyone in the world and did not mind, indeed seemed to enjoy, being the butt of them too.

Rose fell for him.

It has been said that loves which come after the first are

not so involuntary – which is a subtler and more truthful way of saying that the first cut is the deepest. Certainly what happened to Rose was involuntary – a falling indeed, a plunge, a helpless dropping through an unsuspected trapdoor.

The first time he kissed her, she was so utterly surprised at it, and so utterly surprised at the realization that she wanted this more than anything in the world, that she could only stare dumbfounded into his face for what seemed several minutes.

'Well,' he said, 'next time I'll just pull a gun on you. It won't be so drastic.'

'You shouldn't have done that,' she said, finding a voice at last.

*Why?* He did not say the word, but he looked it just as effectively. He had curved expressive eyebrows that were themselves like question marks. Why . . . She never answered. But if she had been capable of doing so she would even at that moment have said, *Because you've started something that can't be stopped.*

It all happened in the course of the summer of 1915, yet, in looking back, Rose seemed to see it as a winter episode. She knew there had been sunlight and greenery, but she could not picture them. Instead the whole thing seemed to be wrapped in an intimate, shielding darkness that had something of the night before Christmas about it – a huggermugger atmosphere of whispers and shining-eyed excitement, urgent and not entirely real.

She had not thought of herself, before it happened, as in the market for romance. And she found, despite the equivocal reputation that entertainers had, that there was nothing especially romantic about the Orpheus Follies. There was a good deal of quite physical hard work, there was a surprising monotony of rehearsal and re-rehearsal, and there was a certain amount of minor backbiting and feuding. The scent of chalk-dusted tap shoes and perspiration was stronger than any whiff of glamorous sensuality. And she acted as a musical accompanist to the enterprise very much as if she were the cook in a busy café. It made the plunge into a love affair all the more startling.

But then the love affair was very much a thing apart. It was apart from everything: from the rehearsals in the Pier Theatre where the boom of the waves about the iron columns beneath them vied with the thunder of dancing feet on the salt-softened boards; from the concert trips to the camps and hospitals where players, props and instruments squeezed into a petrol van public-spiritedly lent by a local haulier. At these times Rose and Alec appeared completely neutral in their behaviour towards one another. And it was a thing apart also from the rest of Rose's genteel, irreproachable Shipden life, making bandages and socks and selling flags and eating boiled bacon and new potatoes with her mother in a provincial Sunday peace rippled by the sound of church bells and the cries of watercress-sellers.

The apparent neutrality was, of course, the calm above a seething surface. When Alec came to the piano and leant over her shoulder, casually discussing some detail in the score, there was a sensation in her that she could only think of as the pleasant equivalent of wanting to be sick. At such times the knowledge, with its attendant anticipation, that a few hours later she would be in the arms of the man with whom she was coolly discussing accents and segues was almost unbearable.

Much later, when Rose was pregnant with Elizabeth and Alec was gone, her mother said to her one day with a mixture of scorn and prurience, 'What I don't understand is how you ever managed it.' This was in a way understandable. Shipden was a small, watchful community, and neither of them lived alone. But they managed it, of course; they managed it very easily. Their stretch of coast abounded in deep heathery woods and secluded seashores; and Alec, naturally, had the keys to the Pier Theatre.

But even without these opportunities, they would have managed it, simply because Rose at that time was driven by her blood. Her mind and her heart were involved, of course, but they were subordinated to her blood: she thought and she felt intensely, but narrowly, and with one end in view. It was a time of great freedom and also a time when she was a slave. Self-slavery, slavery to one overmastering passion, was an alarming thing – so she thought in retrospect: at the time she had seemed to be filled with spectacular courage. There was nothing she could not face.

The same could not be said of Alec Taverner.

Later she wondered whether she had ever trusted him; and concluded that she had probably not. But she had trusted love. Love too was a thing apart. It was something in which you placed a trust quite different from the trust you placed in a bank or family ties or the law. Alec Taverner was – she knew it – unreliable, careless, and fatally changeable. But he also stood beside her within the charmed circle of love, and this must make a difference: you only had to look at the difference it had made to her.

'To be honest,' he said the day she told him she was pregnant, 'I really never bargained for this. Phew. This calls for a cigarette. Crikey.' He sat down on a tree stump. They were at a favourite clifftop spot set amongst pines, overlooking the sea: the combination of pine resin and salt in the air was unique and to catch the faintest scent of it years later was to bring the whole scene back to Rose in nightmarish detail. 'Well. You're sure, I suppose? Of course you are. Good grief. This is something – well, to be honest this is something I really never dreamt of.'

It was impossible to be sure, but she thought it was about then that something turned in her – turned in the sense that milk turns, souring and spoiling. She suddenly noticed that phrase 'to be honest', and realized how often he used it. And staring out at the sea she wondered, with the same curious lucidity, why a person should need to say that they were honest so much.

'This is a facer. This really is a facer, Rose. Haven't got any more up your sleeve, have you? The Germans landed in Dover or anything like that? Phew. This is – to be honest, this isn't something I ever bargained for. Phew. I don't know what the hell to do.'

Helpless, comical indecision was an idiosyncrasy of Alec's. She had known him carry a second tie in his pocket because he had agonized so much over which to wear and felt he might still change his mind. And so it seemed with this.

'Dear me. Dear, dear me. Listen – don't worry. We'll sort something out. I don't know what, to be honest, but – well, never mind. It'll be all right.' It was as if she had shown him a bag of money that she had stolen from a bank and now did not know what to do with. Yet that typical indecisiveness was in a way reassuring, just because it was typical of him. She knew enough to comprehend that men very often changed when confronted with something like this – that they became, simply, not the man you had known.

But Alec soon showed that he could be very decisive indeed.

'I'm sorry, Rose.' Not the piny salt glade this time, but the Pier Theatre after dark: smells of chalk and fusty costumes and floor polish. 'I'm just not made for fatherhood. I can't even say the word right. Dadhood.' His eyes shone, just as if he were telling her something rather amusing. Perhaps he thought he was. 'I pass fit now and my country does need me. I might not be much of a soldier but I shall be more use there than I can ever be to you. I do mean this quite sincerely – it might not seem likely at the moment but you really won't regret my going away one bit. I truly, absolutely wouldn't be any good at it. I'm simply too unreliable – in fact to be honest I think I'd be a handicap to you. I mean, I shall – I shall send you my pay and whatnot . . .'

Now this, of all moments, was the moment when she should have hit him. Not a slap with an outraged squeal, but actually hit him, as one man hits another: she was strong and he was not big.

She thought about it for probably two or three seconds,

but the thought was curiously remote. Her reactions tended to be deep rather than violent. And the mention of sending her his pay struck so deeply because of what – rightly or wrongly – she understood it to say about their relationship. He was proposing to pay her, in cash, for the times they had had together.

He might as well, she thought, have paid her at the time. Five bob against the railings. She wondered what a soldier's pay was.

It was her outrage at this single aspect of it that carried her through. It was in a way a safety valve. Outrage was at least invigorating. It made the pulse beat. This was important, because everything else about her was deathly. The time before she had told him she was pregnant was dreadful too; but about that dreadfulness there had at least been a suspense of unknowing.

Now she knew all. And what she felt was hard, very hard to put into words, even when she looked back at it from five years' vantage. Her emotions were so many and so tightly intertwined and knotted that they were, in an everyday sense, beyond her. Light helped you see but too much of it blinded you: and so it was with these feelings. They were so strong she couldn't feel anything.

'You let him get away with it,' her mother said, or hissed, the day after Alec went to his training camp. 'I can't *believe* it. Oh, you fool. You absolute, monstrous idiot. You simply – let him – go.' Mrs Jordan could hardly speak. And she wanted, above all, to ask *Why?* but could not trust herself to pronounce the word without a shriek.

Why . . .? It was a fair question, in a way – but in another way, nonsensical. She knew what her mother meant. If a man got you, in that telling phrase, into trouble, you pinned him down at once. He knew it was expected of him and if he wriggled, you insisted: even in a family such as theirs, with no vengeful father to browbeat him into submission, you could apply sufficient pressure to make him give in and do the decent thing. Far from ideal, of course – Mrs Jordan did not greatly relish Alec Taverner as a son-in-law – but the best of a bad job.

And Rose could not explain, or could not be bothered to explain, that once you had to insist, there was no point anyhow. She didn't want to stand at the altar with a man who had been dragged there – though 'didn't want' was too tame a phrase: she fiercely rejected the idea. She simply didn't know, when she fell in love with Alec, whether the altar was the ultimate destination she had in mind. It wasn't like that, it had been swift and stormy and bathed in that breathless night-before-Christmas excitement; but she certainly knew that she hadn't pictured it ending in this sordid way. And the one thing above all that would compound the sordidness, a hundred or thousand times, would be a forced wedding with a man who had already made it clear that he didn't want to be anywhere near her when that baby was born.

Because that, of course, was the screaming centre of her hurt. Alec liked walking with her on the beach and making her laugh with his jokes and his snatches of uncannily accurate imitation, and drinking champagne with her in the candlelit theatre dressing room and making love to her amongst the heather and bracken. But he did not like these things as much as she thought. And nor, of course, did he love her as he frequently said he did.

You could make excuses for him, say he was this or he was that: easy enough; she caught herself doing it a few times before she made herself stop, impatiently. No good: away with him. She had been betrayed and it was final.

And when her mother still could not help complaining that she had let him get away with it, Rose thought about that and came to a very firm conclusion that Alec, whatever happened, would have got away with it anyway. She could have screamed blue murder and threatened to ruin him and threatened suicide: a brace of hulking brothers and a hanging-judge father with a pistol and a shotgun could have come after him. But there was something of Brer Rabbit about Alec Taverner. Just when you thought you had him he would whisk merrily away leaving you grasping a clump of cottony tail, mocking and insubstantial. In this case the war and the desperate call for recruits had furnished him with an escape route, but if it hadn't been that, she was sure, it would have been something else.

She never did hit him. She had an indistinct memory, at their last meeting, of turning on him in fury, screaming somewhat, hurling names at him: it was not like her and had not lasted long. Meanwhile Alec had looked on, with something of the same expression that he wore when the two light comedians of the Follies were rehearsing a routine that was falling flat. The day before he left Shipden, he came to her house, but she wouldn't see him. Not long afterwards, he wrote her a letter from his camp in the New Forest, enclosing his pay. The letter was quite long: 'We were both awfully young' and 'Sometimes people make the most terrible blunders' were two phrases she recalled. She tore the letter up and sent the money back to him. A similar letter came when he first arrived in France with his battalion. That, unanswered likewise, was the last of them.

But about a week after that a curious thing happened. Alec's stepmother came to see her. One somehow expected her to be blowsy and full of herself but she was a thin frail-looking woman, with a nervously placating manner and fish-like eyes. She had heard about it, she said, and she wanted to know if Rose was all right. She kept saying this, and kept saying too, with furtive dartings of the fishy eyes, that if there was anything she could do, not personally perhaps, but by pointing her to someone who could help her . . . if she could do that . . . she did know someone who was very helpful . . . in these matters . . .

Slow at first, Rose caught on. She said, chiefly to get rid of the woman, that she would think about it.

She thought about it; but even leaving aside the perils of such a course, she had by that time already done a lot of thinking – unconscious thinking, if there was such a thing – about the baby. Mrs Taverner, absurdly enough, left her card: the name *Taverner* printed on it in embossed and curly italics looked as if it might belong to a hairdresser or a tailor seeking your custom, someone whose name you might vaguely remember being brought to your attention, rather than the name of the father of Rose's unborn child; but she never used it anyhow. Rose had decided that she would have the baby and keep it.

And this plan was quite distinct from what had happened between her and Alec. It was not a continuation of anything. She was quite firm about that. If she had detected in herself any sign of wanting to cling on by proxy to that summer, to perpetuate in another form the love that had died, then she would have seriously thought again. But it was not so. There would be love when the baby came – she knew that – but it would be a fresh and new love, not connected to anything that had gone before. If the child happened to resemble Alec, then so be it: it was simply neutral chance; she felt like that about it.

'There are people who want babies,' her mother kept saying. 'Don't you see? That could easily be arranged. And it would be good for the child. You must see.' Mrs Jordan was desperate and uncomprehending. She wanted Rose, like some eighteenth-century courtesan, to retire into the country to have the baby and then have it adopted at once. This plan was the partly rational plateau to which she came after a good two months of hysteria, during which she scaled peaks of fury and plumbed troughs of despair. The fury and the despair came from the same cause – the unbearable fact that this should happen to her. Once it became clear that Rose was determined on staying where she was and openly having and keeping the child, Mrs Jordan sank again into a sort of resigned, gnawing sullenness, like a trapped animal.

Looking back, Rose felt very sorry for her mother – sorry indeed for what she had done to her. Mrs Jordan did not want a shameless slut of a daughter, living under her roof with her illegitimate child. In fact if you had asked her what was the thing she least wanted in the world, that would probably have been it. And even though what prevented her from throwing Rose out on the street was mostly a dislike of being alone, nevertheless she did not throw Rose out on the street. And Rose knew that she was lucky: that girls of a lower social class than her own, who lacked a sheltering parental home, could end up incarcerated as mental delinquents for doing what she had done.

So in her way Mrs Jordan stood by Rose, even though it meant the end of all she valued in life – which was being able to hold her head up high, or stick her nose in the air, whichever way you wanted to look at it. She was hardly to be blamed if she found relief for her disappointment in continually and venomously reproaching Rose for what she had done to her, both before Elizabeth was born and after. In this, after all, she was merely echoing Shipden's general opinion: disapproving of Rose was the only opportunity that remained to her of being the voice of society.

The charitable ladies, of course, had withdrawn from her in horror. Everyone did. Though Rose kept silent, it was soon common knowledge who the father was; but to the absent Alec there attached no more than a faint and generalized discredit. He was a man, after all, and connected to the loose-living stage; and anyway, he had gone to serve his country; and anyway, the girl must have thrown herself at him. There was even an undercurrent of sympathy for him that she should be so brazen about having the baby: that showed there had been something peculiar about the business.

All this was made clear to Rose, directly or indirectly, before Elizabeth was born and to a lesser extent after it. It hurt, but there was no point in getting worked up about how outstandingly unpleasant people could be to each other. Over in France young men were being culled in their thousands for what increasingly seemed like no sane reason at all. This was the way things were. Rose put up with the snubs and was appreciative of the kindnesses. Many of these came from Aunt Dolly, who knitted and crocheted madly, and whose increased presence in their lives Mrs Jordan regarded as a sort of secondary cross to bear. Kind too was old Dr Vickery, who saw Rose through her pregnancy and delivered Elizabeth himself. He was a conventional enough man, no social maverick; but his profession seemed to have given him a broad view of human frailty and its ironies. His dry priestly manner suggested that he was not much impressed by anything either way: we were all going to die anyhow. Occasionally his ingratiating daughter, Sylvia, called too, but she seemed to want to take Rose up as a Case, or a Cause, and Rose kept her distance.

Born at home in April 1916, Elizabeth came into the world lusty and healthy. There was nothing written on her soft brow to say that she was a child of shame. She was just Rose's child, and beautiful. The tiny hands that patted Rose's face in weak exploration were also mighty: they swept away for ever any faint possibility of regret. They took on the world on Rose's behalf, and beat it hollow.

Early in 1917 Rose bumped into Alec's stepmother in the High Street. Mrs Taverner told her, in between dubious glances into the perambulator as if Rose had some exotic and dangerous pet in there, that Alec had been awarded the DSO for valour at the Somme. Perhaps she had seen it in the *Shipden and Saxburgh Post*: Lieutenant A.J.G. Taverner, Eighth Norfolks . . .? No, Rose hadn't seen it. She didn't know what she was supposed to say.

'Would you like me to write and tell him about the baby?' Mrs Taverner said, with another doubtful peer beneath the hood of the perambulator. Your step-grandmother, Rose thought inconsequently, shushing Elizabeth. Or grand-stepmother.

'I don't see what difference it would make,' Rose said.

'Well.' Mrs Taverner gave Rose her fishy look. She still

seemed a little put out that Rose had not responded to the news of the medal. 'I think he'd like to know.'

Rose did not see her any more: soon after that she sold up and moved to Lowestoft. The buyers of the clifftop hotel found, on beginning to remodel it, that it was unsafe and would have to be demolished. The sleek old men and their young ladies had been dancing the turkey trot on a potential landslide.

Just once or twice, Rose allowed herself to dwell on this, to wonder how it would have been if Alec Taverner had been swept down the cliff to the sea before she had met him. No, she decided; because then she would not have had Elizabeth. Still, this did not mean she felt gratitude to him, far from it.

Shortly before the Armistice in 1918, Dr Vickery began to be very busy. A virulent strain of influenza had taken in Shipden during its tour of war-sapped Europe. It seemed, Dr Vickery observed in his dispassionate way, to attack young people in the main. Poor Mrs Jordan, who had doughtily fought off wrinkles with creams and face packs and had shed actual tears of joy on being told insincerely that she looked no more than thirty, might perhaps have taken a last comfort from this. She caught the youthful plague and died a week before the guns fell silent.

'She was a great lady,' Aunt Dolly said loyally and inaccurately, gathering Rose and Elizabeth to her heavy bosom, 'a great lady.'

Shipden welcomed back its surviving heroes, but Alec Taverner was not amongst them. The *Shipden and Saxburgh Post* carried an account of his deeds – he had been awarded the MC – and mentioned that he had returned to England on his discharge. And that was the last Rose had heard of him until Millie Watlyn told her of his return to Norfolk as they walked the Saxburgh shore.

Lowestoft was, as Millie said, a good way away. Still, it felt disturbingly close to Rose, when she first heard the news.

Later – a couple of days later – after some thought, she felt that she had put it into perspective; and told Dolly about it, quite casually. And it was typical of Dolly that in her crashing ingenuous way she put her finger on the very question that Rose had been evading.

'Goodness – goodness – whatever would you do?' Dolly puffed, agog. 'Whatever would you do if you saw him again?'

And Rose could only reply, outwardly, 'I don't know,' and internally too: I don't know. I really don't know.

# EIGHT

Elizabeth's little bedroom smelt of horehound and soup, the smell of illness. A nightlight burnt in a saucer by the bed, feeble against the oppressive darkness of the small hours.

'Is she sleeping now?' Aunt Dolly said, coming in as softly as she was able.

'Yes. Finally,' Rose said.

'I know what you're thinking, dear. But I haven't heard of any cases of that for a good while now.'

'No. I know.' Rose drew a deep breath. 'She just looks so very pale.'

'So do you. You've been looking a mite peaky yourself lately. Been fretting?'

Rose shook her head and trimmed the wick of the nightlight. 'I wish it would get light,' she said.

'It's always darkest before the dawn,' said Dolly, offering the adage simply as a piece of meteorological observation.

'And she's so hot,' Rose said, stretching out a hand to the child's burning forehead.

'Too much sun, perhaps.'

For a moment Rose wanted to scream, 'She hasn't been in the sun.' But it was only the reaction of anxiety: she had gone through these very same explanations in her head, ever since noticing that Elizabeth was poorly around teatime.

Except that she hadn't taken as much notice as she might have. She had come home from work very tired – Madame Carette had had one of the periodic fits in which she wanted the whole stock of the shop rearranged and then decided it was better as it had been – and she had been absent-minded with Elizabeth. Even, yes, a little snappy: she had thought Elizabeth was just being whiny and difficult until she had noticed the hoarseness in her voice and the damp fringe of hair sticking to her forehead.

These were the times – these long night watches by the bed of the person you had brought into the world – when you fell prey to the worst misgivings about yourself. At such times, a niggling voice told Rose that she should never have tried to bring up a child like this. You have to work, and so you're not here to keep an eye on her, and when you do come home you're tired and fit for nothing, and it's so unfair what you put on Dolly's shoulders, and really the whole thing was nothing but selfish stubbornness and a determination to have your own way without a thought for the poor child's welfare at all . . .

The voice nagged on as Rose sat, heavy-lidded but anxious beyond sleep, in the little basket chair by Elizabeth's bed. She hoped for the morning to dispel the voice as it dispelled darkness. Things always did look better in the morning: it was one of the few old saws that were true.

A milky light came at last, shortly after the first stirrings of birdsong. Elizabeth seemed to be sleeping soundly now. Rose left her for a little while to wash and get herself ready for work at eight o'clock: the rest of the time she could spend with Elizabeth. As she hastily brushed her hair in her bedroom adjoining Elizabeth's, her thoughts kept revolving around the question of a doctor. She had no doubt that Elizabeth must be seen by one. But she wished it were old Dr Vickery rather than this new doctor whom she did not know. Dr Vickery was familiar, a fixture of Shipden life since her own childhood: he somehow made illness less alarming, he domesticated it.

But it was silly to think like this. She would fetch the new doctor: perhaps, if Elizabeth were still sleeping comfortably this morning, run out from the shop at lunchtime to call on him.

She walked into Elizabeth's room. Brilliant, startling daylight had replaced the milky dawn, and it showed her an Elizabeth looking tiny, ashen, bloodless.

'Dolly. I'm going to fetch the doctor now.'

'But it's barely seven, dear—'

'I can't help that.' Rose distantly heard the querulous note in her own voice, an echo of her mother's. They said you came to resemble your mother without realizing it.

She suffered a flash of memory: her mother on her last sickbed, shaking her head as Dr Vickery spoke of the influenza epidemic and wailing, 'But how did *I* come to get it?' over and over, in frustrated disapproval, as if she had been sent the wrong bill.

'I won't be long, Dolly . . .'

The new doctor lived at the rear of the town, at the top of a steep road above the station. The house, a roomy but oddly shaped villa on a triangular corner plot close to the road, had belonged to an old lady who had never opened the curtains, hiding in darkness with a horde of cats. It had stood empty for some time after her death. Rose's calves were aching by the time she reached it. At the last moment, as she placed her hand on the iron front gate, she realized she had come out without a hat. In her distracted state, she experienced a moment of curious panic at this, perhaps her mother surfacing in her again: no hat! As if the doctor might take her more seriously if she were nicely dressed.

She walked, panting a little, up the overgrown brick path and knocked at the front door. The day was already warm and only now did she realize how overheated she was. The door was opened promptly by a tall, greying woman in a pinafore, heavy-set and severe in the Anglian way.

'I'm sorry – I know it's very early – only it's my little girl and I wondered, I'm rather worried and if the doctor could possibly . . .'

Rose found herself gabbling: for all she knew she might have been talking Chinese. But the big woman seemed to understand.

'Come in,' she said. 'I'll see.'

Rose stepped into the hall. It seemed very dark in there after the brightness outside and she did not see at first where the woman went. What she noticed at once was the wonderful coolness of that hall on her heated body. The effect was as instantly relieving and welcoming as if she had been handed a cool drink. Her anxiety diminished a little: absurdly, it seemed that if the house could do this then the doctor must have similar powers.

Her eyes adjusting, she found that she could see right down a long passage and through a room at the rear with french windows opening on to the garden. And in the garden, the big woman was talking to a man in shirtsleeves. He was standing on the lawn and eating something off a small plate. It was odd to see someone standing up to eat like that, in the middle of the garden, and curiously engaging.

All at once Rose felt that she shouldn't be looking: it was like spying on privacy. She turned, and ran her eyes blindly over a glass-fronted bookcase that stood in the hall, thinking of Elizabeth and how good she had always been when she was ill and Dr Vickery was called in. Elizabeth did not have many fears: doctors, the dark, water, creepy-crawlies, none of these troubled her. It was good. Rose wanted her to grow up strong, unafraid . . .

A tall shadow fell across her. Expecting the woman, she looked up to see the man in shirtsleeves.

'How do you do? I'm Dr Blanchard.'

'Oh – how do you do? I was wondering if you could possibly come and see my little girl – Elizabeth, she's four – I'm sorry it's so early . . .'

Gabbling again, she made herself come to a halt, and only then did she realize she hadn't given her name.

'What are her symptoms?' Dr Blanchard said.

She told him about the sore throat, the feverishness and lethargy; and in a burst of desperate frankness added, 'I'm probably over-concerned but two years ago I lost – I lost a close relative to the Spanish influenza.'

He didn't try to breeze that away; just nodded, his face pleasant and uncommunicative, and said, 'I'll come now. Is it far?'

'Princess Street.'

'I'll get the car out. We'll be there in two shakes.'

'Oh – that's all right, I'll walk back.' She felt somewhat shy of him, and too worked up for the kind of social contact a car drive would entail.

'You might well get there ahead of me if you did. I'm not much of a driver. But please—' He smiled, made a friendly shrugging gesture. 'No point in tiring yourself.'

The car – the self-same car that Madame Carette had pointed out to her so eagerly – was parked at the side of the house. Rose got into the passenger seat, feeling very strange, while Dr Blanchard, having cranked the engine, darted into the house to fetch his bag. At the last moment the big woman came out and called to him.

'Doctor – your jacket.'

He was still in shirtsleeves. He glanced down at himself. 'Oh, it doesn't matter,' he called back, pulling out.

It couldn't have been meant that way, but it made Rose feel better about being hatless. Still it was strange indeed, driving in an open car with the new doctor through the streets of Shipden. The few people who were about turned their heads openly; and it occurred to Rose, as a kind of parenthesis in the midst of her anxiety, that he surely couldn't know who she was. She was relieved, though, to have secured such prompt attention for Elizabeth. Being only human, she took that in itself as a good sign, just as we open a prompt letter unthinkingly but look suspiciously at one that has been delivered late.

Elizabeth was awake, coughing, and looking sorry for herself, but not as sorry as an adult might look. The patience of children in illness, Rose thought, was humbling: it was as if they accepted this as their inheritance. Dolly was with her, and as soon as the doctor came in jumped up and began blundering around the room grabbing at things and snorting about 'Making a clearance . . . Awful state, you know how it is . . . Miss Jordan, by the way, how do, we haven't met, one can't meet everyone of course—'

'I'm Dr Blanchard,' he said, going over to the bed; and a faint note of conscious pride was audible in the words. 'Hello. You're Elizabeth, yes?'

Elizabeth, all eyes and heartbreakingly tousled hair, nodded.

Dr Blanchard sat down in the basket chair, and touched the head of the rag doll on the pillow. 'And who's this?'

'Rebecca,' Elizabeth said hoarsely.

'And who's this one?' Dr Blanchard said, picking up the clown doll that had slid on to the floor.

'Hasn't got a name,' Elizabeth said, unapologetic as only a child can be.

Dolly was still noisily circulating, dropping things and whacking her shins.

'Oh, Miss Jordan,' Dr Blanchard, glancing into his opened bag, 'forgetful of me – could I trouble you for a teaspoon or something of that kind, as long as it's clean, so we can take a peep at the young lady's throat?'

Dolly stomped eagerly off. Rose glimpsed a wooden tongue depressor in the doctor's bag just before it was closed.

While he listened to Elizabeth's chest, Rose winked encouragingly at her, her mind full of random thoughts. The will was not all; motherhood had its limitations: she could wield that stethoscope but it would tell her precisely nothing useful about the health of the child who meant the world to her – that fell instead to a stranger with no personal interest at all. How different he was from deliberate old Dr Vickery, who had always been stony, mask-like, in his examinations. And yet this man was unreadable too, though so brisk and apparently open. His hands looked brown against his white shirt and there were fine fair hairs on them, a sort of dark-gold fairness as on his head – bronze perhaps, or nearly cinnamon, how weak and inexact the words for human colouring were, what would she do if it was the influenza, would she go wild and mad . . .

Dolly was back with a spoon.

'Silver,' she huffed, 'the one I was born with in my mouth, or not as the case may be, ha-ha.' When she was nervous, Dolly made jokes like this that weren't jokes.

'Thank you. Now, Elizabeth, if you could open your mouth quite wide . . . that's it . . . All right.' He patted Elizabeth's hand. 'You've been very good. I'll leave you in peace now.' Picking up his bag and getting up, he added, 'Goodbye, Rebecca. And goodbye whatever-your-name-is.'

Signalling to Rose with his eyes, he was out of the room and downstairs in a twinkling. All his movements seemed to have this swiftness and economy about them.

'I don't think you need be unduly worried. I saw a whooping-cough case not so long ago and I wondered if it might be another, but it's definitely not that.' Opening his bag on the parlour table he took out a notepad and a pencil. 'Nor do I think it's likely to be the influenza, though I do understand your concern. She has a badly swollen throat and she's going to be in some discomfort. Ask the chemist for this, it should ease her a little. Keep the room aired and give plenty of liquid. Warm flannel round the throat might help. If there's no improvement by Friday, call me again. I'm sorry, I don't believe I have your name.'

Rose's own throat was so tight with relief that for a moment she could hardly speak.

'Jordan – Rose Jordan,' she got out.

'Well, we'll keep a close eye on her,' he said, snapping shut his bag, 'but as I said, I'm sure you needn't be too concerned.' Again there was a slightly proud touch in his voice, a bright note of assertion.

'Thank you so much . . . I was rather worried . . .'

'Of course.'

She found her hand being shaken, and then he was on his

way to the door. Just before she succumbed to a slightly tearful fit of relief, she noticed the departing Dr Blanchard's shoes, and recognized them. And she realized that she hadn't said 'Miss Jordan' and wondered if she had disguised that deliberately, and wondered why it should matter.

Back home James attempted to resume his breakfast, which he had been taking in the garden standing up and roaming around as was his habit when the weather was fine. He could comfortably read on his feet like this too: it was something he had not been aware of until Mrs Penn had pointed it out to him the other day. 'Just like my late husband, Doctor,' she had said with her sad dignified smile. 'I used to think he was itching to go somewhere. But he said he was comfy up on his legs – just like a horse.'

Soon, however, James found that his appetite was gone and instead he strolled about the garden smoking a cigarette. He felt strange. A vivid and frequent dreamer, he half-suspected that the young woman he had just seen was a figure from one of those dreams, the involved nocturnal sagas that, however naturalistic in their detail, had an unmistakable flavour that separated them from reality.

Quite simply, he had never come across anyone like her. Her circumstances, which seemed to be those of a war widow and mother eking out a living with an old relative, were all too common nowadays: her anxiety for the little girl in a land where influenza had tried to finish the work war had begun was understandable and unexceptional too. Yet the image of her would not leave his mind. It was not just the remarkable, self-possessed beauty of which she seemed so wholly unconscious, but something about her spirit, something strong and luminous. So often women in her position clung to the shreds of gentility: struggling to make ends meet, they struggled also to make an impression. James was disposed more to sympathize with this than to judge it; but for the woman named Rose Jordan he felt not sympathy but

100

admiration. Bare-headed and plain-spoken, she had come to ask for his services: she had been half-frantic with worry for her child but had not taken this as a cue for palpitating helplessness. James liked dignity, by which he meant not pompous reserve but the ability to be oneself, and Rose Jordan had lots of it.

Other things, too, which kept recurring in his mind all that day. That proud and graceful walk; her strong slender hands; the force in her serious dark-lashed glance. The name kept coming back to him, too. Rose Jordan: he thought it fitted her perfectly, expressed her indeed. Then he had to remind himself that it was, surely, her married name and so given her by her late husband and not really hers at all. And at that thought he felt stranger than ever – restless, dissatisfied, and curiously unhappy, as if he had lost something and could not be at peace until he had found it.

# NINE

For three days Elizabeth looked very poorly, and Rose walked a tightrope. On the one hand, the reassurances of Dr Blanchard that it wasn't serious; on the other, her own lurking, irrational fears.

She turned up for work, but was always running home to check on Elizabeth; and it was fortunate that Madame Carette was at her most sentimental, and took the child's cause to heart.

On the fourth morning, Rose woke up with a dreadful thump of intuition that she would have to fetch the doctor again. Going into Elizabeth's room, she found the little girl sitting up in bed, bright-eyed and pink-cheeked, talking to her doll and looking transformed. Rose hugged her, prompting one of Elizabeth's very grown-up admonitions that she should be careful not to catch it.

With a child's swiftness Elizabeth had leapfrogged into apparent health. Rose, though it felt dreadfully hard, preferred to err on the side of caution and insisted she stay in bed one more day.

'Tomorrow,' she said. 'You can definitely get up tomorrow, sweetheart.'

'All right . . . Can we go and see Auntie Millie then?' Elizabeth said. An astute negotiator, she saw an opening for concessions.

'We'll see.'

Rose's anxiety over Elizabeth had kept her from thinking much about what Millie had told her, but a letter came from

103

Millie that morning, reviving the subject. She was troubled: she hadn't wished to upset Rose, and was afraid she shouldn't have said anything.

Rose couldn't truthfully say she was upset. There was a curious unreality about the news of Alec Taverner's return to Norfolk. That past had been so effectively put away that to find it cropping up in her present life, even so remotely, was ineffably strange: like looking down and finding yourself dressed in clothes you had thrown away long ago.

Now that she had time for it, Rose entertained the possibility – it was no more than that – that Alec might wish to see Elizabeth. He certainly knew about her, from his stepmother; and though he had made no attempts at contact in the past four years, it was not necessarily certain that he never would.

She asked herself how she would feel if he did. And answered herself promptly.

She didn't want him to. She didn't want Alec Taverner to have anything to do with her or, most of all, with Elizabeth. Paternity was a large, empty word. Elizabeth happened to be a result of Alec's enjoying himself amongst the summer ferns with a girl who mistook eagerness for sincerity, and as far as Rose was concerned that wasn't much of a link between them. It would be like staking a claim in someone's life over the fact that you once lent them five bob.

Thinking of it in those terms was hard, and bruising to her own self-esteem. Luckily, seeing Elizabeth well again reminded her of what mattered and what didn't: her illness, or rather the illness it didn't turn out to be, stopped any self-pitying reflections at their source.

So Rose wrote back to Millie assuring her that the news hadn't upset her in the least and adding that four years was a long time. This was true: it seemed, indeed, much longer since Alec Taverner had been a part of her life. Perhaps it was because the circumstances of that time had been so completely erased. Her poor mother, who had held her infant granddaughter with a rueful look as if she were a piece of flawed china that she had paid too much for, taken by the epidemic; the war over and all its grim paraphernalia of black-bordered Christmas cards, khaki, tear-jerking songs and tinned beef swept away as if it had never been; even the last posters advertising the Orpheus Follies, which had remained salt-shredded but legible around the town and had given her a shudder until some time after Elizabeth was born, had finally been papered over. The Follies had not long outlived Alec's departure for the war. The rest of the male performers had been called up, the chanteuses and danseuses had drifted off to work in munitions or as bus-conductresses, and by the weary close of the war the town's entertainments were moribund. With the peace and the revival of the resort, the Pier Theatre and the management of a new concert party had been taken over by a middle-aged man named Ernie Crimmins, who had entered what he called 'the business' with the cinema shows in the old drill hall, and who cut a very different figure from Alec Taverner.

The role of impresario sat uneasily on Ernie Crimmins' narrow shoulders. Seedy, bespectacled and harassed-looking, with an unmistakable gait – a speedy hobble like that of a man walking barefoot on a hot pavement – Ernie Crimmins darted about Shipden in a permanent tizzy of overwork, slouch hat set back on his head, greasy overcoat flapping, an everlasting cigarette trailing ash behind him. He soothed his jangled nerves by nipping throughout the day into Shipden's many pubs, where he would often get swiftly, roaringly drunk and end up in a row. People teased him simply because he was so easy to tease, and a common Shipden sight was Ernie Crimmins exiting backwards from a pub door, shouting, 'I won't have it! I won't, you know! I'll not be spoken to in that way and if you think I will then you've got a shock coming to you, that's all I can say!' Like many people, he did not see that when he stood on his dignity he squashed it.

He had, naturally, much business at Madame Carette's

shop, and on Elizabeth's first day out of bed he came in, smoking and agitated, to see about a new piano for the Pier Theatre.

'Can't put up with that old one any longer. Rotten tone it's got. It's donkey's years old, of course, and then there's your salt air, but still. Rotten tone.'

Rose remembered that, because she used to play it for the Follies. She suffered a momentary renewal of memories she could have done without.

'You ought to hear it,' Ernie Crimmins said obliviously, bustling amongst the pianos, lifting the lids and picking an abrupt chord here and there. 'Set your teeth on edge, it would. I don't know. All the things I've got to do. It's too much for one man to think of.' He sat down at a Broadwood and began strumming. 'Nice tone. Now there's the town council coming down on me on account of the Kinema. Place isn't safe for public exhibition, they say. Fire risk, they say. Rubbish.' A shower of sparks fell from the cigarette clenched between his teeth, and he impatiently scattered them. 'I don't know. This is nice. Nice tone. How much did you say? Well, I shall have to get back to you. I shall have to see what the bank says. It's all projections, you see, it's all depending, it's getting a return on your investment, d'you see? I don't know. Need a good season. That's what we need – the whole town.' He gave a cough that sounded like someone kicking a concertina. 'Need it. Need a scorcher.'

Rose liked Ernie Crimmins, for some reason she couldn't place, and hoped he would have his scorcher; and walking home that day she felt that it was likely. The cold spring winds had ceased and there was a tranquil warmth that was almost southern in its softness. Already the first visitors to the resort were ambling about in linen suits and straw hats. Rose seemed to catch in the air a poignant breath of promise, an emanation from the future: other days, other experiences. She breathed it in, not minding if it was not for her. She was sick of the past.

At home she found Dolly red-faced and indignant.

'All right then, my lady. We'll see. You tell your mother what you told me and we'll see.'

'I never took it.' Elizabeth, half-tearful and half-defiant, clutched proprietorially at Rose's skirt. 'I never did.'

'Look at this,' Dolly said, extending her hand. Something bright and sharp lay in the roughened palm.

'Where on earth did that come from?'

'The doctor. It's a tiepin. And that is an emerald if I'm not much mistaken,' Dolly said with angry triumph. 'Elizabeth had it.'

'It came off,' Elizabeth said, plainly not for the first time. 'It came off when he was looking in my mouth. It was in the bed and I found it and I kept it. I never *took* it.'

'If you keep something that doesn't belong to you,' Dolly grumped, 'then it's the same.'

Dolly was in one of her 'cross' moods: she looked righteous and bitter. Rose remembered that Mrs Snell, of the acid taste in colours and even more acid tongue, had been due for a fitting today.

'Why didn't you say?' Rose said to Elizabeth.

'It was nice to look at. When I was laying in bed. I put it on Rebecca's dress.'

'Much nicer to look at,' Dolly huffed, 'on the person it *belongs* to.'

'Dolly,' Rose said, 'she's been ill.'

'Oh, everyone's been ill. That's not so exceptional. I've had the arthritis so bad I can hardly pick up a thimble.'

'She's only four years old, Dolly, for heaven's sake.'

'One can never be too young to learn honesty.' Dolly's lips went thin. 'You're too soft with her, that's your trouble.'

'Please don't tell me how to bring up my daughter,' Rose said before she could stop herself.

Dolly just lifted her chin and gave a loud sniff. Unspoken things seethed, not the least of them the obvious rejoinder, *You wouldn't be able to do it at all if it wasn't for me.*

'Elizabeth,' Rose said, 'you know that ought to go back to the person it belongs to. You can't keep it for ever.'

'I never said I wanted to.' Elizabeth was clever enough to see that the focus of contention had shifted from her, and to seize the advantage.

'I'm sorry you've had this trouble, Dolly,' Rose said.

'Born to trouble as the sparks fly upward and so forth,' muttered Dolly, making a grab at the tea-kettle and promptly bashing it over.

Quarrelling with Dolly, even to this extent, left Rose feeling bruised: Dolly too looked chastened as she crashed about the kitchen, and it was partly so that they could cool off that Rose decided to take the tiepin back to Dr Blanchard's at once.

She felt, also, that it was something to do with reputation: without going so far as to say she didn't want to be thought a thief as well as a hussy, Rose felt the need to be strict about these things.

'I shan't be long, Dolly.'

Dolly, making tea as noisily as if she were using a hammer and chisel to do it, murmured something that sounded like, 'Take care.'

'Mummy,' Elizabeth called out at the last moment, 'I've thought of a name for my clown. Higgins.'

Rose gave Dr Blanchard's house a closer attention this time as she approached. Peeling window-frames and cracked panes, legacies of the old cat-loving lady, showed that there was still much for him to do. The front gate made a rusty screech as she shut it behind her.

This was going to be awkward and she rather hoped he would be out. Then she could just hand the tiepin to the big woman, who she presumed was the housekeeper, and be gone.

To her surprise and embarrassment, she turned from the gate to look up into the face of Dr Blanchard. There was a tall topiary shrub in the middle of the front lawn, and Dr Blanchard was atop a ladder that was propped against it.

'Hello there, do you need me?' His tone was friendly, welcoming.

'Oh – not really, it's just . . .'

'How's Elizabeth coming along?'

'She's better – thank you, she's heaps better. Up and about. Just a bit of a cough.'

'That's splendid. I'll be down in just a minute.' He leant out, clipping. Twigs pattered down.

Drawing nearer, she said, 'Shall I hold the ladder?'

'No, no, quite safe!'

The boyish way he said this made her smile.

'It doesn't look it,' she said, noticing how it wobbled.

'Ah, but I can hold on with one hand. See? Sheep-shears – you only need one hand for them.'

Again there was something of the pleased boy about him.

'That's a good idea.'

'How's it looking?'

She dimly remembered the topiary, from the days before the place fell into disrepair, as shaped like a cockerel; but it certainly didn't look like that now.

'It looks fine.'

'Little more off here, do you think?'

'Er – yes, I think so.'

He clipped wildly. 'Now then. Look out below. Coming down.'

He was in shirtsleeves again, and somehow this coincidence helped to overcome her embarrassment. She put out a hand to steady him as he hopped off the last rung.

'I thought it was a shame to leave it ragged,' he said. 'You don't see much topiary nowadays. Now . . .'

He stepped back, screwing up his eyes – first against the sun, then in disbelief.

The hedge looked as if it had been ripped to pieces by a storm.

'But that's terrible,' he said. 'It's supposed to be a cockerel. It doesn't look anything like it.'

109

She met his eyes, and after a moment they both began laughing.

'It could be a rabbit,' she said helpfully. 'Sort of lying on its back . . . with a hat on.'

'Or a map of Iceland . . . Perhaps I'd better just cut it down. It'll frighten the horses.'

'Oh – no, don't do that. It would be a shame to cut it down.'

He looked younger than she remembered him – perhaps because at their previous meeting she had seen simply the doctor, the figure of authority. He had cool luminous blue eyes, which made a striking combination with his slightly foxy fairness. His face was squarish, with clean pronounced bones, and a wide well-shaped mouth. Again his presence gave her the impression of something quick, dapper, mobile and decisive, even when he was at rest.

'So, what can I do for you?'

'I – I am sorry about this.' She took out the handkerchief in which she had wrapped the tiepin and opened it. 'I think you must be missing a tiepin.'

'Good Lord. I thought it must have gone down the drain or something. That's very kind of you. Where did it . . .?'

'It was in Elizabeth's bed. I'm afraid she – she let her doll wear it until we found out.'

'Ah – Rebecca.'

'That's right.'

Dr Blanchard hesitated. 'Well, you know, I feel rather bad about taking it back – I'm sure it looked better on Rebecca.'

'No, no,' Rose said, 'I wouldn't dream of it – please,' and as he made no move to take the tiepin she put it into his hand.

'Well – if you insist. I'm glad Elizabeth's feeling better.'

'Yes . . . I feel rather fussy and silly for fetching you that morning.'

'You can't tell with children. It's better to be safe than sorry. A child can be in the most shocking pain and will only call it

110

a tummyache. Please don't hesitate to fetch me whenever you have the slightest uneasiness about her. Or bring her here, of course – I've got my consulting room set up. You can't be too careful of a small child's health. Besides, I need the patients.'

The sudden droll switch left her floundering for a moment.

'Oh – surely people are coming to you, aren't they?'

'Slowly. Suspiciously. I am an outsider, after all. How long, would you say, before Shipden will accept me as one of its sons?'

'I'm afraid unless your great-great-grandfather was born here you're out of luck as far as that goes. We're like that in Norfolk.'

'H'm. Hope I haven't spoken out of turn.'

'No, no. I mean, I'm a native myself, but . . . let's say I'm in Shipden but not of it.'

'Detachment, eh?' he said with a keen look. 'Best way.'

'People will soon get used to you, anyhow.'

'They'll have to,' he said, in a quiet downright way that she rather liked.

'Dr Blanchard!' The big grey woman had appeared at the door of the house. 'There's the telephone for you.'

'Oh, I mustn't keep you,' Rose said hurriedly.

'Thank you for bringing this – it was very good of you coming all this way. And I'm glad Elizabeth's better. Say hello to her for me.'

'I will. Oh, by the way, the clown has been given a name. Higgins. She wanted you to know.'

'Higgins.' His eyes crinkled, most attractively, in amusement. 'Well, I hope we'll meet again.' He sounded warm and sincere and the look in his face confirmed this. 'If that doesn't sound too ominous. This is the thing about being a doctor. You can't really say you look forward to seeing someone again without it sounding as if you're wishing an illness on them.' He shook her hand, already starting towards the house. 'Goodbye, Mrs Jordan.' At the last moment he turned to wave.

Rose opened the rusty gate and walked down the quiet

street. It was full of long shadows and smelt, dustily, of sun on sandy brick and new leaves.

Mrs Jordan.

She hadn't corrected him.

Did that count as a lie? If so, it was her first. Well, she could look on it as getting into practice, if she did move away and live under a married name.

But now more than ever the idea seemed an impossible monstrosity. Even this faint touch of a lie hurt her in ways she did not understand.

# *TEN*

Tom Cherry was one of the first patients to come to James when he set up his new practice in Shipden, and one of the most troubling to someone who had chosen medicine, as James had, in order to make a difference.

In his experience not all doctors did. Dr Vickery, for example, seemed in his dour priestly way to regard illness as something like original sin – our inescapable lot, and something against which the medical profession could only fight a rearguard action.

Dr James Blanchard wanted to change things. Even though he had chosen general practice, his view of medicine was Promethean, heroic. He had always thought *Frankenstein* a miserably abject and specious story, with its meek moralizing about usurping the prerogative of the Creator. James did not think the Creator exercised his prerogative particularly well – if there was one at all, which he doubted. This was not something that had troubled him. At the age of fourteen he had gone to his father one day and said he wished to be excused church from now on.

'Why is that, James? Is it because you don't believe in God?'

'Yes.'

'I see. Very well then.'

'I needn't go?'

'No. If that's what you want. I asked you why, in case you didn't want to go to church just because it's full of ladies in flowery hats or because the vicar's a fool or something like that. That would have been different. You'll always have to mix with ladies in flowery hats and foolish vicars so it's as well to get used to it. But if you don't believe in God, very well. I may say that I don't either. But it's best to keep it quiet, if only to save yourself being lectured.'

James tended not to believe in dramatic turning points and moments of revelation – real life, he thought, was not like that: but he admitted, if only to himself, that the death of his mother had had a decisive influence on his choice of medicine as a career and his attitude towards it.

He was at that time ten years old, and away at school. An urgent message that his mother was ill brought him quickly home, but not quickly enough. She died before he got there – died, he later realized, when he was entrained somewhere between Oundle and London. That we could make trains run on time but had no power over mortality struck him as obscene.

The doctor who had attended his mother was at her funeral. Never mind that he was a family friend: something seemed to James profoundly out of joint in this also. The man had not seemed oppressed by his failure to save. If you built a bridge that collapsed, James thought, you would hardly be at the scene looking on and saying what a pity it was. Later these feelings moderated, but a stubborn seed had been planted.

He felt its full growth within him when faced with a patient like Tom Cherry.

'I'm all right sometimes. And then other times thass like I'm breathing through a straw. I'm fighting, fighting like beggary, just to get the air in my lungs.'

'How about coughing? Does that help, or make it worse?'

'I get a coughing fit now and then. Nothing come up. And then there's my breath. Sometimes it stink something horrible – I know it does, you don't have to pretend it doesn't.'

'That would be the effect of the gas on the lungs too, I'm afraid.'

'But thass years ago now. This is what get me. All right, they gassed me in the war. But that was then. Surely I can't have the gas still in me.'

This was what James dreaded: the look of expectancy, the never-extinguished hope that he, the doctor, would suddenly pull a medical rabbit out of the hat. But there wasn't anything to be done for Tom Cherry: the only thing anyone could have done was prevented him being sent to the trenches in the first place. Mustard gas – perhaps German, possibly our own – had permanently impaired Tom's lungs, and had given his breath that sickening sweet tinge. He had been returned to civilian life by the army as a 'fit man', which he was in so far as his limbs and eyes were intact; and as a fit man he had landed a job, at last, as a porter at the Grand Hotel on Shipden seafront. He was lucky to get it – lucky in the same sense that he was fit: it was a poorer job than any he had had before the war.

'The gas does have long-term effects.'

'You mean it'll get worse?'

'Not necessarily.' James winced as he pronounced the words he had always sworn he would never say: 'I'm afraid it's something you'll have to live with.'

Tom Cherry blinked twice at him, but there was only the faintest note of disappointment as he sighed and said, 'That's what Dr Vickery said.'

'Does it affect your work badly?'

'Oh, no. I manage that. Manage that easily.' A big, blunt-nosed, beetle-browed man of thirty, there was yet something of a youth's innocent bravado in Tom Cherry. 'All up-to-date in the Grand now. The War Office left it all done up with electric lights, brand-new lifts, geysers – military efficiency, you see.'

'Ah yes. Military efficiency.' The same, James supposed, that had sent men into gas-filled trenches with no more efficient respirators than handkerchiefs soaked in urine.

'There's my skin, though.' Tom opened his shirt. 'That come up sometimes when I get in a sweat – from running up and down stairs, you know.'

About to say, 'What about the new lifts?' James stopped

himself. Stupid. The lifts, of course, were for the well-heeled patrons of the Grand – probably the same people who had sent Tom Cherry into battle.

'Thass where the gas got trapped under my tunic one time,' Tom said, indicating a broad patch of tight, shiny redness across his chest. 'Blistered something chronic. It still flare up now and then – when I get in a sweat, when I have a bath, in bed sometimes.' He buttoned his shirt and went on in his rapid way, 'I know there's worse. Poor ole boys with hardly no skin left, have to lie covered in grease from head to foot day in day out. Still it do grind you down. I mean, I used to be a picture of health, ask anybody, never a day's sickness.'

'I can give you something to make you sleep better at night,' James said. 'If that would help.'

'That would help, yes.' Again the smothered hopeful glance, as if James might be holding something back.

'Other than that . . . well, you could go and shoot Haig and the generals.'

It was a tactless remark and at once he felt it so. Meaning to express solidarity, he sounded as if he were belittling the soldiers' sacrifice, to himself at least. Tom's expression was mixed. He understood, but ties of loyalty and comradeship tugged at him.

'I don't know,' he said honestly. 'Sometimes I get mad at what happened, but then who am I to say? Were you there, Doctor? In the show?'

'Military hospitals,' James said, uncapping his pen and staring blankly at his prescription pad. 'Not at the front, though.'

'Ah. Well – you were sent where you were needed, of course.'

Was I? James thought afterwards, as he washed and dressed, preparing to receive his first guests.

The Great War for James had been more frustrating than traumatic. Newly qualified when the war broke out, he had found himself marked up as too valuable to be cannon fodder. He was taken at last by the RAMC, but never sent abroad, instead doing duty in the clinical wards of hospitals and rest homes for invalided and convalescent soldiers. The war had given him a broader medical experience than he could have hoped to gain in peacetime, and the servicemen he had treated had seldom shown him anything less than respect and gratitude. Still the consciousness of not having soldiered weighed heavily on him at times. There were men, he supposed, entitled to feel worse in this regard: he had a friend in London who had spent the war working in a bank, his job given the status of reserved occupation and his applications to the military continually turned down. Bloodthirsty ladies had handed this friend white feathers in the street, poison-pen letters had been sent to him, and he had greeted the Armistice in a state of near mental collapse.

It was much easier for James. War needed doctors to be doctors. Yet it was also this easiness that troubled him. Nobody ever would call him a shirker or a base-wallah, except perhaps himself; and sometimes he could not quite look men like Tom Cherry in the eye. Put it all together and it made very little sense, especially as he had concluded quite early on in the war that it was a fruitless slaughter that would shame civilization.

Yet it made a little more sense, perhaps, when he brought to mind a single episode of the war – as he did, reluctantly, now.

While working at a London hospital he had fallen in love with, and become briefly engaged to, a V.A.D. nurse. She was a pretty delicate girl named Lisette who had had to overcome the opposition of old-fashioned and even tyrannical parents in order to nurse, and was justifiably proud of her victory. In London, dark and Zeppelin-haunted, James had tasted romance, and found himself filled with a strange urgency that yet had something unreal about it. He was perhaps more in love with love than with her – though in first love this is pretty much the rule rather than the exception. Caution had slipped the leash, and he had suggested that they run off and get married. Lisette had backed away. Deeply hurt at the time, James afterwards saw that she might well have detected that core of unreality about his feelings.

But this, while charitable, was not the whole truth. Lisette had volunteered for war nursing more out of enthusiasm for war than nursing. She had a brother who was a captain in a distinguished regiment. She was closer to her parents, both emotionally and in her ideas, than her defiance suggested. When James proposed the quick marriage, she told them about it – having omitted, as it turned out, to tell them of the engagement. None of it was approved of. James as a doctor might be respectable enough, but still he was not in khaki. Whether it was Lisette's father or mother who hinted that her suitor might be seeking marriage as an extra insurance against being called up, the bitter fact was that Lisette did not angrily reject this but actually put it to James. It was possible she even believed it.

Inevitably the engagement was broken off. But James was left in an emotional quandary. If her love was conditional on his being a soldier, then it wasn't a love worth having – his self-respect insisted on that. But that didn't stop him applying for, and once again being turned down by, the armed services. Probably he was trying simply to put an end to the mess of it all, but it felt like failure. And soon afterwards Lisette became engaged again – this time to a former patient at the hospital, a convalescent lieutenant who had been decorated for gallantry and whose self-sacrificing deeds were spoken of with a respect unusual in that establishment, where the wounded men were sceptical and glory-boys little esteemed.

This had cut deep – not least because James knew how much exhausting effort the medical staff had put in to restore the shattered hero to health. James had too much energy to be disabled by bitterness, and he told himself that it was foolish to carry a torch after Lisette's final dismissal of him. But in trying so hard to be civilized, he glimpsed the places in his heart where he was not. He experienced for the first time the sickly thrill of jealousy: it was horrible and he hoped never to meet it again.

The episode left him, also, with a hatred of conventionality more profound than that of a flagrant rebel.

As for Lisette's wounded hero, James had liked him. Man to man they got on well – exactly the case with Tom Cherry. But still there was the lurking consciousness of difference.

That the problem was his alone, and not a general one, was plain from Mrs Penn, his housekeeper's, attitude towards him. The war had taken her husband and the home they had had together, leaving her to work for and live in the house of a man whom the war had spared. But she had established an immediate rapport with James on coming here. And when he had told her that he had invited the Vickerys to dinner Mrs Penn in her quiet stoical way had caught on to the wry humour of the situation. She saw that his ability as a bachelor to entertain would be under scrutiny.

'Something a little bit special, I should say, Doctor?' she said, planning the meal. 'Not plain. A proper dinner.'

'That's the ticket, Mrs Penn. We'll do the thing in style.' She was, as it happened, an excellent cook. He could imagine what capital Sylvia Vickery would make out of stodgy puddings and a generally cheerless board.

Sylvia could, however, make capital out of anything. Her remark on first seeing the well-appointed dining table that evening was, 'James, all this for us? But that's so sweet of you. To think of you planning all this here on your own – I call it sweet, I really do.' Thus she made him the lonely bachelor, going overboard when he had a chance of company.

He had invited the Vickerys out of simple friendship and because he wished to return their hospitality, and in spite of his resolve not to be taken too smotheringly under their wing. Looking around his house he wondered if it had not been a little too early. The place was still being redecorated and such furniture as he had been able to afford stood solitary and shiny and rather obvious. He didn't mind it; though there was a trace of the dandy about James, who was personally immaculate, he could happily live in disorder. But he saw that he had laid himself open to insinuations about home-making. He got them.

'I always think men are stuck in the nomadic stage of civilization,' Sylvia said over the soup, her restless, deceptively unfocused eyes taking everything in. She was wearing a mauve crêpe-de-Chine frock which James had not seen before. 'They simply pitch their tents wherever they fetch up. I'm sure if it wasn't for women there wouldn't be any settled societies at all. We'd still be roaming the plains like Genghis Khan.'

'I'm afraid poor Miss King must have left the house in rather a sad condition,' Mrs Vickery said. 'She grew rather eccentric in her old age. You must have had your work cut out to refurbish it, James.'

'Some parts I've just let alone for the time being. I have my consulting room, and this room and Mrs Penn's room have been finished. My bedroom's habitable. For the rest it's just a question of closing the doors and not looking.'

'Of course, there's no point in giving the house a thorough overhaul just yet,' Sylvia said. 'Just for your own occupation – that would make no sense. And of course, it's more economical.'

'Well, I wish I had the money to bring the whole place up to scratch,' James said, 'but that's quite beyond me, I'm afraid.'

'It's cheaper to do it piecemeal, anyhow,' Sylvia said. 'It actually costs less when you do it that way. People always think bulk spending is more economical, but it isn't really, not when you think about it.'

'Our grocer discounts large orders very handsomely,' Mrs Vickery said. 'I wonder he can afford to do it sometimes.'

'Oh, I know that, Mother. I'm not disputing that. But it doesn't necessarily work out cheaper, you know. Not when you consider the waste you get from large amounts of things. It's actually more expensive when you think about it.'

'And your consulting room, James,' Dr Vickery said, taking

his soup with grave consideration, as if he were diagnosing it. 'Does Shipden beat a path to it? Or are folk still chary of you?'

'I have a fair patient list now. I dare say I shall have to wait until the winter chills for a full schedule.'

'It gives one pause, doesn't it?' Dr Vickery said. 'To think that one's livelihood depends on others suffering to some degree.'

'That's true of everyone, surely,' Sylvia said brightly. 'The grocer's livelihood depends on people suffering hunger pangs, if you think about it. The solicitor depends on people being in legal difficulties. Even a painter's in the same boat, really.'

James could not think why. But knowing that Sylvia would find a reason if it took her all evening, he chose not to pursue it.

'Have you had to deal with any influenza cases?' Dr Vickery asked.

'None certain. I saw a fisherman over at Saxburgh who I believe was on the mend from it, though he'd actually called me in because his wife had hurt her ankle and said he'd had nothing but a touch of the shivers. Camphorated oil had set him up, he said. There's never any telling which constitutions will withstand it. Oh, and I had a mother come to me in some anxiety over her little girl, but luckily it was pretty plainly a throat infection. She'd lost a relative to the influenza, so she was understandably worried.'

'Oh, who would that be?' Sylvia said. 'I don't know anyone who's had a sick child. A girl, you say? Not Cora Betts' little Olivia?'

'No, Jordan was the name,' James said. The name came readily to his tongue: he realized how much it had been in his mind the last few days. 'Mrs Rose Jordan.'

'Dear, dear,' Mrs Vickery fluttered.

'Poor James,' Sylvia said. 'I'm afraid she put one over on you, as the Americans say. Rose Jordan isn't a Mrs. Miss Jordan she remains, I'm sorry to say.' Sylvia made a great show of not saying any more, whilst plainly preparing to say a good deal.

'Oh. Well, come to think of it, she didn't say she was Mrs Jordan,' James said. He felt irritated with Sylvia's look of smug knowledge, and this prevented him seeing what else he was feeling. 'No, she didn't. That's my mistake. I just . . .'

'You assumed, very naturally,' Sylvia said. 'If a woman is in that unfortunate position, one somehow doesn't expect her to be quite so – well, undisguised about it. But that's Rose Jordan for you. One feels sorry for her, but I don't think she'd like to know it. I really believe she wants people to *admire* her for what she did.'

James had a pause for thought while Mrs Penn took away the soup dishes and brought in the Dover sole. What the newspapers called war babies had been a common subject for discussion a couple of years ago, before other things had been found to wax moral about, like dance halls and women smoking. James had always thought the outcry a prime piece of hypocrisy, but that was in the abstract. Here his feelings were engaged, and they were complex. He was eager to know more of Rose's story – but he was reluctant to expose her, even in absence, to the judgement of the Vickery ladies.

'She has managed very well, I think,' Dr Vickery said judicially. 'Bringing up a child in those circumstances is not easy.'

'Oh! I don't dispute that,' Sylvia said. 'I think anyone would agree with that. Why she should choose to do it, here in Shipden, is a different question. It's a sad little story, James. I hold no brief either way, so you may as well hear the facts of it. You're sure to hear some garbled version of it in a town like this. It was during the war – I think it would be 1915. There was a man named Taverner – his people were in the hotel trade, he arranged concerts and so on. Something of a fascinator, so one hears, though nothing very discreditable. Rose Jordan was a perfectly nice girl – her father was a schoolmaster and her mother bore up very bravely when she was widowed even though it was common knowledge that the poor things hadn't a bean – and all in all it was a tremendous shock when it turned out that Rose had, ahem, danced the night away with this Taverner, as the yellow-back novels would say. Enormous shock. Though as it happens I think I was one of the few people who wasn't surprised. People used to think she was rather a bluestocking if anything, what with her being musical and so on, but I saw through that quite early on. I remember when everyone was talking about what a surprise it was the way she'd turned out, I simply thought: but couldn't you *see*? Surely I'm not the only one who saw?'

Greedily she searched James's face for reaction. James helped himself to potatoes.

'Anyhow, her beau turned out to be rather a reluctant beau when it came to . . . you know. Some people said it had all been a plan on her part to pin him down but I don't know about that, I'm just giving you the facts. The father-to-be joined up with patriotic promptness and poor Rose Jordan was left . . . well, to say left holding the baby is just too frightful, so let's say left in a pretty pickle.'

'And he was killed in the war, I suppose?' James said.

'Oh no! That's precisely it. That's precisely the irony.' Sylvia was all worldly, kindly amusement. 'He came through it. Decorated several times, I believe. They say distance lends enchantment and poor Rose's beau seemed to wish to stay enchanted. In other words, he never came back. As far as one can gather, he never intended to. There. You've been made privy to one of Shipden's sadder little scandals, which is a step towards honorary citizenship.'

James felt intrusive simply hearing this. But the question came unbidden, as he remembered the handsome, strong-looking woman with the unfathomably dark eyes. 'How does she manage?'

'She works at the music shop in the High Street,' Dr Vickery said. 'Mrs Jordan died in the first wave of the influenza. Rose lives with an aunt now. It was all a sad business. But she has managed very well and has faced down her – her lapse. I delivered the child myself. It was in the middle of the war and all one heard about was death. Any new life was heartening. Of course, the social stigma remains. Some justification can be found for it: a woman who throws away judgement in that way must forfeit a certain amount of respect.'

'More than that,' said Mrs Vickery firmly. 'It is much worse than that, my dear.' Having no brains or feelings worth mentioning, she substituted for them a devoutly merciless morality: asleep all her life, she woke only when this was touched.

'Well, she must be a courageous woman,' James said.

'Exactly what I've always said,' Sylvia rapped out. 'I said that from the beginning. It took a good deal of courage, I always thought, to bring up an illegitimate child here, where everyone knows her, where everyone knows the whole pitiful story. She has to walk down the street in the knowledge that she sacrificed her whole good name and character, her entire future, for a man who didn't wish to know her once he had got what he wanted. A lot of people call it common shamelessness, but they don't do it in my hearing because they know I'll stick up for her. I defend her.'

James privately hoped he would never be unlucky enough to have Sylvia Vickery defend him.

'The man in the case seems to have got off pretty lightly,' he said. Though he meant to speak conversationally, the words came out with sharp emphasis, and this had the effect of revealing to him his own feelings. He found he felt not just indignation but a personal animosity to this man whom he had never met. 'Scot-free, in fact.'

'Mmf,' said Sylvia: she was eating fish, but this sound was a warning signal to the others not to speak as she was just about to. 'Exactly what I've always thought. But then that's the way. It *is* different. Nature is nature, and so forth. If a woman throws herself at a man, and I use that phrase merely as fact and not in any derogatory way, then it's hardly surprising.'

'It doesn't absolve him from blame, though,' James said.

'Oh, I'm not disputing that! I agree absolutely. But it isn't surprising, that's what I mean. I remember people were very surprised at the time, the way the man behaved, but I wasn't, not for a moment. I don't know why, I just seem to see into these things. I can't do anything about it, it's just a thing I have.'

'I believe that Jordan woman flaunts what happened,' Mrs Vickery said, 'just to insult respectable people.'

James's curiosity had turned Rose Jordan into a dinner-table topic. This was not what he had intended; but the whole exchange also had the effect of crystallizing his feelings about her. Emerging from surprise and wonder at the story, he found himself holding a sturdy respect for Rose, while his respect for these people, who were so loftily judging her, had diminished. Feeling that he did not want her name bandied about in their mouths any longer – and her name inspired in him a lot more than respect – he deliberately changed the subject.

'I believe I forgot to mention,' he said, 'my father has promised me a visit soon.'

'Oh, your father, how is he?' Sylvia said eagerly. 'Did he sort out that unfortunate business about the foreman stealing from his firm? That must have been terribly worrying for him. I'm surprised, you know, that he doesn't retire. He's worked so hard all his life. I think he's entitled to some peace.' Sylvia had never met James's father. She wouldn't have known him from Adam.

'He says he's like the old carthorse that falls down if you take it out of the shafts,' James said. 'He enjoys his work, at any rate – always has. The foreman's still there, by the way. Father didn't press charges. The man had been at Passchendaele. He had always seemed quite without mental scars but his house told a different tale when the police visited

125

it. He'd been hoarding literally everything. There were old cigarette packets neatly stacked up to the ceiling. It was some painful impulse to squirrel everything away.'

'Even things that didn't belong to him,' Dr Vickery said with a dry lift of his eyebrows.

'Well, he's receiving treatment, anyhow, and Father's happy for him to keep his job,' James said, putting down his knife and fork. He had suddenly had enough of elderly cynicism and finger-wagging. He felt young and impatient.

'A lot of these ex-soldiers seem to be the complaining sort,' Mrs Vickery said. 'They're forever bewailing their lot. What, I wonder, would the men who didn't come back make of them?'

'I don't know,' James said. 'Probably they would wonder what it was they died for – seeing their comrades slaving away in poor jobs, or with no jobs at all.' Oh, he did not like this, not one bit; and he did not like it either when Sylvia promptly hurried over to his camp, crying, 'This is precisely it – they're discontented because they thought they were fighting to make a better world. Of course it can't be helped that there aren't enough jobs, but they can't be expected to see it that way.'

'Mind you, there is lots of work to be had if they want it,' James said. This was not his belief: he said it out of deadly mischief, to see if there was any position Sylvia would not adopt.

'Of course there is,' Sylvia said readily. 'There's more work than ever. But they think it's beneath them, after being war heroes.'

'They should be ashamed,' Mrs Vickery said. 'At least they came back.'

With an acute dart of shame, James remembered that Sylvia's fiancé was one of those who had not come back. He struggled to make a hasty reparation, saying, 'Anyway, when Father does come up to Shipden, I'd love you to meet him. I've told him a lot about you.'

He felt bad about this cravenness, and worse when Sylvia leapt at it so eagerly.

'I'm longing to meet him,' she said, her eyes intently seeking his. 'I feel as if I know him already.'

James had a complete mental picture of it: his father shaking Dr Vickery's hand, Sylvia flourishing her personality at him, the two families firmly linked, the whole thing so clear cut and relentless and inevitable . . . He felt stifled, and also guilty. His habitual detachment had made him naturally polite: these were decent people who had been kind to him; why then this urge to run away?

He forced himself to dismiss the picture, told himself he was fretting about nothing, and concentrated on playing the host. But that evening he encountered in himself an unsuspected something that could only be called loneliness.

He had never been aware of it when alone in the house. That the company of people should bring it out suggested that they were not the right people. He did not follow this conclusion up, but he kept thinking about the woman who had stood beneath the topiary looking up at him with a gaze that was half grave and half humorous. There was life in that look. It had struck him and tantalized him and now that he had heard her story he was more tantalized than ever.

'James, I've been thinking,' Mrs Vickery said after dinner when they were drinking coffee and James was trying not to look at the clock. 'Your father being a printer – how does he decide which books to print?'

'He isn't burdened with that choice. Publishers do that. He simply prints what they pay him to print.'

'Oh. I see. But suppose it was something offensive or indecent? Would he print it?'

'Oh yes, I dare say,' James said. It was not true, but all at once he had had a bellyful of prurience, and for the first time in his life experienced a mad wish to tear off all his clothes, gallop away naked, and feel disapproval wash coldly over him like a clean invigorating wave.

127

# *ELEVEN*

'I did what you said.'

These are always alarming words. They alarmed Rose greatly when Angelica Harwood spoke them, immediately on entering the music room.

'He's been away,' Angelica said, seating herself at the piano stool and pulling off her gloves. 'Visiting some relations, I think. But he came over on Saturday with Clive and Clive invited him to dinner. And before dinner Clive told me to go and show him the orangery. Which is a bit odd as he's seen it heaps of times.'

'This would be Freddy Collymore,' Rose said, her misgivings growing. This was the terrible thing about giving advice, even unwillingly. You became responsible.

'Yes. Well, it was awful. He started talking about how much he'd missed me and – well, it was such nonsense. He doesn't even know me. And then he said didn't he get a kiss to welcome him back.'

Rose remembered the horrid wet lips.

'So I said very politely, no, I didn't think that would be a good idea. I was shaking all over. But I stuck to it. He tried again and I said no. He went into a bit of a huff but he didn't say anything more, not to me anyhow. But Clive took me aside a bit later and wanted to know why I wasn't being nice to Freddy.'

Rose studied Angelica's pretty, defenceless face, noting a new animation in it. She felt torn between a number of emotions. There was instinctive sympathy – she pictured the egregious Freddy as not unlike Leo Liddell, sidling and predatory. There was admiration too, for an act that had plainly required a good deal of courage from a girl no more accustomed than a caged bird to asserting herself; but part of her wished with a selfish anxiety that she had never said anything, and pictured the monstrous Clive coming after her with a horsewhip.

'What did you say?'

'Well. I was shaking like a leaf again but I came out with it. I said that I was nice to Freddy, I was polite to him as I would be to any of Clive's friends. But I said I didn't want to be nice to him in *that* way, and that it wasn't fair of him to try and make me.'

The selfish part of Rose gave way to an inward cheer. 'What did Clive say to that?'

'He wasn't pleased. He wanted to know who'd been putting these ideas in my head.'

Rose swallowed.

'Well, I thought that was rather too much. I adore Clive and he's much cleverer than me of course, but the fact is it wasn't him who was having to put up with it. It was me and I didn't like it. Well. He was quiet a minute and then he said he was disappointed because Freddy was a good friend of his and he didn't like to think of us not getting along because we were both so dear to him. That made me feel rather awful.'

'I think it was meant to,' Rose said before she could stop herself.

'Do you?' Angelica knotted her fingers. 'You see, I didn't want to cause trouble. I still don't. I know I have made rather a habit of disappointing people. First lieutenant of the Awkward Squad, Clive calls me sometimes. And I don't want him to feel let down.'

Rose had a thought. 'What does your father think of Freddy Collymore?'

'Oh, Daddy died ages ago.' Angelica's voice grew low. 'I

still miss him, actually. But everyone said he was too soft on me and I dare say he was.'

'My father died too,' Rose said. 'And I miss him . . . I think if a man tried to kiss me who I didn't like, my father would have been very angry with him.'

Angelica stared at her fingers.

'Freddy Collymore makes the most unpleasant jokes,' she said. 'About Jews and so on. I don't think they're at all funny. Clive tells me not to be such a prig.'

Clive, Rose thought, seemed to like telling people what to do more than anything in the world.

'I wasn't rude, though,' Angelica said. 'I've thought about it and I wasn't rude. I just said what I felt. That's the main thing, isn't it?'

'Yes,' Rose said. 'What you feel is important.'

'Clive hasn't said anything more about it. And Freddy's away again. But he's coming back on Saturday. Mummy's having a little party for her birthday and she said she specially wanted him to be there.'

First Clive, Rose thought, and now Mummy. The Harwoods sounded increasingly like the Borgias with Norfolk jackets.

'Well,' Rose said, 'let's hope he's taken what you said to heart.'

'Yes . . . When I say a little party, I mean rather a big party. Dancing and so on.' Angelica began to blush: it was a process, delicate and fascinating as sunlight staining a cloud. 'I do wish you could be there.'

Rose was for a moment too taken aback at the image of herself disporting in a blue-blooded ballroom to be flattered.

'I – well, thank you. It's not . . . a likely thing, I'm afraid.'

'No.' Angelica smiled in rueful acknowledgement. 'Different circles, I know.'

She didn't know the half of it, Rose thought with amusement.

'The way we live . . . it's always the same people. Like a club. I just think it would be nice to have someone to talk to.

Someone different from Effie Bressingham. She's jolly nice of course but . . . it's not the same.' A frown, distinct and evanescent as a bird's footprint in snow, appeared on Angelica's smooth white forehead. 'Effie says it's silly to get worked up about these things. She says it comes with time – you know – liking a man. You learn it, she says, though you might not like him at first.' She gave a troubled smile. 'Like the piano, I suppose.'

'I don't know about that. I think there has to be something – perhaps not love at first sight, but a spark.' Rose believed this, but only tentatively. Speaking of these things brought her to a recognition that her experience – though in Shipden's eyes it made her as worldly as the Wife of Bath – was actually very limited. The only knowledge it had given her was negative: the signposts only told her where not to go.

'I don't particularly want to learn,' Angelica said candidly. 'Not just at the moment. I don't want to – meet a man and all the rest of it.'

Well, that was another thing they had in common. Rose did not perceive that a month ago she would have strongly felt this, whereas now the thought was only a reflex.

'Ah, she looks all the time more beautiful,' Madame Carette sighed, when Angelica's lesson was over and the chauffeured Bentley had spirited her away again. 'How sad the world is! Well now, *ma petite*,' she said, turning from the window, 'do you know, I could fancy a little pastry? Now isn't that strange? Just a little pastry or a tart or something like that. Isn't that a funny thing? I don't know how it came into my head.'

Two or three times a week Madame Carette said this, her pretty eyes always glittering in anticipation while she feigned surprise at this curious craving of hers.

'Why not pop into Hyde's?' Rose said, as always. 'I'll be all right in the shop.'

'Do you know, I think I will. Why not?' And Madame Carette set out for the confectioner's, laughing at the oddity of it.

While she was gone Rose sold, with some labour, an album of sheet music to an old lady who wanted a song by Tosti she did not know the name of and who was tone deaf. 'It goes like this,' she kept saying, and crooned what sounded like no music ever composed.

While Rose played through several Tosti songs on the piano, the old lady craning over her with an expression of wincing concentration, she became aware that someone else had entered the shop.

It was Dr Blanchard.

He was examining the display of gramophones, with a tactful air of having plenty of time. His presence made Rose self-conscious in her playing, and she hit several wrong notes – which, however, settled the matter for the old lady. 'That's the one,' she said, 'that's it – you've got it,' and went away very happy with her purchase.

'Hello,' Dr Blanchard said.

'Hello again.' She did not know where the airy unconcern with which she said this came from.

'How's Elizabeth?'

'She's very well.'

'And how are you?'

'I'm very well. If—'

'I—'

'Sorry.'

'No, sorry, you.'

'I was just going to say if I wasn't well, you'd soon know about it.'

'Ah, of course.' He laughed. Rose laughed too. She was rather appalled at the sound that came out of her mouth. It sounded like somebody laughing in an opera.

'I was thinking of buying a gramophone,' he said.

'Yes? Well, the three you see here are quite representative of the range. Would you like to hear one? What kind of music do you like?'

'Oh, anything,' he said, a little taken aback by the brisk

133

way she bore down on him. 'As long as it's cheerful.'

'You don't like sad music?'

'I like it very much,' he said, 'unfortunately. I'm a bit too susceptible. Sometimes I can't listen to it if it's very sad – and, you know, beautiful.'

'I'm like that with some. Schubert's "Ave Maria" – sometimes I can't listen to that.' She wound up one of the gramophones and set a record on it. 'This is Caruso singing "Che gelida manina".'

They listened to the ardent tenor, Dr Blanchard with his arms half crossed, one long forefinger touching his lips.

'This model is the Decalion,' Rose said. 'It has a spring-winding motor. As you can see, the diameter of the horn is a little bigger than on these Columbias. The price is twelve guineas.'

'It sounds wonderful,' he said: he looked impressed. 'I feel very extravagant, though.'

'You can make the purchase on easy terms – two guineas down. We carry a large stock of records, so you need never get bored listening to the same ones. Also replacement needles, in packets or singly.' There was a certain safety in inhabiting the saleswoman's role like this, though she didn't know why it was safety she sought.

He turned to her. 'What do you think I should do?'

'Have one. But don't forget, I work here.'

He laughed. 'I feel like a greedy boy in a sweetshop with a half-crown. I don't know . . . there are lots of dreary practical household things I ought to be buying.'

It crossed Rose's mind that this was rather an odd thing to say, for hadn't he come in purposely to buy a gramophone? 'You shouldn't feel bad about treating yourself. Besides, it will help you relax in the evenings, and that will make you work better. So it's a practical purchase really.'

Again he laughed, a satisfying and musical sound.

'I can't argue with a sales pitch like that. I'll take it. And the Caruso record too.'

Rose went to the counter. 'I'll make out the invoice. Oh – your initial, sir?'

It was the first time she had sirred him. There was a look of perplexed amusement on his face as he said, 'It's James.'

James, she thought as she made out the invoice and placed the money he paid over in the cashbox. James. It fitted him . . . but nonsense, she didn't even know him.

'Would you like the gramophone delivered?'

'I've got the car in the square. I may as well take it with me. Should give people something to look at when I carry it out.'

'I'm afraid so. But it's not the sort of thing I could wrap very easily . . . Mind you, if it was a comb you'd bought it would still be all round the town in an hour.'

'I know what you mean. I dare say I shall get used to it, but I'm still rather amazed at the – the watchfulness.'

'It must be very different from London.'

He raised his eyebrows. 'Now how did you know I was from London?'

'The grapevine, of course,' she said smiling. 'How else did you know I worked here?'

His own smile was wry, a little inward, as if it came over him in spite of himself. Rose found it very attractive: but then she had learnt to mistrust the ready smile.

'You play wonderfully well,' he said. 'It's a great talent. I had a friend when I was a medical student who could play the violin like Kreisler. At least, it sounded it to me. I envied him. And yet he only did it for recreation: what his heart was really set on was orthopaedic surgery. That was a thing I could never understand. To have a talent like that and disregard it. Still, I suppose it's the same with my talent for gardening.'

'You haven't chopped it down?' she said, laughing.

'The recumbent rabbit with the hat on? No, I haven't chopped it down.'

His hands, she thought randomly, looked like a violinist's

themselves. She thought she had never seen such beautiful hands.

'Perhaps I could sell you a violin as well,' she found herself saying, with a quick aversion of her eyes.

'Then I really would be cleaned out. My friend tried to teach me, but I never got very far. I suppose you have to learn when you're young, like most things.'

'Not everything.'

'No, not everything. Well . . .' He turned back to the gramophone. 'I'd better be going. Not raining, is it? I suppose that would ruin it.'

'I don't think it would do it any good.'

They laughed again. He seemed to be havering.

'Well – anyhow, thank you very much.'

'A pleasure,' she said. 'If you ever need cleaning out again, you know where to come.' Watching him carry the gramophone to the door, she had a sudden thought. 'When you go out with that, I could run across the square after you shouting, "Stop thief!"'

The picture this called up made them laugh once more.

'Don't,' he said, 'I shall drop it.'

'Don't do that. Oh, nearly forgot – your record.' She hesitated, then tucked the disc under his arm. 'There.' She held the door open for him, aware that her hands were not steady.

'Thanks so much. Goodbye.'

'Goodbye.'

The door closed. Rose drifted back to the counter. Well, Madame Carette would be pleased with the sale, she thought absently. Gramophones were expensive items, and sometimes she complained that all they did was take up shop space and gather dust.

The doorbell jangled.

James Blanchard, unencumbered, was back.

'I – I want to ask you something. It's the first summer concert at the Winter Gardens next week.'

He blurted it out so abruptly that for a moment they were both nearly laughing again. Not quite, though.

'Summer concert at the Winter Gardens,' he said, shaking his head. 'Doesn't make sense. Anyhow.' With a look of almost pained concentration he went on, 'I wanted to ask you whether you'd like to come with me. To it,' he added.

'Me? I . . . oh, that's very kind of you, but I . . . Thank you, but I really couldn't. I'm so sorry.'

Rose was utterly surprised. It was the sort of pure, blank surprise that was supposed to render you speechless; but something had already spoken for her.

'But thank you for asking,' the something added.

James Blanchard was nodding, rapidly, as if she were giving him an answer he vehemently agreed with. 'Well – never mind. I'd, er, better go back to the car in case someone runs off with the gramophone. Got the top down, you see.'

'Oh – yes, you'd better. That would be terrible.'

There was a sort of suspended, mutual hesitation between them, which was suddenly broken by Madame Carette coming in. She gave a purr of surprise, her pastry-sated eyes lighting up when she saw who was there.

'Ah! It is Dr Blanchard, I think? Madame Carette. So glad to meet you at last. What can we do for you? Please, come in, come in . . .'

'Oh, I've been in – er, thank you. How d'you do? I've bought one of your gramophones.'

Madame Carette's eyes lit up even more brightly.

'Indeed? I hope everything was to your satisfaction, Dr—'

'Yes, very much so. I must be off . . .' He was gone as he spoke.

'Thank you, Dr Blanchard, for your custom!' Madame Carette called after him, her voice carrying across the square. 'Well, well, my dear Rose – what a black horse you are! I go out for a little moment and not only does the new doctor come in after I've waited to meet him all this time – but you sell him a gramophone!' She roamed silkily about the shop, pleased and speculative. 'Now, he will want records and needles, of course, so we will see him again . . . A very beautiful man, is he not?' She snapped her fingers. 'No, no, of course, the word must always be handsome when it is a man. Very handsome, is he not?'

'Yes,' Rose said.

She thought Madame Carette had been right the first time.

'And a record too,' Madame Carette said, examining the invoice book. 'Caruso – good, good, not that filthy ragtime.'

'Shall I write to the wholesalers for another Decalion?' Rose said.

'Oh, time enough. He is thirty-two, I understand? He looks younger, I think, don't you?'

'I'll write to them now. We can catch the last post,' Rose said. She ducked into the office, which was a tiny cubbyhole at the back of the shop screened by a bead curtain. She needed a minute to think.

Not that a minute would be enough, not for this humming swarm of thoughts.

She sat down at the desk, occupied herself with hunting out a new pen nib. Her heart was beating wildly, as if she had just experienced some physically perilous near-miss.

Totally unexpected; she had been overcome with surprise. Now the surprise was at herself, for the intensity of her own reaction.

She hoped she hadn't put her refusal rudely, because his manner of asking had been wholly polite. She kept trying to remember what she had said.

'I couldn't' – had that been it? She thought so.

Well, it was right, at any rate. She couldn't: it just wasn't possible.

There must, she thought, be a mistake somewhere. A pity, but never mind. Hopefully they could still be on friendly terms.

But the more she thought about it, the more mysterious it became. He must know about her – her history. They had laughed about the efficiency of the Shipden grapevine. Surely he knew.

Well, perhaps he did; perhaps he knew, and didn't care. Good, if so: she would not accept any other terms, whether it came to friendship or anything else.

Or perhaps he knew about her, and drew the conclusion that Leo Liddell had.

No. She violently repudiated the idea. James Blanchard was no Leo Liddell. A sceptical voice asked how she knew; but her heart answered emphatically that she just knew – as well as if she had known him all her life.

Not that it mattered. She simply couldn't, as she had told him. This wasn't for her. He couldn't know that, perhaps, but that didn't change the fact that she simply wasn't in the market for that sort of thing. Elizabeth, and the life the two of them had together – all her emotional stock was invested in that. She should, perhaps, have explained that to him, so he would not go away with the wrong idea.

But it would have been difficult explaining it to him when she could hardly explain it to herself.

Fairy tales, she thought, belonged only in Elizabeth's storybooks.

A reminder: Elizabeth needed new shoes. She made a note on a piece of scrap paper, then fell to doodling.

Rose snapped upright. She would have to put this out of her mind. It could be done: she had had plenty of practice at disciplining her thoughts.

Meanwhile there was her heart, which felt swollen and full of a ticklish pain.

# TWELVE

James's car was parked by the church. The bonnet was sticky with odorous blossom from the tall horse chestnuts that grew in the churchyard. He brushed a few off, then gave it up. He checked that the gramophone was safe in the back seat, then sat at the wheel smoking a cigarette, preparing to go and not going.

A tap at the windscreen jolted him out of a deep abstraction. For a leaping moment he thought it was Rose Jordan.

Instead he saw it was Mrs Porson, district nurse and midwife and general, inexhaustible medical factotum: a sturdy sharp-eyed woman in sober tailor-mades, like a little black hen. To be on bad terms with such a person was doom to a new doctor, but luckily James had liked her at once on meeting her. She began telling him about a woman she had just visited who was expecting her sixth child.

'Not that she've ever had any trouble with 'em – takes every one in her stride. Nell Henning her name is, fisherman's wife. Sort of. Bit of a character, if you know what I mean. She's due in a week or so. I've a feeling it might be a breech, but I wouldn't like to say it for certain.'

'I'll take a look at her,' James said.

'Would you? You'd be doing me a favour. She's as strong as an ox, but you never know. I doubt she can afford fees, mind.'

'Not to worry. Where does she live?' He was glad of this, after what had just happened: glad to switch himself off and be nothing but the doctor, cool and objective.

'The Rows. Number five. Tain't very sweet in there, but

there's no harm in her.' Mrs Porson nodded humorously at the gramophone. 'If I pay a penny, do I get a tune?'

The Rows was the oldest part of the town, at the other end from the pier and the grand hotels. This was Shipden as it had been before the effects of sea-bathing and gentility: a cluster of fishermen's cottages, crudely built of flint and tile, dark and cramped and huddled round noisome courtyards.

After knocking for some time at the door of number five he turned to see a tiny old woman, no more than four foot six, in a sacking apron and children's boots, peering out of the open door of the cottage across the yard.

'Is this Mrs Henning's house?'

'Knock and goo in, dair – just knock and goo in. She's at home. She don't answer the door. Just goo in. I'm Mrs Scace. Doctor, is it? Ah, course, she's near her sixth. Poor stick. All on her own, shame that is.'

'Is there no Mr Henning?'

'Well. Well now. There was. Only he cleared off. Don't know where. Yarmouth herringers maybe. Beautiful-pretty fisherman he was. Poor stick. Cleared off, he did. Two year ago come July that'd be.'

'Two years? But she's . . .'

'Ah. Well. We're all human, ain't we? I am. You are. Never mind. No harm in her. Yew goo in, dair, take and goo in.'

The cottage was a lightless damp-stained hole with brick floors partly covered by coconut matting, stifling from the fire in the kitchen-cum-living room and from the ammoniac smell of unrinsed nappies hung to dry in front of it. Children teemed. Nell Henning, a large and very fat woman of thirty-odd on whom pregnancy showed as little more than a slight redistribution of weight, was puttering nervelessly about the stove on bare flat feet, and her pretty doll-like face registered only mild surprise at James's presence.

'I can't afford to pay no doctor bill,' she said in a curiously deep gruff voice when he explained why he had come.

'That's all right. I just want to make sure everything's going

142

as it should be with your baby. Mrs Porson said a week, I believe.'

'You mark him, gel.' Mrs Scace had followed him in. 'You take heed. He know what's what. She want to rest up, doon't she?'

'How can I?' Nell Henning said listlessly. 'I got all these kids to feed. And the house to keep clean.'

James noticed a pile of cat droppings on the kitchen shelf near his head. 'I won't keep you long,' he said.

With Mrs Scace as a chaperon – it was necessary to be more strict about this in poor homes than well-off ones – James examined Nell Henning in her bedroom, which was a curtained-off area downstairs. Mrs Henning came temporarily out of her apparent torpor to explain this: 'I can't manage the stairs at the moment. Once the baby's born I shall sleep upstairs again. It ain't decent, sleeping downstairs.'

James thought the birth would be normal, and there seemed little to worry about: Mrs Henning was strong and, as Mrs Porson said, appeared to be taking it all in her stride. But he mistrusted the comforting fiction, common amongst his profession, that for women like this childbirth was like falling off a log and scarcely required medical presence at all.

'Everything's going very well, Mrs Henning. Now you will call me, won't you, if you feel any uneasiness, have any difficulties? Please don't hesitate.'

Nell Henning only gave a blank nod, so James turned to Mrs Scace, hovering at his elbow like an eager monkey.

'I'll make sure she do. Don't you worry. I'm always around, I am. I'll keep an eye on her.'

She scuttled after him to the car. Taking grateful lungfuls of freshish air, he asked, 'How does Mrs Henning manage?'

'Well now. When she's fit, like – you know – in between, she goes charring. Other times she gets a bit here and a bit there. You know. To keep going. We're all human, aren't we? I am. You are.'

He was, though since leaving the square he had repressed

143

the fact. He had let the medical practitioner take over, but as he drove away the man came back.

He drove up to a picnic spot on the heathery clifftop above West Shipden, parked the car, sat on the bonnet, smoked, looked out to sea, and wondered what on earth had come over him.

Well, there was no harm done, he supposed. Except to his pride – and, looking into himself, he found that even that was not badly hurt. He had just made a bit of a blunder.

So he told himself, and didn't believe himself for a moment.

James was an habitually cautious man – which was a different thing from being naturally cautious. He kept his impulses on a short rein because he could not trust them not to run away with him. During his training he had heard a patient suffering from vertigo explain her curious contradictory urge to jump when she found herself at those frightening heights: she had been bewildered by this, but James understood at once. So he consciously kept his distance from the precipitous edges of life, because he was ambitious and determined, and all his beliefs tended towards rationality and detachment. But he knew he had unruly passions in him too: knew the temptation to dash and leap.

Rose Jordan.

He had, quite simply, never felt like this before.

His experience with Lisette, the V.A.D. nurse, during the war offered no comparisons. There had been an element of the willed romance about that: looking back, he saw that he had been very ready to fall in love at the time. When it had all ended in disaster, he had considered himself in a way inoculated. The particular circumstances of it had helped him in this belief: when the war ended, it was possible to see the love affair itself as war-engendered – something that, like rationing and raids, was not part of normal life. The curious unreal glow had faded, and so had the dark resentful bitterness that had followed it; and James had pursued his career.

Falling in love did not seem a possibility that need concern him. And on coming to Shipden, where his bachelor eligibility was constantly, embarrassingly brought home to him, it seemed more remote than ever, simply because it was thus trivialized. The eagerness to match him had made him laugh the whole business off. But in many ways light-hearted and unserious, James was serious about this, he would not deal in trumpery emotions. If he were going to go in for love, he wanted the genuine article. But he hadn't supposed, for a moment, that he wanted it at all. Beginning his career as a general practitioner – more momentous and unnerving than his quietly confident manner suggested – settling into a new district, refurbishing his first real home: these were quite enough to be going on with.

And then he had met Rose.

That air of confidence, that cool polished surface which he presented to the world, meant that there had been little to suggest the vast turbulence of feeling that lay behind the simple act of stepping back into the music shop and asking Rose to go to the Winter Gardens with him. For days previously he had been tugged hither and thither by strong crosscurrents of emotion. The collision of caution and passion had shaken him to the root of his nature, and as he sat gazing at the sea, a sullen rugged grey despite the mellow gentleness of the afternoon, he felt as if he had been through some exhausting battle.

James was not a rebel, but he was not conventional either. His easy accommodating manner concealed the fact that he did not think along the same lines as the society of which he was a part.

After his mother's death, James's whole upbringing had fallen to his father. Mr Blanchard had built up a prosperous printing house from small beginnings, and had discovered himself in the process. He fell in love with books, filled his house in North Kensington with them, and in an unstructured autodidactic way learnt from them. He read into everything, and James partook of this, learning that there was always another side, that accepted views were there to be questioned in the light of vast perspectives of history and science. For instance, cannibalism – why should it bear a stigma? It was an eminently reasonable way of getting that rare resource, animal protein, and few carnivorous animals disdained it.

James would sometimes argue with his father's more extreme conclusions, but meanwhile he was taking it all in, and he emerged into manhood with a firm belief of his own that everything was relative and nothing was universal. Ladies bared their backs at theatres and dinners, believing themselves utterly respectable – in certain Eastern societies that was as obscene as if they had gone bare-breasted. The ex-soldier dragged into the police court for committing indecency with another man would in classical Greece have had his feelings honoured. James liked beer, music-hall songs, Keats, village greens, and even English weather: but he did not think that a nation which considered boiled cabbage a delicacy, which believed stupidity was more trustworthy than intelligence, and which remained infatuated with a particularly ungifted aristocracy whose ancestors had raped it, had very good reasons to pride itself on being the greatest in the world. As for the war to end wars, he tended to agree with Shaw that it would have been better if the troops on both sides had shot the generals and gone home.

Shipden would not have approved of thoughts like these.

And so James would, ordinarily, have listened to Sylvia Vickery's account of Rose's 'downfall' unmoved, beyond a certain admiration for her courage in the face of so much disapproval.

Indeed, he did feel this, when Sylvia told him. But it was more complex than that, because of the effect Rose had had on him from their very first meeting.

From her domestic arrangements, he had at first supposed her to be one of the many young war widows; the absence of a ring was the sort of thing he didn't notice. Learning the truth had thrown him into confusion. Gone was the clear-eyed objectivity on which he prided himself. Suddenly the woman who had struck him more forcibly, more dazzlingly than any woman he had ever seen was changed.

Or rather, James was – and in trying to gauge how much he tried to gauge too the level of his own hypocrisy. He felt he could honestly say that he would, in neutral circumstances, have had no strong opinions or feelings about a young woman having an illegitimate child. But these circumstances were not neutral, because he had fallen for this young woman.

Hence the turbulence. The voice of caution that said, drearily, that this was an unsuitable attachment and that he was playing with fire was easily suppressed, so deeply had he fallen. Far stronger was something he could only call jealousy. Nonsense, perhaps, but he couldn't help it: the thought of a deceased husband would have affected him very differently from the thought of a man whom she had loved enough to bear his illegitimate child.

It had thrown a new light on her character too. She seemed so self-contained, so adult, with something of his own coolness. He liked that: it drew him. Now he had to contend with this newly revealed side of her. Out of the confusion of it all had come a powerful, perplexed attraction and an overwhelming longing to see her again – simply that. It had kept him awake all last night. The gramophone idea had been born of this longing. Asking her to the Winter Gardens had been pure impulse, but an impulse with roots in that attraction; for, seeing her again, he had found his feeling confirmed, strengthened, multiplied a thousandfold.

    *. . . I really couldn't. I'm so sorry . . . But thank you for asking.*

He felt a dull sort of relief, like waking up from a fascinating but mystifying dream. He had assumed too much, he supposed; he had even perhaps played on his position, as doctor to her child.

He thought about the man – Taverner? – who had not returned to her. He wished . . . but that was pointless.

He ought to be getting home: a patient might need him. If you set up as a GP in a small town, where you were the only doctor to be had, you should be prepared always to be available.

But he sat on, smoking, watching the choppy advance of the sea up the beach, as if the motions of that tide might decide something for him.

# THIRTEEN

Five days later, James found himself dressing to go out to dinner, in spite of the fact that he had told himself a hundred times he wouldn't go.

The invitation was from Mr Jarvis Truelove, the solicitor, who had a set of gauze-windowed offices in Shipden High Street and a detached villa on the outskirts of the town. He was a small, plump, rather fierce-looking man – bald except for two cherubic wings of curly hair above his ears – shrewd and quick and rather clever for a quiet provincial town. He had done well by his wife and daughters and was understandably anxious that the daughters – or rather, the one who was not married – should do well for themselves.

Four days ago he had telephoned James personally and asked him to come and see this daughter, whose name was Clara, and whom James had already heard spoken of – sometimes with admiration and sometimes with envy – as the belle of Shipden. The girl he found decorously propped up on lace pillows was certainly very pretty, very obliging, and not very ill.

'A summer cold,' James had pronounced – though even that was stretching it a bit. 'Nothing to worry about. Drink plenty of liquid, and beef tea if you've no appetite.'

'Yes, Doctor,' Clara Truelove said obediently, regarding him with large luminous eyes.

'A summer cold – thought so – just as well to be sure,' Mr Truelove said absently. His mind seemed already to have moved on to other things, and he invited James into his study

149

and set about getting to know him, under cover of polite enquiries about how he was settling in. In his astute lawyerlike way, Mr Truelove had soon extracted from James all the relevant facts: his age; his financial situation; his family, including the absence of dependent relatives; his feelings about joining the Liberal Club, which Mr Truelove seemed to regard as his private fiefdom.

For his part James was making his own mental notes. All the time as he talked Mr Truelove sucked peppermint and charcoal tablets, sometimes rubbing his knuckles just under his breastbone with a motion plainly so habitual it had become unconscious. Occasionally a grimace would pass over his face, like that of a baby with wind. The man was in the grip of grinding dyspepsia: probably his stomach was ulcerated. But when James, observing him popping another charcoal tablet in his mouth, tentatively alluded to Mr Truelove's own health, he was not wholly surprised at the answer he received.

'Oh, a touch of indigestion,' he said. 'Always been prone to it. It's nothing. I've got other things to worry about.'

And the worrying, no doubt, was making it worse; but James could not advise unless actually consulted, and it was clear that Mr Truelove's interest in him was not as a doctor.

'Come to dinner on Monday – we're having a few people over,' Mr Truelove had said; and added, 'Clara should be better by then.'

Since then – and right up to the moment of dressing – James had been thinking up excuses for not going. He was not unappreciative of the invitation: he was simply out of sorts for company, and especially this sort of company – for he knew he would not be the only one on show.

He might have conjured up an excuse, if his mind had not been so occupied with thoughts of Rose.

These were tangled, restless, troubling. At one moment he regretted ever having spoken, and vowed to put the whole thing out of his mind: the next moment he found himself replaying the scene in the music shop, and constructing alternative scenarios for it.

Had he simply been too hasty? Probably he should have 'got to know her' first, whatever that meant. But the strength of his feelings had overleaped such things.

He had been wondering too whether to go into the shop again. Buying a record made a plausible excuse: he could hardly listen to the Caruso for ever (though he had, in fact, played it scores of times). But he felt this would be clumsy, obvious. James had a fastidious dislike of the obvious.

Hearing that the Vickerys would be at the Trueloves' dinner as well disinclined him further, and he might even have cried off without an excuse if it had not been for the letter from his father this morning. Reading the letter, hearing the well-loved rich brown voice in the words, James was reminded of his father's long-ago remark about foolish vicars and ladies in hats, and remembered too that the only times his father was stern with him as a boy was when he was – his father's apt word – churlish. It would be churlish not to turn up, and he was correct about such things.

But before he went to the Trueloves' he told Mrs Penn not to hesitate to telephone him there if he were needed.

After all, he was a doctor.

Driving up to the Trueloves' villa in a sweet-scented evening, James permitted himself to entertain a bitter-sweet image: Rose being there. Meeting her eyes across the dinner-table . . . At once came the realization that that could not happen. Rose Jordan was not invited to the dinner-tables of Shipden.

That thought gave him a curious, sharp, fresh feeling. He could only call it a chivalrous feeling – though such a word was absurd in this day and age.

What do you want to do? he asked himself. Draw your sword on her behalf?

He found that he did.

'Yes – a German band again. And here for the whole season,

it appears. They've taken lodgings at the Star – three months in advance,' Mrs Vickery said.

'It doesn't seem right,' said Mr Truelove, his face inflamed with the pain of eating. 'I must confess, it doesn't seem right.'

'Anyhow, one is always reading in the papers how they're so poor in Germany now and we mustn't be so hard on them,' Mrs Vickery said. 'But it seems they can afford to come over here. And to buy musical instruments.'

'Perhaps they had the instruments before the war,' said Frank Watlyn.

'Oho, I doubt it,' twinkled a young-old man named Askew, who ran the Royal Links Golf Club, had been a captain in the war, and sported moustaches which he waggled racily, like some left-over Edwardian dandy. 'I doubt it very much, you know. I know those fellows. I could tell you a few things if I wanted.'

'I think it's rather nice that they're back,' said Millie Watlyn, the Trueloves' elder daughter, who was on James's right. Clara, the unmarried one, was on his left. He felt like the centre of an allegorical painting. 'The Shipden season wouldn't be the same without a German band on the prom. Besides –' she turned to James with a friendly back-me-up look – 'we're not at war any more, are we?'

'It would be hard to get rid of all the German elements in our national life,' James said. 'The royal family would have to go, for a start.'

'Oh yes!' cried Sylvia Vickery, who all evening kept giving James looks of intimate collusion which he kept trying not to see. 'Even we're German, you know. Anglo-Saxon – those were our ancestors.'

'With Norse and Norman additions,' Dr Vickery said.

'Oh, but they come from the same stock,' Sylvia said. 'Their languages are all related. So it's all German, really, when you think about it.'

'Well, I don't think we should be so quick to forget,' said Mrs Truelove, a handsome horsy woman who seemed to have all the health and serenity her husband lacked. 'Not after all that happened. Remember those Belgian nuns.'

'Yes – you simply can't get them any more,' Mrs Vickery said, apparently under the impression that Mrs Truelove had said Belgian buns.

'We ought to keep out of Continental affairs in future,' Mr Truelove said, gulping his wine. 'They're not like us.'

'That woman who keeps the music shop in the High Street – she's Belgian, isn't she?' his wife said.

'She uses garlic,' Mrs Vickery said in a shocked whisper. 'I've smelt it. I've sometimes wondered about her. She calls herself a widow – but you know. Their morals are different from ours.'

'Oh, that's not so, Mrs Vickery,' Millie Watlyn said. 'Madame Carette lost her husband in the war and is absolutely devoted to his memory. Rose told me, and she knows her pretty well.'

'Oh, you know Rose Jordan?' James said quickly.

'We've been friends for years,' Millie said with a smile. 'We were at school together.'

'Oh! I knew Rose before that,' Sylvia said loudly. 'It's a funny thing, but I actually knew Rose Jordan before anyone.'

'You've met Rose?' Millie said to James. 'And Elizabeth?' She looked pleased. 'She's a darling, isn't she?'

'Yes, she is,' James said: unsure which was meant.

'But you know, James,' Sylvia called, 'going back to this German question, now *you* could throw a different light on this. Being a medical man. Because if you were at a field hospital during the war and they brought wounded German prisoners in, you would have to treat them just the same, isn't that so?'

'Yes, it is,' James said. 'I would, I suppose, be bandaging the wounds that my countrymen had inflicted. Not that the medical conscience is always so broad. There are many doctors who refused to treat the children of railwaymen who were on strike. Presumably these children were more dangerous enemies than the Germans.'

'Well, at least the German band is traditional,' Mrs Vickery said. 'Better that than having jazz-band music in Shipden.'

'There was talk of the Links Pavilion hiring a jazz band,' said Mr Askew, 'but it was pretty firmly stamped on, let me tell you, and quite right too.' But he looked a little regretful.

'I dare say such things are quite familiar to you, Dr Blanchard,' fluted Clara Truelove, turning her searchlight eyes on James. 'Coming from London, I mean. Shipden must seem quite a different world. I wonder why you chose us?'

'I love the coast – the sea, and the freshness. And then I was lucky enough to meet Dr Vickery, who was retiring and wanted someone to take over his practice. So it seemed too good an opportunity to miss.'

'You could say Shipden chose you, James,' put in Sylvia, with one of her significant looks.

'Fate, you might say,' Millie Watlyn said. 'Do you believe in fate, Dr Blanchard?'

'Yes, I think I do.'

Millie looked at him with interest.

'James, *not* very scientific,' called Sylvia.

'I suppose I believe in it in the sense that life seems to hold out to you certain things that were – well, meant to happen; and that they will even if you go out of your way to avoid them.'

'Rather like love at first sight,' Millie said. 'That's not very scientific, but it happens. I know.'

James saw a spasm cross Mr Truelove's face: perhaps indigestion, perhaps something else. He had already noticed that Mr Truelove hardly addressed a word to his son-in-law.

'It does indeed happen, Mrs Watlyn,' said Dr Vickery. 'A thousand unhappy marriages can testify to that.'

'But there's a scientific explanation for everything – isn't that so, James?' Sylvia said. 'Even superstitions – they usually have some basis in fact, when you think about it.'

She was prevented from carrying on by the necessity of

putting food in her mouth, and Mrs Truelove cut in with: 'In these parts there's a very curious superstition about eggshells. You must always crush them after you've eaten the eggs, so that they won't make boats for witches.'

'They must have been terribly small witches, I always thought,' Clara Truelove said, dimpling at James.

'Oh, but that's the point. That was the whole idea about witches, in the old days,' cried Sylvia. 'They could take any size or shape – it's in Shakespeare. Oh no, I was never surprised by that. I always understood that. In fact when I saw pictures of witches in storybooks, and they were human size, I always knew that was wrong.'

The maid had come in and was bending over Mr Truelove's shoulder. He looked up in surprise.

'Dr Blanchard, there's a telephone call for you, it seems.'

'Ah. I said I would be here in case of emergency – hope you don't mind.'

'Not at all, not at all. The telephone's in the hall. Alice will show you.'

'Thank you. Please excuse me a moment.'

It was, as he had thought, Mrs Penn. A rather scruffy ten-year-old boy was at the house, she said, saying that his mother had started her labour and they couldn't get hold of the midwife. Henning was the name: the boy said his mother was 'sweating more than usual', and apparently the doctor had said to call him any time.

'All right, Mrs Penn. Thank you. Yes, you did quite right. Tell the boy I'll be there directly.'

He returned to the dining room but did not resume his seat.

'I'm very sorry – I shall have to leave.'

'Not a bad case, I hope?' Mr Truelove said.

'A childbirth.'

'Who is it, James?' Sylvia said.

'Lady called Mrs Henning. I am sorry for the interruption, but—'

'Good Lord,' Dr Vickery said, 'not Nell Henning – lives at The Rows?'

'That's right.'

'The woman's had a score. Means no more to her than paring her nails. She's as strong as an ox.' Dr Vickery waved his bony hand dismissively. 'Leave it to the midwife, my boy, and sit down.'

'It's just possible there may be difficulties this time,' James said. 'I'm afraid I must go.'

'Oh, the midwife can manage. The presentation probably won't be for hours yet. Finish your dinner, James,' Dr Vickery said.

'Oh, Dr Blanchard,' Clara said, with a charming tilt of her head, 'if it's really not an absolute emergency . . .'

'That I can't tell. I'm sorry.'

'Really, James,' Dr Vickery said. 'I know the woman. I wouldn't hurry to respond to a call like that, and I've been a doctor for forty years. Really, I wouldn't do it.'

'Well,' James said agreeably, 'we must all judge for ourselves.'

He apologized again and said goodbye.

From Dr Vickery there was a displeased silence, while Sylvia burst out, 'James is right, you know. Oh, yes. I knew someone once who had had ten children with no difficulty at all, but the eleventh . . .'

The birth, as it turned out, was straightforward. When James arrived at the cottage Nell Henning was reclining like a vast houri behind her curtain and clutching a bottle of light ale which she sipped, rather demurely, in between the contractions; and she was scarcely less troubled by the delivery itself. The baby was a girl, and as there were three boys and only two girls gathered round to stare at the new arrival this, as Nell placidly remarked, 'evened things out nice'. Mrs Scace hovered in the background throughout, offering cheering advice, and Mrs Porson arrived wind-blown and breathlessly apologetic just before the presentation, but there was very little for any of them to do, except take a sip of the second bottle of ale which Nell sent the eldest boy out to fetch from the Crab Pot by way of celebration.

All the same, James was glad that he had gone. It did no harm to assert your independence of mind.

His only regret was that he hadn't been able to talk more with Millie Watlyn. She had seemed the nicest person there. Of course, he ruefully admitted to himself as he drove down the High Street that night and felt a quickening of his pulse at the sight of the shuttered music shop, he was biased.

# FOURTEEN

Rose welcomed, with an almost hungry gladness, the warm summery weather that began in the week following James Blanchard's visit to the music shop.

Usually she was pretty much indifferent to weather; hard winters and rainy days did not cast her down as they did some people. But this year the tardy spring following the long grey months seemed to have wound something up in her like a tight spring, and she greeted the sun with a sense of passionate release. At every opportunity she was outdoors, taking Elizabeth for walks through the clifftop woods or down to the sea or through the municipal gardens where the war veterans who tended them waited on the first full blooms with something of her own hunger for warmth and colour.

She did a good deal of thinking, on these walks, about what had happened, or rather what had not happened.

Even supposing it was to be considered – which it wasn't, because she had done with all that – even then, the whole thing must surely be based on a misconception. He surely couldn't know the facts of her situation, that was all: she stuck to this, even though she had already told herself that it was highly unlikely.

But then it wasn't even worth thinking of, because of the way she was. Many people had assumed, when she stayed on in Shipden with her child, that this meant she was still carrying a torch for the child's father. It was not so. The torch had gone out – or had been abruptly extinguished – long ago, and she could not imagine it being relit. The news of Alec Taverner's return to the district, for example, had stirred nothing within her. If there were some treacherous corner of her heart that was ready to forgive his betrayal, she had certainly not found it.

But that any new flame could be kindled seemed just as unlikely. Rose had changed from the person who had loved Alec – had in fact put that person quite away – but that did not mean that Alec had left her unmarked. To love again, she felt, you had to be whole-hearted – nothing else would do – and her heart was not whole. She acknowledged this quite unsentimentally, factually, as one would recognize the loss of a tooth or the darkening of hair. And therefore if James Blanchard had asked her to go with him to the concert sincerely and in full knowledge of her situation (which surely wasn't the case) then she had been quite right to say no. It was the only fair, correct thing to do.

Besides, there was a steadiness about her life now that she valued, having known what emotional storm and tempest were like. Looking at Elizabeth, buying her weekly sweets in the confectioner's where ancient Mrs Hyde crouched behind the counter and watched her scarcely less ancient daughter, Miss Hyde, weigh out the liquorice like a malicious old eagle, listening to her first promising attempts at reading, trimming her lustrous fast-growing hair in front of the propped-up mirror that Elizabeth always insisted on, in case her mother should take it into her head to scalp her: all the time Rose was aware that this ordinary and precious routine was a hard-won achievement. This mould was what she had poured herself into; in its shape was fulfilment. Life meant the two of them, Rose and Elizabeth, and anything impinging on that she could not help but see as a threat.

Thus her thoughts. Which were periodically interrupted by a violent, wrenching wish that she had said yes to James Blanchard.

*Yes. I would like that very much.*

She pictured it several times in detail – herself saying those

160

words to him in the music shop. Then she made herself stop picturing it. And then she would think again of moving away – would paper over that bright picture, as it were, with another that was dark with the grey tints of reality.

She lived in daily expectation of bumping into him, and did not know what would happen if she did. Each day, out with Elizabeth, she was sure she would spot the Talbot car, glimpse the tall, loose-knit figure amongst the strollers on the seafront, catch sight of the cinnamon-coloured hair in a shop or amongst the Saturday market stalls.

Each day it did not happen.

Meanwhile the perennial features of the Shipden holiday season appeared: the donkeys and ponies on the beach, the Punch and Judy show, the ice-cream tricycles, the goat carts, the windmill sellers. And the silhouette cutter in her booth at the near end of the pier.

Elizabeth loved everything to do with drawing, painting and modelling, and the silhouette cutter fascinated her more than all the animals and shows. On Saturday, when she was paid, Rose acceded to Elizabeth's long-held wish and they had their silhouettes cut, Elizabeth sitting solemn and commendably still while the silhouette cutter, a gaunt silent woman with her hair dramatically swept into a turban, flourished her scissors at amazing speed, making no sketched outline to begin with and scarcely seeming even to look up at her subjects.

The likenesses were striking: at least Elizabeth's was, and Aunt Dolly assured Rose, who like most people had only the vaguest idea of her own profile, that her own silhouette was remarkably accurate. Looking at them side by side, Rose found herself fancying a third alongside them: a lean yet boyish profile. A family group.

# FIFTEEN

The night was too warm for sleep. Rose had come to bed over an hour ago and at last had thrown back the bedclothes and lay gazing at the purple window-square of summer sky.

Faces came to her as she lay there, half-drowsing: faces that popped up grotesquely like the puppets in the Punch and Judy show she had seen with Elizabeth earlier, randomly and yet as if with some inscrutable purpose to communicate to her. Alec Taverner with his charming droll shrug; Leo Liddell with his matinée-idol gaze; Millie and Frank Watlyn, solid and inseparable; Angelica Harwood, all beautiful bewilderment; Madame Carette sucking sweets with greedy melancholy; Rose's mother, immaculately martyred; Mrs Betts with her raised damning eyebrows; James Blanchard.

Rose became aware that the deep purple in the sky had turned to red. She suffered a moment of panic – it was morning and she hadn't slept, she wouldn't be fit for work in the morning . . .

No. Getting up and peering out, she saw that the red glow was coming from the direction of Pound Street. There was smoke too, and a bell was ringing.

She met Aunt Dolly in her dressing gown on the landing.

'A fire? Heavens above, I hope no one's hurt. I say, it won't spread, will it? I remember when I was a girl one whole side of March Street went that way.'

'It looks a fair way off . . . I'll go down and look. I can't sleep anyway.'

'All right, dear. Be careful. And take the brandy flask with you – just in case someone needs it.'

Rose dressed and went out. The bell had stopped ringing, but the glow in the sky was fiercer than ever, and black smuts touched her face as she turned into Pound Street.

Rose gasped.

The fire was coming from the old drill hall that did service as the town's Kinema, and it was plain at once that it would not provide that service any more. The whole building was lit ominously from within like a dark lantern, and flames were wriggling and darting from the roof. The sound was like nothing Rose had ever heard: a deep purring roar that had something dreadfully suggestive of satisfaction about it. At the same time the scorched smell hit her, seeming to reach into the back of her throat, and she almost gagged as she wondered with horror just what it was that she was smelling.

She was not the only onlooker watching the gallant, doomed efforts of the Shipden and Saxburgh Fire Brigade. The engine was fitted with a steam-pump which directed a powerful jet of water – the volunteers, older men mostly, panted and braced their feet against the sizzling cobbles as they struggled to control the hoses – but the fire was too far advanced. Ernie Crimmins, the proprietor of the Kinema, was darting frantically about and shouting to anyone who would listen that he was done for.

'They didn't come quick enough.' Ernie danced up and down, hands clamped to his hat in despair, as there was a crash of timber and a shower of sparks. Making another dart of agitation, he fetched up against Rose. 'I've told the council time and time again. They need a motor to drive the engine. Any time there's a fire, they have to get the horses out of Pilcher's Meadow to drive the engine: now that's not practical, is it? Yarmouth's got a motor-engine. Even Hunstanton's got a motor-engine.' He threw up his hands, moaning, as the roof fell in with a surprisingly hushed, soft, spattering sound. Sparks whirled and danced, and Rose grabbed Ernie's coat and pulled him out of their reach. 'There it goes,' he said

164

brokenly. 'There goes my living. Goodbye. Cheerio. Ta-ta.'

'Oh, Ernie, how terrible . . . There wasn't anyone inside, was there?'

Ernie shook his head. 'Cleaner left an hour ago. Saw her come out meself. So that's a blessing . . . Still and all. It's a crying shame. I've told the council, time and again I've told 'em, the engine can't get to places quick enough. Now it's happened. Now we see it.'

'What about insurance, Ernie?'

'Eh? What?'

'Insurance?'

'Oh! Ah, that. I've got that,' he said vaguely. 'Plenty of insurance.'

Rose remembered the brandy flask. 'Here. Have a nip of this.'

Ernie took the flask without a word and drained it. 'I told 'em a million times. That's the trouble with the world nowadays. People don't listen.' He handed her the empty flask and darted away again.

There was another spattering collapse from the shell of the Kinema, followed this time by what seemed like a great lunge of pure heat, as if the fire were reaching out to the silhouetted spectators. Frightened, her cheeks and eyes stinging, Rose drew back and stepped up on to the kerb on the opposite side of the street. She nearly missed her footing: a hand grasped her elbow.

She found James Blanchard standing beside her.

'That'll be a blow to the town. Losing its Kinema at the start of the season.'

He did not look at her as he spoke. The light from the fire etched his profile in bronze.

'Yes . . . At least it happened at night. After everyone had left.'

He nodded. 'I heard the fire bell. I thought I'd better run down in case I was needed.'

He was in shirtsleeves again: she could hardly describe the

feeling this gave her except in terms of superstition.

'I couldn't sleep anyhow,' he said.

'Neither could I. It's very muggy tonight. We very rarely get this sort of sultry weather on this coast.' She had a sensation of carefully proceeding across stepping stones of conversation. 'Usually there are some sea breezes.'

He looked at her, for the first time. 'How are you? And Elizabeth?'

'We're well. How – how's your gramophone?'

'He's very well. Settling in nicely.'

They offered each other a laugh.

'I feel rather ghoulish standing here,' she said.

'So do I. I suppose there's nothing we can do to help.' He wiped his brow with his handkerchief: the heat was intense.

After a fractional hesitation, Rose said, 'Shall we walk down to the seafront? See if there's a cool breeze?'

'All right.'

Their footsteps were loud along the deserted promenade. The ironwork lamps were lit, but cloud was obscuring the stars and down below the massive sea wall the beach was an expanse of bluish shadow broken here and there by the shapes of the crab-boats. The tide was out, though the stillness of the night produced the strange aural illusion that the far-off waves were breaking almost at their feet. There was no discernible breeze, but the air that touched Rose's face was fresher.

'I believe I met a friend of yours the other day,' he said. 'Mrs Watlyn?'

'Oh yes, Millie. Where did you meet?'

'It was her father's – Mr Truelove. I went there for dinner. Couldn't stay, as it happened, because I was called out to a patient. Mrs Watlyn happened to mention you.'

'She's a very dear friend.'

'She spoke very warmly of you. Lives at Saxburgh, I think she said.'

'Yes, they have a guest house there. They have a little girl who's great friends with Elizabeth.'

'I'm afraid I rather took you by surprise in the shop the other week.'

He spoke with that little extra volume that comes from nerving oneself up to say something.

'A bit,' she said.

'It was very . . . forward of me, I'm sorry.'

Suddenly Rose found herself laughing.

'What have I said?'

'Nothing,' she said. 'Just . . . forward. Quite a word.'

He laughed too. 'I was trying to think of another one . . . Presumptuous, perhaps. How about that?'

'Well. It wasn't either of those. It's . . . hard to explain.'

'Oh, you don't have to explain anything.'

'No – you see, I think you might have got the wrong impression.'

'About what?'

She cleared her throat. 'About me.'

He said, surprising her, 'Actually that's just what I thought. About myself. After all, I'm a stranger here. You really don't know me from Adam.'

'I . . . I'm afraid I do in a way. You know, word gets round in a town like this.'

'I suppose it does.'

'It must be rather awful for you. In terms of privacy, I mean. You see, it's a small community here and a lot of men were lost in the war. So if the name of Dr Blanchard tends to be on everyone's lips . . .'

'James,' he said, and stopped walking, facing her.

'How do you do? We're starting again, yes?'

'If you like.'

'I'm Rose.'

'How do you do, Rose?'

'Or – Miss Jordan if you prefer. As we're starting again.' She met his eyes nakedly.

He returned her gaze, with a faint hint of a smile.

'I'd like to call you Rose.'

The feeling of his eyes upon her threw her into sudden nervous flippancy. 'Well,' she said, 'a rose by any other name would smell as sweet, and all that.'

'Exactly,' he said, very serious. 'Exactly right.'

They walked on. Rose wondered if he could hear her heart beating: to her each beat seemed as loud as a pistol shot.

'We can't go on to the pier?' he said, screwing up his eyes in the gloom.

'No. It's locked at night.' She had a dreadful moment of memory: Alec unlocking the gate and she waiting, giggling, beside him. Dear God.

'The sea's like a lake tonight. Dr Vickery was telling me they used to call this bay the Devil's Throat.'

'Because of all the ships that were lost here, yes. It was quiet this spring, but when it does turn . . . I've seen waves hitting the sea wall there and the spray rising twenty, thirty feet in the air. And the lifeboat – I've seen it go out a few times.' She pointed beyond the pier to the boathouse, perched above a timber chute. 'It's thrilling. They send a maroon up and then the doors are flung open and the boat thunders down the chute and hits the sea with a tremendous whoosh . . . And yet you know you shouldn't be thrilled because there are people out there whose lives are in danger. It makes me think of that hymn about "those in peril on the sea". They sang that hymn at Shipden church a lot and when I was young I couldn't hear it without wanting to cry.'

'It's that last cadence,' he said, and hummed the tune. 'Chromatic then diatonic – or is it the other way round?'

'That's it. Schubert does that a lot. It has this sort of sad but comforting effect . . . You're more musical than you pretend.'

'No, no, I only picked these things up from my friend at Edinburgh – the one I told you about. He got me started, as I said, but of course I was too old by then.'

'I have one pupil who must be nearly twenty and is just starting. Angelica Harwood. Though we seem to spend more

168

time talking about her love problems than working on the piano.'

'Love problems, eh?'

'Well. Sort of the opposite. She's from this rather grand county family and I get the impression they're keen to marry her off well. But the man . . . he doesn't sound very nice and she's upset about it all. "Horrid wet lips" is the description she gave me, which somehow gives the whole picture, doesn't it?'

'Ugh, it does,' he said laughing.

Looking at his lips, she caught herself in a moment of sensual speculation, and went on hastily, 'Anyhow, she isn't progressing terribly well, but she's a delightful person once her shyness breaks down. I just feel rather guilty and awkward when she tells me about these things because it's as if she wants advice and . . . well, I don't think I'm the person to give it.'

'It's your face,' he said. 'You look . . . like a person who understands things.' It was his turn to catch himself up hastily. 'Anyway, you must have learnt music very early, I should think.'

'My father began teaching me when I was very small. He was a wonderful teacher . . . He died not long before the war. I owe him a lot.'

'Miss him?'

She nodded. 'Yes.'

The simple exchange seemed to close up great distances.

'I was luckier in a way,' he said. 'My mother died when I was quite a child. Memories fade awfully quickly . . . I've always been very close to my father too.'

'Is he a doctor?'

'No, no. You might perhaps have seen his name if you're one of those people who read the flyleaves of books. "Printed and bound by H. W. Blanchard Ltd, London." When I was very small I had an idea, seeing that, that he somehow made the books up too.' He dabbed at his face; smuts from the fire were still drifting in the air. 'That poor fellow. Will he be ruined?'

'Well, he runs the Pier Theatre as well – he has a finger in every pie. But I don't know whether he'll be able to rebuild the Kinema. He seemed rather vague about the matter of insurance . . . How did you get on with Mr Truelove?'

'I think he has an ulcer and it will get worse unless it's treated. But he seems the sort of man who won't look after himself. I tried to give him a hint when he called me in to see his daughter – not Mrs Watlyn, the other one. Clara.' He gave her a wry look. 'There really wasn't anything wrong with her.'

'Oh dear. I'm afraid that will go on until everyone's had a good look at you.'

'Perhaps I should beat them to it.'

She looked at him quizzically.

'Have them all come to me. Some sort of party – get it all over with in one go. How about a garden party? I believe there's room. People could admire my topiary.'

'A good idea,' she said laughing. 'I'm sure they'd all come. As long as you could bear being the prize exhibit.'

'Like a giant marrow . . . Would you come? You, and Elizabeth, and your aunt?'

There was a pause between them.

'Or is that presumptuous?' he said.

'No. But it's as well to be clear about this – I'm not the sort of person you invite to garden parties.'

'You're the sort of person *I* invite to garden parties.'

Again there was that touch of pride in himself, a sort of inward arrogance, but it attracted rather than repelled her.

'I'd love to come,' she said.

The satisfaction was plain in his face, but he went on quickly, 'Now, I must see about hiring a small marquee. I wonder where . . . I shall have to ask Mrs Snell where she gets her dresses from.'

Rose began laughing, and with a wonderful sense of freedom in the open night air.

'You've met Mrs Snell, I take it.'

'I . . . encountered her. Did Mr Snell marry all of her, do

you suppose, or just take out a lease on part of her? Yes, she called me in and gave me a thorough inspection. She was determined to find out whether I was related to the Suffolk Blanchards, whoever they are.'

'Actually my Aunt Dolly sometimes makes costumes for Mrs Snell.'

'Poor Dolly. Where does she get all the material? No, I'm sorry. I just think when someone is such an intolerable conceited snob, they should take care not to look grotesque. It always seems to be the case, though. Glass-house dwellers always are the first to throw stones.'

*He that is without sin among you, let him first cast a stone at her* . . . In the early days after Elizabeth was born, the days of covert glances and sneers, she often used to think of that text with bitterness. Now she was surprised to find the bitterness quite gone, like a toothache that passes without one realizing it.

The church clock began striking. It was one o'clock: she hadn't realized it was so late.

'I'd better go,' she said. 'Dolly will be wondering where I've got to.'

He walked with her to the corner of Princess Street. Smoke still hung in the air, but the red glow had gone from the sky. They turned to face each other, stammering in the awkwardness of parting. At that precise moment a light in the upper window of the house on the corner was turned off; and it was a voice out of darkness, receding, that said, 'Good night, Rose.'

'Good night, James,' she answered, and her hand seemed to tingle where he had gently touched it.

# SIXTEEN

James set himself eagerly to the planning of the garden party.

His temperament was a peculiar combination of the methodical and the impatient. He wanted things done properly, and he wanted them done now. It proved impossible to hire a marquee in Shipden, except for a dull green canvas affair that looked to him like an army pup tent, and he paid over the odds to have a good one sent from Norwich. His domestic arrangements still being of a basic kind, he had to hire glasses and crockery and cutlery too; and he went down to the promenade and bespoke the services of a children's entertainer for the afternoon. In his spare time he worked on the garden himself, mowing and rolling and hacking away at the overgrown flowerbeds.

All this activity, on top of his professional work, effectively stopped him thinking. He scarcely articulated to himself any reasons for this party except the surface one, of getting his introduction to Shipden over with; and that suited him. In many ways an exacting and analytical man, he was content at times to lash the wheel and let his ship take him where it would.

He had invitations printed too, but made the mistake, before sending them out, of mentioning the coming party to the Vickerys when they called one evening.

Sylvia pounced.

'Now. I'm at your disposal. Thinking caps –' she patted her head, frowning humorously – 'thinking caps on, and I think we can make something rather good out of this.'

'No need,' James said. 'It's all in hand.'

'Oh – ho,' Sylvia chuckled, 'it seems it, no doubt. I dare say it seems it. Now. First things first: there must be enough to drink. Obviously there'll be tea and coffee and so on, but some people will expect something a little stronger. What did you plan to serve?'

'Some sort of cup, I thought.'

'No, no, and I'm saying that because I happen to know about this. I knew someone once who served a claret-cup at a garden party. It was too strong for the women and the men didn't like it, and the whole thing was a fairly complete disaster.'

'Well, it doesn't have to be claret-cup. Some other—'

'But you see what I mean. *Any* cup is not a good idea. In fact I'd go so far as to say that claret-cup is probably the best. The others are even worse. Now . . .'

Finally, with great labour, he managed to convince Sylvia that he could manage, but it was like holding a door shut against ten men.

Then she spotted the gramophone.

'Now how much did you pay for this, James? It's well known that that Carette woman overcharges. Now if you'd come to me, I could have advised you about this, because I happen to know. I helped a friend choose one of these and she said to me afterwards that she would have been swindled terribly if I hadn't been there. I always seem to be able to find a good bargain, I don't know why, it's just one of those things I can do.'

'I'm very pleased with the gramophone,' he said, 'and I think it was a fair price. Rose Jordan helped me choose.'

'Rose Jordan again?' Sylvia said with a bright look. 'You seem quite fated to meet that woman.' She laughed pointlessly. 'So, how went the day with Nell Henning?'

Dr Vickery maintained a stiff silence. He had been polite to James, but there was no doubt that James's copybook remained blotted.

'She has a healthy baby girl,' he said. 'I'm going to call on them tomorrow morning, as it happens.' This, though he did not yet know it, was the second unwise thing he had mentioned.

'Well, I'm glad,' Sylvia said, nodding vigorously. 'It's high time somebody did something about her.'

He perhaps should not have been surprised, when he arrived at the cottage in The Rows the next morning, to find Sylvia waiting for him. She had brought a gift of baby clothes and, very much the lady bountiful, marched straight in with James and began belabouring Nell Henning with cheerful advice – which Nell, in her bovine way, hardly seemed to notice at all.

Afterwards, as he could hardly avoid doing, he offered Sylvia a lift home, and in the car she began to speak of Nell Henning as their joint project.

'Now, we must put our heads together and work out what's to be done with her.'

James did not see that there was anything, particularly; but it was clear that Sylvia was determined to take Nell Henning up as a case, with him as medical consultant.

'First,' she said, 'we must find out if she's got family, someone who can help her with the children. If not, that busybody neighbour of hers can play a part, perhaps. Apparently Nell used to do charring before, ahem, nature intervened again. We must look around for openings. And then there's that house – we must see if we can get that into some sort of order . . .'

That evening he worked on the garden again; and at last, satisfied that it would pass muster, he set the gramophone outside and sat listening and smoking. All at once the thought occurred to him: perhaps no one would come.

And then he realized that the thought didn't really trouble him. The one acceptance that mattered had already been made.

# *SEVENTEEN*

Shipden responded favourably to James Blanchard's invitation.

Sylvia Vickery considered the garden party as partly her responsibility, and perhaps even her own idea: she spoke of it as 'our little plan', sometimes in tones of resigned amusement, for days beforehand. Dr Vickery, though not pleased about the way he had been challenged at the Trueloves' – his austere manner covered a fair share of vanity – was prepared to put it down to youth, believing that right judgement belonged only to age; and acquiesced to the invitation readily enough. While he was not about to push Sylvia into James's arms, not being sufficiently interested in her for that, he would take every favourable opportunity as it came.

Mr Jarvis Truelove, though his dyspepsia made public engagements involving food and drink a torture to him, was eager to go. It was a great pity Dr Blanchard had had to leave his dinner party early; he had been getting along well, it seemed, with Clara. Mr Truelove bought her a new frock for the occasion of the garden party, and she put it on obediently, as she would a hairshirt if she had thought it expedient. Clara Truelove had long ago learnt that having no apparent will of your own got you through life pretty well, though she had some very decided opinions of her own inside her groomed head, one of which was that she would happily consider Dr Blanchard as a potential husband, as long as she could do so without compromising her reputation as a model of submissive femininity.

Millie Watlyn was pleased at the invitation that arrived at

the Arcadia Guest House, where the edges of it got a little besmirched with jam as she prepared the Captain's sugar-rich breakfast. She and Frank did not get out much; and it made a nice change, too, to find their little girl, Carrie, included in the invitation.

Mrs Snell, wife of Mr Clement Snell the bank manager, received the invitation merely as her due, indeed supposed it to be the first one sent out. As for Mr Snell, a little pince-nezed man, two parts water and one vinegar, no one asked what he thought. He was an appendage to Mrs Snell, part of her ensemble; no one would have been surprised to see him trimmed with matching feathers or dyed to this season's shade.

Madame Carette sighed a good deal over her invitation, seesawing between acceptance and refusal according to her mood. Mr Seymour Gaze, the barber and photographer, melancholy and besotted, changed his mind about going each time she did.

Mrs Betts, wife of Mr George Betts the auctioneer and land agent, decided she would go, but not take her little girl, Olivia, even though she was mentioned in the invitation. Olivia had been temperamental and sullen ever since finishing her piano lessons with that Jordan woman, and efforts to find another teacher had been unsuccessful. It was all very annoying, but Mrs Betts thought it probably as well to give up the music idea altogether: it was not as if it helped a girl get married.

The vicar of Shipden, the Revd Mr Shillingford, accepted because his wife wished to go, but would gladly have stayed at home. Incumbent of one of the grandest churches in Norfolk, he was dismally conscious of being unequal to the architecture. He was not good at any of the things vicars were supposed to do – preaching, talking in a sonorous voice, remembering the names of children and whether they had been confirmed, lending good-humoured dignity to social occasions. He often wished Mrs Shillingford, who was efficient at all these things and more, could have worn the dog collar.

Little Miss Hyde the confectioner wanted very much to go, having seen very little of life beyond the bull's-eye window of the shop in the High Street, and the thoughtful timing of the garden party – Thursday, early closing – meant that she could have gone. But old Mrs Hyde said no, and that was that. Prim and correct and fiercely respectable, this old lady coolly and deliberately made her daughter's life a misery just as much as if she had got drunk and beat her with a stick every night in the dingy parlour behind the shop.

Mr Ernie Crimmins glanced at his invitation regretfully – it would have been nice for Mrs Crimmins and the children, a noisy good-natured crew who lived in a ripe Dickensian disorder in an old squeezed townhouse behind the High Street – but he doubted he could make time, what with the clearing up of the Kinema fire on top of his usual commitments, and the invitation was quickly lost under a heap of papers.

Mr Leo Liddell, conductor of the resident orchestra, signalled acceptance on his own behalf, though not his wife's. It would be no fun, he thought, with Mrs Liddell there – she was such a killjoy that nothing ever was. As it was his habit to give her a peculiarly painful open-handed slap if she disagreed with him, Mrs Liddell chose not to protest the point.

Tom Cherry, porter at the Grand and patient of Dr Blanchard's, was delighted with his invitation, but doubted very much that his employers at the Grand would let him have time off. Like many ex-soldiers, he already found himself tagged, quite unfairly, as a Bolshie – on being given contrary orders by the undermanager and the head porter he had made the mistake of raising the bemused question of which he was to follow.

Dolly Jordan openly looked forward to a jolly good chinwag – she was aware that the other ladies would patronize her but had learnt not to care – and, privately, to hitting the drink. Elizabeth Jordan was highly excited, as a note had been slipped into their invitation revealing that a children's entertainer would be provided.

Others who accepted were Mr Askew, the golf club manager, who looked forward to waggling his moustaches at the ladies and yarning about the war (both of these activities, which people thought were conceited, were actually the result of a piercing loneliness); ancient Mr Coxon the bellringer and his ancient wife, perennially covered in dog hairs; Mr Gunnell the haberdasher, who was so mean that he lived on sandwiches made of thinly sliced beetroot and was always up for a free treat; and Mrs Porson the midwife, who was robustly free of social fears, having seen the likes of Mrs Snell and Mrs Vickery in very undignified positions and heard them swear like dockers in the process.

One person who could not come, and would have been the first to accept, occupied Rose's thoughts a good deal as she got ready on the day. Her mother. How she would have loved it! The opportunity to dress up and socially parade without having to do anything intellectually demanding like listen to music or play cards, not to mention the chance that the garden party, being by its nature a non-exclusive gathering, gave to sort the social sheep from the goats, with the appropriate snubs and cuts resulting.

And how surprised she would have been, too, to see Rose and Elizabeth invited.

It was indeed an unusual experience for Rose. Putting on her best frock – her one good frock, really – she thought how long it had been since she had done anything like this. And looking at her reflection in the mirror, she had also the simple thought: I'm young. It was a mere fact, but she seemed to perceive it, and feel it deep inside her, for the first time in five years.

She was a little nervous too. She had long kept to a limited circle – the company of the kind and true. Now she would be mixing with the people who had effectively ostracized her. It gave her a good feeling, a glow that was defiant and quietly proud – something like that note she sometimes heard in James Blanchard's voice, when he spoke of being a doctor or set

180

down an opinion. In it there was a refusal to accommodate, though without any showy rebellion: an independence.

James. She had thought of him – and by that name – almost ceaselessly since the night of the Kinema fire. A strange meeting: whilst there had been a polite withdrawal from the position he had so surprisingly taken when he had asked her to go to the Winter Gardens, yet there had been a crossing of a bridge too. She had begun to know him; and an itch of fascination contended with her cautious resolve not to get involved, to shun the heat of the flame.

'Mummy.' Elizabeth, neat in her summer frock, her thick hair brushed but unadorned – Rose was secretly pleased that she disdained the ribbons and beads that could turn delightful girl-children into little primping beasts – tugged at her sleeve and held up her clown-doll. 'Can I take Higgins with me?'

'All right. Mind you keep tight hold of him.'

Setting off to walk to James's house, Rose found herself experiencing a peculiar and uncharacteristic dread of being the first to arrive; but they found a fair sprinkling of guests already there, milling about the lawns and ignoring, with English stolidity, the stiff breeze that kept lifting the tails of linen jackets and the hems of flimsy skirts. Informal formality; she couldn't help wondering what a visiting Chinaman or Aborigine would have made of the strange ritual.

'Hello, hello, glad you could come.'

James looked spruce and cool; but, to Rose's eyes at least, he was plainly nervous too.

'You must have been busy – you've got the garden looking lovely,' she said. It was true: the lawns were trim and the jungle of shrubs had been tamed and the marquee and bunting made a colourful picture under the bright sun. Only the topiary gave a hint that this order had been hastily carved out of chaos.

'Thank you,' he said smiling; then, with urgent despondency, 'I didn't rake the grass enough – look. It's going to stick to everyone's shoes.'

'Oh dear. That'll be a black mark against you.'

He looked at her and then laughed. 'Oh well. As long as nobody actually lies down and rolls in it. Now, let me get you some refreshments – there's tea and coffee and iced lemonade, or there's cider-cup if—'

'Oh, my dear boy, you've far too much to do to fuss with that,' Aunt Dolly said. 'Just point me to the place and I'll do the honours.'

Dolly made a beeline for the marquee. Rose and James exchanged a smile; then he bent down to Elizabeth. 'Hello, you two. Thank you for coming. See that man over there? He's going to be doing a show soon – magic tricks, I think. If you'd like to see it, just toddle over there whenever you want.'

'Do you have to pay?' Elizabeth said.

'No, it's free.'

There were already several children gathered about the terrace where the entertainer – looking, in the usual way of children's entertainers, a little boozy and seedy – was setting up his equipment. Peering over, Elizabeth gave a little shout. 'Oh, Mummy, Carrie's there. Can I go?'

'Of course. I'll be here if you want me.'

She watched Elizabeth run across the lawn and greet Carrie, Millie Watlyn's little girl. Conscious of her reluctance to lose sight of her, she looked up to meet James's observant eyes.

'I shall have to get used to that,' she said. 'Watching her go away from me.' Feeling she had been a little too solemn, she said hastily, 'Well, how does it feel to be a giant marrow?'

'A bit forced,' he said. 'You must be very proud of Elizabeth.'

'I am.' All the more proud of her because she was meant to be ashamed of her. She wondered for a moment whether to say this; but it seemed like thrusting confidences on him, unfair in the circumstances. 'It was nice of you to have a children's entertainer.'

'Well – I think it's a pity when children are left out of things. Seen and not heard and all that.'

He had done it for her. The knowledge of this went through her with an effect that was like an interior blush.

'Damn,' he said, glancing over at the gate, 'here come people.'

She laughed. 'Spoken like a true host.'

'Dear, does it show?'

'I'm only teasing.' She dropped her eyes. 'You'd better circulate.'

'Yes, I shall have to.'

But he did not move and with a sudden lightness of heart she aimed a mock blow at him.

'Well, circulate, then!'

'Careful, we bruise easily, us marrows. I suppose I shouldn't be seen to be monopolizing you, should I?'

'No, you shouldn't. People will talk.'

'Yes . . . On the other hand, they like nothing better, so we'd be doing them a service. You look wonderful, by the way.'

Dolly broke in on her dry-mouthed silence.

'I say, Rose dear, this cider-cup is awfully refreshing – do try it. It was a clever idea of yours, Dr Blanchard, because you see it's stimulating without being heady. I simply can't take heady liquors myself.' Dolly smiled at them both, toothy and eager. 'Normally I wouldn't indulge at all, but with you being a doctor I *know* it'll be wholesome. Goodness, here comes Mrs Snell.'

'So she does,' James said. 'I *thought* the sun had gone in. I'd better present myself.'

Watching him go, Rose was glad of the cider-cup Dolly handed her. If she were going to have this dizzy, half-drunken feeling, she might as well have a reason for it.

Over by the marquee, Mr Seymour Gaze placed a chair for Madame Carette.

'Thank you, Mr Gaze. You must think me a very weak creature, having to be seated like this.'

'Not at all, Madame C. Thass the sun, you know: makes you tired, it does.'

'It is not the sun,' Madame Carette said wistfully. 'I wish it was the sun.'

'The wind then,' Mr Gaze said; then, feeling this was unfortunate, was struck dumb.

'It is not the wind. It is the spirits.'

'Oh? Oh – well, Madame C., what I always say is, if it makes you feel better, then no harm done. I take a drop meself now and then—'

'Oh, Mr Gaze, Mr Gaze!' she said, tapping his hand, a gesture which made him sag visibly at the knees. 'It is not those kind of spirits. It is my spirits. They are low. All these people – all so happy and beautiful.'

'I wouldn't say beautiful – not when you're here,' Mr Gaze said, dipping his badgerlike head.

'Oh, pooh. I am just a shadow – a skeleton at the feast.'

'H'm – well, I wish all skeletons looked like you, Madame C., thass all I can say,' said Mr Gaze – aware, as soon as he said it, that this did not make much sense.

'I should not be here,' Madame Carette mourned. 'My sun has set.'

'Ah. But the thing about the sun, Madame C., is that it always rises again,' Mr Gaze said, congratulating himself on a smart recovery.

'You are sweet, Mr Gaze.'

'Sweet on *you*, Madame C.'

'Oh, nonsense, nonsense. I am like a little withered tree.'

'Well, I'd plant you in my garden, Madame C., any day,' Mr Gaze chuckled, undergoing his peculiar torture, which was to say facetiously what he meant dreadfully.

Mrs Snell, graciously receiving James's greetings, swept the gathering with her eyes, noting whom she could talk to, whom she could speak to, whom she could nod to, and whom she could ignore altogether. The gradations were fine: a tradesman who lived in rooms *above* a shop would get a nod, a tradesman who lived in a house *behind* the premises would get a word.

James, relinquished, watched her sailing across the grass; saw her head swivel in Rose's direction and then turn conspicuously away. Remove those corsets, he thought maliciously, and the flesh would not so much flop as spill.

It was like a pool of fish, he thought, with most of the fish intent, carp-like, on devouring the others. And amongst all the treacherous, stealthy circling, a flash of marvellous beauty.

Mrs Cora Betts – who in the summer months looked diminished without her favourite furs, like a shorn sheep – nudged Mrs Shillingford and said, with a backward motion of her head, 'I'm very surprised to see that woman here. The Jordan woman.'

'Her child's here too,' Mrs Shillingford said. 'I saw her earlier. What can the doctor be thinking of? Do you suppose he doesn't know?'

'Someone should tell him, if not.'

'Well, standards aren't what they were, wherever you look. I blame the war. One sees quite well-brought-up young women aping the ways of the factory girl. I suggested to Matthew that he should preach on the subject. But he says the pulpit isn't the place for it.' Mrs Shillingford, a handsome and forceful woman, waved an irritated hand. It was a standing affront to her that her husband, feeble enough in most ways, still clung on to his opinions: changing them to her own was one of the things she had looked forward to when marrying him.

Dolly Jordan, on her third cider-cup, was pointing out the flowerbeds to Mrs Vickery. 'Do look – now aren't those lupins a picture? And that, I do believe, is mock orange blossom. Goodness, do I see blackfly? My good gosh, I shall have to tell Dr Blanchard – they'll strip it away in no time, little blighters. There, I'll nip a few off for him.' She spoke with excited, tipsy fizzings, lumbering and grabbing at the shrub.

'My dear, you'll soil your gloves,' Mrs Vickery said unconcernedly. Though she would deplore Dolly Jordan to her friends, she enjoyed pitying her. Occasionally Mrs Vickery would hazily grasp at the realization that her husband did not much love or respect her, and at such times it was helpful to think of someone like Dolly Jordan, who was lonely in shabby spinsterhood rather than lonely in well-upholstered wedlock.

Sylvia Vickery, relentless and unstoppable as the tide or the seasons, bore down on James. She dispensed with preliminaries.

'Now, James, I've been thinking about what we were saying apropos of Nell Henning.' Though James was talking with Mr Truelove, she merely blinkered him out. 'The thing is to give her a character; people simply won't take her on without it. Now I'm prepared to give her a reference – I could ask Father but I do think, actually, people would take more notice if it came from me. I don't know why that is but it's just something I've experienced in the past: people tend to come to me about these things. Somehow, I suppose they must simply trust my judgement. I remember someone moving to the district and wanting to know which butcher to deal with and, as you know, everyone deals with Youens', including the very best houses out in the shooting country – but that actually didn't satisfy this friend of mine, because it was *my* recommendation she wanted. She simply said, "If you're happy with them, Sylvia, then I know they'll be all right," which is a funny thing, isn't it?'

'Excellent firm, Youens',' Mr Truelove said agreeably. 'They—'

'So what I wanted to know,' Sylvia said, talking over him, 'is whether you'd give a reference for Nell Henning too? It is better if there are two, you see.'

'Yes, certainly, I'd be happy to,' James said.

'Right. Now, the question is the wording of it.'

'Oh well, I'll just write the standard testimony, I suppose,' James said. 'How about something to drink?'

'Ah. Now this is it, you see. I think it needs to be something a little different from the usual reference. We really need to put our thinking caps on and do this properly. I've a notebook in my bag . . .'

He was rescued by the arrival of more guests, whom even Sylvia's obtuseness acknowledged that he had to go and greet; but she followed him a little way, like a trailing streamer, still talking.

Well meaning, he told himself, forcing down an ungovernable irritation. It was, in fact, not entirely at her. He had failed to anticipate the sheer swamping effect of all these people. Stupid, of course: did he suppose he could invite them and then leave them to their own devices while he concentrated on the one thing that mattered to him? Of course not. So he told himself, rationally; but still he chafed at the unsatisfactoriness of life, on edge, and not entirely happy.

Mr Truelove watched James go regretfully. He liked the fellow: seemed to have a brain, which was not universally the case amongst the eligible young men of the district. The Shillingfords' boy, Victor, for instance, who often partnered Clara at mixed tennis and generally considered himself in the running, if not a clear favourite, for her hand, sometimes drove Mr Truelove to explosive point with his drivelling about cricket. The doctor was different. Good profession, no ties, and something rather nice could be made of this house. It would be a jolly good thing, Mr Truelove thought, if Clara could hook him.

Mr Truelove was less mercenary and more affectionate than this suggested. He was simply driven by pathological worry. He was a man who could not relax. He had married young, as a barely established lawyer with no connections, and that had been a worry. In time he had become one of the most prosperous men in Shipden, transacting legal business for many landed families, like the Harwoods, in the horsy hinterland of the town. So he took to worrying about other things. First there had been his elder daughter, Millie, whom he loved devotedly. He would have done anything to stop her marrying Frank Watlyn, except actually stopping her – he was not that sort of man – and five years after they were married, he still worried. He would lie awake thinking of what would happen if, as was not wholly unlikely, Frank Watlyn went bust. He would get up and go downstairs and reread Millie's latest letter to convince himself that there was nothing between the lines.

And he worried about Clara, his younger daughter, who was so sensible, obedient, accommodating – the perfect daughter in fact – that that in itself was worrying. Now if he could fix her up with Dr Blanchard . . . And yet, no fool, Mr Truelove had a shrewd feeling that the young doctor was not going to take this particular bait. Looking over at him, and then at Clara talking in her polite decorous way to that unfortunate Rose Jordan, Mr Truelove just couldn't see it.

'Yes, it's been the best season I can remember,' Rose said, replying to Clara Truelove's small talk. Devoted to Millie, Rose had never quite known what to make of her younger sister. Something was surely going on behind those gentian eyes, but she was damned if she knew what. 'The hotel people must be pleased. They had such a hard time of it with the war.'

'Oh, yes. It seems such a terrible thing when countries go to war, doesn't it? I wonder why they can't just get along with each other.'

'Perhaps for the same reasons that people don't,' Rose said.

'Yes, I'm sure you're right,' Clara cooed. 'People can be horrid to one another, can't they? That's where the trouble starts. Look at that awful Kaiser. What became of him after they threw him out? I'm sure I remember reading he was in Holland but Victor Shillingford swears it's Switzerland.'

'I think it was Holland he went to,' Rose said. 'I remember feeling surprised that they would have him.'

'That's what I thought. But Victor wouldn't listen. Dr Blanchard!' She beckoned James over with a white arm, like a swan's neck. 'Can you settle it for us? Where did the Kaiser go?'

Before James could answer Sylvia Vickery, gliding across his path as if on swift castors, put in, 'What's this? What are we trying to settle?'

'Where the Kaiser is,' Rose said. 'We thought Holland.'

'No, no. It's Denmark.' Sylvia, all smiling assurance, turned to James, consulting him as if he were a watch or some other piece of entirely private property. 'The Kaiser, though strictly one should say ex-Kaiser, went into exile in Denmark, didn't he, James?'

'Holland,' James said. 'Lives there like a country gent, they say. It'd be odd to have him as a neighbour, wouldn't it? "Morning, nice to see the sun again. Do you know, you *remind* me of someone . . ."'

'No, no,' Sylvia said, 'it's definitely Denmark. Don't you remember, James, we were talking about it the other day? There was something about it in the paper and we said how odd it was that a neutral country would let him in, but of course that's the whole point of neutrality, isn't it?' She nodded complacently at Clara, as if she had challenged her. 'Yes, it is, you know, when you think about it.'

'Well, now I'm confused,' Clara said. 'There was Victor saying Switzerland, and—'

'Oh good heavens, not Switzerland!' Sylvia laughed. 'Good gracious, no, that's quite out of the question. What a funny thing to think of! It's Denmark – I think you'll find that's right. Isn't it, James? We know, don't we?'

'It's Holland – a place called Doorn,' James said pleasantly.

'Oh, wait – now, I see what's happening – you're getting confused,' Sylvia said. 'Holland – yes – you're talking about Kaiser Wilhelm, of course.'

'Of course,' said James, 'the one they wanted to hang.'

'Ah – now I see where the confusion is. I'm not talking about that Kaiser. I mean the old Austrian Emperor. He was called "Kaiser" too, you see, in German. This is what I thought you meant. The Austrian Kaiser – do you see? Now he's the one who's in Switzerland, as I said.'

'But Sylvia, dear, you said Denmark,' Clara said.

'No, no, Switzerland. Now you're getting confused, Clara. Switzerland. That's where he went – the Austrian Kaiser. Not the other one. It's quite simple really, once you get it fixed in your mind. Do you see it now, Rose?'

'Yes, I see it,' Rose said. 'Kaiser Bill went to Holland. That awful Kaiser who would never admit he was wrong.'

'. . . You heard about poor Ernie Crimmins?' Frank Watlyn said to his father-in-law, Mr Truelove. 'No insurance on the Kinema, they say. Didn't keep up the payments.'

'Terrible business,' Mr Truelove said, crunching a peppermint and fighting down waves of stabbing dyspepsia.

'I like the man personally,' Frank said, 'but it's shocking when a fellow doesn't take thought for the future like that. All right if it's just him – but there's a wife and children to consider in his case.' Frank knew his father-in-law's opinion of him – though he thought it entirely unjustified – and he said things like this in the hope of altering it. He did not realize that it made him look merely smug, and made Mr Truelove dislike him even more.

'That Kinema was a ramshackle affair anyhow, as a business venture,' Mr Truelove said. 'It seems to have been regarded as a temporary expedient. But even so, it should have been insured. This is what comes of doing things by halves.'

'Surely,' Frank said. 'Absolutely.' He glanced curiously at his father-in-law's fiery little face, wondering if the old fellow was hinting about the insurance on the Arcadia. A bit stiff if so, he thought. As it happened there was no insurance on the Arcadia, but it didn't seem worth it when they were going to move on to bigger things quite soon.

'Where have you been?' Rose said, spotting Millie Watlyn at last and hurrying over to her. 'I kept looking round for you.'

'Cornered by the Snells, hellish,' Millie said, as they gave each other a quick hug. 'Goodness, you look well. I say, isn't this a nice idea of the doctor's, being able to bring the children? I wonder what made him think of it? Come along, let's get something to drink.'

The imperturbable Mrs Penn, helped by two hired maids, was serving the refreshments in the marquee. Rose decided on another cider-cup, even though she didn't have the strongest of heads. She was on edge, and put it down to the presence of Sylvia Vickery, a woman who had an effect on her like a metal file rasped across the teeth. And then there was the matter of James, and the matter of finding, to her own dismay, that having a ration of him – as was inevitable at a party like this – was not enough. It was like having just one drink: better not to have any.

'Gosh, you have got a thirst,' Millie said. She seemed, in her acute way, to see much; but just then Mrs Shillingford hove into view and smiled a condescending greeting.

'Mrs Watlyn, isn't this charming? We see so little of you. And how is your little girl?'

'Oh, thriving, thank you, Mrs Shillingford. She's enjoying the entertainment, with Rose's little girl. They're the best of friends.'

'Mm?' Mrs Shillingford said, her smile visibly decaying.

Millie did not let her get away with it. 'Of course, you remember Rose Jordan,' she said, for all the world as if Rose had been away for years – which in a way she had.

'Of course,' Mrs Shillingford said, making a vague gesture with her right hand, as if Rose were a pet that she was afraid might bite. 'How – how nice.'

Rose remembered Mrs Shillingford crossing the road to avoid her when she had Elizabeth in a perambulator. It was merely a memory, though: no feeling came with it. Something had changed her.

'We were just saying what a nice idea it was to have a children's entertainer,' Millie said. 'It's rotten if they're left out. And grown-up talk can be so very dull. How *is* Victor, by the way . . .?'

'I like James a good deal,' Dr Vickery said to the Revd Matthew Shillingford. 'But he is headstrong and stubborn.'

'Dear me, is he?' Mr Shillingford said, feeling inferior, as he did to everyone. 'Is he? Dear me.'

'He thinks he knows everything worth knowing,' said Dr Vickery, who believed this of himself. 'But experience will do much.'

'Experience is a great teacher,' said Mr Shillingford. He often talked in platitudes like this, which saved having to think.

'As long as he doesn't make some *very* big mistake before he's of an age to realize it,' Dr Vickery said, dourly sipping sugarless tea.

'Yes, that would be a great pity,' the vicar said, and remembered asking a lady to marry him. It had been the one big decisive act of his life. The lady had said yes, and gone on to despise him. 'Yes, that would be a pity indeed.'

'Millie, you're terrible,' Rose said, as Mrs Shillingford stiffly left them.

'Oh, I don't believe she caught on anyhow. Did she? Perhaps she did.' Millie laughed. 'Well, I've never forgotten her precious Victor trying to put his hand up my skirt during a game of sardines in that awful churchy house of theirs. I knew it was him because he smelt of old cassocks. Anyway, the look the old cat gave you.'

'Really, it doesn't bother me any more.'

Leo Liddell, making his narrow-hipped way past them with two glasses of cider-cup held aloft, paused to donate a smile. 'Afternoon, ladies. Rose, old girl. So you do let your hair down now and then. And there was me thinking you'd changed your ways and turned into an old stay-at-home. Fires still burn, eh? Who's in your sights this time? Mr Happy, the Kiddies' Entertainer?'

'No,' Rose said. 'But don't worry, Leo, if clowns are ever in with a chance I'll let you know.'

'Killing,' he said. 'Absolutely killing, that. Well, must go. Young lady waiting for her drink.'

'Yes, don't keep her waiting. She might be charging by the minute.'

'Rose, dear,' Millie said, scandalized and giggling, 'such behaviour for a garden party.'

'Perhaps I'd better not drink any more of this,' Rose said, half-laughing, but with a peculiar sorrowful feeling too.

'Ah, here you are.'

Suddenly James was there. They looked at each other a moment and then he put a hand out to Millie.

'Mrs Watlyn, I didn't get a chance earlier . . . I am sorry, by the way, about having to skip off the other week from dinner at your father's. It was a great pity.'

'Oh, not at all, only to be expected when you're a doctor. I don't suppose you're ever off duty really, are you? Even at night, which must be dreadful – you know, not knowing when you go to bed whether you're going to have to get up again in an hour's time.'

'That's true. Luckily I'm a light sleeper,' he said, with a significant glance at Rose.

'Yes, luckily I am too,' Rose said.

'Hardly lucky, I'd say,' said Millie, watching them. 'I'm a rag if I don't get my eight hours without fail. Rose, dear, haven't you been sleeping?'

'Not all that well, just lately.'

'Well, that's terrible. Dr Blanchard, what would you suggest?'

'I don't think there's any great harm in it,' James said. 'Not on these wonderful summer nights.'

Millie, looking from one to the other, was about to say something when the voice of Sylvia Vickery silenced them like a screech of brakes. 'James! James, arrivals – your presence is required.'

A kind of tired flinch crossed James's face. 'Excuse me.'

Millie watched him go, her lips parted.

'Millicent Truelove,' Rose said in the accents of their old headmistress, 'you are catching flies.'

Millie closed her mouth with a snap and then aimed a slap at Rose's hand.

'Ow, what's that for?'

'Rose, you didn't tell me. I can't believe you didn't tell me.'

'What?'

'You've made a conquest. Oh, my dear girl, you've made *the* conquest.'

'Oh, hush, rubbish,' Rose said, with a painful laugh.

'My goodness, *how* jealous everyone will be! What did you do? Not that you needed to do anything. I don't blame Dr Blanchard a bit, in fact I thoroughly approve of his taste, but – I mean, whatever are you going to do? Could you – you know, consider it?'

Rose drained her glass and stared into the bottom of it. 'I don't know, Millie.'

'Do you like him?'

'A good deal more than that,' Rose said, hearing her own voice husky and almost unrecognizable.

'*Well* then.'

'I don't know whether it's enough though,' Rose said in sudden urgent confession. 'I mean – I keep wondering whether what happened with Alec just – took something away from me that won't come back.'

Millie studied her, searchingly but kindly.

'Judging by the look you just gave him,' she said, 'there's quite a lot left, even if so . . .'


'The drink is the trouble, you see,' Sylvia informed James. 'What little income Nell does get is mostly wasted on drink. And so she can't really plan her budget. This is the problem we've got to address.'

Growing deeply tired of this, James said, 'It isn't really our business. If she wants to drink, than I don't see why she shouldn't.'

'Oh no! I'm not saying that. Of course that's right, in fact that is what I actually said to Father just the other day. But I was just trying to get to the bottom of the problem, you see. Because I don't want us to waste our efforts when the solution's staring us in the face. That's where we've been going wrong with Nell, I think.'

There is no *we*, James thought wearily. The host's duty of circulating should by rights have enabled him to shake off Sylvia, but she simply circulated with him, sticking to him like a shadow. Or a hostess.

'Dr Blanchard.' Ancient, tiny Mrs Coxon leant out of a lady-cluster and plucked at his sleeve, the wax cherries on her hat waving under his nose. 'Will you back us up? We were thinking of presenting a petition to the District Council asking that no new licence be granted for another Kinema in Shipden.'

'Oh, why?' James said.

'Film shows are a vulgar entertainment,' Mrs Vickery said, 'and often, I hear, indecent. I'm sure this is something Shipden could happily do without.'

'I don't know about that,' James said. 'They're everywhere now. And visitors to a seaside resort in particular expect to find one. I understand Yarmouth has several.'

'We are not Yarmouth,' quavered Mrs Coxon. 'And the visitors we welcome are not of that sort.'

James was familiar with this stuff, and disliked it. No doubt these people wanted to go back to the days of operations without anaesthetic and sweeping-boys up chimneys. He reminded himself that they were his guests, but the stubbornness of his nature would not be suppressed.

He said, 'It's a new world. We can't hold back progress even if we should want to. And personally, I'm afraid, I'm rather fond of the films.'

There was a moan of reproach, but James heard a note of

real hostility in some of the cries against him. Progress meant workmen who did not know their place and books without a wedding at the end. They did not like it.

'What will become of craftsmanship?' Mr Coxon quavered.

'Well, doesn't that just mean a combination of deference and low wages?' James said.

'And all this hurry, hurry,' lamented Mrs Vickery, 'this modern worship of speed.'

'True,' he said, 'but no one ever minded servants and waitresses hurrying. They tended to sack them if they didn't.'

'Oh, Dr Blanchard, now you're teasing,' Mrs Vickery said, thin-lipped.

More people gathered, and peppered him with remonstrances. He rather enjoyed it, though he wished his father were here to help him; and he found a surprising, or perhaps not so surprising, ally in Clara Truelove, who piped up, 'I agree with Dr Blanchard. I think we should have a Kinema, and jazz-dancing too. It would just be silly to go back to the past. The world's always moved forward, hasn't it?'

Throughout all this Sylvia Vickery found herself somewhat pushed out, at least by her standards. Usually she talked loudly over people until they gave up and let her take centre stage, but here, with the passions of respectability generally aroused, she could not manage it. It might have been as a direct consequence of this, or perhaps simply as a result of impatiently thrusting herself forward in an effort to be heard, that Sylvia abruptly spilt her whole glassful of cider-cup over the gauzy skirt of Clara Truelove's expensive pale blue silk frock.

It broke up the talk very effectively. Now Sylvia, loudly apologizing, cursing her clumsiness, holding out Clara's skirt to inspect the stain, was the centre of attention – Clara in the meantime meekly murmuring that it didn't matter.

'Oh, but it does – your lovely new frock, what a terrible thing. It'll be all right though, I've had experience of this as it happens. All you need is a damp sponge – lightly sponge it down and it'll be as right as rain . . .' Sylvia looked up, and her eyes lit on Rose, who had been standing at a little distance listening with amusement to James defending the modern world. 'Rose – Rose, dear, could you fetch a sponge? If you're not busy with anything else, could you bring us a damp sponge?' And then, before Rose could say anything, 'You are? Oh good heavens, my mistake! I thought – what a fool – I thought you were, you know, one of the hired help. I just assumed— How silly of me . . .' Sylvia started laughing loudly, one hand to her cheek. 'Honestly, I feel a fool. I'm sorry, James, for some reason I just thought Rose was part of the help—'

'No, Sylvia,' James said, his face tight and pale, 'and I'm not the butler either.'

Rose said distinctly, 'No, it's all right. I'll fetch a sponge, if you like. If you could tell me where, James?'

Their eyes met for several moments.

'I'll show you,' he said.

They went into the house together. Intrigued eyes stared after them, while Sylvia continued to deplore her mistake with noisy hilarity, though by now no one was listening.

It was cool in the house, and seemed very dark after the sunshine outdoors. Rose hesitated in the hall, her eyes half blinded.

James touched her elbow. 'Down here.'

There was a brick-floored scullery and laundry room at the end of the passage. She found a sponge and ran it under the tap. James stood in the doorway, breathing hard.

'Rose – please, leave that.'

'No, no, I may as well. Poor Clara's dress will be stained.' She squeezed out the sponge and turned to face him. 'I'm not angry, you know.'

'I'm angry,' he said, pale and taut as a whipcord. 'It's all bloody well gone wrong.'

'There's always some sort of hitch at a big party.'

'This isn't a big party. The whole point was . . . As far as I'm concerned there's only you here. That's why – that's what it was all for. So I could see you.'

For a few moments there was only the sound of his quick breathing.

Unable to look at him, Rose kept on pointlessly squeezing the sponge over the sink until he came over and tried to take it from her.

'Leave that damn thing—'

'No, I've got to—'

Their hands got entangled: the sponge fell on the floor but their hands stayed together, clutching. Her head came close to his. She felt his breath on her hair and then she found herself putting her face in his neck.

'Oh – Dr Blanchard.'

Mrs Penn had come silently in. It was as impossible not to spring apart as not to close the eye against flying grit.

'Sorry, Doctor.' Grey, pleasant and inscrutable, Mrs Penn came forward and picked up the sponge. 'I'll just take that for the spill on the lady's dress, shall I? A dab is all it needs.'

When she had gone they looked at each other with eyes made brighter by the flush on their faces.

'They'll be talking about us, I dare say,' he said.

'Yes.' Simply uttering a word seemed to cost her as much effort as a shout. The flush felt as if it were spreading down her neck and across her chest.

'Do you care?'

'No, I don't care. Do you, James?'

'I . . . only care about one thing.'

With a last flash of nervous inconsequence she remembered the dapper shoes in the High Street and realized, as they drew together, that they were doing so like dancers, feet in position, his arm encircling her. Then, kissing him, she didn't think about that any more.

'James,' she said at last, her mouth against his face, 'you do realize, there are two of me.'

'Yes.' He took her hand, studied her smiling. 'Let's go and see the other one.'

They found Elizabeth sitting in a ring with the other children and applauding as Mr Happy, accordion slung round his neck, came to the end of a rather wheezy and clattery rendition of tunes from *HMS Pinafore*.

'Mummy,' Elizabeth said, greatly impressed, 'he can play music just like you.'

This made them laugh so hard that Elizabeth, though she didn't know why, laughed along too.

'You can't do magic, though, Mummy,' she added.

'No,' Rose said. 'I'm afraid I can't.'

'Does Mr Happy live in your house?' Elizabeth asked James.

'No. I wish he did. I don't know, though. He might magic things away.'

'What things?'

'Your dinner, just when you're going to eat it. The bedclothes off the bed.'

Elizabeth giggled.

Half-shy, half-proud, Rose looked over at the other guests, catching a rapid and self-conscious movement of heads which gave an effect like a ripple across water. She seemed still to feel a tingle on her lips and face where James had kissed her; she wondered if anything of that showed. What she was feeling was hard to put into words. It was an enormous, embracing happiness, but of a sort so long forgotten, so little expected, that she almost felt a twinge of warning in the bright heart of it.

# EIGHTEEN

They had been dancing at the Winter Gardens. It was a high summer night, still light when James parked the car at a picnic spot on the craggier heights overlooking the sea west of Shipden.

Because they faced north here, the sun both rose and set into the sea. It had disappeared from view some while ago, tucked into a pocket of sultry western cloud just above the horizon, but a bronze glow still shone off the bay and reflected on to their faces and hands, so that when Rose looked down at herself she found her skin gypsy dark against the white of her dress.

'We didn't miss one dance, did we?' she said. 'My feet are aching.'

James, as she had thought, was a light deft dancer. To the eye he always gave the impression of not weighing very much, though on touching him you found a surprising wiriness.

'Beautiful night,' he said.

The scent of pine reached the ferny clearing where they were parked in intermittent wafts like long sighs from land to sea. Rose was aware that this was a spot she had once visited with Alec, but that seemed, rather than a bad omen, a proof of providence, a defiant snap of the fingers in the face of fate.

'I've had a wonderful time, James. I'm sorry I said no before. I'm glad you asked me again.'

At the Winter Gardens Leo Liddell, conducting, had clearly spotted them. But then they had spent every spare minute together since the garden party, so they were probably already the talk of the town.

Well, Rose was no stranger to that anyway.

James took a travelling rug from the car and laid it on the heather. Sitting down beside him, Rose was conscious of stretching the insecure seams of her dress, which she and Dolly had hastily run up for the occasion from an old pattern.

'I'm glad I asked again,' James said. 'It is difficult, though. To know the right moment to ask.'

'Especially with me.'

'Why? I don't think so. You always seem so open – truthful.'

'Well – because of my situation.' She leant back, lightly holding his hand. 'You see, I hadn't thought of having anything like this.'

'Ever again?'

'I don't know. Perhaps some day. I suppose that's what I kept on thinking – "some day" – but never getting nearer to the day . . . Yes: never again, in fact. Oh, not because of what people say, not because of shame or guilt or any of that. I just felt it wasn't for me.'

'You were hurt very badly,' James said, his tone halfway between question and statement.

'Perhaps in my pride more than anything else. It's not pleasant to feel that you've been made a fool of. Or that you made a fool of yourself . . . It feels strange to be talking about this to you.'

'Does it?'

'It's such a different world. Like another life . . . It wasn't another life, though, James.' Rose, one of those people who could shift from lassitude to urgency in a moment, sat up quickly, gripping his hand and engaging his eyes. 'It wasn't another life. That was me. The very same person who's sitting here with you now, even though it doesn't seem it even to me. Some men would – find that difficult.'

James returned the pressure of her hand and then said, looking out at the sea, 'I'll confess, when I first heard about it, I felt . . . strange. Jealous. Resentful, even. I had this intense and I dare say rather conceited wish that I'd met you first.

202

But then – perhaps it simply wasn't meant to be that way.'

They both felt the inadequacy of this, and as a supplementary gesture she kissed him.

'The thing is,' she said, 'I can't wish things different. Because of Elizabeth. As a result of what happened, I have Elizabeth. So there really can't be any regrets.'

'She's a dear child. Does you credit . . . What was he all about, do you suppose? Just as a matter of interest, what was he, really, about?'

He seemed to be speaking in a spirit of detached enquiry, though she saw emotion there too. He was good at disguising this, and probably only her love-sharpened eyes would have seen it.

'Sorry,' he said as she hesitated, 'it really isn't my business.'

'No, no. I'm just trying to think, because it's something I've – I've tended to put out of my mind . . . The thing about Alec was – I believe he genuinely was fascinated by women. In that sense, at least, he couldn't help himself.' She shrugged, covering a shiver that came from she didn't know where. 'He was irresponsible. He couldn't see cause and effect. If you put a pan on the stove and leave it, you and I know that sooner or later it's going to boil over or burn. But there are some people who just don't see that. They don't think it's going to happen, simply because they don't want it to . . .' She frowned and plucked a piece of heather. 'You'd better tell me the version you've heard. No,' she said as he protested, 'no, I know you'll have been given the story, if you've lived in Shipden for more than a week. It would be amazing if you hadn't.'

He drew a deep breath. 'All I know is that it was a man called Alec Taverner, that he was in charge of the town's entertainments, that it was during the war. You . . . became pregnant with Elizabeth. He went to the war and didn't come back.'

'Because he didn't want to,' she said, a little harshly. 'That's the important part of the story. That's the twist, if you like. And I decided to stay here and have the baby. My mother wasn't pleased. I don't *think* I was really forgiven when she died – I may be wrong. But she did stick by me, which I know wasn't easy for her. Then I went to live with Aunt Dolly and began working for Madame Carette. I've never heard from Alec since, though I know he survived the war and came back to England with some medals. And I don't want to hear from him. Ever.'

After a silence, James said, 'Ever read *Tess of the d'Urbervilles*?'

'Yes. My mother said it was shocking and indecent, so of course I read it.'

He smiled. 'I was just reminded of that scene where she tells that strait-laced husband about her past, and he makes such a big fuss. Of course, he's already told his, which I haven't.'

'You don't have to give me any confessions.'

'Well, there isn't much. During the war I became engaged, briefly. She was a V.A.D. nurse at the hospital where I was working. We broke it off and she married someone else. With hindsight, it was probably just as well. My feelings were a bit unrealistic. But at the time it was . . . well, a bit bruising. He was a soldier,' he added with seeming casualness. 'My position's the same, really. I didn't expect this. I wasn't looking for it. I met you and – it just happened.'

'Glad it did?'

'Yes. A little frightened too.'

She nodded: she understood. 'When you found out – it didn't change anything?'

'I can't pretend I didn't think a lot about it. Because, as I say, I was jealous.'

'You don't have to be,' she said very seriously, 'believe me.'

'Well, perhaps that jealousy was a good thing in a way. It fired me up somehow – so I ended up asking you to the Winter Gardens that time. Which happened to be the wrong time.'

'Not necessarily. I wanted to say yes. But I was all confused.'

James kissed her, his lips lingering about her face for several moments. 'And now?'

'I'm not confused now.'

He sat back a little. 'Then I wonder if this is a good time . . . to ask you to marry me.'

'Oh!'

He didn't move; he kept his eyes on hers. Suffocating waves of feeling beat over her and prevented her from speaking. It was very much as if she were drowning.

'Oh – say something!' she gasped, breaking the silence.

He shook his head. 'It's not my turn.'

Recovering her breath, Rose had a rapid mental image of women in this position, what they said and did. *I shall have to think about it* – that was a traditional one. They palpitated and hesitated – just as she probably seemed to be doing.

And yet what she felt, as she returned James's level gaze, was something clear and adult and strong, impelling her down a straight road of decision.

The glow of dusk had faded, and all near at hand was shadowy: only the white-shirted, lambent-eyed figure of James was truly visible to her. And this was right. Many other things waited in the shadows of life, presently to be illuminated and considered – Elizabeth, Dolly, the phantom of Alec, the new family and new life built on the foundations of the old . . . many things. But in front of her, and all that she could see or needed to see, was James.

She remembered as a girl standing on the breakwater and looking down into the waves and choosing, gladly electing to jump. In the same way, she found she wanted to leap into him.

'Yes,' she said. 'Yes, James, I will.'

He held her, and there was not only delight and relief but a kind of boyish pride in the way he breathlessly exclaimed, 'So – I did pick the right moment after all!'

'Oh, my dear, we'll have a drink on it. That calls for a drink, my goodness it does – oh, my dear girl, I don't know where I am.'

Aunt Dolly made a little dancing twirl about the kitchen, sending every movable object in the room flying, and then galumphed into her workroom, coming back with a brandy bottle.

'I keep this in my sewing-machine case, you know,' she said disingenuously, 'for safekeeping. In case of emergencies. I quite forgot it was there. You'll have one, won't you, dear? Just a little, as a nightcap, can't hurt anyone. And after all, it's not every day we have news like this!'

True enough, Rose thought dizzily, coughing a little at the strength of the drink Dolly poured her. She was in a daze. She had walked in, after James had dropped her off, and blurted it out to Dolly all at once, like an excited schoolgirl, though on the drive home she had made careful plans about how she would announce it.

Dolly drained her drink and poured herself another, gabbling, 'Of course one wouldn't normally do this, but under the circumstances . . .' Suddenly she stopped and looked at Rose, curiously deadpan.

'My dear, you're not marrying him out of gratitude, I hope?'

'What?'

'Oh, that's not me talking, dear. I'm giving you a taste of what people may say. You *know* what they're like as well as I do. And the drift of it will be, "Good heavens, not many men would take on another man's child like that. I hope she counts herself lucky." Do you see?'

'Yes. I do count myself lucky – but not because of that.' Stimulated by the brandy, Rose interrogated herself. Was there any trace of that feeling? No. No and no. Though, of course, the question of Elizabeth was crucial. She could not have answered yes to James if she had had any doubts about relations between him and Elizabeth. Luckily, though, a rapport had already built up between them: he had a good way with children. And just before they had parted, she had brought this subject up, saying gently, 'James, just to be a complete wet blanket for a moment – I know you don't need reminding but . . . it will mean being a husband and father in one go.'

'I'm happy about that,' he said, 'if you are. I know I can only be a stepfather really, but – well, I'll be everything I can.'

'No, Dolly,' Rose said now. 'I'm not marrying him for that. As long as I know it and you know it, then everyone else can—'

'Go and boil their heads!' cried Dolly with one of her sudden hooting laughs. 'Of course, my dear. I just thought I'd be "the voice of Shipden" for a moment. Personally I think he'll be an excellent father to Elizabeth. Oh, my dear – what a nice life you're both going to have!' she added, her face beaming with a pure childlike pleasure at the thought.

'I think so. But – oh, Dolly – I shall be leaving you,' Rose said, and burst into tears.

'There now,' Dolly said, hugging Rose to her, 'there now. Jolly well glad to be free of me, I dare say.'

'Never,' Rose said. Cradled on Dolly's vast bosom, wrapped in a scent of talcum and brandy, Rose thought of what her aunt had said. A nice life . . . Now that she was away from James and the spell of his touch and voice, she made herself examine her heart, dreading to find any trace of dishonesty, any faint suggestion that in saying yes to him she had grasped at an easy way out. There was no denying the material advantages: a father for Elizabeth, a secure home, 'respectability' and all the freedoms and comforts it brought with it . . . no more problems or worries about the future . . .

She was a stern judge. But she acquitted herself. She had said yes to James, gladly, unhesitatingly – and that was the point. Any clouding of her motives, any tickling of her conscience, and she would have said no straight out.

Half-tearful, half-wry, Dolly said, 'How pleased your poor mother would have been!'

'Yes . . .' Things did not always happen, after all, at the right moment.

'I'm so happy for you, dear,' Dolly said, relinquishing her with an awkward pat. 'Oh, and *how* wild all those old cats will be! Won't they just seethe when they find you've hooked him! Oh, I can't wait to tell Mrs Snell!' Dolly's eyes were alight; and Rose saw that she had handed her aunt a most gratifyingly powerful weapon. 'Of course you'll want to announce it properly . . . but could I just tell her, Rose? Could I?'

'Of course, Dolly,' Rose said; and being only human, could not help feeling her own share of vengeful exultation. 'Tell everybody you like.'

Could this really be happening? Should she pinch herself – was she dreaming? It was strange, she thought as she went up to bed, how you only posed those questions when nice things happened. When something terrible happened, you knew it was real all right. Perhaps that said something about life.

She felt a little light-headed, drunk not so much from Dolly's brandy as from fatigue and excitement.

Elizabeth, who Rose sometimes suspected had some psychic sympathy that adults lost, seemed to feel her excitement simply by Rose peeping into her bedroom to check on her. Her eyes opened, and her hand came out over the bedclothes, beckoning.

'Sorry, sweetheart,' Rose said, going forward to kiss her. 'Didn't mean to wake you.'

'Mummy,' Elizabeth said, 'your eyes are all shiny,' then dozed again.

Young, Rose thought, stroking her hair; adaptable. Who knew, perhaps she would call James Daddy in time: she was of an age for new beginnings. It might even be just as if she were really his, and he had happened by some mischance to miss her first four years; and Alec Taverner, in effect, would never have happened at all.

She felt optimistic, and when something so marvellous had happened, even this impossibility seemed likely.

# NINETEEN

Angelica Harwood walked into the music room and, as fiercely accusing as her look of a vague angel would allow, cried, 'Miss Jordan, it can't be true.'

Ah. Madame Carette must have told her, when she entered the shop, that the lessons would be coming to an end. Rose could imagine the way she had done it. Since learning that Rose would be leaving her, Madame Carette had been a trial – alternately sulking and wheedling.

'Madame says you're leaving. And you won't be able to give me piano lessons any more.'

'Yes. Not yet, but soon. I'm going to get married, you see.'

Angelica burst out, 'How perfectly awful!'

'Well,' Rose laughed, 'I'm afraid I don't see it that way.'

'Oh, I'm sorry – of course.' Angelica came glumly to the piano and sat down. 'Congratulations. I do mean that, you know, very much. Who are you marrying?'

'His name's James Blanchard. He's a doctor.'

Angelica shook her head. 'Don't know him, I'm afraid. Or anybody, come to that. Our doctor comes to us from Norwich. He's frightfully old and his hands shake, but he's connected to the Lewis-Dunns or something.'

'Well, James isn't frightfully old and his hands don't shake. So you see I just had to accept him.'

Angelica smiled sadly at her. 'You look happy . . . I am a selfish pig. No, I know I am – Clive's always told me so. When I heard the news, all I thought of was myself.'

209

'Madame Carette intends to find someone else to give piano lessons here.'

'That won't be the same,' Angelica said, beginning to pluck at her fingers.

'Well, no. Whoever it is might well insist on a little more attention to the piano . . . No – I shouldn't tease. I shall be sorry not to see you any more, Angelica. I wish—'

'When did he ask you?' Angelica said suddenly. 'Do tell me about it.'

Rose told, briefly.

'And did you know – at once?' Angelica said, studying her as if she held the answer to existence.

'Yes.' Rose thought again about the evening on the clifftop. Did it have that effect of a lightning-bolt from a cloud? It had seemed clearer, calmer, saner than that. She felt there was fairness to James, rather than disloyalty, in these thoughts. She loved him, and wanted to marry him: she only wanted to be clear in her mind what love meant, this time around.

'How awfully romantic,' Angelica breathed; then, lowering her eyes again, 'I hope you'll be very happy.'

'Thank you. I . . . hope you will come to the wedding.'

'That's kind of you. I don't suppose I shall,' Angelica said, with resignation. 'I'm not really able to receive invitations on my own account because I'm not properly out yet. There's talk of London next season . . . but I don't know. Clive says we should see how things go.'

'Meaning, with Freddy Collymore.'

'He hasn't given up,' Angelica sighed. 'Clive, I mean. Freddy hasn't been – well, since he tried to kiss me and I stopped him he hasn't been half so bad. But Clive keeps saying how he owes a lot to Freddy – as a friend – and how I'm putting him in a difficult position.'

'No, you're not.' Be damned to caution, Rose thought, and minding her own business and all the rest of it; Angelica was a friend and she would speak out for a friend. 'It's he who's putting you in a difficult position. Pushing you towards a man you don't care for, and using moral blackmail to do it.'

Angelica looked surprised. 'Is he?'

'Yes he is. He can't do it, Angelica. Nobody can make you do anything you don't want to do. Not if you hold out firmly for what you want and don't want in life.'

'No – that's true. Of course it is. But you see . . . I can think all this now, when I'm with you. Then when I'm at home, and no one's there I can talk to, I— How awful of me. I am a perfect beast. Here you are preparing for this wonderfully happy event and I'm spoiling it. Don't take any notice of me. I'm so stupid I ought to be – jolly well buried up to my neck in sand or something.'

'Good Lord, that's a bit strong. Is that one of Clive's?'

'One of mine.' Angelica gave the sad smile again. 'Well, I'd better get practising, if I'm going to learn to play a tune by the time you leave.'

Rose asked James about Angelica that evening, when they were walking on the beach.

They had already agreed that Rose would not work at Madame Carette's after their marriage: though it would be sad to say goodbye, Rose relished the chance of freedom at last, of not being forcibly separated from Elizabeth by the working week. But James hoped very much that that would not be the end of music for her.

'A piano,' he said. 'That must be our first piece of married furniture. If you can have such a thing as married furniture.'

'Yes – you can have a single bed.'

'Perhaps Madame Carette will give us a discount on a piano.'

'H'm – the way she's taking it, she's more likely to overcharge us. And attach a booby trap to the pedals.'

'Well, I can't blame her. She's losing you, after all. Who wouldn't be desolated?'

'Oh, you silver-tongued cavalier, you . . . If we did have a piano—'

'Which we will.'

'—then do you think I could still give lessons? To selected pupils, I mean. Well – Angelica Harwood in particular.'

'I don't see why not. Mind you, it sounds as if it's talking to you she likes, not learning the piano.'

'Well, I think she'd prefer to have the pretext. And by the sound of her family they wouldn't let her go anywhere without a reason.'

'All right then. Home tuition it is.'

Home . . . As so often now, her thoughts were filled with a bewildered, speculative excitement. She recalled first going to that house on Hill Rise, desperate with worry, to fetch the man she then knew only as the new doctor, and how remote and absurd the prospect would have seemed that she would actually live there. In fact, she did not tend to think of it as James's house: as he freely admitted, he was no nest-builder, and in the short time he had spent there had set very little impress on the building. 'It will start being a home,' he had said, 'when you and Elizabeth live in it.'

Elizabeth had taken the news of this dramatic change very well – indeed, apparently with an excitement of her own. Probably she didn't fully understand it all yet – only grasped that something new and interesting was about to happen. Rose was hopeful of the result. Elizabeth was not a shy child: she responded readily to people, and could even chatter them to exhaustion, as Rose and Dolly well knew; probably she relished the prospect of another listener.

Leaving Dolly, to whom Rose owed so much, was a sadness; and she had pretended not to notice Dolly having a sniffle over her sewing machine more than once. But there was no doubt that having a growing, lively, talkative child in the house had begun to put a strain on the old lady; and at least she would have privacy now, and would be able to tipple and concoct her cheese-feasts whenever she wanted.

'Doctor! Doctor, come and look!' Elizabeth called across the beach. She had found something – not, Rose hoped, either dead or obscene – that had been washed up by the retreating ide. While James went to look, Rose considered the question his raised – what was Elizabeth to call him, once they were married? It was too soon for 'Daddy'. And the thought of a little girl calling an adult 'James' brought images of aristocratic brats ordering their servants about. Perhaps 'Doctor', odd as it was, would do for now: they both seemed happy with it.

'It was a very tiny crab about the size of your thumbnail,' James said, coming back. 'I said it was a baby crab, though I don't know. Maybe it was a very small species of crab, grown-up. Had to pretend I knew, of course.'

'You'll get asked tougher questions than that.'

'I'll bet. I can remember as a boy innocently asking my father what an orgy was – God knows where I came across the word.'

'What did he say?'

'"A licentious Dionysian ritual of antiquity." That shut me up.'

Slipping her arm through his, Rose said, part playful but with a certain dogged purpose too, 'James, why me?'

'Why what you? Or why you what?' he said laughing.

'You know.'

'Well, why not you?'

'Plenty of reasons. For a start, it could have been someone else – like, I don't know, Clara Truelove—'

'Pah.'

'Also I have – well, what they call an encumbrance. Charming phrase.'

'*They* would.'

'Plus – your family can hardly have thought of you marrying like this—'

'Listen,' he said, squeezing her arm, 'I've told you. My family is my father, and he thinks for himself, always has. I know he'll love you. So no worries on that score. Anyway, I could just as well ask, why me?'

'Because,' she said distinctly and seriously, 'you are the first man I have loved.'

213

His eyes lingered on hers, searching, while his hand lifted hers and kissed it.

'Where do you suppose he is?' he said after a moment.

He spoke casually; but she had already noticed that he never used Alec Taverner's name – it was always 'he'.

'I know he came back to England and was demobbed: that was in the local paper,' she said. 'Beyond that, I don't know.'

It was her first lie to him: the knowledge of it brushed her like a bat's wing. But she felt it was more right than wrong. This was their beginning. Let that old ghost go away and haunt someone else.

# TWENTY

'"A son is a son until he takes a wife, but a daughter is a daughter for the rest of her life",' Mr Blanchard said. 'It was my grandmother who used to say that. You wouldn't remember her, James – lived at Slough. Quite a character. Had a gloomy saw for every occasion. Are these grandmothers born or made? Can she, I wonder, have dispensed these bromides as a pretty young girl? Did she respond to hopeful suitors pressing her lily-white hand in one of those overcrowded Victorian conservatories with a direful mutter of, "There's many a slip 'tween cup and lip"?'

Chuckling, Mr Blanchard took the cup of tea James handed him and sipped noisily.

'Still, I must be careful. After all, I'm a grandfather now, or shortly to become one. A very unexpected development.'

He did look like a grandfather, Rose thought – big-bodied, tweedy, with a ruddy face and thick white hair; but there was a youthful spring in his movements, and something very young, too, about his blue eyes, bright and guileless and almost boyish behind the tortoiseshell spectacles.

'Still, quite as unexpected for the little girl, I dare say. She has a very quick brain.' Elizabeth had monopolized Mr Blanchard for much of the day – he had arrived by train that morning – and had so tired herself out that she was now having a nap upstairs, in the room that would be hers after the marriage next month. 'Has she started schooling?'

'Not yet,' Rose said. 'Come September, I thought.'

'Don't let them teach her rubbish, will you?' Mr Blanchard

said. 'We are a strange civilization: we don't educate our young. We fob them off with a ration of scholastic nonsense, vaguely hope for experience to fill in the gaps, and then get surprised when they turn out the way they do. Also we expect them to profit by our example yet not to make our mistakes.'

'I wouldn't have thought you'd made many mistakes, Father,' James said.

'Ah, you don't know, my boy. I have a great many regrets. For example, never learning German. Oh, yes, our destinies are linked with theirs whether we like it or not, yet no one makes an effort to understand . . . I think, too – and this is with the greatest respect to your mother's memory, James – that I should have married again.'

James was surprised. 'Really? I didn't know you felt that.'

'Your upbringing was too male. Men shouldn't be together too much, it makes them hidebound. Yes, I should have married again, but there we are. I never found anyone who suited.'

'Well,' James said, 'I think you did a pretty good job all in all.'

Mr Blanchard said nothing to that, but gulped his tea down and then gave Rose a long, close, interested look, as if she were a striking picture. Rose felt the best thing was to look right back.

'I suppose,' Mr Blanchard said with a slight smile, 'that you two have set tongues a-wagging, eh? Charming as this little town looks, I don't imagine it as a place where you can sink into comfortable anonymity. Does that bother you?'

'No,' Rose said.

'James?'

'Not at all.'

'Good. Now, I'll have some more of that Dundee cake, if I may. A good big slice, James, that's it. I am rather greedy when it comes to food, my dear,' he added to Rose. 'But I refuse to feel guilty about this. Eating a lot used to be praiseworthy. The pre-modern period had the admiring phrase "a good trencherman". Even in Johnson's day a hearty appetite was approved. Then along came the Victorians and the Evangelical movement and it was deny the flesh, feed the spirit and all that nonsense. Well, I'm not fooled.' Mr Blanchard chomped cake vigorously. He had the immodesty of the auto-didact, but it was not dislikeable. Rose, who had been more nervous of this meeting than she had admitted, had warmed to James's father at once; though she could never tell what he was going to say next, and that in itself kept her on her toes.

'I dare say you were nervous of having to meet me, my dear,' he said, as if reading her thoughts.

'I was rather.'

'Understandable. You thought I was going to come up here and inspect you. Well, I suppose I have in a way. But only in a spirit of friendly scientific enquiry. Anyhow, fathers usually like their sons' choices. It's the mothers who don't approve, traditionally. There must be some anthropological basis for this: possibly the cave-mother looked askance at the bride which her son proudly brought home by the hair, wondering what sort of blood she was going to bring into the stock. Is that the telephone I hear?'

It was, and Mrs Penn came in a moment later.

'Lady at Saxburgh, Dr Blanchard. Husband collapsed after sawing wood. He's sitting up and talking but she's worried.'

'Tell her I'll be there in a few minutes, Mrs Penn,' James said jumping up. 'Sorry about this. I shouldn't be long.'

'Not at all, my boy,' Mr Blanchard said. He winked at Rose. 'It will give us a chance to talk all about you.'

Rose felt a renewal of shyness when James had gone, but Mr Blanchard, utterly without uneasiness, said, 'Let's walk in the garden, my dear. I must get away from this cake, otherwise I shall eat it all and be sick.'

In the garden, where dry weather, added to the trampling of the garden party a few weeks ago, had all but annihilated the lawns, Mr Blanchard gave her his arm and smoked a cigarette in an amber holder.

217

'Next month isn't long, my dear,' he said. 'Have you done all those things a bride is supposed to do? Preparations? Trousseau, and so on? That word, very unfortunately, is derived from the word "truss". Not a happy conjunction of ideas.'

'I think everything's in train. My Aunt Dolly's helping with the dress.' White, they had decided: why not? 'It might seem a bit soon – but we didn't see any point in waiting.'

'Absolutely. I like decisiveness. Besides, you're both responsible adults. You're what, twenty-five? That's good. It's my firm belief that adolescence continues until about the age of twenty-three: our species simply doesn't mature until then, a fact that we've tried to ignore in our social arrangements, and which accounts for a lot.'

'That sounds reasonable . . . Mr Blanchard, when you asked us whether it bothered us – about the talk. You must know that I've been thinking the same thing about you – I mean, whether it bothers you.'

'What bothers me, my dear? Your situation? The fact that you have a "child of sin"?'

'If you like. Yes.'

'And what would you do if I did disapprove?'

'I would marry James anyway.'

'Jolly good. I thought so.'

'But obviously – I would prefer things to be all right with his family.'

'Naturally. Well, my dear, as far as I'm concerned the concept of "sin" in that sense was invented by a gang of itinerant Hebrews three thousand years ago to reinforce tribal cohesion and exclusiveness. Basing our morality on the superstitious beliefs of a primitive people so distant and alien to us seems to me the height of folly. We don't live in deserts, and we know that thunder is produced by atmospheric conditions and not by Jehovah getting cross. As for marriage, if you leave aside all that holy business it's simply a legal convenience, mainly to do with property.'

218

'But you got married,' she said smiling.

'Oh, surely. I don't think James's mother would have had me any other way, and besides, I don't claim to be free of the infection of conventionality. No one escapes. For instance, it's a warm day, and you and I would probably be more comfortable walking round the garden in just our drawers – but we wouldn't dream of it. It's simply too much effort to try to overcome received ideas like that. So you see, my judgement of you isn't completely free of prejudice. I think you probably have an irresponsible streak, for example.'

'Doesn't everyone?'

'No. A lot of people would be improved by it, though. You see what I'm saying, my dear: even my ideas have got mixed up with society's. No doubt I would have chosen for James some young girl, pure, spotless, conventional. And very probably I would have chosen wrongly. Thank heaven parents *don't* choose any more.'

'It's funny . . . James is *exactly* what my mother would have chosen for me. And exactly what she thought I would never get, after what happened.'

'Life is stranger than we can imagine, isn't it? My dear . . . promise me something. Promise me you'll never let yourself feel that James has *rescued* you in any way.'

'I don't think I would,' she said honestly. 'I am marrying James for love – not respectability.'

'I can see that, and it's marvellous. And bless you both. But please, don't ever let that idea in. James, you know, is rather a knight of old. He idealizes.'

'Perhaps. But I like that. I'm not keen on second-best myself.'

Mr Blanchard beamed at her. 'I like you, my dear.'

'Thank you.' She found herself blushing, and they laughed.

'I think,' she said presently, 'that I will have a good life with James.'

'You might. In spite of what I've said, I can't pretend I really know him. There's another myth – that parents know their children. They do not. Probably they know them less than anyone. After a certain age the most important lesson a child learns is to hide itself from its parents. Because if they don't have that privacy, what privacy do they have? Which reminds me. I know your father's deceased, but do you have any uncles or male relations?'

'None at all.'

'In that case,' Mr Blanchard said, making a courtly little bow, 'would you allow me to give you away?'

Love was making him, James thought, a better doctor. The man at Saxburgh had, pretty plainly, fainted from heat and exertion, having been sawing up timber under the full sun for several hours. His pulse made healthful music and he was generally in good fettle. Previously James might have felt a twinge of impatience – at the man's foolishness, at the woman's panicky concern. But he viewed with new eyes. His patient had been sawing timber because he wanted to please his wife with a little summerhouse; and who would not panic on seeing their loved one collapse in a faint?

It certainly shouldn't be that way, he knew, but many doctors had very little patience with human frailty. He had perhaps begun to fall into that trap himself. Not now, though.

As he drove back to Shipden he wondered how Rose and his father were getting along. Introducing them had been stranger than he thought. His father, for all his unconventional thinking, came from a world where a woman like Rose was beyond the pale. James himself, for all his proud determination to form his own judgements, came from that world. Love had come upon him like a revolution inside, and seeing Rose and his father together had demonstrated to him just how complete had been the overthrow.

Rose in a way disturbed, almost frightened him in the effect she had on his previously cool nature. He supposed that this was indeed how love should be. Still, it was alarming when he had schooled himself so carefully in caution and self-knowledge.

He was deeply excited, though, at the prospect of his new life, including its challenges. Foremost among these was Elizabeth, and he did not underestimate it; but he was already fond of the child, and felt prepared, even if not adequately equipped, to try to be a father to her. It was not this, indeed, that troubled him so much as the fact that she was another man's child.

All the rationality of his nature told him that this was a mere biological detail, that to speak of fatherhood in relation to that man was nonsense by any standard. Unfortunately he wasn't all reason: there was a part of him that was intensely and even blindly emotional, and very absolute. It was the part that had made him love Rose and snap his fingers in the face of the society which, he knew, would be shocked at his choice – in that sense, perhaps, the best part of him; but it was also the part that made him unable to think dispassionately about Elizabeth's paternity.

And sometimes too it gave him a perplexed, frustrated feeling when he kissed Rose and looked into her eyes – a frustration at the mystery there, the thoughts and feelings that were inaccessible to him; the painful knowledge that some part of her was for ever beyond understanding, incomprehensible, other. And sometimes he would even catch himself thinking: what did she look like five years ago, when it all happened? Different, the same?

But then he would pull himself back, and simply marvel at his good fortune. James had a share of his father's immodesty: he did not think of himself as ordinary, and had never really expected to find someone both extraordinary and compatible as Rose was.

For they were good together. Whether dancing, talking, falling companionably quiet; whether in their cordial, tolerant, and firm dislike of the world of Mrs Snell and all its works, or their mutual agreement that it was better to laugh at it than cry over it; it all fitted. He simply could not live without her: to have her in his life was everything.

Even if it was not all of her.

# TWENTY-ONE

In August, the height of Shipden's season, the town was really two towns. One consisted of the visitors, the other of the residents – many of whom, at this time, were discussing with various emotions a wedding invitation that had dropped through their doors.

Oblivious of this, the visitors came and enjoyed and, in the way of seaside visitors, idly looked at property prices and wondered about coming here to live – thinking that the residents had their holiday feeling all the year round, and that life here was play and not earnest.

Branch-line trains brought them through a surprising Norfolk landscape – wooded, mellow, secretive, with glimpses into lush meadows ablaze with poppies – past the parks of country estates and golf links and into a sudden broad-skied, northern-bright bay. Taxis took them down from the station into a world of balconied villas and bougainvillaea, of loggias and fuchsias in terracotta tubs, clock golf and bowling greens; or to the seafront with its zigzagging ramps down to the beach, the elegantly outflung arm of the pier, the grand hotels exuding a stately leisureliness. They came to a world that was small but opulently laid out, quiet but not fossilized, secluded yet embraced by that powerful sea from which the crab-boats came bucketing right on to the beach. Here, surely, was life with the unpleasant parts taken out. At night, the view from the esplanade back to the row of grand hotels, lit in each window, was such as to suggest some Continental watering place – except for the noble church, quintessentially English, raising its vast flint tower beside them. A wonderful church! If only they had a church like that at home, the visitors thought, they would attend more regularly. As for a wedding in that church, it would be heavenly.

They did not know that the very next wedding to take place in that church was prompting some very earth-bound discussion all over the town.

The vicar's wife, Mrs Shillingford, had something of an altercation with her husband over this subject. She was sure there was something against a woman like Rose Jordan having a church wedding – or if there wasn't, there ought to be. Matthew Shillingford stuck to his guns, or at least hid behind them. The couple had been to see him, and had been charming. Also he was something of a hypochondriac, and did not want to get on the wrong side of the doctor. So he said he was going to marry them, and that was that.

'No one will go,' Mrs Shillingford said, resolving to go so as to see she was right.

'We shall not go,' Mrs Snell said to Mrs Truelove, gobbling *petit beurre* biscuits – their daintiness giving an effect of disproportion, as when an elephant eats a bun. 'If Dr Blanchard wants to go ahead with this folly, then we can at least spare him the indignity of having it witnessed.' In fact, being old, fat and resentful, and in some corner of her unpleasant mind seeing herself still as a young girl yet to make the mistake of marrying a nondescript like Mr Snell, she had already resolved to hate whomever Dr Blanchard married.

'Well, you know, it was wartime,' Mrs Truelove said temperately. 'When Rose made her . . . mistake. It would be a shame if she had to pay for it for ever.' She knew Mr Truelove was disappointed: possibly Clara too, though the girl was so self-controlled it was hard to tell. 'I think we shall go. Millie, of course, is Rose's great friend.'

Mrs Snell snorted crumbs. 'If you can bear it, my dear,

then good luck to you. One supposes the child will be at the church too – what a disgrace!'

'I suppose the little girl will be at the church,' said Mr Seymour Gaze to Madame Carette: he had been booked to take the wedding photographs, and was feeling pleasantly included in it all. 'Nice for her, that – they like to get dressed up at that age, don't they?'

'I don't know. I don't care. I shan't go. I shall be too upset,' said Madame Carette.

'Oh, but thass a happy event, surely, Madame C.?'

'Not for me,' Madame Carette sighed, asserting the true human principle. 'I am to be alone – deserted. Everyone leaves me. Everyone . . . drops off. I tell you, I am a withered tree, parching.'

'A lovely pink cherry blossom – thass what you are.'

'Tut-tut, nonsense,' Madame Carette said, with genuine impatience. She did not want to be cheered up; she wanted someone to be miserable with her.

'Buck up, Madame C.,' Mr Gaze said; and with a wink at Albert, who was sweeping out the shop, 'You've still got old Albert here. He ain't gooing anywhere.'

'Al-bare will leave me too,' Madame Carette sniffed. 'A girl will catch his eye, and take him away.'

'Oh no she will not,' said Albert very distinctly.

Mr Gaze suffered a wild impulse to ask Madame Carette, then and there, to walk down the aisle with him: it made him tremble for several seconds. Then the head fell off Albert's broom with a clatter, Mr Gaze came to himself, and he lost the courage.

'Anyhow,' he said weakly, 'you'll still see Rose, you know. She ain't gooing nowhere.'

'It won't be the same,' Madame Carette said, and disconsolately nibbled at Turkish delight.

'It won't be the same without James,' Mrs Vickery said.

'He's marrying, my dear,' said Dr Vickery. 'Not sailing for Patagonia.'

'I don't call it marrying,' Mrs Vickery said. 'Throwing himself away, I call it. Anyhow, I can't be expected to meet the woman socially.'

'Why not?' Sylvia said.

'Because she has an illegitimate child!'

'But it'll be different, Mother. She'll be a married woman. That's respectable, isn't it? That changes everything, you know.'

'I must say you're taking all this very calmly, Sylvia,' Mrs Vickery said, pouting.

'Well, certainly. Because it's no surprise to me. I knew. The only thing that amazes me is how surprised everyone is. I saw it from the start, the very first time James mentioned her, in fact. Really, I think it's quite funny.'

'I wish I could see it so,' Mrs Vickery said, huffily.

'My dear,' Dr Vickery said with a thin smile, 'anyone would think you meant to bump me off and marry James yourself.' Dr Vickery had no thoughts on the morality of it all. It was James's choice, and that was that. But he found all this upheaval distasteful, not to mention the thought that James had been motivated by passionate feeling. Dr Vickery had chosen his own wife because she was pretty and had a little money and it was the done thing to get married. This attachment of James's smacked of flamboyance, which Dr Vickery disliked above everything.

'Of course we shall have to go,' Sylvia said. 'To support poor James. I'm afraid he'll be snubbed a bit. We shall simply have to rally round him and, well, just behave normally. Put on a front. I can do that, always have, but some people don't seem to be able to – which is odd. I can't understand it.'

'Do you suppose she's done again what she did last time?' Mrs Vickery said. 'To trap him? And this time it's worked?'

'Good heavens, Mother, what a thought,' Sylvia said. 'Rose waddling up the aisle, you mean? Really, that's priceless.' She began laughing; and continued to laugh for a long time, loudly and gaily. Her father studied her. He was not insensitive and saw plenty, but people's lives, he considered, were their own.

'Well, there must be some explanation,' Mrs Vickery said. 'Things like this don't just happen.'

Things like this just happen, old fellow,' said Leo Liddell to Ernie Crimmins, in the bar of the Victoria Hotel. Ernie was complaining again about the loss of the Kinema, and Leo Liddell, short on sympathy at the best of times, was tired of it. 'No sense in getting worked up.'

'Easy for you to say,' Ernie Crimmins said, lighting a fresh cigarette from the butt of the old one. 'You ain't got my responsibilities. Wife, kiddies.'

'I have responsibilities,' Leo said coldly. 'I have a wife.'

'No kiddies though.'

'No.' Leo set down his gin glass with a bang. 'Well, nobody made you have them, old boy.'

Ernie looked at him in foggy surprise. 'What's up with you?'

'Nothing,' Leo said, massaging his temples. 'Bad head. Working too hard.'

'You want to see the doc about that.'

'Him? I wouldn't trust him.' Leo made a face as if he were sucking something nasty. 'Hitching himself up with Rose Jordan – shows you what his judgement's like. What a laugh. Poor sap. She'll be rogering somebody else in six months' time.'

You wish, Ernie thought but did not say.

'You mark my words. You watch.' Leo called for another gin. 'Six months' time.'

'In six months' time,' Millie Watlyn said to her father, who was visiting her at the Arcadia, 'it will all have been forgotten about. People's memories are very short.'

Mr Truelove, whose memory was not short, grunted and looked over at Frank Watlyn, who was playing lotto with little Carrie at the dinner table. Millie was darning a tablecloth –

their own, Mr Truelove guessed: the guest stuff was always immaculate.

'I'm happy for them both,' Millie said. 'Rose deserves her chance and they make a lovely couple.'

'Or threesome,' Mr Truelove said. 'No, I've no quarrel with it. They're grown-up people. Dr Blanchard has a good profession and can support her and the child well. It's not as if he's going to lose patients either, when he's the only doctor in town – which has probably occurred to him.'

'Oh, Pops, I'm sure they wouldn't be that calculating,' Millie said.

'No, no, dear, after all, one has to think of these things,' Frank said. Like many dreamers, he prided himself on his hard-headedness.

Mr Truelove grunted again. He didn't like it when his son-in-law agreed with him: he preferred a settled antipathy.

'No harm in a bit of forethought for the future,' Frank said cheerfully. 'Look at poor Ernie Crimmins – lost the Kinema and no insurance.'

'Poor Ernie,' Millie said.

'Well, I've given him a quote for the cost of rebuilding,' Frank said. 'Came straight to me.'

'I thought you said there was no insurance?' Mr Truelove said.

'Oh, he's going to raise the money somehow,' Frank said vaguely, 'and we can come to some sort of arrangement.'

Mr Truelove felt his ulcer gnaw at him.

'Six months' work there at least,' Frank said, looking pleased.

'Six months,' Mrs Betts said to her whist party. 'I give that marriage six months.'

228

# TWENTY-TWO

James insisted on carriages for their wedding.

The Hotel Metropolitan still supplied the traditional turnout as in its Edwardian heyday, with a team of greys with plaited manes and white ribbons; and in James's determination to have these he and Rose, oddly enough, almost came to their first disagreement. For Rose, though so proud and indeed defiant about her marriage, felt curiously shy at the thought of going through the streets to her wedding so very publicly.

*Oh, my dear, if he was absolutely determined to take her on, at least he could have done it in decent secrecy.* Yes, she could hear the voices: and yes, she wanted to dismiss them as she had always done. And yet she felt reluctant about the carriages.

'It might be the last chance,' James said. 'Tom Cherry was telling me they might do away with carriage hire altogether next season.'

It would undoubtedly please James: and it was undeniably romantic. A turnout from the Metropolitan was the dream of every Shipden girl. Rose wasn't a girl, of course; and probably could never feel as one of those girls – her own past self included – would have felt at the occasion, deeply as she loved James. But out of that love, she agreed to the carriages; and so there was a carriage outside Dolly's house in Princess Street on the wedding morning.

It had already picked up Mr Blanchard, who had come up by train last night along with James's best man – his old student friend, a fresh-faced Scot named Mackay – and it was Mr

Blanchard who with old-fashioned courtliness handed Rose in.

'James and his friend kept exchanging doctors' talk over dinner last night,' he said. 'Hope you know what you're letting yourself in for, my dear. Colostomies and prolapses over the lamb cutlets. Did you know, by the way, that you look absolutely wonderful?'

'Thank you.' Her dress, though white, was of a simple modern style rather than a full gown with train: still she felt glowingly self-conscious.

'All aboard the jolly old *Skylark*,' puffed Dolly, who was wearing a huge straw hat and a brightly coloured costume, and who made a complicated business of climbing up into the carriage. 'Come along, Elizabeth. The horses won't bite you.'

Elizabeth, after being half-sick with excitement, now looked solemn and even a little tearful.

Rose had had a long talk with her last night, making sure she knew where she stood. They had been many times to their new home. Elizabeth had inspected and approved the room that would be hers, and she had been reassured that they would still see lots of Aunt Dolly. And she seemed to be taking it all in her stride.

Yet it was a good deal to take in. It was scary. It was scary for Rose, let alone a little child. Rose had to be certain Elizabeth was all right: she couldn't begin to be happy unless she was absolutely sure of that in her heart. Some people – even Dolly – thought no further than the simple proposition, 'It'll be nice for her to have a father.' But it had to be better than that for Rose: it had to be a father and a situation that Elizabeth was happy with.

And James too, of course. The presence of a child could certainly be a barrier to romance: she hoped he wouldn't see it that way. But he had been understanding when the question of a honeymoon had come up. Rose had never been away from Elizabeth, and she feared that it would be too much change for the little girl all at once – the marriage and the new home, plus a fortnight's absence from her mother. She had hardly begun to explain this when James anticipated her.

'She'd be quite justified in thinking me an ogre if I took you away from her straight after marrying you,' he said, and kissed her. 'We'll have lots of time. As you told me: there are two of you.'

Remembering this warmly as the carriage started off, Rose took Elizabeth's hand and squeezed it.

'Are you all right, sweetheart?'

'Bit scared.'

'So am I. We'll have to look after each other, won't we?'

The drive to the church was short. Holidaymakers waved their hats, pleased with everything. In the churchyard Mr Blanchard, with a nimbleness like his son's, jumped down and held out his hand to Rose.

'Come along, my dear. The bride's traditionally late, but not too late.'

'Oh, better late than never, that's what I always say, ha-ha,' said Dolly, in her nervousness making one of her jokes that weren't jokes. Then she realized the application of this remark, and turned brick red and hastily rearranged the flowers at her bosom until they were squashed flat.

Rose took Mr Blanchard's arm, and they began to walk up the crunching gravel path to the church door. Her wedding day: it was meant to be unforgettable, and everything did have a tremendous full-daylight intensity – all that had gone before it seemed misty and shadowy in comparison, with the spectral half-light of a dream. Looking back, she found it impossible to say how she had arrived here, at this point in her life: there was nothing relentless and consecutive, like the steps of a board game. It was all separate, surprising, new.

This, she thought, was a beginning. Even though much had gone before it, it was a beginning.

The churchyard grass had been cut that morning, and Dolly

began a spectacular sneezing-fit. Rose, to her relief, heard Elizabeth giggling.

The church was half-full, which was not a bad turnout for its vast size. Rose saw Millie turn and give her a smile. Elsewhere there were different looks. One or two appeared to be wishing she would fall flat on her face. But she had no intention of doing that.

And there was James.

He looked nervous. The effect of this on him was to make him pale rather than flushed. His Adam's apple bobbed beneath his stiff collar as he swallowed.

She stood beside him. After the first tender smile something – propriety, shyness, fear of bursting out laughing, perhaps a combination of these – made them avert their eyes. Rose looked down at his shoes, and remembered those dapper shoes in the High Street just five months ago, and again she was struck by the sheer mystery of how things happened.

All around the altar were flowers. Their colours looked incandescent, like burning candles, against the venerable greyness of the ancient church.

As the organ introduction ended Rose became aware that someone was crying. Not Elizabeth, thankfully; it was poor Dolly. 'I shan't blub,' she had kept saying this morning. 'I don't blub as a rule.'

The Revd Mr Shillingford took the service in his watery Sunday-school voice. It made what they were doing seem mild and unspectacular, rather than the stuff of wide-eyed gossip as it undoubtedly was. When it came to his asking whether anyone knew of any just impediment why they should not be married, Rose had a fleeting half-delirious image of someone shouting: 'Yes! Black sheep should not marry golden boys!'

Well, he was golden to her. She only hoped she could convey this love and admiration to him. She knew that, after these past five years, open tenderness and warmth came a little haltingly to her, simply because they were associated with betrayal. His name was easy on her lips, but she did not as yet use 'darling' or any other endearment – that was part of it too. And while she was physically drawn to him, found him beautiful, and loved his touch and kiss, she was nervous of the consummation, not knowing how she would feel about it after all this time. That too was a subject burdened with association. She had been a passionate woman five years ago; and the Rose of five years ago was not a person she could ever trust to be in the same body as herself.

She noticed that her responses were getting fainter as they went on. It was intimidating, speaking out in that great church, and felt somehow wrong, as if only clergymen should do it.

But the words began to get to her. Her own faith was equivocal and James's, she suspected, non-existent; yet the solemnity of the occasion lit her from within. James gave his responses with that slightly proud, conscious way of his. He never gave the impression that anything he did was unimportant: it was one of the things she loved about him.

'. . . I pronounce that they be Man and Wife together.'

In the intensity of her emotion, which came to a point in the kiss that found them both trembling and without breath, she had forgotten that anyone was there; and when they turned, to see that large and attentive body of watchers, she was as startled as if they had just that moment stolen in.

'We did it,' she whispered to James, holding him; and they laughed softly together, the vibrations of their laughter passing between their bodies.

Outside, Mr Seymour Gaze took photographs, his brilliantined head looking more badger-like than ever as it bobbed beneath the camera hood. Aunt Dolly became suddenly camera-shy, and had to be cajoled into the shots.

'It shouldn't be me,' she clucked, laughing painfully at herself. 'It should be your mother – it should have been your mother in the photographs, dear.'

'That's why I want you in them,' Rose said, pressing her rough damp hand.

Elizabeth had cheered up a lot, and smiled into the camera

without shyness and even with relief. Perhaps she had thought something dreadful was going to happen in the church – Rose remembered her own childhood dislike of the deathly places – and was pleasantly surprised: her mother had come out in one piece and nothing seemed to have changed.

The carriages took them back to James's house – their house – for the reception. There were flowers everywhere and amongst them Mrs Penn moved grand and solemn, like the housekeeper of a stately home conducting a guided tour.

Here, though the formality of the service was lifted, Rose and James could not be so much together. Passing amongst the guests, receiving congratulations, exchanging chit-chat, the intensity of those moments in the church became diluted, especially among so many guests. The congregation of half a church made a houseful, and everyone invited had accepted. But Rose and James already had the silent semaphore of couples, and signalled to each other, 'This is nice, but it isn't the main thing: soon we'll be alone.'

Millie Watlyn, bright-eyed and sentimental and slightly tipsy, said, 'Be happy, you two. It's actually quite easy. As long as you remember the important things and don't get bogged down with the unimportant ones.'

'James,' Sylvia said, 'we're going to have to think about this question of Nell Henning. I went the other day and she was drinking again. This can't be good when she's nursing' – just as if there were no wedding at all. It was James's best man, Mackay, who prised her away and bore the brunt of her talk – which, on her discovering his nationality, took the form of a lecture on Scottish customs, Sylvia strangely turning out to know more about them than he did.

Quite soon it was time for their honeymoon train. Mr Gaze took a last brace of photographs in the garden, with Rose in her going-away clothes and James sharing her smile of relief that they would not be on show for much longer. It was nice to be surrounded by warm wishes, and even piquant to be surrounded by wishes that were far from warm; but she could

234

not wait for their lives to be their own.

On the train Elizabeth fell asleep, and Rose and James talked over her in soft voices, their hands gently clasping. James reached up and picked a piece of confetti from her hair.

'Do you feel different?' he said.

'I feel very different.'

'Good.' He smiled. 'That's what I want. To make a difference.'

A honeymoon at the seaside would have had something of coals to Newcastle about it, and instead James had booked a suite at a London hotel, the Tavistock. They would have a week of outings, trips to the zoo and the sights, matinées, everything the capital had to offer. Today, however, had been too tiring for much more than a walk up to Covent Garden after dinner. This also had the effect of making Elizabeth so drowsy that she had to be carried back into the hotel, half-asleep on James's shoulder: fortunate, for it meant that there would be no problems about sleeping in a strange bed. She was deep asleep before Rose had pulled the coverlet over her.

In the next room she and James sat softly talking over a nightcap. Rose kept fighting an impulse to go and check on Elizabeth, which James did not miss.

'Sorry,' she said. 'I shall get out of this habit, I'm sure.'

'She's taking it all in her stride,' he said, sitting back, neglecting his drink and simply drinking her in.

'She's never had a holiday before.' Rose fiddled with her glass, then deliberately set it down and met his eyes.

Unlimited privacy is not necessarily conducive to passion. Being slightly alert and on the qui vive to the next room gave, as it turned out, an edge both to appetite and satisfaction.

Rose had forgotten how physically draining lovemaking was. She lay afterwards with thundering heart, his tousled head on her panting chest, feeling as if she had been hurled around by a tornado.

Well, that was all right too. Nothing, in fact, was going wrong: there seemed no shadows across her path. They had overcome their obstacles simply and plainly through love, and she could not imagine that power proving inadequate to any challenge.

# TWENTY-THREE

The season was, as Ernie Crimmins had hoped, a scorcher, and when Rose and James returned with Elizabeth to Shipden late in August, the golf links around the town were as brown as tobacco and the veterans who spent the whole summer there looked, as they sat imperturbably outside their beach huts, like some dried, smoked, cured, thoroughly kippered Norfolk delicacy.

The house on Hill Rise seemed to respond to people in it. Now it began to be truly inhabited, and to be a home.

Rose, accustomed to cramped quarters, greatly appreciated the roominess of the house, and Elizabeth even more: she was forever roaming and exploring, and especially loved the garden which, because of the way the house stood on a corner plot, extended in a horseshoe around it and was full of child-attracting nooks and angles. Inside the house there was always a pleasant smell of waxed wood, not only from the floors of the hall and landings and the heavy chocolate-brown staircase but from the deep skirting boards and the many wood-framed closets and tallboys. Downstairs there was a long sitting room which faced the garden and which always seemed to be filled with sunlight, a dining room half-filled by a large mahogany dining-table with piecrust edges which James called a monstrosity and planned to replace, the kitchen and pantry and laundry room, and James's study and consulting room. This had its own door opening through a little lobby to the gravel drive at the darker side of the house, where James kept the car, and was the only place out of bounds to Elizabeth.

He did not dispense much but still there were medicaments and instruments in there that a child should not meddle with and there was, besides, the risk of infection from patients who came to call.

Upstairs Rose and James's bedroom was above the living room and was, in the same way, full of sun. There was a small dressing room attached and across the passage was a bathroom – James's first, immediate and urgent installation when taking the house, for he was particular about cleanliness. On the other side of the dressing room was Elizabeth's room, decorated in fresh white and apple-green and with, her particular delight, a window seat: down the passage were Mrs Penn's room and two small guest rooms at the rear.

It was James's habit to keep his work separate from his domestic life – despite Mr Blanchard's warning, there was no talk of pathology over breakfast – though Rose found it interesting and began to help with the keeping of his patient records. She was biased, of course, but she thought him a good doctor. In addition to this, she continued to take a few pupils for lessons at the new piano in the living room, including Angelica Harwood. The chauffeur now parked the gleaming Bentley in the drive, where it dwarfed James's Talbot, and drank tea in the kitchen whilst Angelica, almost shrivelling with delighted shyness, continued her dogged struggle with an art she found as incomprehensible as unattractive.

The town, very slowly, began to get used to the idea of Rose as Mrs Blanchard. It was an adjustment of identity that Rose found surprisingly easy to make: the words 'my husband' came easily to her lips and when she drove into the town with James it almost felt as if they had always been doing this, so natural did it seem.

For James and Elizabeth there was perhaps a more profound adjustment to be made, and not one that would progress without a hitch. James was not cut out to be a heavy father, or stepfather. He tended to treat Elizabeth pretty much as if she were an adult, or at least possessed of an adult rationality and proportion. So Elizabeth, who was not short of spirit, began after a little while to push her luck, even to boss him. Rose was troubled by this, James amused; but there was no showdown, yet.

And there was much for them to enjoy as a newly made family. They reaped the benefits of a seaside summer: they took frequent picnics to the cliffs or down to the shingle at Saxburgh and were often on the beach, Elizabeth swiftly turning as brown as an egg. On Sundays Aunt Dolly came to lunch, and would be heartily nervous and clumsy until James had poured her a generous sherry and then absently left the decanter within her reach.

Rose was happy. And she believed James was happy too, though sometimes finding him a little difficult to read. He had, as it were, more surface than her, a result perhaps of living alone. She was quick to spot it when there was something amiss with him, but he preferred not to admit it and to cover it with his light easiness of manner. While she recognized that this was probably meant as a courteous consideration for her, it could also be seen as a cutting of himself off. One evening, when his last patient had been Tom Cherry, she detected this mood in him, and it was almost bedtime before she pushed down his casual screen and found out what was troubling him.

It was to do with Tom Cherry – who came to see him practically every week, continually ground down as he was by ill-health brought about by the war.

'He was discharged fit,' James said, 'yet in essence, he's still walking wounded. Might as well still be on the battlefield. Better if he was, in a way, because he would have the entitlements of a soldier. As it is he's neither fish nor fowl – just always in pain, always in a semi-nervous condition, and wondering why the hell he can't feel normal like anyone else.'

'It's terrible,' she said. 'But you do your best to help him.'

'Yes, I try. There's the awful thing. He looks to me for help.'

'Why awful? You're a doctor.'

'Oh, well,' James said, taut and tense and smiling in a bare thin way, 'he fought, and I didn't. One can't help feeling bad . . . He was in it – I was at home.' He made a gesture as if he would snap his fingers, but put his hand to his lips instead.

'Thank God you were,' she said. 'I might not have met you otherwise.'

He smiled more gently and stroked her hand, as if she had simply said something conventionally loving. But it seemed to her that it was an extremely important thing for her to say, and she hoped he had taken it in.


In September it was time at last for Elizabeth to begin going to school. There was a decent day-school for younger children behind Shipden church, and Elizabeth had long looked forward to going there. But now there was a change. The novelty of her new home had not yet worn off, and she wanted to stay in it. James, with his slightly naïve faith in logical reasoning, took it on himself to explain why she had to go, and there was a sharp scene which ended with Elizabeth stomping upstairs with a loud retort of, 'Shan't! You can't make me – you're not my daddy!'

So it had come at last, Rose thought. Ruefully she noticed James's hurt, stung look. Having approached Elizabeth as an adult, the remark had hit home just as if an adult had flung it at him.

'I'll speak to her,' said Rose. 'She's getting cheeky. But she would not have said that if she'd thought just how horrible she was being.'

'My fault,' said James, trying to hide his upset. 'She simply isn't ready to see me as her father. I shouldn't have assumed . . .'

Rose went upstairs and found Elizabeth lying pink-cheeked and expressionless face down on the bed rather like one of her own dolls.

'That was nasty, you know. Saying James isn't your daddy.'

'He's not,' Elizabeth said smartly. 'He's new and you have a daddy from the start. When you're a baby.'

Rose sat down. 'Well, that's true.'

'Where's my daddy then?'

'I've told you. He went away. Sometimes that happens.'

'Why did he go away?'

Not for the first time Rose was confronted with the impossibility of explaining.

'It was the war. He went to the war.'

'Did he die?'

'No. He didn't die. As I said, sometimes it happens. But a daddy, a real daddy, is someone who lives with you and Mummy and looks after you. That's what James is – that's what he wants to be. He wants to try and be your daddy, because he likes you very much and me too. That's the way it should be.'

Elizabeth was silent. It was difficult to tell whether she was thinking this over or sulking. She was a normal little girl, and had learnt the art of long sulks before walking.

Well, Rose thought, the prospect of Elizabeth going to school as an illegitimate, fatherless child had caused her worry enough – but here were difficulties she had not anticipated. It was an ironic riposte, at any rate, to those who said – she knew it – that she had married James just for the convenience of giving her child a respectable home.

On the great day Elizabeth presented herself, brushed and combed and mutinously acquiescent, to be taken to school. Much to her surprise she found an inducement or bribe, in the shape of a new doll, bought by James.

'I admit it,' he said wryly to Rose afterwards. 'Trying to buy her over.'

'I don't think you'll need to, you know. Not in the long run.'

'A wrench for you too, I should think,' he said, lightly but feelingly, 'her first day at school.'

'She's never gone anywhere alone before,' Rose shrugged,

hearing and disliking the plaintive quaver in her voice. 'I'm possessive, I know.'

'That's natural. Just as it's natural that it takes time for her to get used to me. After all . . . I *wasn't* there from the beginning.'

Elizabeth came back from school full of excitement. School, it seemed, was a tremendous experience, and a whole evening was scarcely enough to tell what had gone on there. She clung constantly to the doll James had bought her; and before she went to bed she elected to give him a kiss.

Rose, when she came down from seeing Elizabeth to bed, gave him a kiss too.

'Thank you for being so patient.' She put her hand to his face. 'What you said . . . about not being there from the beginning. I do wish . . . But you know, that isn't a thing that can ever be.'

'I know. I – well, I love you so much that I want to have your past too.' He smiled, to take the glare off his statement. 'Can't, I know.'

'No. But you can be there from the beginning when you and I have a child.'

'I'd like that.'

'There are lots of new beginnings,' she said slipping under his arm. 'Before I met you I didn't think there could be.'

She was happy, and easy as she found it to fit into her new life, its wonderful strangeness would sometimes burst on her like a sudden light. Sometimes she would catch herself looking at James and thinking how handsome he was and then, with a start of surprise, thinking: it's real; we are together. And if she hesitated to say such things directly to him, it was because she still found it difficult to break down her own reserve, to venture just yet beyond the bounds that had been set by disappointment and betrayal. They made love with tenderness and sincerity, but did not speak much at these times: instead there was a quietly urgent drawing together in darkness.

Her newlywed life was self-contained and did not need much of the world. She hardly noticed the ending of the season, and it was with seeming suddenness that she found, on one of their beach walks, the blue bay replaced by a sea the colour of gunmetal and shadowed by a heavy swell, and knew that autumn was here.

One night soon after this they were woken by the deep *crump* of a maroon going up. A few moments later, standing at the open bedroom window, they heard the whoosh of the Shipden lifeboat setting out to sea.

James wondered if he ought to go down to the waterside in case he were needed when the boat came in, and Rose said she would go with him. They took a flask of brandy, and a blanket in case it should be chilly; but the night turned out to be quite mild, as if patches of summer remained. They walked up and down the esplanade for some time, looking out to sea, but there were no lights visible. The town behind them was silent, and the swell on the sea seemed to have beaten itself out, and it was difficult to imagine that anything direful was happening out there on the breast of that murmuring darkness.

Presently the lifeboat hove into view, heading back to Shipden. A shore crewman, waiting at the dock to the boat station, read the signalling light on deck and told them it was a false alarm. 'Somebody got in a tizzy, thass all, I reckon. You can goo back to bed, Doctor, there's noobody been broke.'

They did not go back to bed yet, however: they were not tired and it was pleasant to stroll down the beach under the stars, taking a nip from the flask, talking in the ease of pure companionship; and there was, besides, the memory of a night not unlike this one which was very sweet to her.

For a moment Rose imagined lying down here, in this dark seclusion, and making love: for a moment she was going to suggest it.

Then she thought that it was perhaps, after all, a little chilly – and after all, she was older now, and not like that.

* * *

She put this from her mind and only thought of it fleetingly when, later in the week, Millie Watlyn came to call and said in her likeably robust way once they were alone, 'Well? How is it? Love, married life, toothbrushes in the same glass, and all the rest of it? You *look* jolly well on it, but of course I want the whole story.'

'It's good. It's wonderful,' Rose said. 'Different, of course – it's not the same as when you're young.' It was Rose's habit, not always to her own comfort, to answer a question honestly and fully.

'Oh, but my dear, you are young. You're only twenty-five.'

'Yes . . . but you know what I mean. It isn't like when you're really young and new and beginning; but that's what's good. I don't want it to be like that.'

She had, of course, found herself drawing comparisons, not deliberately but idly and at random moments. There had been two love experiences in her life. Being married to James, loving James, did not erase the fact that she had loved before.

And it was different, yes. She saw nothing amiss with that. If she had felt precisely the same each time, then *that*, she felt, would say something rather alarming about her.

'Well . . .' Millie said, studying her with a slight smile, 'I *think* I know what you mean. But all I can say is you look jolly well on it. And James too. He looks like the cat that got the cream. Well, no – more like someone whose dreams actually came true.'

'I hope so,' Rose said.

For she wondered, just occasionally, whether James wanted of her something that she could not give. He had about him, as Millie said, the sort of glowing exultation of someone who has won their coveted prize. Only Rose seemed to glimpse, in the depths of it, a shadow of doubt that it was really, truly his.

# TWENTY-FOUR

Nell Henning did not ask much of life. All she wanted was to potter around in the friendly disorder of her cottage, brewing tea when there was no money for something stronger, giving a lusty shout at the kids when they got over-boisterous, gossiping with Mrs Scace next door, stewing up the remains of the catch that the local fishermen sold for pennies late in the day, and when necessary doing a bit of skivvying for the cheaper hotels and rest homes of the town. Beyond that there were men, now and then, for a laugh over a drink and if possible for money – though Henning, not a bad lot for all he had done a bunk, sent her an envelope containing a ten-bob note every now and then. FOR CHILDERN, he always wrote on the back. This latest wasn't his, but then the second wasn't either; and she wasn't entirely sure about the fourth.

This was all she wanted from life – this, and to be left alone. Nell did not feel very strongly about anything, but she did dislike being meddled with as Sylvia Vickery continued to do through the summer and into the autumn.

The woman brought gifts of food and clothes, which was all right. Nell took them but wouldn't have cared if they stopped. Being bossed about and told what to do was different – but then again, being so placid, Nell never got irritated enough to tell Sylvia to sling her hook. If she really wanted to keep hanging about The Rows, then so be it.

In a shrewd unmoved way, Nell could understand why the woman kept coming. It was all to do with that young doctor. When the baby was new, Sylvia was forever fetching the doctor to her, saying she had this or she looked that – none of it true – the new one was as healthy as all Nell's children.

The doctor was married now. And so Sylvia had no reason to continue to haunt Nell's place as an excuse to get near him. Yet she did, of course. It would look obvious, Nell thought, if she simply stopped.

This was true; but as for Sylvia, she had avoided self-knowledge so successfully it was doubtful if she saw it. She had taken up Nell Henning for reasons of her own, and all her reasons were of course good, and so she stuck to it with all the narrow tenacity of her nature. Also she convinced herself that Nell could not manage without her.

It meant, too, that she was still somehow near James, and her restless brain simply grasped at that. It was intolerable to think that she had had a yen for him and he had fallen in love with and married someone else. So she did not think it. Such a thought meant she was not the centre of the picture any more, and Sylvia could not envisage such a picture. The story was still her and James's story, which Rose Jordan had somehow entered from the side.

It was the same with the death of Sylvia's fiancé in the war. She could not see this as part of any larger tragedy. She entirely lacked fellow feeling, not through callousness to others but through self-concentration. She had met many people who had suffered a similar loss, but had never shared grief or shown sympathy. If there was talk of this kind, she would go silent and adopt a secret aloof look. Her emotions were fuller and finer than anyone else's, and she felt that they would be cheapened rather than ennobled by being universal.

As for the waste of her fiancé's young life, that all came back to her too. It was wasted in the sense that it was cut off before he could marry Sylvia Vickery: the tragedy of his death was that it prevented him spending his life with her.

This did not mean she did not feel the loss intensely: egotism is very emotional, more so than unselfishness, which is by nature tepid. And the loss gave an extra twist to her feelings towards Rose. The man who had given Rose her child had not come back either – but he had not been killed. Sylvia felt that rejection was preferable, because more dramatic, than loss, and this fuelled the envy she suffered when Rose married James Blanchard.

And yet Sylvia could not admit the envy to herself. A good, downright, envious hatred of Rose would have implied that Sylvia was vulnerable and fallible and not one step ahead of everyone else. So she invented the fiction of prior knowledge. She had always known it would happen, knew the course it would follow and how it would end. Knowing all was her prop.

'But of course they would do that, Mother,' she would say, when Mrs Vickery gossiped about the Blanchards' doings. 'That was inevitable. I could have told you they would. It was on the cards.'

Meanwhile she took charge of Nell Henning, striding about the cottage and making changes to its arrangements, which Nell would simply undo as soon as she was gone. 'Silly ole busybody,' Nell would say to Mrs Scace, without rancour, 'silly ole spinster.'

And in this way Sylvia clung to her link with James, for if, as was surely not unlikely, one of the Henning children fell ill, she would be there. She had no calculating end in view – Sylvia's mind did not work like that – she just ploughed on under the steam of her unhappy, selfish intensity, seeing what would happen. Strictly speaking she did not mean any harm even though she would, for example, have tempted James to infidelity without a second thought if it had proved possible. That would just have been one of those things: it would have been on the cards.

'You don't get 'em that way,' Nell Henning remarked phlegmatically to Mrs Scace, after Sylvia had left saying she was going to call in the doctor to one of the children for no reason at all. She grunted with unconcerned humour. 'Poor ole cow. You don't get 'em that way – I could tell her that. Even if you're desperate, the thing is not to look it.'

# TWENTY-FIVE

'I brought these for you,' Angelica said, placing a little basket of luscious Victoria plums on top of the piano.

'Oh, how lovely, thank you,' Rose said, surprised.

'They're from our kitchen garden. Clive saw me taking them out and wanted to know who they were for. Mrs Blanchard, my piano teacher, I said. Just like that.' Angelica gave a bashful smile. 'And do you know, he didn't know what to say.'

Rose saw that in this small piece of assertion an important victory had taken place.

'Well, that's a very kind thought.'

'I thought your little girl might like them too.'

'I'll bet she will.'

In coming to Rose's married home for her lessons, Angelica had undergone a revelation. Her first sight of James had thrown her into the worst of her old tongue-tied shyness, but she was easier with Elizabeth; and had said at last to Rose, 'What a sweet little girl. Did Dr Blanchard's first wife die?'

'James hasn't been married before. Well, if he has, he never told me,' Rose had said, laughing, and not understanding.

And then she understood.

'Oh, I see. No. Elizabeth's my daughter,' she had said simply.

That Angelica had never known about this was not, perhaps, so surprising. The Harwoods in their crested and acred hauteur were far beyond the tattle of Shipden. Perhaps in their aristocratic way they were not even troubled by such things: being born on the wrong side of the blanket seemed, as far as

Rose could tell, more acceptable in that sophisticated world than in the burgher solidity of a place like Shipden. Still she wondered what Angelica's reaction would be. The girl had formed with her a friendship that included on Angelica's own part a good deal of confessional. Perhaps she would feel her confidence misplaced.

If so, however, there was no sign of it. Angelica seemed, if anything, to look on Rose with renewed respect – which made her uncomfortable, as she had never felt the old respect was exactly deserved. But she did not learn that a new dimension had been added to Angelica's view of her until the day of the plums: the day when Angelica, after some more than usually halting attempts at piano practice, gave it up and turning round to Rose said directly, 'Mrs Blanchard, I couldn't say this to anyone in the world but you and please don't be cross that I'm – burdening you with these things again but you see you're the only one who would understand.'

'Is it – is it Freddy Collymore again?' Rose said; although she already had a presentiment that it was not.

'Oh, Freddy . . . he's still hanging around, poor fellow. I think it's Clive who keeps pushing him and he'd really rather leave it alone. No, it's nothing like that. Or I suppose it is . . . I've met someone.'

She gasped it out and then stared at her hands, almost doubled over with shyness.

'Yes . . .?' Rose said, feeling herself to be moving into uncharted waters.

'He's awfully nice,' Angelica whispered, 'and I like him very much.'

'Does he know?'

'Yes. And he likes me very much as well. That sounds awfully big-headed,' Angelica added hastily, 'but you see I . . . I know.'

'Well, that's wonderful.'

Angelica beamed. 'There you are, you see – that's why I can talk to you about it. Other people would . . . He isn't at all like Freddy.'

'Different lips, I should hope,' Rose said.

'Oh golly, yes . . . He's a sort of cousin of the Ferriers – oh, not the Hampshire Ferriers, the others.'

Rose, mystified as ever by these Byzantine distinctions, could only nod.

'He's an artist, sort of. The thing is he wasn't decommissioned from the army till quite recently because he had to stay and watch the Germans or something and so he isn't really established in any way and he hasn't any money.'

'An artist? That's interesting.'

'Oh, he's like nobody I ever . . . well, he's like nobody I ever met except you, Mrs Blanchard.'

'Good heavens,' Rose said, laughing and self-conscious, 'that doesn't say much for him. I'm afraid I'm no artist—'

'Oh, but you mustn't say that. You're different, that's what it is, and so is he and he's a person you can really talk with instead of it just being chit-chat and shooting and – and he wants me to run away with him and get married.'

Rose stared at Angelica's lowered Botticelli-beauty head. Through her amazement she grasped at the realization that her advice was being sought and that this, undoubtedly, was serious.

'When . . .' She cleared her throat. 'When did he suggest this?'

'The other day.'

'And what did you say?'

'I said . . . well, the idea is quite mad of course and I simply couldn't say, "Yes, all right," but it does sound – well, it sounds wonderful. And I do so want to be with him and I said I'd think about it. It's – you see, it's all happened so fast.'

'Yes,' Rose said. 'Yes, it does.'

Angelica gave her a glowing look. 'I knew you'd understand.'

Uncomfortable again, Rose said, 'Where does he live?'

'Well, he's staying with the Courtneys at the moment, over at Holt. But he has a little place in London, with a studio and so on. As I said, he isn't really established.'

'What does Clive think of him?'

'Oh, he doesn't think of him at all. Not in that way.' Angelica's eyes were large and solemn. 'Nor Mummy or anyone. He simply isn't a person they would take much notice of. Not in that way.'

The unknown artist immediately went up in Rose's estimation. 'So there couldn't be any question of him going to your family and—'

'Oh good heavens, no,' Angelica said, her eyes wider than ever. 'No question. He knows that as well as I. Which I suppose is why he asked me to . . . elope.' Angelica pronounced the word with a sort of thrilled anguish.

'Well,' Rose said, 'I'm flattered that you should tell me about this, Angelica. It's very . . . it's a big thing to think about, isn't it?'

'Too jolly well big. Which is why I just had to tell you about it.'

She had said 'tell you' and not 'ask you'; but the searching look she gave Rose left no room for doubt.

'Angelica, I . . . you know I can't tell you what you should do.'

'Oh no, of course not,' Angelica said – gazing hopefully at her still.

'Whatever you decide, it has to be your decision alone.'

'Yes, of course.'

'Really I'm the last person who should say . . . I've made some dreadful mistakes in my life.'

Angelica looked at her as if she had said she could fly like a bird.

Helplessly, Rose said, 'What's his name?'

'Edward. Edward Stapleton.'

Well, there was certainly no doubting Angelica's feelings. Simply from the burning, conscious way she spoke the syllables, one could tell . . .

Rose pictured Clive and Mummy and Freddy and all those tweedy Machiavellians whom Angelica, without any direct description and with absolutely no malice, had conjured up in all their dreadfulness. Then she pictured the ardent artist suddenly entering the dreary scene. Run away with me . . .

'Is he nice to you?' she said. 'Edward?'

'He's nice to me in a way that – that nobody has ever been, except you. He makes me feel . . .' Scarlet, perplexed, Angelica lapsed into finger-twisting silence.

Rose knew the sensible answer. Angelica should think about it; she should not do anything hasty; she should remember she was very young and this was her first experience of such things.

Hearing the sensible answer in her head, Rose disliked it. Even the practical considerations, which the struggle of the past five years had taught her never to dismiss, did not seem very pressing. The artist might be unacceptable to Clive and Mummy, but he was still hardly a workless coalheaver. And she knew that when someone of the Harwoods' class said 'no money', it meant something quite different to them than it did to her – as did a 'little place' in London.

Of course it would mean great changes for Angelica. Even taking the artist's pennilessness with a pinch of salt, she would be in a different world from the landed, chauffeured, rarefied opulence of her family home. As for the family, Rose doubted they would be forgiving. Clive obviously had profitable plans for Angelica. The artist might have to be everything to her in a different way than he was at the moment.

This carping and caution was all very well, but the girl looked happy. Couldn't she be happy for her?

She could, and was. And Angelica needed something of her.

'Angelica, I'm so pleased that you've met someone and that it – it sounds so wonderful. As I've said, I can't tell you what you should do, and it wouldn't be right if I did. I'm not even going to say "follow your heart" because besides that being an awful old chestnut your heart sometimes points in different ways. But when your feelings are very strong I've never seen any point in denying them. All I can say is that . . . if one day you didn't turn up here any more then I should be very sad but I would be – enormously happy for you too.'

Angelica did a most uncharacteristic thing. She seized Rose's hand and burst into tears.

'It was very hard to know what to say,' Rose said to James in bed that night. 'I've built up a rather fearful picture of this family of hers and I can imagine them hunting me down with beaters if they find out I encouraged her to run off.'

'Well, it doesn't sound as if you actually encouraged her.'

'I did try to be very careful. Because it *has* got to be her choice. But in a way I wanted to come right out and say, "Do it, don't think twice, take the chance."'

'Did you?'

'Oh, yes.' She laid her head drowsily against him. 'They're young, after all. Life's short. Even if there are regrets, it's better than being old and grey and regretting that you never did anything at all.'

'Yes, I suppose so.'

'She had this spark about her today, you see. It was nice to see it and . . .' she yawned, 'it would be a pity if it went out.'

James lay gently stroking her hair while her breathing deepened. He was wakeful.

He had often been so in the first weeks of their marriage: it was all so amazing that she was here with him that the sheer fact of it somehow disinclined him to sleep. Love was still for him a grand and somewhat awesome experience, much more so than his manner suggested; and marriage had magnified it. If he was assailed by any doubts, they were about himself.

And that was why he was wakeful tonight. He was in a troubled, gnawing mood without quite being able to put his finger on why.

Probably it had something to do with seeing Tom Cherry again today. Tom was very low at the moment and the nerve tonic James had given him seemed to have had no effect. His breathing difficulties made him irritable and his sleep was disturbed by nightmares of the war and the comrades he had lost in the trenches. Big, young and robust, Tom was forced to live life like an old man and James could not help him.

'I don't know,' Tom had said, slumped in the chair, his eyes listlessly roaming around the consulting room, 'I reckon it would've been better if they'd finished me off. I'm no good here. They should have put a bullet in me head and finished me off.'

It was all very well for James to protest that he shouldn't think like that. The fact was, as polite Tom had so far refrained from pointing out to him, he couldn't know what it was like. James recalled the old mocking soldiers' song:

> You was with the wenches
> While we were in the trenches
> A-facing our German foe . . .

The consciousness of not having fought in the war had been troublesome to James before. Never mind that it was a futile barbarity against which the reasonable mind revolted; never mind that the authorities had insisted on keeping his skills well away from the battlefield – at some deep irrational level, not having fought set him at a disadvantage. But it had never preyed on him so much as it had done lately. It might have had something to do with seeing Tom Cherry. It might also have had something to do with Elizabeth's father, that enigmatic unplaceable figure, who had fought and won medals.

James had the self-awareness to spot at once the twinge of inferiority he suffered when Rose told him this. It was dangerous to let such a feeling in, he told himself; also somehow disloyal to Rose.

But he couldn't help it. The feeling stole over him now, as he lay beside Rose listening to her breathing deepen into sleep.

She is with you, he told himself, from her own free choice:

what more? But a miserable whining doubt replied that the choice was only second best.

He might have crushed that doubt if it had not been for her earlier words about Angelica Harwood and her beau. In them he felt he had detected an unmistakable note of regret. *They're young . . . Life's short . . . It would be a pity if the spark went out . . .* He had seemed to hear a gentle, resigned envy, a wistful longing for the romance and excitement that, by inference, she had recognized as being for ever lost to her.

Again he felt disloyal and treacherous, thinking these things as she lay beside him with her body lightly touching his at hip and arm, a faint smear of moonlight on her cheek. He loved her desperately, but he could not help his thoughts; and having been solitary for a long time, he did not suppose that unspoken thoughts had any power, for good or evil.

# TWENTY-SIX

Tom Cherry had been working at the Grand Hotel long enough to know most of the types who came to stay there. There were the old bodies who had been coming here since long before the war, leftovers from old Queen Victoria's time, stuffy and snooty but with a bit of something about them all the same. The men had walrus moustaches, the ladies huge hats and creaking corsets, and they plodded stiffly about looking as if nothing had ever made them raise their eyebrows in their lives. Their luggage was always musty and bulky and looked as if it had come out of the ark. They certainly weren't chummy with hotel porters, but they had a correct formal way of treating you that, Tom supposed, came from always having servants. He preferred them on the whole to the newer sort who arrived in natty motors and who liked to flash their lolly about – the women all hard-faced and covered in jewels, and the men with fat necks and thick watch chains stretched across their paunches. They tipped well enough but you were lucky to get a civil word out of them; and Tom couldn't help associating them with the base-wallahs and the money-grabbers of the war, the people who didn't care if the mud-soaked, blood-soaked slogging went on for ever as long as there were plenty of men like Tom to fight it for them. He thought this was probably unfair, and was perplexed at himself: he always seemed to be festering with a sense of bitterness and unfairness lately. He had always been rather easy-going and it was this feeling of an unwanted change within himself that was perhaps the hardest legacy of the war, harder than the rawness of his skin and the perpetual fire in his lungs.

Those were the older types. The younger types included the honeymoon couples, who were always friendly; the young families who twenty years ago wouldn't have been able to afford the Grand and who were still a bit bashful about their step upward and kept saying thank you to any member of the hotel staff who came near them; and the young things who, he guessed, didn't think much of either honeymoons or families – the women with bobbed hair and dancing shoes and a very free way with cigarettes, the men a little dandified and speaking some sort of slang that he didn't understand. They were always very chummy with him – almost unnaturally so – though he had a feeling that they would just as easily laugh at him, if the drink they knocked back so plentifully took them the wrong way.

So he thought he knew all the types, and could recognize them straight off; even when you were being the dutiful porter, see-nothing, say-nothing, you could get the measure of them in a few minutes.

But the chap who arrived very late that Friday in early October, when the season was really over and the guests were thinning out and the maids were busy closing up one wing of the hotel for the winter, did not fit any of these categories.

Tom did not take much notice of him at first. His breathing had been especially bad that day and it took all his concentration to keep the labouring and wheezing under control. There was an impatient pride in this and also a practical necessity. He knew that the head porter and the undermanager did not like him and would pass up no opportunity to get rid of him, especially with the off season coming up. Unfitness would do very nicely.

So when he was beckoned forward to take the gentleman's bags he kept his mind fixed on the battle with his lungs.

'This way, sir.'

A cursory glance, as he picked up the bags, showed Tom

that this chap did not fit the usual types. He was youngish, but not the usual brilliantined boy: smartly dressed, but no hard-faced moneybags. He had a lean, travelled, confident look. He appeared to Tom, practised in quickly assessing people, as if he had seen a few things.

But he didn't think any more of this, occupied as he was with the struggle to get air smoothly into his lungs, until they were at the door of the gentleman's room. About to open and carry the bags in – they weren't large and it embarrassed Tom that he was making such heavy weather of them – he found the gentleman putting a hand on his shoulder and saying, 'You all right, old fellow?'

'Perfectly, sir,' Tom said with an effort.

'Here, give me one of those. It's nonsense me being waited on like this.'

'No, no.' With an obscure idea that it would get back to his superiors that he had let a guest carry his own luggage, Tom hefted the bags and carried them in.

His lungs felt as if they would burst, but he was more than ever determined not to show it. He stowed the bags with care, taking the time to collect himself.

'Will there be anything else, sir?' he said, turning at last, and unconsciously standing very straight.

The gentleman gave him a direct, friendly look, as if they had known each other all their lives.

'I should think you and I have been in the same place, haven't we?' he said.

'Beg pardon, sir?'

'It's hard to settle back, isn't it?' the gentleman said, shrugging off his coat. 'A lot of things back home don't seem quite real, even now. Were you with the Norfolks?'

'Oh – yes, sir.' Tom found himself relaxing; and again noticing the guest's tanned, wiry look. Of course, he should have known. 'You were at the front, sir?'

'I should say so. Front, they called it. More like the arse-end of somewhere. Where'd you cop the gas?'

'Passchendaele.' Even pronouncing the word seemed to relieve the pressure on his chest. That was the trouble nowadays – nobody wanted to hear about these things any more. It was all over, they seemed to say, and should be forgotten; to talk about it was to be a complainer, a bore, a Bolshie. And somehow Tom knew, from the gentleman's look, that he understood this.

'Christ,' the gentleman said. 'I was spared that.'

'It wasn't so bad,' Tom said.

'Of course. That's what we have to say, don't we? So as not to make people uncomfortable. I was at the Somme. Now it's just a river again. People's memories are short.'

'Can't blame them, I suppose,' Tom said, feeling a glow of vindication. 'Did you cop one, sir? Over there?'

'Only this scratch –' he pointed to his left eyebrow, which was broken – 'and a blast in the backside that kept me out of the line for precisely three months. To be honest, when it hit I was hoping it was a Blighty one. Windy of me, I know, but I'd had enough.'

'Everybody felt windy at one time or another,' Tom said. 'Liars if they say they didn't, I reckon. Oh, no thank you, sir,' he added as the gentleman proffered a cigarette case, 'not on duty.'

'Sorry, I was forgetting. All these damn rules and regulations – the army was nothing to it. Take one for later.'

He passed Tom a cigarette in an easy soldierlike way that made it very easy to accept.

'Thank you, sir. Staying with us long?'

'It could be.' The gentleman went to the window to look at the view, then turned and winked. 'Long enough for you to drop the sir, anyway.'

A few more guests like that, Tom thought as he went away with a handsome tip, and his job would be a lot easier. It was just that sort of camaraderie that he missed, and that made him so confused and frustrated in a post-war world that seemed ready to forget it had ever fought a war at all.

Descending the narrow ill-lit stairs, he noticed that his breathing felt better.

The gentleman, having seen to his own unpacking, went down to the dining room to see if they were still serving dinner. They were, and he ate alone amongst the palms and pier-glasses and marble, taking half a pint of champagne with his dinner. While he ate he looked about him with an expression of relaxed, chipper interest, not appearing lonely or bored: there was something about him that suggested he had resources at hand and plans in mind. He was a little under medium height, compactly made, dark, thin-faced, and with something attractively wry about his expression which the broken eyebrow tended to accentuate.

After dinner he thought he would take a walk down to the promenade and see if Shipden had changed much in his absence. 'Though,' Alec Taverner said to himself with quiet amusement, 'I rather doubt whether it has.'

# TWENTY-SEVEN

The first week of October saw a spell of lovely weather. Blue skies, rarefied by autumn, gave an impression of eternity. Instead of glaring and blazing, the sun became an artist, creating everywhere ripples and dapples, adding to the tints of nature an endless variety of rich golds, and endowing even the most commonplace object with a fragment of its radiance, so that a tin kettle or a water-tap glittered like a precious artefact.

It was impossible to resist the call of the open air, especially as this would probably be the last of such weather for six months or more. On Sunday, instead of entertaining Aunt Dolly to lunch at the house, Rose and James invited her to join them on a picnic.

Instead of the beach or clifftops, they decided this time to drive inland to a spot they had found earlier in the season. It was a dell-like meadow half enfolded by magical copses where butterfly orchis grew, and opening on the other side to a broad rolling prospect of cornfields.

When they had visited the spot earlier, the cornfields had been wonderfully sprinkled with poppies, thousands of the scarlet blobs seeming to extend to the horizon: but now the harvest was over there was only bronzy stubble to be seen.

'Oh! What a pity,' Dolly said, shading her eyes with her hand and looking out over the fields as James pulled the car up. 'The way you described it to me, Rose – I was so looking forward to seeing it.'

'I should have thought,' Rose said, crestfallen too. 'I should have realized they'd be gone. The weather was so beautiful I kept thinking it would be just the same.'

'Wait, though – wait – look there,' cried Dolly, pointing heroically like a general on a bridge, 'I see something.'

She was out of the car and off, galumphing down the slope and crossing the ditch to the unfenced field by a duckboard bridge that sagged ominously beneath her weight.

'Where's Auntie Dolly going?' Elizabeth said.

'I don't know,' Rose said. 'We'd better go and see.'

They followed, Rose and James holding Elizabeth's hands on either side and from time to time as they went, lifting her up off her feet so that her legs pedalled in the air. It was a thing she loved and Rose remembered the delightful sensation of it from her own childhood, on the few occasions her mother would consent to do it.

'Look. Look, dears.'

There was a footpath running through the stubble field and several yards along it Dolly was standing facing them, her hands out in a displaying gesture and her face triumphant.

'Look, dears. The last of the poppies. Isn't that a heartbreaking sight? Doesn't that just suggest – oh, a poem or something?'

All along the edge of the path, where the gleaning had reached its furthest limit, were dead poppies, like a border on a handkerchief. The sun had dried them and when Rose bent to pick one up it felt like some marvellous confection of paper.

'See,' Dolly said, turning and pointing to where the path arrowed across the field, bordered all the way by the fallen poppies, 'isn't that a picture? All the way along.'

'They'll grow again next year,' Rose said to Elizabeth, who was handling a dead poppy with a downcast look. 'Lots and lots of them, all over, all bright red. We'll come and see them.'

'What do they grow them for, Mummy?' said Elizabeth, who was of a practical turn of mind.

'Well, they don't grow them on purpose. They grow wheat

'I'm afraid Dolly was sozzled today, anyway,' she said.

The whole of the case . . . As she kissed him she sensed a subtle untruth in these words, something crucially omitted. Elizabeth was her child, she might become James's child, but she was still a child born of an earlier love; and it was that, some deep part of her knew, that he could not come to terms with. They had spoken, but they had not addressed this, not quite.

But she began to respond to his kisses. 'Come here,' she said, 'come into bed,' and it was easy to slip into the compelling fiction that there is a physical truth which goes beyond words.

The contrary emotions of the day had left her very passionate, and the same thing, it seemed, had occurred in James. They slept only intermittently and presently there was daylight in the room and she was lying lazily watching James dress.

'You look nice,' she said.

He bent and kissed her. 'So do you.'

'Oh, not me, I look a fright,' Rose said, half-burying her head in the pillow: mostly she was free of physical inhibition, but she had a shyness about the morning uglies.

'I wonder how Dolly's feeling.' He fastened his collar-stud.

'Seedy. Very seedy. And . . .' it was easy to say it in this frank sensual contentment, 'and probably remembering what she said with dreadful embarrassment.'

'Oh well, I suppose it's natural,' James said. 'She must have known him, after all.'

'Yes,' Rose said. 'Not all that well, but . . . yes.'

'Is it a strong resemblance?' James said, doing up his tie. 'I was just wondering, you know, just as a matter of interest, really. Does Elizabeth look like him?'

'Sometimes,' Rose said after a moment. 'But it doesn't matter anyway, does it?'

'Oh no, of course not. Doesn't matter at all,' he said. 'I'll see about some breakfast.'

Well, he had given the answer she wanted. But more important, it seemed to her, was the question he felt he had to ask.

# TWENTY-NINE

Days on which something bad began ought, Rose thought afterwards, to bear some sort of outward sign. There ought to be the thunderstorms and birds of ill omen that had warned the Romans – or at the very least pictures in the fire to foretell what was coming.

But this was a perfectly ordinary day with the quiet grey resignation of autumn about it, and when she walked down to the town in the afternoon to collect Elizabeth from her school she had no inkling of what was to come.

Which was not to say that she was entirely easy in her mind. She had not been, in fact, since the day of the picnic.

No drastic changes in her married life had proceeded from that day. But there was no doubting that a seed had been planted in James by that outburst of Dolly's, and what growth it might take she could not tell.

If he had altered at all in his behaviour towards Elizabeth, alarm bells would have rung indeed. Rose would have had to speak out regardless of the consequences. But there was no sign of that: he was as kind to Elizabeth as ever. Whatever jealousy he was feeling, it was not so intense and distorted as to lead him to take it out on the child, and Rose could hardly have stayed with him if it had.

No, the change, or rather shift, in James's behaviour was towards herself. That was the way the seed was growing. And if she had not spoken out about it, it was partly because she could not be sure she had not fostered its growth by lacking that last degree of emotional openness towards him.

And also it was because there was nothing she could put her finger on. James was a subtle man and the change in him was subtle. It chiefly took the form of constrictions. She noticed that if the subject of the past came up in conversation, even in the most incidental, anecdotal way, he tightened. He would not speak freely or respond freely. One day she had found herself speaking, quite lightly and without thought, about the cravings she had suffered when she was carrying Elizabeth, and when she looked up his face had assumed an expression that she could only call stony politeness. At once he changed the subject.

Little signs and tokens.

He was having his consulting room refurbished, and got carried away talking of it: suddenly looked at her – she was dreaming rather than bored – and clammed up, saying, 'Sorry, this is all rather boring. The dizzying glamour of the medical profession.'

He had instituted a weekly child welfare clinic in the church hall, which Rose attended to give him support. A mother at a loss to explain her child's partial deafness protested that there was none in her family, and afterwards Rose innocently asked James whether these things came through the male line. 'Well, of course they do,' he said almost snappishly. 'It takes two to make a child.'

She found a photograph of herself taken when she was eighteen, and he studied it with a loverlike attention.

'How young you look,' he said.

'I was young,' she said, looking at the picture with mixed though not troubling emotions. 'Frighteningly young.'

'My God, you wouldn't have thought much of me then,' he said. 'Dull stick coming out of med school and conning textbooks over cocoa.'

'I thought medical students were always rather wild, like in *Pickwick*.'

'Some are,' he said.

And she thought: what did he mean? That if she had met

him first, she wouldn't have been attracted to him? And that, in effect, she had only married him because she had a child and sought security rather than excitement and didn't mind taking second best to achieve it?

Insulting to both of them. Yet the very framing of this idea made her question herself, and set off a corresponding doubt within her own mind. Could it be that there was some truth in it? Her heart answered no – she had married for love and no less – but that niggling doubt was not so easily got rid of. It was irrational, but so was James's lurking jealousy. And it was because of the doubt that she could not have it out with James. Could she deny, after all, that she would still have been with Alec if he had not rejected her?

Part of her knew that questions like this were nonsense. The fact was that Alec *had* rejected her, and so opened her eyes to his true nature, and so love had died – certainly not overnight, but quickly and completely. But the doubt undermined this knowledge. She was beginning to see that the poison of jealousy acted on both sides.

And yet there was still an abundance of love and even trust. James was above all a reasonable man and the signs and tokens were like cross-waves in the tide. Rose could only hope that time would work for her: that as the day of the picnic receded into the past its effect on him would weaken and the suspicion that had been planted stunt and wither.

She was jolted out of her reflections by the sight of something new in Pound Street. The site of the Kinema, for so long a forlorn and blackened shell, was all activity. Scaffolding and tarpaulins had gone up all round it and workmen were unloading a builder's lorry in the street in front. Rose paused to watch, thinking how nice it would be to go with James and Elizabeth to see a film, now that Elizabeth was old enough. She hadn't seen a film in the past five years, and before that she had only made one or two furtive visits, her mother considering moving pictures vulgar.

275

Suddenly she recognized the man supervising the builders, and hurried over.

'Frank!'

'Afternoon, Rose. Looking well.'

Frank Watlyn, self-consciously businesslike in shirtsleeves and braces with a pencil stuck behind his ear, beamed at her and made a modest backward nod of his head at the sign, *This Renovation F. N. Watlyn, Builders, Saxburgh*, that hung from the scaffolding. 'What d'you think, then, eh? Not a bad little job to land.'

'Oh, I'm so pleased for you – congratulations.' This was good news indeed for the Watlyns, with the end of the season meaning that the Arcadia would be less than a goldmine for the next six months. 'Is it to be a kinema again?'

'I should say so,' Frank said importantly. 'And no half-and-half job. A proper picture palace, tiered seating, balcony, everything. Going over the plans just this morning.'

'But that's wonderful. I didn't think Ernie Crimmins was going to be able to do it.'

'Oh no – not Ernie Crimmins. The site's been sold up to a, well, to another buyer. No, not old Ernie Crimmins.' Frank took the pencil from behind his ear, looked at it in puzzlement as if he couldn't think how it had got there, whistled through his teeth, and then looked up at the scaffolding. 'Yes, big job this'll be. Big plans.' He looked, amazingly for Frank who was normally as open as a friendly old hound, both furtive and evasive. 'Anyway, better be getting down to it. Millie's well, by the way. Carrie too. Still. Must get busy.' Whistling, he sidled away.

It was strange, so strange that as soon as Rose had brought Elizabeth home from school, she telephoned Millie at the Arcadia. The use of the telephone still did not come naturally to her, and it was a measure of how disturbed she was that she picked it up without a second thought. She couldn't think what had made Frank so odd – unless the rebuilding of the Kinema was some speculation of his own which was going to land them deep in debt. Though Frank had never been sheepish even about his most disastrous ventures – always there was a Micawberish belief that this one was copper-bottomed and foolproof.

When Millie answered, however, there seemed no constraint in her voice. After some general chat Rose said, hoping to keep her own voice light and casual, 'Oh, I saw Frank at the Kinema site today. He told me he'd got the contract for rebuilding – that's good news, isn't it?'

The hesitation on the other end of the line was momentary – but very noticeable. 'Yes,' Millie said, 'yes, isn't it? Did he – did he tell you all about it?'

'Well, just that the site had been bought up, and he would be doing the rebuilding, and it was all going to be on a grand scale . . . Millie,' Rose said, 'it – it *is* good news, isn't it?'

Millie sighed. 'Oh damn, I was going to fib but I can't, Rose, I just can't. I do wish it didn't have to be me again . . . It's Alec Taverner. He's the one who bought the site. You know I told you he'd come into some money and I suppose . . . Well, anyhow, he's moving back to Shipden. Frank had a big powwow with him last week. I'm sorry, Rose, I didn't know whether to tell you or what to do . . .'

A voice inside Rose said *I knew something like this was going to happen.* But it wasn't true. She hadn't known. The voice was more like some desperate denial that events were beyond her control.

Which, of course, they were. There was absolutely nothing to prevent Alec Taverner returning to Shipden, if such was his choice. She had known this, at least, since Millie had told her he was back in Norfolk, but had suppressed or disregarded it. It had seemed, at any rate, unlikely. Unless he had strong reasons.

'Rose – are you still there?'

'Yes . . . yes, sorry, Millie, I'm here . . . Millie, did you see him?'

'No, not me. Frank's been full of him, but of course that's

277

understandable – it is a big contract. All I know is that he's coming back to settle here and he's using his money to restart the Kinema, perhaps other things too, Frank says. Of course he was always in the entertainments line, wasn't he?'

'Yes,' said Rose. 'He was.'

'Oh, my dear, it is awkward for you . . . Do you think he'll want to see Elizabeth?'

'This late in the day?' Rose said, and was surprised to hear in her voice a bitterness she thought had gone. 'I shouldn't think so. If he does – well, we'll see.'

'I am so sorry to be the messenger again, Rose. I must admit I was rather knocked back when Frank told me who'd been to see him . . . Rose, you'll try not to worry about this, won't you? You've got your own life now and a damned good one and I hope he realizes it. And if he doesn't I should think – well, I should think you'll let him know.'

'Yes,' said Rose. 'I'll let him know.'

After she had rung off she went into the garden, where Elizabeth was playing with a toy battledore and shuttlecock. Rose played with her a while, managing to laugh and run, but she was heavy with the news.

Alec Taverner back in Shipden. She could hardly believe it. She felt a chill as if the past had physically laid a cold hand on her neck.

Her first heart-stopping thought had been, indeed, of his somehow turning up at the door and demanding his share of Elizabeth; but a little reflection soon quelled that fear. She was not sure about the legal details, but she was sure about Alec. He had shown no interest in his daughter over the past five years and had never liked taking on any responsibility that might cramp his style. No, that was hardly likely. On the other hand, he was incorrigibly sentimental, and she could well imagine him making one misty-eyed pilgrimage to look wistfully, like a small-town Byron, on the fruit of his youthful indiscretion.

Well, she was prepared to deal with that, directly, herself.

That was straightforward enough. Even if it came to Elizabeth wanting to know the facts of the situation, Rose was prepared to face it. More problematic was the reaction of James. Shipden was a small talkative town and even if Alec kept out of the way James would, sooner or later, get to know of his presence. See him; perhaps meet him.

All unexpectedly, Rose felt a little leap of hope.

For she suspected that at the root of James's problem lay the sheer absence of Alec Taverner. Back when James had first proposed to her she had thought of Alec in terms of a ghost and the image was apposite. James was, if only in a subtle way, haunted. The small, seemingly casual questions he kept asking her must mean that he was trying to build up a private picture of the man who – there was no denying it – exerted a powerful influence on his life, if only because he had left his mark on Rose's. And imagined fears were greater than real ones: the imagination was a great torturer. From the self-deprecating, faintly resentful remarks that James had let slip lately, Rose suspected that the picture he had built up of Alec Taverner was a dazzling one – irresistibly romantic and life-enhancing ladykiller wearing the ribbons of a war hero.

Well, the real Alec Taverner, she thought, couldn't come up to that. The war might have made him a hero but it had also been his escape route: and as for the ladykilling skills, they had depended back then on the lady being barely out of her teens, and might well not have progressed. Most of all, he was a normal, fallible, unexceptional human being. And perhaps seeing that – and that he was a human being in whom Rose had no interest – would be the very thing that would rid James of this niggling fixation that was taking away part of the man she loved.

It might be; it might well be. No starry-eyed optimist, Rose still considered this a reasonable hope, and took a firm grip on it. She even shouted down an inward lament that this should happen just when they were settled – because could they really be called settled, when James nurtured this secret jealousy? It

might have simply gone on festering, whereas the return of
Alec, whatever happened, might at least bring it to a head.
And by temperament Rose preferred things out in the open.

So: hope.

'Mummy. Mummy, will you play a bit more?'

Rose flailed at the shuttlecock – she was the most complete
duffer at sports and games – and while Elizabeth with a patient
sigh went to pluck it out of the flowerbeds she looked up at
the house, where a light was glowing in the kitchen as the
afternoon grew shadowy. Smoke was rising from the chimney,
and already the sight of the place touched her feelings directly
with warm and loving associations. And while it was all very
well for her to be hopeful and to proclaim that Alec Taverner
was just a human being like any other, she could not help but
feel, superstitiously, that his coming cast a shadow that touched
this place, where all that she loved and valued was
concentrated.

More than anything she wanted to keep her home inviolate.
And that was why, when she heard James's car approaching,
her courage and perhaps good sense deserted her and she
decided that she would not tell him about Alec Taverner, not
yet. Time enough. Not yet.

# THIRTY

It had been for James a dispiriting day, during the course of which some words of advice spoken by a lecturing surgeon in his training days at Edinburgh came vividly back to him: 'I would remind you that the medical profession is, by its very nature, the only one that is engaged in a losing battle. Remember that, when you go out of here thinking you are little gods.'

That afternoon Tom Cherry had come to him in distress. He complained of his nerves, refused an examination, roamed about the consulting room, and at last told James with lurching, shuddering tears that he had been sacked from his job that morning.

'I know I shouldn't have spoke like that. I know I shouldn't have got over my collar. But I said so – I said I was wrong and I was ready to apologize. Surely that's worth something, ain't it, Doctor?'

Little by little – Tom, unusually, had had a drink and was not coherent – James got it out of him. That morning an elderly guest had been preparing to leave the hotel and Tom had taken the man's luggage down to his car. The man had told him to place his golf bag in the bottom of the boot and the cases on top of it. Tom, thinking this to be a mistake, had done the reverse.

'It made sense, thass all. I tried putting stuff on top of the golf bag and it started to bend the heads of the clubs – it was just too heavy, it was going to damage them. So I stowed 'em the other way round. Then he comes out and sees what I've done and starts on me. My man this and my man that. I tried to explain that I'd done it that way so as the golf clubs wouldn't get damaged. He went wild. "Don't you answer back to me. You do just as I tell you" – oh, he had this red face like some bloody stubborn ole pig, I'm sorry but he did – and I just snapped. I started shouting at him. "Oh yes, I know this game," I says. "Ours not to reason why, ours just to do or die." I know it was stupid but I couldn't help it. It just brought back so many things. Puffed-up old buffers like him giving orders that didn't make any sense . . . Maybe it wasn't men getting sent to their deaths this time but it was the same, it was just the same . . .' Wiping his face, Tom looked up at James and as if anticipating a protest said, 'It might seem a bit much to you, Doctor, but you see you weren't there – in the war, I mean.'

'No,' James said, 'I wasn't there.'

Tom seemed at once to regret this. 'Mind you,' he said clumsily, 'thank God you weren't. If it hadn't been for the doctors I'd have lost a lot more pals than I did . . .'

'Go on, Tom. What happened then?'

Tom slumped back. 'He went to the undermanager. There was a ruckus . . . That's when I tried to apologize. It was like whatever got into me just all drained away and I couldn't hardly believe what I'd done . . . No good. I got the sack there and then. I don't know.' Tom's big fresh-coloured face was pale, his lowered eyes hollow. 'Perhaps I deserved it. Perhaps I'm losing my mind.'

James got up. 'Come on. Let's go to the Grand. The undermanager, did you say? That wasn't a fair dismissal,' he said at Tom's surprised look. 'You're a war veteran and you've been under strain from it. They've got to take that into consideration.'

Tom winced, half-reluctant, half-hopeful. 'I'm not an invalid. I don't want no special treatment as if I was.'

'Fair treatment. My God, if a man's good enough to risk his life for his country, he's good enough to be treated fairly when he comes back to it.'

Tom seemed impressed, a little startled by the sharpness of James's anger. Perhaps he did not see, as James himself only half saw, into the twisted roots of it.

The undermanager of the Grand turned out to be a cold-eyed, whey-faced man of forty who had a clinical smell of soap and who looked, with his tailcoat and the fingertips of his antiseptic hands pressed showily together, like some grim conjurer. In his mahogany-polished office he listened, silent and expressionless, to what James had to say.

'I'm sorry, Dr Blanchard,' he said at last. 'I'm afraid I don't quite see the application of what you're telling me.'

'A patient of mine,' James said, drawing an impatient breath, 'has been sacked from this establishment. For behaviour which as his physician I can explain.'

'Yes,' the undermanager said, 'but the behaviour is not suitable for the position of hotel porter. Therefore Cherry was dismissed.' He frowned faintly, as if James were talking in riddles.

'Mr Cherry is an ex-soldier with a sterling war record. He was gassed at the front, and still suffers from the effects of this. Among these effects may be an occasional nervous irritability which—'

'Cherry's record does him credit, I'm sure, Dr Blanchard, but he is not the only man who was in the war. I served at the front myself, in the artillery, for over two years.'

James tried to find some expression in the aloof grey eyes.

'Then you'll understand,' he said, his heart sinking.

'I understand that some men have returned to civilian life with a grievance, and a belief that the world owes them a living.'

'You must understand the state of Mr Cherry's health—'

'I'm sorry, Dr Blanchard, but I understood he was discharged as fit. He was certainly employed on that basis, and you will appreciate we cannot employ a man who is not.'

'He is fit,' James said. 'Entirely so, but—'

'If a man is fit enough to do a job,' the undermanager said, 'then he is fit enough to abide by the rules of that job. Of which the strictest courtesy is one, in this case. Believe me, if there were any way . . . but I'm afraid there isn't. I am not unsympathetic.' He got up from his desk. 'As I said, I was in the war myself.'

James felt the failure bitterly. Tom, who seemed to have settled into an apathetic resignation, thanked him for trying and was good about it; but then, James reflected, Tom was used to his doctor being unable to help him.

James wondered as he drove home just what it was that was making him feel so bad. Tom's misfortune – or his own humiliation?

Brooding, he was surprised on reaching home to find Rose running out to the drive and flinging her arms round him and kissing him passionately.

'My God,' he said, 'what have I done to deserve this?'

'Oh, I don't know – everything.' Her eyes were shining like a cat's in the dusk, and he noticed the tick of her pulse in her smooth neck. He felt a keen love and desire for her which even his mood of self-disgust could not quite stifle.

She was bright that evening, almost restlessly chatty and affectionate. No, she hadn't been doing much today, she said in answer to his enquiry: just thinking of him. Several times, however, he saw her glance over at him as if she were about to tell him something.

But he didn't press her again; and when she asked about his day he refrained from telling her about Tom Cherry. He was rather afraid lately that when he talked of these things he was dull – banging on about his patients and their problems.

They went to bed very loving, scarcely having communicated with each other at all.

# THIRTY-ONE

Every Wednesday morning Rose went to visit Aunt Dolly. The old lady had decided to take in a lodger and was constantly interviewing candidates, none of whom so far had come up to scratch, for various and curious reasons. 'Smell of onions,' Dolly would say of the latest, or 'Tapped her fingers while she was talking – says a lot about a person.'

So when Rose arrived this Wednesday, she thought at first that Dolly was talking of a prospective lodger when she greeted her with the words, 'Someone's been here – not more than an hour ago – you just missed him.'

'Oh, have you found someone to suit?'

'I wouldn't call it that.' Dolly, festooned with lengths of half-sewn fabric, looked incongruously solemn. 'My dear, he was – he was asking for you.'

All at once Rose knew.

'Ah,' she said. She sat down.

'It was that Alec Taverner. Who would have thought it after all this time? You could have knocked me down with a feather.'

So he had been in this very room . . . in this house where Rose and Dolly had struggled to bring up his child. Looking round, Rose felt – she didn't quite know why – an acute shudder. Perhaps this was why people were so afraid of ghosts. It wasn't so much the supernatural element as the sheer unnatural fact of the past coming back. Nothing was so dead as the past.

'Asking for me, did you say?'

'Afraid so, dear.' Dolly, wide-eyed, sat down beside her.

'What did you say?'

'I said you didn't live here any more, of course. Goodness, you wouldn't recognize him. Well, that's not true, you would, of course you would, but he's so much more mature-looking, very tanned and fit, really rather a striking figure . . .' Dolly caught herself up hastily. 'Anyhow, he was asking – about Elizabeth too. Well, of course I told him that you were married. He wanted to know all about it.' Stealing a timid glance at Rose's face Dolly went on, 'I had to tell him – he was awfully polite and friendly, and after all . . . My dear, he's coming back here to live. He's come into money, apparently, and he's rebuilding the Kinema and looking about him for some other prospects in the entertainment line. He wants to jolly the old place up, he said. I must say I can't blame him for that. He's staying at the Grand while he looks for a place to live. Well, he said thank you and so on, and chatted a while, and then he went off . . . My dear, do you think he wants to – you know, stake a claim in Elizabeth, as it were?'

'Did he say so?'

'Well, no . . .'

'Good,' Rose said. 'I'd kill him before he'd do that.'

'Oh!' Dolly said, her eyes opening wider. 'Well . . . After all, he may not have any such thing in mind, you know. It's only that he's coming back here to live. And anyway, you're happily married now, and it's all changed, so really there shouldn't be any difficulty, should there?'

'No,' Rose said, 'there shouldn't be.'

She wished it were as simple as that.

In a way the scenario conjured up by Dolly's words was a dream come true. To be able to confront Alec with her head held high, to snap her fingers in his face and show him that the woman he had left with nothing now had everything . . . And yet just now she dreaded meeting him. She had a superstitious feeling that he would read in her face what she didn't like to admit – that everything *wasn't* perfect; and that

286

his merry knowing eyes would pick out just where the deficiency lay.

It was going to come, though. She couldn't pretend about that: he was looking for her. The only question that remained was why. She had already convinced herself that he couldn't seriously have designs on Elizabeth; that he had designs on her seemed equally unlikely, unless he thought her a complete idiot. Which was, however, possible: God knew she had shown all the signs of drivelling idiocy five years ago.

But the likeliest explanation seemed, as she had thought the other day, sheer sentiment. Alec was a showman, the director and star of his own life, and surely could not pass up the opportunity to add a bitter-sweet episode to the production.

Well, let him get it over with, and then perhaps she and Elizabeth and James could get on with their lives. Though she dreaded the meeting, in a way it could not come too soon, like an appointment with the dentist.

But Rose knew now, urgently, that she must tell James first. And with the same urgency she cursed herself for having delayed it.

She left Dolly's as soon as she was able and hurried home. She found James putting his bag in the car, just about to go out on his rounds.

'Hello, darling. How was Dolly? Found anyone who doesn't smell of onions yet?'

'No, not yet . . . James, there was something I wanted to talk to you about.'

'Could it be later? I'm running a bit behind as it is.'

'Well, I really wanted to . . .' She breathed painfully. She knew this was probably not a good time, not a good way to tell him; but she had stoked herself up for it now and could not stop. 'It's something I heard that I thought I'd better tell you. I mean it doesn't make any difference to anything but you're sure to hear sooner or later.' She laid her hand on his arm. 'Apparently Alec Taverner's come back to Shipden.'

He looked at her, his eyes hard and pale.

'You've seen him?'

'No. He went to Dolly's. But I – I heard from Millie the other day that he was back, you see he's bought the Kinema and Frank's doing the rebuilding so . . .'

It was not the first time her honesty had done her no favours. James frowned.

'You didn't tell me.'

'No. Well. I didn't think it – I didn't think it should have anything to do with us and I just hoped it would go away, if you see what I mean. But now he's been to Dolly's, and—'

'And he's been looking for you, I suppose?'

'Yes. I don't want to see him. I don't want him having any part in my life, our lives. But I thought you should know that – well, he *is* back.'

James leant his arm on the bonnet of the car.

'I see,' he said.

'I can live with it,' she said, studying him, 'if you can. It's a small town but not that small. And he's nothing to do with us.'

He glanced bleakly at her. 'Not entirely true. There's Elizabeth.'

'He's nothing to do with her either. And I shall tell him so if he thinks otherwise.'

James stared for a long time at the ground and then, visibly, came out of himself, like a man stepping out of darkness. He met her eyes.

'Poor darling,' he said. 'Rough on you.'

'Not really,' she said stoutly. 'I've got a new life. He can't touch that.'

'No . . . Still, it must have been a shock.'

'Yes. I really never expected that he would come back after all this time. It feels strange. But it won't make any difference.'

'Hopefully not . . . But that really depends on him, doesn't it? And what he intends to do.'

'He can't do anything.'

'How long has he been in Shipden?'

'I don't know. Not long, I don't think. Dolly says he's staying at the Grand until he finds somewhere to live.'

James gave a little mirthless smile. 'I've probably walked past him in the street. Little did I know. Lucky really. And lucky I don't carry a gun.'

'No.' Rose held on to his arm. 'No, James, I don't want that.'

'What, me shooting him? Don't worry, I've never fired a gun in my life, probably end up shooting myself—'

'I mean I don't want those feelings. There's no need for it, in either of us. Yes, I've got – I've got bitterness, more than I thought; and I most definitely do not want him near Elizabeth. But it's not a question of revenge or confrontation or anything like that. It's all a dead letter and I want it to stay that way.' She added, with a sense of dropping a veil of caution, 'It might be a good thing in a way. It might . . . lay some ghosts.'

'Yes,' he said, drawing a deep breath, 'it might do that.' He looked at his watch. 'I'd better go. I'm glad you told me. You don't – have to hide anything, you know.'

'No.'

Again he seemed to withdraw into himself, and then step out of darkness. He took her hand. 'Are you all right, darling? Has this upset you?'

'Surprised me. Not upset me.'

Getting into the car he said, 'Do you suppose he'll come to the house?'

'I suppose he might. I – I don't know what he'll do.'

'What will you do if he does?'

'Tell him to go away.'

She spoke confidently, and she blew him a kiss as he drove away; but she felt a twist in her heart at the fact that he had to ask.

# THIRTY-TWO

That afternoon Angelica came for her lesson. She was more diligent and less communicative than usual, and Rose, preoccupied and troubled, did not feel up to digging anything out of her.

But the girl had a kind of secret glow that suggested something was afoot; and when it was time for her to leave, she stood for a while fiddling with her gloves, glancing up at Rose and then away again.

'I'll see you next week, then?' Rose said.

'Yes – I think so. I mean, I think next week but I don't know after that . . . There's a good deal going on at the moment and I think there – there may be a change soon. I can't tell you when because I don't know myself yet.'

'Ah. Well, as long as you're happy. The two of you.'

'Yes,' Angelica said, with a sort of gasp of well-bred embarrassment; and then, 'Are you all right, Mrs Blanchard?'

'Yes, of course,' Rose said a little shortly. She was faintly irritated, not so much by the question as by the assumption behind it that she always was all right. That was the trouble with being a confessor-figure. Wasn't it within the bounds of possibility that she should have problems too?

Angelica's look of instant contrition reminded her that the poor girl was all too used to being slapped down.

'I'm a bit headachy today,' she said, summoning a smile. 'So, you can't let me in on the secret?'

'Oh, I will – as soon as it's settled,' Angelica said. 'I must say I do feel awfully underhand at home, but . . . it's exciting.'

Yes, Rose thought as she saw Angelica out to the car and waved her off, she remembered that excitement. Going about your daily business with the secret knowledge inside you . . . For the first time she wondered, with a sudden critical adultness, whether she would have fallen for Alec at all if it had not been for that faint sense of the furtive and forbidden. She had never regarded herself as a rebel, but looking back, had there not been a little provocative defiance of her mother's ferocious conventions in the way she had embarked on that affair?

It was frightening to think how little your own motives and desires could be known to you, she thought, turning to go back in.

She stopped and looked back. Someone was coming through the gate.

It was Alec Taverner.

She stood still and waited.

It was five years since she had seen him. She had been deserted by him, she had borne his child alone, and until she had met James his influence had determined practically everything about her life. And indeed, though she was married and had begun what should have been a new chapter, his influence was at work still. While he walked up the path Rose had a swift, clear apprehension of all these things; and yet for a few moments all the turbulent emotions she should have been expected to feel were quiescent within her, like dough that failed to rise. It was as if she were simply stunned by the fact of his continued existence – almost as if some famous historical figure had walked into her garden.

He came to within a few feet of her, then stopped. He was dressed casually in sports jacket and flannels and was bareheaded, but he seemed to feel the absence of a hat in the way he put his hand up to his hair and then, with a certain schoolboy awkwardness, scratched his head and said, 'Hello, Rose. I hope you don't mind me dropping in. Only I thought . . . as I was back in this neck of the woods . . .'

He offered a smile, the one that made the wry crinkles at the edge of his mouth and eyes. He was not changed: though he was, as Dolly said, tanned and fit-looking, and seemed to have an extra veneer of worldliness, he was still the same Alec; and the way he spoke was as if he had last seen her a fortnight ago. It was that which finally brought the emotions seething to the surface.

'I don't,' she said, 'quite know how you dare.'

'No,' he said with a little laugh, 'I don't either, to be honest. The fact is, I'm moving back to Shipden.'

'I know.'

'Mm. Of course, should have remembered, news travels fast here. Well, I thought that we were bound to bump into each other sooner or later, so it seemed best to break the ice, as it were.'

She glared at him. It was so impossible that he should be standing here, in her garden, in her life, talking as if nothing had happened . . .

'*Why?*' she burst out. 'Why come back?'

'Well I heard about the old Kinema being up for grabs. I've some money and I've been looking round for a likely prospect in the old line and Shipden seems as good a spot as any – better, really. More opportunities, seeing as the old place is a bit backward and sleepy. And besides, it was my home.'

'You weren't very reluctant to leave it before,' she said, disliking herself, because she didn't want to give him anything, any answers, any signs of what she was feeling, any glimpse into herself. Yet it was impossible to keep the bitterness down.

'Oh yes I was,' he said. 'Part of me was. I was young, Rose. Stupid. Confused. That isn't meant to be an excuse, by the way.'

'Good. Because it's a very poor one.'

He looked up at the house. 'Is your husband at home?'

'No.'

'And – Elizabeth? My stepmother told me her name,' he said at her look.

'She's at school.'

A flicker came into his eyes – perhaps a regretful realization which, she had to admit, was probably genuine.

'I imagine you probably don't want to ask me in,' he said. 'But there are things we need to talk about and it seems silly to do it here as if I were selling bootlaces or something. Besides, someone might see us, and talk. If I remember my Shipden, they love to talk.'

She didn't want him in their house. But it would be, she was resolved, the only time. And it was certainly true that they had things to talk about. She wanted Alec Taverner to know exactly where he stood.

She stood aside, somehow not wanting to turn her back on him, and gestured to the door. 'This way.'

In the living room he sat, uninvited. Rose stayed on her feet. He gave the room an amiable, incurious look, and then his eyes lit on the piano.

'Oh, you still play?' he said conversationally.

'Yes.' Something you didn't destroy, she thought; and then was annoyed with herself. These mutinous thoughts were getting in the way. 'Look, I don't know why you came here, but I can say all I've got to say to you quite quickly. I'm married, and Elizabeth and I have a very happy home and we're settled. There really isn't any place for you in the scheme of things and I hope you've got the sense to realize that. Maybe we'll be living in the same town but I don't see that we need have anything to do with each other, now that that's straight between us.'

'Is he good to you?'

'What?'

'Your husband. A doctor, I think Dolly said. Is he good to you?'

'Yes, very.'

Alec nodded, thoughtfully. 'I wasn't good to you. I know that. It didn't mean, though, that I stopped loving you.'

She let out a scornful breath. 'Oh, please . . .'

'No, hear me out. As I said, I'm not in the market for excuses. I'm just trying to explain how it happened. We were – we were both very young—'

'I grew up fast, Alec. Believe me, I grew up fast.'

'So I can see. But you were probably more grown-up than I was even then. I just got – scared. This tremendous, overwhelming thing – becoming a father. Me, a father! God knows, I wasn't fit for it. Even I knew that, and I was pretty good at hiding things from myself back then. And so I ran. It was bad, I know – unforgivable, probably; but surely understandable. I'm only human. And it didn't alter my feelings about you, not deep down.'

'Of course it did,' she said. 'You were very keen on me when I wasn't pregnant and not at all keen on me when I was. I'd call that a pretty significant alteration, wouldn't you?'

He sighed, hanging his head: gave her a rueful glance. 'You always did see things more clearly than me.'

She turned to look out of the window. Having him here was almost intolerable. She felt like a bomb on the verge of explosion.

'It was years ago. It's all over. There are no feelings of any sort, either way. That's all. Just get that into your mind, and then go.'

'There is something else, Rose. Elizabeth. I really would like to see her.'

'Why?'

'Well, it's natural, isn't it? She is my kid after all.'

'I don't see that she's yours in any way that can—' Rose stopped herself. 'I told you, she's at school. And I don't see why you're so eager now. I heard you came back to Norfolk some time ago. You didn't rush to see her.'

'No . . . Didn't have the guts, I suppose. But now that I'm here – I can't help thinking of her.'

'And you want to take her by the hand and tell her you're her daddy, is that it? Don't try it, Alec. I mean it.'

He frowned a little. 'I'm not a villain, Rose. I dare say you're

295

quite justified in thinking I am, but I'm not. I made a mess of things and acted badly, no doubt, but I'm still just a person like anybody else. I've got a kid and I'd like, just once, to see her. Of course I can't make you let me see her if you don't want to, but I'm just saying how I feel.'

He was making her seem like the unreasonable, unnatural one: it was a pretty good trick.

'I don't want you to see her,' she said.

'If I'm going to be living in Shipden, I surely will sooner or later.'

'I know. But I don't want you to see her in the way you mean. What would be the point of that? You're nothing to do with her. She has a father now.'

Alec leaned back, watching her. 'How does he feel about that? Your husband?'

'He loves Elizabeth very much. We're a family.'

'Doesn't resent the kid?'

'Not at all. You see, this time I picked a good one.'

He laughed in a melancholy way. 'Touché,' he said getting to his feet. 'Listen, Rose, the fact is I am going to be around. But I can promise that I won't bother you, if that's what you want. I'm not utterly obtuse. And I'm not looking for a way back, either.'

'Oh good,' she said, with a high broken laugh that was not far off a sob.

'No. That would be stupid of me – nearly as stupid as I was before. After all, you're married now.'

'There would be no way back for you even if I wasn't.'

'Really?' He looked closely at her. 'Well, you know, there's one point you've got to give me.'

'Yes?'

'Yes. You got married: you found someone else. Me – no. I never found anyone else who came close . . . Oh yes, I've been around, but . . . there's never been any comparison.'

'Even if it mattered, I don't think I can believe that.'

He shrugged. 'All right. But the one thing I never did was

lie to you. I'm glad, anyway, that everything came all right for you. I just wish – you know, that things had been different.' He went to the door. 'I think Elizabeth's a lovely name, by the way. Goodbye, Rose.'

# THIRTY-THREE

It was possible to believe you were strong, to act as if you were strong, to convince others that you were strong, and yet not be strong at all. So Rose found after Alec had gone – for she sat down and burst into tears, and for some time felt so weak and wobbly that she simply couldn't get out of the chair.

This wasn't how it was meant to be. Alec Taverner's power to affect her in any vital way was supposed to have died long ago. But she hadn't reckoned with the sheer disturbing strangeness of having him sitting a few feet away from her, of speaking to him, of knowing that this was a man to whom she had given herself and whose child she had had and who had cast a long shadow over her life – and yet who still existed in the everyday world, mundane, casual, no more dramatic or demonic than the man who brought the coals.

And as is usually the case with anticipated encounters, she had thought only of what she would say to him, not what he would say to her. What he had said did not impress her or even surprise her – looking back at it, it was pure Alec in its easy plausibility – but it was still upsetting to have to listen to. It provoked emotion, and she did not want to manifest emotion in his presence. She wished to be a stone to him, a carved image.

At last she went upstairs to wash her face. On the landing she met Mrs Penn, who had just finished changing the laundry: but one of the many virtues of Mrs Penn was that she never saw or heard anything unless you wanted her to. Rose was some time at her dressing table making herself presentable; it was nearly time to collect Elizabeth from school and she didn't want the little girl to see any signs of her mother's distress.

Elizabeth. There was, damn him for it, a definite resemblance, as Dolly had said.

With bafflement Rose wondered whether, as he had seemed to suggest, he had really believed he had a chance with her again after all that had happened. Had he, over the past five years, become deeply stupid – which he had certainly not been before?

Perhaps she should take it in the same spirit as his talk of the Kinema and the entertainment line. It was a matter of opportunities. Alec was above all an opportunist, who would take whatever came his way. Almost without being able to help himself, he had made a quick assessment of his chances. It was a more likely explanation than believing that he had spent the past five years in an agony of regret.

Horrible meeting. At least it was over; though she could not feel that that was the end of it. He had wanted to see Elizabeth, and he might stick by that, if he wanted to keep his foot in the door of her life. There was no telling.

One thing was certain: she wouldn't run. She was settled and happy here, James had his practice, and the little panicked voice that had suggested begging James that they should move away had been swiftly quashed. If there had to be a fight to keep the new family together, then let it be here on their own ground.

She set out to collect Elizabeth from school. At the foot of Hill Rise she heard the toot of a horn behind her, and James drew up alongside in the Talbot.

'Hop in,' he said, 'we'll go together.'

'You've finished your rounds?'

'Yes, all hypochondriacs. Told 'em to pull themselves together.' He kissed her as she got into the car. 'You look and smell wonderful.'

'And I flower all the year round,' she said, putting her arms round him. The fresh scent of him was attractive too. After the distressing business she had just been through, it made her heart ache sweetly like the sight of home after long exile.

'Rose, what we were saying earlier – you know, about him—'

'I've seen him,' she said: this time there must be no hesitation.

James shut off the engine.

'Where?'

'He came to the house this afternoon. I'm glad,' she said, fixing James's eyes with her own. 'I'm glad we got it over with straight away.'

'We?'

'Yes . . . Alec and myself. I've told him where he stands. I've told him to keep away. I made it all very clear to him, and he went away.'

James's hands tapped restlessly on the steering wheel. 'Came to the house . . . my God, the bloody impudence of the man.'

'I know,' she said. 'But he went away and that's it.'

'Is it? He's still going to be living in Shipden, I suppose?'

'Yes. But as I said to you earlier, I can live with that if you can.'

'What . . . what precisely did he want? Coming to see you like that?'

She hesitated, then wished she had not. 'What he said was, we were bound to bump into each other since he was coming to live here, and that it was best to – break the ice, as he put it. And he said he wanted to see Elizabeth. I said I didn't want him to. He seemed to accept it but I don't know whether he'll try again. I think he was just being sentimental – just let me see her once and that sort of thing.'

'Oh, the heart bleeds,' James said, and his lips were uncharacteristically thin for a moment. 'Did he . . . upset you?'

'I don't think he meant to. But it's not something I can just shrug off – seeing him like that after all this time.'

'Of course he meant to upset you. Don't defend him, Rose. That man doesn't need any special pleading.'

The sharpness of his tone surprised her.

'I'm not defending him,' she said. 'But this is what I mean – he's just a person, a person I was once involved with. He's not some curse or – or phantom that's going to haunt us. He can't have any influence on our lives unless we let him.'

'Can't he? He's already been in our house. He wants to see his daughter. He wanted to see *you* – didn't he?'

'I suppose. But it doesn't matter if he did. I'm not interested in anything he's got to say.'

'It's just the thought of him there . . . Did you have to go and let him in?'

'Yes, because we're grown-up people and I wanted to set him straight and – and the last thing I want to give him is a drama.'

Frowning, James said, 'I'm surprised you'd want to see him after what happened.'

'I didn't – don't want to see him. But it had to happen.'

'Yes,' he said, staring at the road. 'It had to happen.'

'James. You're the man I married.'

'I know . . . but he wasn't around then, was he?'

'That's a ridiculous thing to say.'

He ran his hand irritably through his hair. 'I'm sorry . . . I'm sorry, I am truly sorry, I – I just can't be reasonable when it comes to that man.'

'Alec. Alec Taverner. He's going to be around, so it's best to get used to his name.'

'Obviously.'

She stared at him more in perplexity than anger. 'James, you knew right from the start how things were with me. You knew that I had a *past*, as they say. I don't see what's changed.'

'Yes, but that past never really ended, did it? There was never a firm line drawn under it. He was still around, and there was Elizabeth, and – and it didn't really end.'

'It did for me,' she said, angry now. 'If you can't understand

302

that, then you can't understand anything about me.'

He blew out a long breath. 'If he hadn't found you married when he came back,' he said, 'do you think he would have tried to get back together with you?'

'That question doesn't apply,' she said, a little uneasy.

'Hypothetically, then. Do you think he would?'

'I don't know. He might. But even if I wasn't married to you, he wouldn't have any chance.'

James sighed, and said in a tone more like his own, 'It isn't that I doubt you. I know it might seem that way but it isn't so. I just keep thinking of him and – well, he must have had something about him, a good deal about him, for what happened between you to have happened—'

'Yes. I fell head over heels for him. Is that what you want to hear? I was very young and rather innocent and I'd never known anything like it and it was all wonderfully exciting. And it ended in disaster. A mistake. Didn't you make a mistake yourself?'

'Yes. But that was different. That was never – a great romance.'

'Didn't you say the girl married a soldier?' Rose said.

'That has nothing to do with it.'

'And you were very hurt?'

'Not that much. Like I said, in my case it wasn't a great romance.'

She knew that James could be intensely stubborn; but this stubbornness was like flint. 'I don't know what I can do or say,' she said.

'Tell me not to be such a bloody fool,' he said, lighting a cigarette.

'Would you listen?'

'Yes, I'd listen.'

'Don't be such a bloody fool, James.'

'All right.' He looked at his watch. 'We'd better go and pick Elizabeth up.'

She breathed a little easier, but she was not taken in. He

was putting up a front for her sake, but what was going on behind it she could only guess.

Elizabeth was highly delighted at being picked up in the car. 'Daddy,' she said, 'I wish I could ride home every day!'

It was the first time she had called him 'Daddy' spontaneously. But looking at James's face, Rose saw that this didn't have the effect on him it should have had. It had been spoilt.

# THIRTY-FOUR

It was early evening a few days after this when James received a telephone call from the undermanager of the Grand Hotel. He knew the cold precise tones at once.

'Dr Blanchard, I'm sorry to disturb you at this time, but we have a little trouble here and I wonder if you could come over at once.'

A guest taken ill, James supposed. 'I'll come. What's the trouble?' His own tone was short: he did not have the friendliest feelings towards the undermanager.

'I'm afraid it's Cherry – our late employee. He seems to have taken leave of his senses. He entered the building, quite against permission, and has climbed out on to a balcony on the third floor. He's threatening to throw himself off.' There was a pause. 'I really don't know who else to apply to.'

Dear God, thought James. Guiltily he recognized that his mind had been wrapped up in something else entirely recently, to the exclusion of poor Tom Cherry, and that fact gave him an irrational feeling that this was all his fault.

'Emergency,' he told Rose as he hurried out. He didn't want to say more: he felt too responsible.

At the Grand the undermanager was waiting for him in the lobby, and at once ushered him skywards in the hydraulic lift.

'I don't know how he got in,' he told James. 'No one saw him. I do hope you can help us, Dr Blanchard. This is really not what one wishes to see in a respectable hotel. We have our reputation. Fortunately we haven't a great many guests at this time of the year.'

James looked at the bloodless face. He was going to say something, but decided it probably wasn't worth it.

They entered an unused guest room on the top floor. Two maids were there, gawping as if at a free show. The window that gave on to the balcony was blocked by the blue-clad figures of two policemen.

'. . . Don't be a fool, lad,' one of them was saying, in a rumbling monotone. 'Don't be a fool, now. Come on in. Don't be a fool.' He sounded almost bored.

They stood aside to let James through. The balcony was about five feet square, with a wrought-iron railing. Tom Cherry was perched on this like a man sitting on a five-bar gate, his hands loosely gripping the railing, his knees up. Below him, there was a long drop to the concrete sea wall.

Tom was humming. The tune sounded like 'Champagne Charlie'.

'Tom,' James said. His heart was in his mouth, and he was desperate not to startle Tom into movement. 'It's me.'

Tom turned his head very slightly, like a blind person, towards the sound of James's voice.

'I'm not cracked, Doctor,' he said, 'if that's what you're thinking.'

'I know you're not.'

'Course you do. You're a doctor. You see?' he said raising his voice. 'The doc says I'm not. So it must be right.'

The back of Tom's hair was sticking up, and his ears were red from the cold. He had on a stiff collar and tie. He reminded James, heartbreakingly, of a little boy.

'Tom – there's no need for this. Truly, there isn't.' James tried to keep his voice steady, but he was desperately nervous: he had no experience of this kind of thing. He had known that Tom's state of mind was depressed and unstable, but he had not supposed it plumbing depths such as this; and there was no room now for another misjudgement. He could feel chill perspiration all over his body beneath his clothes. Dear God, he thought, not Tom – not after all he had been through.

'Well, don't jump to conclusions, Doctor. I haven't made up my mind to do it, you see. I'm sort of getting the feel of it . . . I'm pretty certain, though,' he added reflectively, rocking a little. 'I'm pretty certain.'

James threw a furiously questioning glance back at the undermanager, who shrugged fastidiously. 'He can have his job back,' he said, 'I've told him that.'

'I can hear you. I'm not deaf,' Tom said.

'Tom,' James said, 'I know the job isn't everything – but perhaps it's a start. Perhaps—'

'Job,' Tom said. 'Well, of course they're going to say that when I'm perching up here. It don't make any odds anyway. It's too late for that. I've had it. Not wanted on voyage. Oh, I dare say you can give me plenty of reasons for living. But not *good* reasons. Not for the way I feel.'

'Tom, I'm not going to say I know how you feel, because I don't. No one can know how you feel. But what I can say is that pain and suffering – no matter how bad they are, how unbearable they seem – they can be made better. Things can always be helped.'

'You believe that, do you, Doctor?'

'I wouldn't do this job if I didn't. I know I've failed you as far as the pain in your lungs and your skin goes. They're as bad as ever, aren't they? But I want to go on trying, with your help. You've overcome such a lot, Tom. You fought through the world's most terrible war and you came through. I believe you can overcome this.'

'That's nice of you, Doctor,' Tom said, and gave a quick jagged smile over his shoulder. 'The thing is, I don't believe you.'

'Please, Tom. Come in.'

Tom shook his head, looking down with a dreamy expression. Voices could be faintly heard down below: people walking the seafront under the gaslamps had spotted him and were gathering.

Suddenly Tom leant forward. The policeman behind James

made a move, but James stopped him.

'Hello there, sir!' Tom was waving downward. 'Me? Oh, I'm just – just hanging around.' He chuckled.

Faintly, James caught the shouted words from below: '. . . Don't come down – I'll come up!'

'Now then, lad, what's going on?' the policeman said, as if he suspected Tom of being in the midst of some subtle crime.

'Very nice fellow coming up to see me,' Tom said. 'I wouldn't mind a word with that fellow, you know. If that's all right. He is staying here, so I should *think* he's allowed in.'

James looked at the undermanager, who said, 'What's the gentleman's name, Cherry?'

'Why, Mr Taverner, of course. A real decent sort.'

James felt the blood rush to his face.

'Anna,' the undermanager said to one of the maids, 'step out and see that Mr Taverner can find us.'

'Decent sort,' Tom was muttering into the empty air, 'not many left.'

'In here, sir,' came the maid's voice down the passage, 'asking to see you, apparently . . .'

So, at last, this was the man. James tried to show nothing of what he was feeling. In fact he felt guilty for feeling anything, in such a situation; and it was a measure of how much the thought of this man had got under his skin that his jealous resentment overcame his concern for Tom for several moments, and he could hardly bring himself to look round at the newcomer.

'Mr Taverner, sir,' the undermanager was saying, 'would you be so good as to . . .? So sorry about this, but Cherry insists . . .'

Suddenly James was brushed aside, his place at the window taken by a dark man of medium height, about his own age.

'Tom!' Alec Taverner said. 'What the devil are you doing?'

Tom looked over his shoulder with a faint sheepish smile. 'Just making my mind up, sir.'

'To do what? Chuck yourself off? Oh, you bloody fool.'

'Now don't start trying to talk me out of it,' Tom said. 'I'm sorry, sir, but please don't.'

'Oh, I'm not, don't you worry.' Standing in the window so that the lights from below silhouetted him, his hands jammed in his pockets, Alec Taverner seemed no more than mildly irritated. He had an outdoors smell about him. Older, thought James randomly, older than he had supposed: images of a young Lothario. This man was sturdy, mature.

'I just thought better of you, that's all,' Alec Taverner went on. 'But you go on and jump, if that's what you want. Be a coward.'

Different – entirely different from the way he had pictured him. My God, thought James, here is poor Tom about to kill himself and you're chewing over your obsession with this man. What does that say about you?

'Perhaps I am a coward,' Tom said. 'I don't particularly care any more. Ask the doctor, there. Go on – you ask Dr Blanchard. Ask him if I'm right – right in the head.'

'All right . . . Dr Blanchard?' Taverner turned, gave James a quick glance, no more than a soldierlike signal. 'Is Tom right?'

'Right as rain,' James said.

'No, he's not,' Taverner said, turning back to the balcony. 'He's cracked in the head. Of course you are!' he barked, as Tom protested. 'Why else are you perching there and threatening to do yourself in, man? Why else would you choose to throw your life away, when all those pals of yours who died would have wanted you to live? What do you think they would say to it – their old mucker Cherry surviving that bloody show in France and then coming home and deciding to throw his life away for nothing? They'd say you were cracked and they'd be damn well right.'

'It ain't for nothing,' Tom said. 'You don't know – you don't know what it's—'

'Of course I bloody know. I know all about it. Cracked – you must be cracked, Tom, that's all I can say. Simply because good honest decent fellows like you don't do this sort of thing.

Come down here, look me in the face and tell me you're not cracked, and I might believe you, but not when you're flapping about up there.'

Tom began mournfully beating the palms of his hands against his temples. 'You don't understand . . .'

'What's amiss then, Tom? You tell me. Lost a leg? Can't see? Can't get a girl? I doubt it, but tell me if so. Or is it your work? Can't be something as trivial as that, surely? Or just angry at the big bad world? Want to hit out? Well, maybe you're scared to, and that's why you're up there. You want to hit out but you're scared to. Well, come on. Come and take a pop at me if you're so full of it. Come on – take a pop. Scared? Come and hit me, Tom, or are you too yellow? Or are you just cracked in the head?'

Bellowing like a bull, crimson-faced, Tom jumped down from the balcony and went at Alec Taverner with windmilling fists. Taverner caught hold of him, gripping him tightly by the arms, and for a bizarre moment it was as if they were dancing. Then Tom's body slumped and he began weeping.

'All right, old fellow. All right.' Taverner had his arms round Tom's shoulders now, and guided him gently into the room. 'That's it. I do understand, you know. People do. That's what you've got to remember. Sorry if I was a bit hard on you, but it seemed the only way – one old comrade to another. Let's have a drink on it, eh? Let's go down to the bar and have a bloody good drink and a talk about old times. Come on. Come with me.'

Tom Cherry followed him like a tired child. At the door Taverner made a face as if to say, 'I'll look after him.' The maids goggled.

'Well.' The undermanager sniffed. 'I'm sorry, Dr Blanchard, it turns out you weren't needed after all. Anna,' he added with a fastidious gesture at the window, 'sweep that balcony and clean the sill, there's mud on it.'

James found he wanted a drink too, but not here. He

descended alone in the lift, and leaving the Grand walked along the esplanade to the Victoria.

He hated himself, for he was not thinking about Tom Cherry and his anguish, but about Alec Taverner.

In the lounge bar of the Victoria, dim and chintzy, a frosty barmaid served him gin, banging the cash drawer shut as if he had insulted her. A couple of mustachioed men, the types who had their own tankards above the bar, stood jawing about the fire with their legs propped showily on the fender.

Different, thought James: entirely different from what he had expected. Yet in a way he could not say, because he had never built up a single coherent picture of Alec Taverner in his mind. Like the sea-serpent, he had been a jumble of half-mythical images: the irresponsible charmer, handsome, debonair yet democratic, easy, confident, smiling . . .

Instead there was this lean, mature, quietly dressed, rather sharp-featured, entirely unclassifiable man who was both less and more than James had imagined.

Tasting the juniper tang of gin, sitting back, James saw in a single lucid moment that he could stop this now. He could simply face up to the absurdity of his jealousy as an emotion – its indignity, its pettiness – even leaving aside whether it was justified or not: simply view it as something he would not like to have within himself, and master it by an act of will. Overcome it, as Tom's despairing impulse had been conquered by Alec Taverner. *Now you've seen him: now stop it.*

Yet he had no sooner set about erecting a barrier than the old sick tide of jealous speculation came flooding back.

James could understand Rose's bafflement at his behaviour – because, after all, this thing hadn't troubled him at first. He couldn't quite explain it himself. He had simply found that as time went on he couldn't stop thinking of the man who was Elizabeth's father. It had grown on him like a bad physical habit. And it had come to a head, he knew, with Dolly's careless comment at that picnic by the path of poppies.

Probably it had begun with a simple possessiveness born

311

out of the passion of his love for Rose: he just didn't like to think of anyone else with her. Then, after Dolly's remark, he had found himself imagining Rose and Taverner together – and had imagined them somehow as *natural* together as he and Rose were not. In this way he convinced himself that she would never have thrown caution to the winds with him as she had with Taverner. It just wouldn't have happened. He did not exert that magnetism. In bed he would torment himself with such thoughts. From these feelings it had been a swift transition to the next stage – of thinking that Rose would surely recognize what he would recognize: that she would feel the lack of that magnetism, that she would wake up from this marriage and realize she had made a mistake.

With feelings like this upon him, to James the return of Alec Taverner to Shipden was like the fulfilment of a doleful prophecy.

James thought again about the man he had just seen. He tried to view him as an anonymous individual, shorn of his associations; but he could not do it. Taverner was for him no more a neutral figure than a pantomime villain in a circle of flames. And it was hard that this first encounter should see him, in effect, beating James at something. James's sense of irony was usually well developed and would have kindled at this, seeing the whole thing as too wry for anything but laughter; but jealousy destroyed irony, and in the scene in the hotel room he could see only an ominous reflection of their positions. Because he already had it fixed in his mind that he had to compete with Alec Taverner – whether in the flesh or as a ghost of the past – their first meeting was inevitably a contest, and James had lost.

He had another gin. The grim barmaid glared at him, as if seeing his thoughts, and that brought him back to a realization of just how unworthy they were. Don't you trust your wife, then? he asked himself. Don't you trust Rose?

He told himself that he did, and he believed it. But when she told him that Alec Taverner meant nothing to her now, he took this as an expression of loyalty rather than truth. He believed that she genuinely wanted to love him, but was hampered by a smothered longing for what had been.

Well, he thought, who could blame her? Obviously the man had something.

Finishing his drink, James debated whether to have another – and debated it an unusually long time. It was a reflection in miniature of his general state, for James was almost literally in two minds. One side of him knew quite well that he was being ridiculous, brooding like some petty provincial Othello. But the other side was in the ascendant. Unfortunately, for a very rational and logical man James was burdened with a vivid imagination. If he had been more mentally sluggish he would have been happier.

As a result of this, he was beginning to withdraw emotionally when at home. He thought of this as a safeguard, even as an act of fairness to Rose – if he were harbouring such thoughts and feelings, he ought to keep them away from her, who had done nothing to deserve them. So he withdrew, and did not think that in the spaces he left, misunderstanding could develop. He had already decided that when he went home he would say nothing of having seen Alec Taverner. He thought this would be the mature thing to do.

It certainly never occurred to him that maturity – not worldly maturity, but maturity of the heart – was what he lacked, or that in this regard he and Rose were at different stages. He was thirty-two, a successful man in his profession, and a married householder: and he couldn't see past all this to the painfully young, desperately emotional self inside. And if he did happen to glimpse it, he did not suppose that Rose would love or like or understand that self – let alone greet it with tender recognition.

# THIRTY-FIVE

In November Sylvia Vickery went to a drinks party at the house of Cyril Askew, the manager of the golf club. It took all her considerable persistence to persuade her parents to go. The idea of a drinks party was not trusted; in Shipden any social taking of drinks was an inevitable precursor to a heavy dinner of brown Windsor and saddle of lamb. Just going to someone's house to take drinks seemed rather racy, perhaps rowdy – as Mr Askew, in his innocently rakish way, very much hoped.

Dr Vickery might have gone along more readily if he had thought there was a chance of offloading Sylvia on Mr Askew. But that had been in the air for a couple of years now and had come to nothing. Mr Askew, lonely, gallant and touching forty, was probably still keen, but Sylvia had never seemed to give him any encouragement.

Sylvia knew Mr Askew's feelings very well, and it suited her that they should continue. He was not for her: it would look too second-rate, and to Sylvia how it looked was all-important. But to have him thinking he was in with a chance, and doggedly dancing attendance on the strength of it, was pleasant to her highly developed sense of self-importance.

Besides, it was just not in Sylvia to refuse any invitation. If it were possible, she would have been out all the time, and in fact would never even have gone to sleep if that had been socially required of her. Nothing less than being the absolute tyrant of a powerful nation with an aggressive foreign policy would have absorbed the full measure of Sylvia Vickery's unfocused will and energy. Instead she had to dispose of it, somehow, in the small minglings of provincial society.

So she got her way, and the Vickerys went up to Mr Askew's house, which was a redbrick villa up by the links, set about with pines and hopefully named Folie à Deux. Inside the place was of rather a sporting character, with mounted trout in glass cases and oars from Mr Askew's university rowing days on the walls, but Mr Askew had done his best to create a modern atmosphere: he served strong mixed drinks and was continually darting about to offer Balkan cigarettes and wind up the gramophone.

Quite a few Shipdenites had braved this social experiment: the Trueloves were here and Leo Liddell and the Crimminses and even the Snells. All were old familiar faces, in fact, except one – and that one was very interesting to Sylvia.

She had only known Alec Taverner to exchange a greeting with, back before the war; but she homed in on him at once as if they were old and firm friends, and cornered him. Since hearing of his return to Shipden she had been eagerly waiting for this, and now she would have tied him down rather than let him get away from her.

Dr Vickery watched his daughter, wondering. Mr Truelove, following his gaze and reading his thoughts, said in a low voice, 'Funny to have that chap back in Shipden. Think he's been tamed a bit?'

'It would seem so,' Dr Vickery said, lip judiciously jutting. 'The war, of course, will have done that. He was made captain, and decorated, I understand.'

'Come into money too. Going all out with the Kinema. It's good to see an entrepreneurial spirit in Shipden, I think. It was unfortunate about that business with Rose Jordan, but that's all in the past, I suppose. Or is it once a rogue, always a rogue? I wonder . . .'

'You're absolutely right,' Sylvia was saying, her eyes glued to Alec's face. 'The old place *does* need shaking up. It's what I've always maintained. We're far too stuffy here.'

'That has its charm, of course,' Alec said. 'I wouldn't want Shipden to lose its character. But we need modern entertainments if we're going to compete with Yarmouth and Hunstanton for visitors. Times are changing. The people who used to fill those thumping great hotels can just as well go abroad now. We'll have to attract the less well-to-do. Shipden will have to become – ' he whispered it ' – democratic.'

'Oh, and not before time. I've always been democratic,' Sylvia said. 'I can mix with anyone, always have. Just today I was down at The Rows, visiting a woman there who's a bit of a favourite of mine. Some people would say how could you, but it doesn't bother me a bit.'

'The Rows, eh? They were pretty grim when I left, as I remember. Hasn't the council done anything about them? Stupid question, I know.'

'You'll have to join the council yourself, Mr Taverner.'

'Alec. Think they'd elect me?'

'I don't see why not. You're a property owner – and a native of the town, come to that, even though you were away from it for a while. But then lots of men were, with the war.'

'H'm. Not all of them were – under such a cloud,' he said, after seeming to debate for a moment whether to say this, and then flatteringly to decide he could.

'A cloud . . .? Oh good heavens, that.' Sylvia looked worldly. 'Well, yes, there was a lot of gossip – when isn't there? – but I wouldn't say you were under a cloud.'

'Well, it was all a sad business, and I acted like a damn fool, I'm afraid,' Alec Taverner said. 'My only excuse is youth, plus wartime – which is no excuse, really. But then there's no point in hiding or pretending. What happened happened. I can talk of this to you because you've obviously got sense, and aren't about to throw up your hands in scandal at the mere mention of it . . . Anyhow, it all seems to have turned out all right in the end.'

'With Rose? Oh – I suppose so. In a way.'

Alec raised his expressive eyebrows.

'Well – really, Alec, I don't know how much you know.'

'Just that she married pretty well. This doctor chap – Blanchard.'

'James. You've met him?'

'Briefly. Seems a decent sort.'

'Oh, yes. Our James is sterling. We know him well – actually we know him better than anybody. And so if anyone could have warned him, we should; but of course, you simply can't tell people how to run their lives. Still – as you say – it hasn't turned out too badly, all things considered. To all appearances, anyway.'

'What – they're not suited, you mean?'

Sylvia half closed her eyes, looking consciously tactful. 'I don't think I'm speaking out of turn when I say it was something of a marriage of convenience. But what can one do? Regrets come after, as they say.'

'I must admit, I can't quite picture Rose quietly married to some sobersides doctor. She was always so full of life.'

'Exactly. And I believe she still is, which . . . Well, I've said too much. It may yet turn out all right.'

'I suppose everyone has to settle down eventually,' he said, after giving her a close look. 'I never thought I would – but to be honest, I'm rather enjoying domesticity. Yes, I've taken a house in Shepherd Street, up above the station. Just a bachelor sort of domesticity at the moment, but it's a start. I'm afraid I'm not the tidiest of men – and I've been so busy with the Kinema and whatnot – so really it's just a den at present.'

'Really, Alec, what men *are* tidy? You all make dens for yourselves, and go to pot without someone to look after you. What you need is a woman to come in daily and clean up and cook you a meal.'

'My dear Sylvia,' he said, with a twist of his wry brows, 'it's very kind, but I couldn't hear of it.'

'Oh my goodness gracious, not me! Oh my Lord, I didn't mean me – ha ha ha . . .' Laughing, Sylvia threw her head

318

back, so that the laugh, and the high old time they were having, were visible all over the room.

Not *that* democratic, then, thought Alec. He had a swift, thumbnail way of measuring people up, and Sylvia Vickery he thought a tasteless bloodsucking sort of woman who, in a phrase he had picked up in the army, he wouldn't touch with somebody else's. But he was a social animal, who genuinely liked talking to practically anyone, and he had besides something of Sylvia's acquisitiveness in people. For Alec all human contacts were both potentially useful and fascinating on their own account: he could no more deliver a snub than a miser could forgo picking up a penny from the pavement. He was in fact rather like Sylvia in his combination of voracious curiosity and self-concern, though where Sylvia moved blindly in a fog, ignorant of her own motives, he knew very well what he was about.

'No, no,' Sylvia chuckled, 'the woman I was telling you about – that's who I mean. My Nell Henning. She's a gem really. A lot of people would write her off, but I spotted her. I saw what she was really like – that's a talent I've got, I don't know where it comes from. She's a splendid woman really, a terrific workhorse, and very much in need of extra earnings. Now I happen to know that one word from me, and she would take the job like a shot.'

'I didn't know I'd advertised the vacancy,' Alec said with a light laugh.

'Oh yes, you have. You have, you know. Tell me this – when was your kitchen last cleaned?'

'Ah . . . I give in.'

'There you are, you see. Now, Nell Henning. What I can promise you is that you won't have to pay over the rate. And I'll be personally responsible for her. She'll report to me and so on, and answer to me if she's not pulling her weight. Like I say, she's a bit of a protégée of mine. Right, now when can she start? I'll bring her to your house, and introduce her. Tomorrow? How about tomorrow?'

'All right. Tomorrow it is. I say, you don't waste any time, do you?'

For a moment there was an edge, a hint of mocking innuendo, which even Sylvia's obtuseness caught. She coloured, and looked flustered. Alec, being fundamentally not unkind, quickly erased the moment by saying, 'Actually, this is the answer to a prayer. I can let you in on this – I'm hoping to take up more than just the Kinema in the property line. And if I'm ever to entertain investors and so on, I'll need a decent household.'

'Entertaining? Like the sound of it,' put in Mr Askew, presenting his sad-jolly moustache between them. 'Just what we need. More of that the merrier. What do you say, Syl? We need a bit of a spark in us, eh?'

'Oh, some of us have it already,' she said airily, with a glance of collusion at Alec.

She was enjoying being cruel, Alec saw. He did not miss much.

This was what Alec Taverner was like. People were all to him. He did not care for anything that was abstract: animals, or music that had no voice part, or scenery or solitude. He had been called a philanderer and perhaps was – but this did not take into account the fact that he was absorbed by people as others are by books, and would just as readily finish one and go on to another.

Nor was it fair to call him calculating. At a young age he had discovered that his boyish grin, which came to him quite naturally and was not in the least studied, had an effect on women; he had appreciated it and employed it accordingly, but it was still natural. His amorousness, which was strong, was like the exercise of a personal talent; there was nothing in it, as with some womanizers, of resentment or of self-doubt masked as self-assertion. He was drawn to women not because he hated them but because he liked them. He did not get on greatly with men, unless in some specific situation where their roles were defined, like a theatre company or an army unit. He had never really had a friend and did not much want one. Human relations in which there was no sexual element – at least as an exciting potential – struck him as dull and dry.

Certainly Alec Taverner was changeable, unsteady, difficult to pin down. He knew it – though this did not trouble him because, from the adoration of a doting stepmother to the passionate attachment of several young women to the devoted loyalty of his unit in the trenches, he had long been accustomed to thinking of himself as fundamentally lovable, faults included. But besides, this changeableness did not mean that he was trivial or detached in his feelings. Rather, each new idea, each new project, each new romance engaged him totally: it engulfed him: it was the greatest thing ever. And so, naturally, was the next. Giving something up was easy: he made a dramatic renunciation, without regrets, and moved on.

About the matter of Rose Jordan there were regrets, but they were couched in sentimental terms. Alec concentrated most of his selfhood on love and its ramifications, very much as women are represented as, or accused of, doing. Because of this, nothing in his emotional landscape loomed much larger than anything else. It was all peaks – in other words all level. Rose's pregnancy was a poignant episode in the romantic novel that was his life, as were his going to war, coming back to find her married, and sighing over the fact of his five-year-old child who had never called him Daddy. He did feel this quite sincerely, but his feelings were so circumscribed within narrow romantic limits that it was only with a sense of pathos. The coolness of tragedy and irony were beyond him. It especially touched him that the child was a little girl; he would perhaps have not felt quite so sentimental about a little boy.

As for Rose, he believed – for he had a sharp realism in him too – that she had been better off without him. Going away in 1915, he had said this quite seriously and not out of pusillanimous excuse-making; though at the time he had certainly not wanted fatherhood and all that went with it.

Now, perhaps, he felt differently. Seeing Rose again did bring home to him what he had lost, though again in sentimental terms. Because he had great confidence in himself and a ready disposition to fall in love with women, the loss did not seem irreplaceable or worth a lifetime of anguished regret.

All the same, something stirred. They had been good together. Alec did not plan ahead: he believed in serendipity. The Kinema was an opportunity that had happened to come his way, and he had taken it. He followed his impulses, believing that whatever the heart said must be right. Again rather like Sylvia Vickery, Alec thought that whatever happened, for good or ill, was simply on the cards.

# THIRTY-SIX

Nell Henning was happy enough to take on the charwoman's job that Sylvia Vickery got for her. The gent seemed an undemanding sort, and privately agreed a higher rate than the one Sylvia had proposed. And a man on his own wouldn't be picky, Nell thought; it was the women who were always sniffing round and making sure you'd dusted properly. It was easy enough: go to the gent's house each day at around noon, clean, see to his laundry, and have a meal ready for when he got in, whilst Mrs Scace minded the kids.

Nell knew there was more to it – of course there was, with that Vickery woman – and this was confirmed after the very first day, when Sylvia descended on her as soon as she got home and pumped her for everything she knew about the household and Mr Taverner's comings and goings. Nell cottoned on at once: she was to be a spy for Sylvia, for whatever reasons.

'Got her eye on him, you reckon, gel?' Mrs Scace said, when Nell spoke of this.

'Might be,' Nell said unconcernedly. 'Don't think she know what she's about, really. Meddling, always meddling of some sort. Do her no good, whatever it is.'

Rose still came to the church hall with James each week to the infant welfare clinic. This, and her lessons with Angelica, which still continued despite Angelica's increasing sense of nervous expectation, made a shape to Rose's week. She helped with weighing babies and untying tiny laces and buttons, and sometimes in getting the shyer mothers to talk about what was on their minds. She seemed, he thought, to enjoy it; though he had begun now to mistrust all his assumptions about her.

Several weeks had passed since he had first set eyes on Alec Taverner. He had seen nothing of him since. In the meantime there was between himself and Rose an unrestful peace. He had seen nothing, either, of Tom Cherry – and was surprised to find him waiting outside the church hall when they left after the clinic.

'Doctor – can I have a word?' Tom said, tipping his hat to Rose, and meeting James's eyes urgently.

'I'll see you in the car,' Rose said.

'Doctor, I just . . .' The pavement was thick with fallen leaves and the thick rind-like skins of conkers fallen from the chestnut trees around the church. Tom rustled about in them with the toe of his boot as if he were searching for something lost. 'I just wanted to say sorry. You know. Dragging you into all that malarkey the other week.'

'Not at all, quite all right. How are you? You haven't been to see me at the surgery of late.'

'Tell the truth, I felt embarrassed,' Tom said, still poking earnestly amongst the dead leaves. 'I'm all right now though – shaped meself up.' He lifted his head at last, and smiled shyly. 'I've got a new job.'

'That's marvellous. Not – at the Grand?'

'I couldn't go back there, not really. Even though they offered, it was . . . well, it didn't make sense. But anyhow, this is better. I'm working at the Kinema – refitting the insides. Mr Taverner gave me a job there – and he says I'll have a job with him as long as I want it. He's a real good sort. Helped me no end, he did. He get you talking and, I don't know, you get things off your chest somehow. About the war and that . . . it's like he understands . . . Anyway!' Suddenly breezy, Tom squared his shoulders. 'I wanted to let you know, and to say I'm sorry about all that daft business.'

'It wasn't daft,' James said. 'I'm . . . just sorry I couldn't have been more help.'

Rose, waiting in the car behind the church, noticed the stoniness when James rejoined her.

'What was that all about?' she said.

'Nothing. Just Tom Cherry wanting a word about his medicine.'

It had happened again, she thought – that withdrawing of himself from her.

She was disappointed. She had thought they were slowly getting back to safer ground these past weeks, with no more interference from Alec Taverner. And tonight they were to go to the mayoral charity dance at the Town Hall, an event she had been looking forward to. It was ordinary enough, but going dancing with James had a special feeling for her; and it had seemed, when the tickets came, exactly the sort of occasion to help close up the distance between them.

Yet his withdrawn mood persisted as they got ready that evening. James seemed to be clamping something down, hard, within himself. She suspected that the encounter with Tom Cherry had something to do with it, but she saw no point in quizzing him. Usually he came to himself when he was like this. And she was determined to enjoy the evening come what may.

When she came out of the dressing room, wearing her new georgette dress and garnet earrings that he had bought her on their honeymoon, it was as if he were seeing her for the first time.

He was sitting on the bed aimlessly toying with his tie, and it was with a startled look that he said: 'My God, you look wonderful.'

That was more like it, she thought; and, naturally sanguine, she began to feel that things would be all right. Only one anxiety hummed like a bass note beneath her uplifted mood: would Alec be there tonight?

In a way she half hoped that he would. If she and James

could be in the same place with him for an evening and get through it in a normal fashion, then much would be achieved. But when they arrived she realized it would be hard to spot Alec quickly. The town hall chamber was already very full and, Shipden still going in for evening dress, the men all looked the same – though it was noticeable that few could wear it with ease as James did: their stiff shirtfronts and dancing shoes made them move like awkward pigeons. The boiler had been stoked too high and there was a languorousness about the room, something a little suppressed and stifling. On the dais a small band played a waltz, reedy and slow, making the rhythm more like a limp than a dance step, and accompanying it there was a slushy sound as feet brushed against some paper streamers that, insecurely pinned, had fallen from the ceiling.

Millie and Frank Watlyn were here, bright and high-spirited, and came over at once; Millie's sister Clara joined them too. This, Rose thought, was how it should be – friends, openness, laughter, her husband beside her – it tasted good. Even James seemed to relax – until he saw Sylvia Vickery across the room, unengaged and on the lookout for prey.

'Oh God, there's Sylvia,' James hissed. 'If she gets hold of me, it'll be that damned Henning family again, I know it, there'll be no end to it.'

'We'll save you,' Rose said.

'Yes, we'll come and rescue you,' laughed Millie.

'There is no rescue from such a fate. Even the damned fire brigade can't rescue you from that,' James said, laughing too, but in a cross-grained way, looking nervously about him.

Rose said, 'Come and dance.'

They danced, but James's body was stiff and he seemed to go off into an abstraction, head up above hers.

She tapped his shoulder.

'I wish you'd come down and join me,' she said.

He looked at her, summoned a smile. 'Sorry. Is it that bad?'

'A bit of a chill. Despite this heat.'

'Fierce, isn't it? You look cool, though.'

'Do I? I feel as if I'm – what's the ladylike term for sweating?'

'Glowing?' he said.

'That's it. Well, I'm glowing like a horse.'

He laughed, and she loved the free young sound of it.

'James – what happened with Tom Cherry?'

He gave her a rueful smile, and was about to answer when Sylvia, dancing with Mr Askew, leant into him and shouted, 'James! I'm glad you're here. We really need to talk about Nell Henning's youngest. After this dance. It is important.'

'Damn that woman,' James gritted, his jaw shutting tight.

Unusually for Shipden, the band was not good, and it was hard to keep time. Another occasion they might have laughed about this, but tonight the effect on James seemed to be like the winding of an already tight spring.

'Filthy band, isn't it?' Leo Liddell said to them as they came off the floor. 'I could have found them some better players than that. The Mayor's doing, I think – probably paying back some favour. Hark at that deadly off-rhythm – you'd know, Rose. Still keep up the music? Just don't have to pay the rent from it, eh? Jolly good. Good old lady of leisure. I say, you used to do a bit of the dance-band stuff yourself, didn't you? During the war, it was. Tinkling the ivories for the Follies.'

'That's right,' Rose said.

'Thought so.' Leo cocked his head at James. 'No end to your wife's talents, you know.'

'I know,' James said. 'I think she must have got someone else's share as well. Darling, would you like an ice?'

The ices were melting so rapidly in the stuffy heat that they dribbled off the spoon. It was doubly difficult to manage them in the crush and once James gave a furious glare when an elbow went into his back.

'. . . to be honest, I think the live stage has a fight on its hands with moving pictures . . .'

Rose knew the voice at once. Alec must be very close to them, though she couldn't see without turning right round. Her earlier feeling that it would be a good thing if he were here trickled dismally away like the ice she was struggling to eat, and her palms grew clammy. She confronted with new misgiving the fact that she had never before been with James in his presence; and the overheated air felt too electric, dangerous. Another time, perhaps; but not tonight.

Yet she refused to take the easy way out, to plead a headache and say they should go home. Running away never did any good. She abandoned the ice, and James found her a chair while he went to the men's room. Another dance had started, and after a moment she saw Alec in the midst of the twirling figures, dancing with Clara Truelove.

Suddenly Millie was at her side. Her kind eyes looked at Rose and then swivelled significantly in Alec's direction.

'I know,' Rose said. 'It really doesn't matter.'

'Makes you think, though,' Millie said. 'He's welcomed back with open arms. No nasty remarks and pointing fingers for him.'

'Water under the bridge,' Rose said. Another time she might have allowed herself some bitter reflections on this very point, but just now she was more concerned with James's reaction to his presence.

But then, as far as she knew James had never set eyes on Alec Taverner and wouldn't know him if he did see him. So there was a choice: should she say nothing – or simply say, 'That's him,' and hope they could continue with the evening? Millie had left to dance with Frank, but before Rose could give the question any thought, she found Alec standing in front of her.

'Rose. You're looking marvellous. How is it you never got any older? Oh, I know, stop it. All right. I just wanted to say – you know, what we were discussing the other week—'

'Mr Taverner, will you come and meet Mr Snell's cousin from Wymondham?' It was Mrs Snell, oozing. 'He was in the same regiment as you, I believe – dying to meet you.'

'I will, certainly, in just one minute,' he said agreeably, not moving.

Mrs Snell gave them both an interested look, tiny eyes glinting, and then wheeled her bulk away.

'About what we were saying the other week,' Alec resumed calmly.

'I think we said everything,' Rose said.

'Yes? Well, maybe not quite.' He looked sober and serious. She noticed for the first time a touch of grey at his temples. The eyes were the same, though: restless, greedy eyes. 'I ought to add that I won't pester you. That's all. I'll keep out of your way – as long as you tell me that's what you want.'

'That's what I want.'

The eyes, like sharp fragments of jet, dwelt on hers.

'All right,' he said. 'But if it's ever *not* what you want, just give me a shout. I'll be there. I've got myself a place now, by the way. Shepherd Street, number nine.'

*I'll be there*, she thought with amazement. She was on the point of letting her bitterness out by saying that as far as *being there* went, he was the last person in the world she would count on, but he had deftly slipped away.

'So, old chap,' Leo Liddell was saying to Ernie Crimmins, 'you've lost out to this Taverner fellow, then?'

'Lost out?' Ernie Crimmins, cigarette ash besprinkling the greyish front of his dress shirt, blinked at Leo Liddell through steamed-up spectacles. 'What on earth d'you mean?'

'Just what I say, old bean. He's taken on the Kinema, hasn't he? Your old baby?'

'Oh, I disposed of that particular concern, yes,' said Ernie Crimmins, noting with a righteous sniff that Liddell smelt of drink (which Ernie, for once, did not). 'Best move I ever made. Leaves me free to concentrate on the Pier Theatre, see. Moving pictures are only a sideshow anyway. They're fairground stuff. The novelty's going to wear off. The legit stage is what people always come back to.'

'From what I hear, Taverner's got ideas that way too.'

'You hear a lot,' Ernie said huffily. 'Anyway, he's a fly-by-night. I remember him years ago. No bottom to him. Bit of a brass neck coming back here and all, I reckon – it was him who got Rose Jordan into trouble, wasn't it?'

'Well, so they say,' Liddell said, smoking theatrically, eyes narrowed. 'But from what I hear, that could have been any one of a number of fellows.'

'Get out of it.'

'Oh yes! Afraid so.' Liddell nodded, looking pleased with himself. 'I know Rose pretty well, you see. Oh yes . . .'

Sylvia Vickery had slid into the vacant seat beside Rose, and said in her characteristically earnest tone, 'I think you're bearing up well, Rose. Very well.'

'Am I?'

Sylvia nodded significantly, head back. 'You don't have to say anything more to me than that. I understand, you see, whereas some people are so thick-skinned they can't spot an awkward situation. They can't feel it, and so they make the most terrible blunders.'

'Oh, I don't find anything awkward here.'

'You're like me,' Sylvia said – this was her very highest accolade. 'It's the only way, isn't it? Making the best of things. It's no good wishing things were different – you just have to show some strength of character. Some people wouldn't know where to put their faces in such a situation – but you're like me, you face it out. Ah!'

That was for James, who was back, and did not look best pleased to find her there.

'Now, James, at last. About Nell Henning's youngest – I've been meaning to have you see her—'

'If there's anything wrong,' James said, 'I'm sure she can call me in herself.'

'Well, that's just it. She doesn't spot these things.'

'A mother will know if her child's ill, Sylvia,' he said.

'Well, actually, no – it's an outsider who's far more likely to spot these things, because of the different perspective. That is an actual fact.'

'Is that a real fact,' James said, 'or one of those facts you make up?'

'Sorry,' he said to Rose, after Sylvia had gone off with the appearance of someone who has just spotted a long-lost friend across the room.

'You don't have to apologize for telling Sylvia Vickery what's what,' she said. 'I've wanted to do it myself.' And she didn't mind, at all; but still she was uncomfortable, for him and about him. The uncharacteristic rudeness showed like physical pain on his face.

Feeling an urgent need to be open, she said quickly, 'James, Alec Taverner's here.'

'I know. I just saw him.'

'. . . You know him?'

'Yes – I happened to meet him the other week.'

'You didn't tell me.'

'No. Well, he's nothing to do with us, is he?'

'That's true,' she said, 'he's nothing to do with us.' But she suspected he meant it in a different way from her.

Soon after that she danced with Frank Watlyn, and James with Millie. He did not know Millie very well yet, but he liked her; and when she said conversationally, 'Rose is looking very beautiful tonight, isn't she?' there was no reason on earth for him to resent it. But he did.

'Yes,' he said. 'She's certainly made the effort.' He was being stupid: the stupidity was pointless and self-lacerating and yet he could not help it – the spring inside him was coiled so tight. This was the most dismal revelation to James, who had always valued self-control – the revelation that there were limits to it; that the self could be a stranger, the body and mind mutinous beyond discipline.

'She doesn't need to,' Millie said, though without reproach. 'She's a natural.'

He murmured something. A deadly resentment was on him

now. Though he took care not to look consciously round the room, all the time he was scanning it for Alec Taverner. Every now and then the man would come into sight – dark alert head turning, smiling, looking self-contained and cool. Several men there who had seen service in the war wore their medals with their dress suits, but not he. An air of modesty and good humour surrounded him – a prince gracing the homespun shindig. James remembered Tom Cherry's words, uttered with a worshipful look: *he understands . . .*

'I say, Rose,' Frank Watlyn said as they danced, 'I hope you don't think badly of me – you know – taking on this contract. I actually didn't realize who the chap was at first, and then . . .'

'Of course not, Frank. Don't think that for a minute. I'm pleased for you.'

'It is a good contract . . . So it's water under the bridge, eh?'

'Water under the bridge.'

That phrase seemed to be mocking her tonight. With a doleful plunge, she wondered: did the past ever let you go? Were you to be fashioned by it for ever?

No, she wouldn't believe it. She and Elizabeth had come so far – to within hailing distance of true, solid happiness. That past *must* be conquered – even if now it had taken a substantial form instead of a ghostly one.

More ices, along with bowls of fruit cup, had been placed on the refreshment tables. There was quite a crush to get to them and James, who felt half-frantic with thirst, found himself squeezed alongside Leo Liddell as he waited.

'You know, old man, about what I was saying earlier,' Liddell said, a whiff of whisky on his breath. 'If your wife ever wanted to perform in public again – we've been trying out quite a few arrangements with piano obbligato. The new thing – nig-style, you know. Rather like this.'

He nodded his sculptured head to the band, who had begun a tune in a cautious jazz style. Glancing back, James saw that

Alec Taverner was the first to take the floor and attempt the novelty, along with Clara Truelove. Everyone seemed to be watching, with admiration.

'I don't think so,' James said.

'No? Well, you know best, I suppose.' Liddell maintained his easy, sketchy smile. 'I just wondered. I do know Rose pretty well, you see. Pretty well. We go back a long way.'

And he gave a broad, man-of-the-world wink.

Probably Liddell would not have gone so far if he had not been rather drunk. And if he had not been rather drunk, he might have made an effort to dodge the swinging punch that James threw at him. As it was, the punch landed right under his sleek chin and knocked him flying backwards. He cannoned into the unyielding bulk of Mrs Snell before hitting the floor.

'He broke my jaw!' Sitting up in a pose that ludicrously recalled the Dying Gladiator, his brilliantined hair spectacularly dishevelled, Liddell seemed to feel more outraged indignation than pain. With trembling appeal he cried, 'Did you see that? He broke it – broke my jaw!'

Dr Vickery slipped in and began helping Liddell up, running a swift professional hand over his face. 'You're all right,' he said. 'Come on, enough of this.'

'The man's mad!' Liddell said, again with an indignant appeal to the onlookers, desperately smoothing his hair.

'Yes, I'm mad,' James said. 'And I don't even have the excuse of shell shock.'

He pushed his way through the crowd to the other side of the room where Rose was standing motionless, gazing at him in as much perturbed astonishment as if he had suddenly ripped off a mask.

# THIRTY-SEVEN

She had never been so angry with him. The anger surged through her in waves that were like attacks of chronic pain, receding only to leave her trembling at their return. And James's short, tight answer to her question, that Leo Liddell had 'said something', did nothing to stem the tide.

Because even if what Leo Liddell had said had been about her, it was not *about* her, not really. There was only one thing that this was all about and she spoke it bitterly, with a harsh tang of understanding, when they were home and alone.

James began, mixing a drink, to say something about being sorry for hitting Liddell when she stopped him with: 'That's all very well, but it wasn't him you were hitting. Was it? It was really Alec Taverner. That's who you were hitting out at, James.'

'No.' James was curt. 'Liddell was insulting.'

'No doubt. I can imagine in what way. I know what he's like.'

'Oh, do you?'

She ignored that.

'It was nothing to do,' James said, and gulped his drink before he pronounced the name, 'with Alec Taverner.'

'Everything is. Just now, with us, everything is to do with Alec Taverner.'

'I can't help it if it is. The man's come back into your life, so what is there for me to do?'

'Not into my life. Perhaps into our lives. If we let him.'

'Oh, he's always been there. It's just that now it's in the open.'

'Tell me. Did you see me dancing with him? Did you see me even looking at him? All I wanted was an evening out with my husband.'

'Which I spoilt. I know. I'm sorry.' He spoke this sincerely enough, as if with a sort of forgetful lapse into his normal courtesy.

'It doesn't matter. It shouldn't be the only one, after all. There should be others . . . But I'd hoped – in a way I'd hoped that he *would* be there tonight. And then we could overcome this thing that's . . . If we could just carry on normally, with him in the same room, and prove to ourselves that he'd got no power – James, it should be easy. Just show that we're strong enough to brush him aside, instead of – well, instead of us ending up quarrelling over him. Which is exactly what we're doing.' Sadness invaded her anger. She sat down, wearily. 'I wish to God he'd never come back.'

Standing at a little distance, half-turned away, he said, 'I don't make a habit of throwing my fists around, I swear.'

'I know you don't. That's what's so alarming, because . . .' She stared at his taut figure: she felt love as she did so, but it was painfully twisted into a knot of bafflement. 'James. I will say it now if you will listen. Alec Taverner means nothing to me. I'm not going to say he didn't once. You can love someone very much and then things change and time passes, and it ends. You don't love them any more, or feel anything for them. But that can't take away the fact that that *happened* in the past.'

He reached out to turn up the gas, and his profile was silhouetted in the brief glare as he said, 'They say nothing ever comes up to first love.'

'Perhaps it's true. I don't know. I'm not being given a chance to find out.'

He made an impatient movement. 'You can't accuse me of not loving you, of not—'

'Not trusting. How about trust?'

'It's not that simple. That man – he's *part* of you in a way I can't be.'

'Trust is easy, James. You either trust, or you don't. Tell me, what did Leo Liddell say?' As he did not answer she added, 'Something about me and him?'

'Something along those lines.'

'You believed him?'

'Of course not,' James said with sudden heat. 'He's a dirty bloody liar, and that's why I hit him.'

'But if you'd really, utterly had trust it wouldn't have got such a reaction from you. You'd have known he was just stirring the pot. But Alec was there and it was Alec you were angry at because you know that there *was* something between me and Alec.'

'Well, he's got a lot on his side, hasn't he? The charm, the medals—'

'Oh, for God's sake.'

'All right, never mind the medals. He's just got that way about him. He *must* have.'

'All right, perhaps so. But I didn't choose to marry him.'

'You didn't really have the choice at the time, did you?'

'No.' She was deeply hurt now; and that such hurt should come from James was also somehow shocking, as if her own flesh had turned against her. 'No, I didn't. Well, I have the choice now, don't I? I could run to his arms right now if I chose. It might be a bit of a scandal but that's nothing new. It would be easy to do. I could have done it last week, yesterday, this very evening. Why in God's name,' she sobbed, 'do you think I haven't?'

He had never seen her cry. It visibly shook him. He knelt and clasped her hands.

'I did that,' he said, his voice unsteady. 'Oh, God, I made that happen.'

'You can – make it stop if you want to.'

'I do want to.'

'It's you who's got the power, James. Not bloody Alec.'

He gripped her hands tightly. 'Rose – if I've got the power to make you happy – if I've got that . . . Have I?'

'Yes, damn you,' she said, leaning her forehead against his. 'I wish you'd bloody well use it!'

For some time they stayed like that, in the sort of joint-wrenching position that only high emotion makes bearable. There was a calm, and she was too grateful for it to wonder whether it was the sort that comes after a storm or precedes it.


'Extraordinary behaviour of Dr Blanchard's,' Mrs Snell said as the guests left the dance at the Town Hall. 'Do you suppose he was drunk?'

'Liddell was,' Mr Truelove said, handing his wife her wrap. 'He often is. One doesn't know what went on.'

'All the same,' Mrs Snell said, 'it's hardly what one expects at a respectable function.'

'It all dates from when he married that woman,' said Mrs Betts, shrugging on her furs, which in the heat of the Town Hall chamber smelt like a slaughterhouse. 'One couldn't expect any good to come of that.'

'They make rather a charming couple, I think,' Clara Truelove said. 'And Dr Blanchard seems quite devoted to the little girl.'

'Liddell's always making trouble,' her father said. 'I feel sorry for that wife of his.'

'I feel sorry for James,' Mrs Vickery said. 'Now that the father of that child has come back – what must he be feeling?'

'I feel sorry for Rose,' Clara Truelove said. 'It can't be very nice to have to see the man who – well, who nearly ruined her.'

'It takes two,' Mrs Betts said. 'Anyway, she must have thrown herself at him. Mr Taverner doesn't seem a bad lot to me.'

'I think he's got a nerve,' Mrs Truelove said. 'I know it was wartime, and a long while ago, but all the same, to see him walking around as bold as brass . . .'

'Well, he may have been a bit of a rogue in the past,' Mr

Truelove said. 'No one's denying that. But he has drive and enterprise, which is what this town needs.'

'If I had a grown-up daughter,' Ernie Crimmins said, 'I wouldn't let him near her.'

'Oh, the war's sobered him up a good deal, I think,' Dr Vickery said. 'He'll settle down quite respectably.'

'I wonder the doc didn't hit *him*,' Ernie Crimmins said.

'Well, Dr Blanchard should keep a careful eye on his wife, that's all I can say,' pronounced Mrs Snell. 'A leopard doesn't change its spots.'

Unusually, perhaps uniquely, Sylvia Vickery was present throughout this but did not say anything: just listened.

# THIRTY-EIGHT

December brought damp sea fogs, and with them bronchial conditions. James's services were required not only in Shipden and Saxburgh but all along the north Norfolk coast. His practice, after a tentative start, was doing well now, partly because of his readiness to heed any call: his only rival was an elderly, good-living doctor at Saxburgh who was reluctant to stir more than a mile for anything less than a life-threatening illness.

It meant that James could be absent from home at any time, and that plans were often thrown out. It happened thus on a Saturday morning, when he had promised to take Elizabeth to see a Christmas display at a department store in Norwich. Elizabeth was remarkably understanding about these absences, but still she waited patiently for James's return, and when around noon there was the sound of a car engine she ran to the front door and flung it open.

Following her, Rose saw the figure of Alec in the doorway, very precise against a background of spectral grey mist, looking down at Elizabeth.

'Hello,' he said. 'You must be Elizabeth.'

He seemed to tear his gaze away with an effort, and met Rose's eyes.

'All right to leave it there?' he said. Standing to one side, he pointed to the bonnet of a motorcar in the drive. 'Nice little job, eh? Picked her up by auction over at Aylsham.'

'What are you doing here?' Rose said.

Before he could speak, Elizabeth said, 'How did you know my name?'

341

Rose glared at Alec, daring him.

'It was a lucky guess,' he said. 'My name's Alec, by the way.'

Elizabeth, unfortunately, was at the stage of mock tea-parties and elaborate etiquette. She said, urbanely, 'Would you like to come in, Alec?'

It was smartly done: in a twinkling he was in the hall and had closed the door behind him. Elizabeth began to lead a ladylike way down the passage.

'You shouldn't be here,' Rose hissed at him. 'I don't want you here.'

'Look, it's not what you think, I just wanted to ask you something – a little advice. You're the very person.'

His eyes, as if magnetized, sought Elizabeth again. He followed her to the living room.

'I can't think what it could be,' Rose said, following in turn, 'but just ask it and then go.'

Her anger at his being here, and at that soulful gaze he was directing at Elizabeth, was intense. It amounted in fact almost to hatred; and she had never expected to feel that, after all the long hard ground she had had to cross.

He was bending over Elizabeth's platoon of dolls, ranged along the window seat.

'That's a nice dolly. What's her name?'

It was the one James had bought her on her first day at school. Rose snatched it from his examining hands.

'You've got a nerve,' she muttered. 'And you know very well that just now I can't say what I want to say to you.'

Alec gave his mischievous, little-boy-caught-out look. 'Rose,' he said, with faint amused reproach, 'I just had to see. I had to see for myself – just once. That's natural, surely.' He looked down at Elizabeth, who was busily arranging the dolls for inspection. 'She's beautiful.'

This sentimentalism irritated her more than anything. 'Children tend to be,' she said. 'What was it you wanted to ask?'

'Oh,' he said with a sigh, his eyes still on Elizabeth, 'it's about the Kinema. It's nearly finished, and we'll soon be ready to set up our first screening. We need a good piano accompanist. Someone with the technical ability and the imagination – not just tum-ti-tum for the chases and "Liebesträum" for the spoony scenes. I wondered if you could recommend anyone.'

She looked at him blankly. 'No.'

'No? I just thought, you still being involved in music, perhaps there was an ex-pupil or—'

'No. Is that it? Is that what you came here for, after all I've—'

'All right, it was an excuse.' He held up his hands. 'I admit it. Look, Rose, I may have been a pig in the past but you can't deny me my natural human feelings.'

'Oh yes, that's it, isn't it? Everything's natural and we're only human and we all make mistakes and all the rest of it. Everything's forgivable, in other words, and nothing is more bad than anything else. It's a pretty good philosophy, isn't it? You can get out of everything with it.'

He looked at her with a gentle perplexity. 'Hard, Rose. Rather hard. You know, you never used to be hard.'

It was not true he had no power: he still had power to wound her. 'If I am,' she said tightly, 'it's no wonder.'

'We were both very young,' he said, spreading his hands – and again it was that *c'est-la-vie* sentimentalism that pricked her to fury.

'You've never been young,' she said. 'You were a little crafty glad-eyed man when you were ten years old, I'll bet. Go now: don't come back.'

'No, it's no wonder you're hard,' he said, looking sadly on her. 'I don't think you would have been, if I hadn't gone away. That's my regret, my true regret.' He looked around him with an open-handed gesture. 'Nice home for Elizabeth. I'm glad . . . But is it really you, all this, Rose – truly? We did have some high old times, you know. Never think about them?'

343

She was silent. She was trying to maintain enough self-control to prevent herself screaming at him; but he took it another way, and his old knowing smile dawned.

Then there was the sound of a car engine, and Elizabeth jumped up.

'Daddy!'

With an unreadable expression Alec watched her running from the room.

'Right then, who's for Norwich?' came James's voice. He entered the room swinging Elizabeth in his arms; then, seeing Alec, stood still and gently lowered the child to the floor.

'Dr Blanchard,' Alec said, 'we've met, I think.'

'What are you doing here?' James said, his face closed, very slightly pale.

'I just dropped by to ask Mrs Blanchard's advice,' Alec said readily. 'I'm in need of a pianist for the Kinema, and—'

'Just get out, Alec,' Rose said.

'Well, I could do,' Alec said after a hesitating moment. 'But really, it might be as well to stay a little. I think we ought to talk this thing through, don't you?' He addressed this to James, with a look of bright politeness.

'Elizabeth,' James said, not taking his eyes off him, 'could you go and see Mrs Penn – ask her to make some sandwiches for us? You help make them – choose what you want in them.'

Elizabeth went obediently to the kitchen, leaving the three of them standing there at roughly equal distances from each other – the eternal triangle, Rose thought, with a kind of grim, hysterical inward laugh.

'Er – you know who I am, obviously,' Alec said.

James nodded. Rose saw that he was exerting the very maximum of his considerable self-control.

'Well.' Alec tried for lightness. 'All rather awkward, isn't it?'

'It needn't be,' Rose said, 'if you just go away.'

'Well, yes and no,' Alec said, again directing his appeal to James, 'you see – I can do that to a certain extent but Shipden is still where I live. That's the fact we've got to take into account. And that's why we should sort this out. Now, Elizabeth is my kid – no, no, I know she isn't in any way that makes sense. This is – the first time I've set eyes on her, which you've got to admit is a pretty big thing for me.'

James said nothing; he did not move a muscle. He was a tall, tense, pale concentration of attention. Rose felt a sickness at the base of her stomach. Neither of them was an uncivilized man, but still there was something crude, nightmarish and atavistic about this situation.

'I'm not going to say that blood's thicker than water,' Alec went on. 'But obviously it's – it's something to think about. Knowing I have a child. And so – I admit it, I came here wanting to see her. Just to see her.'

'Now you've seen her,' Rose said. 'So go.'

'But we simply can't be forever at daggers drawn like this, Rose,' Alec said. 'It just isn't—'

'What else did you have in mind?' said James, and his voice came out mechanically, as if it were an instrument he was unsure how to use.

'Well, a friendly peace. *Entente cordiale*. Whatever you want to call it.'

'And with me?' James said.

'I've absolutely nothing against you, old chap,' Alec said, very reasonable, 'I'm glad to meet you and all that, and I hope—'

'Well, I'm not glad to meet you,' James said. He took a tiny step forward, then seemed to regret even that much betrayal of himself and kept quite still. 'I may as well tell you that I hate you like I've never hated anybody or anything in my life. You're going to say I don't know you? It doesn't matter. I hate you and everything about you and I'd burn this house down before I'd see you set foot in it again. Now, if we can sort something out, as you say, then it will have to be on those terms.'

'You know, I'm really not that bad a fellow,' Alec said. He

gave his alert monkey-like look from one to the other. 'I don't see why there should be quite such hatred. Oh, I believe you, all right, I don't doubt you mean what you say – I just don't quite understand.'

'No,' James said, 'you probably wouldn't.'

'What about you, Rose?' Alec said.

Rose felt James's gaze on her like a distant flame.

'I've told you,' she said, 'I don't want you here.'

'Oh well, that's pretty straight, I suppose,' Alec said, spinning his hat on his finger. 'I must confess I don't see why it has to be like this. We're all grown-up people, aren't we?'

James, staring, did not respond.

Alec shrugged and said, with a little laugh, 'Well, I hope to God I'm never in need of medical attention.'

'Yes,' James said, and he was deadly serious. 'You're right. Don't call on me.'

With a last assessing look from one to the other, as a man might study the state of play on a chessboard, Alec went silently out.

They did not speak until the sound of his car had dwindled into the distance.

'I'm sorry that had to happen,' Rose said.

'It didn't have to happen,' James said, unmoving. 'You let him in again.'

'I couldn't help it. Elizabeth opened the door – it just happened—'

'That's always the way with that man, isn't it? You can never help yourself. It just happens. What is he, a hypnotist? Does he make a conjuror's pass and you lose all power of will?'

'He came here without my knowledge or consent,' Rose said, and thought with that same grim hysteria: my God, why am I using these legal phrases, as if I were on trial?

'To talk about the piano,' James said.

'That was an excuse. He wanted to see Elizabeth.'

'And you let him.'

'I told him not to come here!'

James did not sneer – his face was not made that way – but his expression was near enough to it, and sufficiently unlike himself, to give Rose a horrible shock. 'Oh,' he said, 'you must have said it *very* convincingly.'

'You're terrible,' she said trembling, 'you're terrible, saying a thing like that!'

'I meant what I said to him,' James said. 'He'd better not call on me if he's sick. Damn the Hippocratic oath and the duty to save – I'd forget it in his case. I'd watch the man drown.'

He stalked out.

A hellish Sunday followed. Aunt Dolly now had a lodger to whom she gave dinner on Sundays, so there was no company to divert them or draw the poison from the atmosphere. It was just them, frozen against each other. Rose had never before realized the agonizing unrestfulness of two people in a house who were at odds, and how they could tear at each other without any direct utterance or action.

Though James was good at maintaining a front, eventually Elizabeth saw something was amiss. When her mother was angry with her, it was all in the open: before James's closed coldness Elizabeth retreated in bewilderment.

This was too much.

'This isn't fair,' Rose said when they went to bed on Sunday night. 'It isn't fair on Elizabeth – she doesn't understand. She thinks it's her.'

'I'm sorry. Of course it's not her fault.'

She watched him lie down. There was a studied normality about his movements that did not fool her for a moment.

'Whose then?'

'No one's. It's just a bloody mess.' He turned over.

# THIRTY-NINE

On Monday afternoon, with no break in the clouds at home, Rose went heavy-hearted to collect Elizabeth from school. She was standing at the gate in a sombre dream, children and mothers milling cheerfully about her, when she became aware of a figure at her elbow.

She looked up to see Alec.

'I just wanted to . . .' He held out a parcel wrapped with pink ribbon. The words 'To Elizabeth' were written on the tag. 'Just the one present. She doesn't have to know who it's from. Just indulge me in this, Rose. It's fair enough, isn't it?' He pressed the parcel into her hands. 'Bye.'

She was so stunned that she did not see him go; and a moment later Elizabeth was tugging at her arm.

'Mummy, what's that?' She could easily read her name, and gave a coo of excitement. 'A present? A present for me? Ooh, can I open it?'

'No.' Rose put a hand on her head, looked all around, but there was no sign of him. 'No, darling – wait till we get home.'

'But can't I just—'

'Do as you're told.'

Elizabeth looked hurt at her tone. But Rose couldn't help it. She grasped the little girl's hand and hurried her home, the parcel feeling like a burning coal under her arm.

The gift was a doll – a large china doll with delicately sewn skirts trimmed with lace. Elizabeth loved it.

What could Rose do? How could she snatch it away and smash it, as she wanted to do? Elizabeth would be heartbroken

. . . which, no doubt, Alec had known very well and counted on.

And yet she wanted, so much, to throw that damned thing on the fire when she thought of Alec trying by such means to insinuate himself into Elizabeth's life. It was evil of him – no less.

And in this dilemma over the doll there seemed to be crystallized, suddenly, all the tortuous wretchedness of her present situation. It presented itself to Rose, as she watched Elizabeth murmuring to the doll, as a simple imperative: this was unbearable. She couldn't stand it any more and would have to do something. That was all.

'Mrs Penn,' she said going into the kitchen, 'where's Dr Blanchard?'

'Called out to an emergency, mum – over Blakeney way.'

A good distance. She had time.

'Would you watch over Elizabeth for me, Mrs Penn, and give her her tea when you're ready?' Rose said, pinning on her hat. 'I shouldn't be long.'

She soon found the house in Shepherd Street: an unpretentious bay-fronted villa with an overgrown buddleia covering much of its front window. As she mounted the steps, Rose resolved that if he wasn't in she would wait for him, for however long it took. Though she couldn't be sure that she wouldn't demolish the place while she was about it. She pictured his face. *What's wrong, Alec? You're destroying my home, so it's tit for tat.*

The door was opened by a fat lank-haired young woman in a grubby pinafore.

'Is Mr Taverner in?'

The fat woman moved languidly aside to let her in, then shuffling down the parqueted hall said almost as an afterthought, 'Who shall I say?'

'Mrs Blanchard.'

A door to the right opened. Alec must have heard her voice; he came out eagerly.

350

'Rose! This is a surprise!'

'It shouldn't be.'

She stared at him. He was in his shirtsleeves, tie unfastened. Half smiling, studying her, he made an ushering gesture into the front living room.

'Sorry about all this,' he said, waving a hand at a dropleaf table covered with ciphered papers, an overflowing ashtray, coffee cups. 'The place isn't all it should be yet. I'm afraid I'm not much of a home-maker.'

'No. Try home-breaker.'

'Now that isn't fair. I've told you. I won't bother you any more.'

'You bothered me this afternoon.'

'That was different,' he said. She had ignored his invitation to be seated, and so he stayed on his feet – a little uneasily, for him. 'I wanted Elizabeth to have something from me.'

She hated the easy way he used her daughter's name. 'It's rather too late for that,' she said.

'Now, be fair, Rose. I did send money in the beginning – you know I did.'

'Yes, and I sent it back. That should have told you everything.'

'It told me you were proud. So I respected that.'

There was a holiness about this that infuriated her.

'What if I told you,' she said, 'that Elizabeth isn't yours?'

'What?' he said sharply.

'Well, let's think about it. You don't *know*. So just suppose you weren't the only one, back then.'

'You're not serious.'

'No. I'm not. But I want you to picture that. Just fix it in your mind for a minute. You'd not bother to have anything to do with Elizabeth then, would you?'

He shrugged, looking faintly displeased. 'No.'

'Well, then, keep that picture – permanently. Because that's how I want you to see it. Elizabeth isn't yours, just as if someone else had fathered her back during the war.'

He stood back and regarded her critically, as if she had just put on a hat or coat and he were judging the effect. 'All right,' he said.

'And that means, don't come near her.'

'All right,' he said mildly, nodding. 'There's something you should know, though, Rose. Before you go off feeling you've thoroughly put me in my place. Even if that little scenario you drew were real – even if Elizabeth weren't mine – I would still be the same. I'd still have great difficulty in keeping away from you. *You*, Rose. That's what it's about, I'm afraid. Seeing you again.'

She frowned at him, not knowing what to believe. She couldn't honestly tell whether he were lying, trying to have the last word, chancing his luck – or whether he made himself believe something simply by saying it. If that were so, then he genuinely couldn't help himself, any more than a person with a chronic disease.

But she did know herself. She had begun to doubt herself since the venom of jealousy had entered her marriage: she had questioned herself, analysed her true feelings, probed half-fearfully the secret places of her heart.

But now she knew. No flame: not even embers. All gone.

'Well, I'm sorry, Alec,' she said, 'but we all want things we can't have: and you can't have me. And isn't that, really, the attraction for you?'

He smiled, moved swiftly across the room, and kissed her on the lips.

Rose didn't move.

'That's attraction,' he said. 'Isn't it?'

She shook her head, glad that she had not shrunk or flinched or shown anything at all. 'No, it isn't.' She went to the door. 'I won't ask you for your word not to come near us, because I can't trust it. But you have my word that if you wreck my life – and that includes Elizabeth's life and my husband's life – then I'll make you suffer for it.'

\* \* \*

'I only said I *think* he kissed her. It was hard, peeping through the crack in the door. Look here.' Nell Henning padded heavily over to her kitchen door, half closed it, and peeped at Sylvia through the narrow gap between jamb and hinges. 'That sort o' crack. Thass what I mean.'

'Oh, but it must have been,' Sylvia said, impatiently patting the sticky head of a little Henning who was attempting to show her a dead frog. 'Oh yes, definitely. You can't mistake a thing like that.'

'Well, I dunno,' Nell said, stumping back to her chair by the fire. 'From what I heard of 'em talking, they weren't very lovey-dovey. That sounded more like she was telling him to sling his hook.'

'That,' sighed Sylvia, 'is significant in itself, I'm afraid. Yes, I'm afraid so – I've got experience of these things. You have to read between the lines. Very often what people mean is the opposite of what they say.'

'When I say a thing,' grumped Nell, wishing she could get on with making her tea, 'I mean it.'

Sylvia shook her head in her most knowing way. 'Dear me, dear me . . . terrible thing. Going to his house like that, in the middle of the day. It's a wicked world, it really is . . . Oh well, it's none of my business,' she said, gathering up her coat and bag and looking curiously pleased with herself. 'It's a wicked world though, Nell my dear, it really is.'

That it ain't, thought Nell: it's the people in it. For a moment she regretted having told Sylvia anything – she didn't like this spying business. But she very much wanted her tea, and didn't think of it any more.

# FORTY

She might really be ill, James thought after Sylvia Vickery had telephoned and asked urgently to see him at morning surgery. She might really be ill, and reluctant to speak to her own father about it. It seemed unlikely, but he was prepared to give her the benefit of the doubt – or to listen to another trumped-up tale about Nell Henning's children, if need be.

James felt bad about his behaviour at the mayoral dance; bad about his behaviour since; bad about everything. But whatever black dog had him in its jaws would not let him go, and the confrontation with Alec Taverner seemed only to have tightened its grip. A blight had been cast across his marriage, and each day saw him staring stubbornly into the same dark tunnel, fretted with shadows of doubt, mistrust and self-disgust; and with all this upon him, Sylvia Vickery seemed the least of his worries.

When she entered the consulting room, his first thought was that she really was ill after all. She held her stole tightly about her throat as she slipped in, her eyes preternaturally large in her pale face.

'Well, now, what can I do for you?' James said encouragingly as she took a chair.

Sylvia looked down at her hands, swallowing hard.

'Is it yourself? I hope I can help, if so.'

Sylvia shook her head.

'Er – is it the Henning family, perhaps?'

'James,' Sylvia said huskily, 'it's you.'

'Me, good heavens. What about me?'

Sylvia gave him a misty look, as if from a long distance. 'This is so painful to me. But one has to do what one thinks is right. I've had to face some . . . hard choices before and hopefully I've always made the right decision in the end. And I think it's as well you hear it from me rather than anyone else because you and I go back a long way and other people, I'm afraid, wouldn't know how to put it. I'm not sure how to put it myself and I'm usually good at this sort of thing.'

His frown was more absent-minded than impatient, but seeing it she stirred and said quickly, 'It's Rose. She's been meeting Alec Taverner.'

'How do you mean?'

With a look of patiently bearing a load of suffering, Sylvia said, 'At his house.'

James stared down at his desk blotter. He found he was shaking slightly, but he kept his voice level as he said, 'I thought you'd come here with some genuine reason, Sylvia. Not to pass on stupid gossip.'

Sylvia shook and shook her head, both meek and solemn. 'Not gossip, I'm afraid. Oh, my dear James, I'm afraid it isn't. Nell Henning's been doing housekeeping for Alec Taverner. She's seen it all. All of it . . . and I'm afraid I do mean *all* of it.'

Her large, tireless, merciless eyes dwelt on his face, daring him to disbelieve.

And James knew that she was malicious: he knew that he should not give her the satisfaction of showing in his face that he believed. All that was reasonable in him said: I do not believe this.

But there was doubt too – a crack, a tiny hole in a great firm dam; and like a hole in a dam, all that was needed for the deluge.

'I thought you ought to know,' Sylvia said. 'It wasn't easy for me, James, not at all.' She paused, and there was a slight pout as if her feelings were not being adequately considered.

'But I can say this for myself – I have never shirked at doing what I think is right.'

'Oh, yes. It was very public-spirited of you,' James said, and the expression on his face was such that even Sylvia flushed. He lowered his eyes to the desk blotter. If he could just stare at this whiteness, think of nothing, until she was gone, then he would be all right: he would not fly apart like a bursting shell. 'I've got patients to see, Sylvia. I'm sure you understand.'

When he looked up a minute later, she was gone.

Rose was surprised when she looked up from the keyboard at the grandmother clock: the last of his patients for morning surgery had gone some time ago and there was still no sign of James. Usually, unless he had rounds, they shared lunch at this time.

Not that anything could quite be called 'usual' since the shadow of Alec had come between them; but Rose had high hopes that after her action yesterday, their life together might stand at least a better chance of getting back on an even keel. She believed that she had finally dealt with Alec. Just as importantly, she had dealt with the burrowing goblins of her own self. She felt toughened after that encounter in Shepherd Street, and ready to carry the fight for her marriage from that ground to this.

Different weapons, of course: on that ground, a towering indignation that had contained a surprising element of hatred; on this ground, love, a love which also still had the power to surprise her. But she must wield them both with the same amount of determination.

She knocked at the consulting room door, looked in.

James was sitting at his desk in a curious slumped position, as if he were on the point of falling asleep from enormous fatigue.

'James? Do you want some lunch?'

'Lunch?'

He lifted his head and looked at her as if she had suddenly proposed some abstruse philosophical question.

'Yes, I thought we could have it together. If you're finished for the morning.'

'Yes . . . yes, I'm finished.' He sat up, picked a pen from his desk and examined the nib. 'Rose . . . have you got anything to tell me?'

'What about?'

He suddenly tossed the pen up in the air so that it clattered down on the desk. It made her jump.

'Did you go to Alec Taverner's house yesterday?' he said, sounding almost bored.

Rose took a deep breath. So it had come to his ears. Very well: this could be overcome. 'Yes, I did,' she said. 'I'll tell you why. Will you listen? James, will you listen?'

'Yes,' he said, his eyes heavy-lidded, 'I'll listen.'

'Will you believe me?'

He didn't answer.

She went out and came back carrying the china-faced doll.

'Look. He gave this to Elizabeth. So I went to his house to tell him: no more. It was the only way. I threatened him, if you like. It was up to me to do it and I did it, and that's the end of it. I won't ask you how you got to hear about it. If I'm being spied on, it's no surprise.'

'Don't you need to be?' James said.

His voice was quite cool, even neutral. It was as if she were a person whose answers were so habitually untruthful that he could barely be bothered with them.

And suddenly, horribly, Rose saw that she was not going to win. It was something like staring at an oncoming train and knowing that it was going too fast for you to get out of the way: a stark, clear, instantaneous knowledge of her own helplessness. Plugging away at this was no good, just no good. This suspicion of James's was a rock she could not move. And she was no longer sure she even wanted to.

'Is this the price of staying married to you, James?' she

said, trying to swallow down her emotion and be distinct – because she did want to be clear about this. 'That I have to beg and plead with you to believe I'm telling the truth? Is this how it's always to be?'

'How can there be any talk about *our marriage*?' he said, his voice coming gusty, high-pitched, almost cracking. 'As soon as my back's turned you go to him. Not a very good lookout for *our marriage*, is it?'

'I want to save our marriage, James. But not at this price. Not at the price of trust. I went to Alec to tell him, once and for all, to stop or else. I'm asking you to believe me, but I'm not begging. I shan't beg you any more. Now you give me your answer. Do you believe me?'

Silence swelled between them. The heavy-lidded eyes rested on hers, unkindled, hollow. There was a faint movement in the muscle of his jaw, but that was all.

'Then I can't live with you any more,' she said, the words shaken out of her like a shudder. She turned and went out.

James sat on at the desk, unmoving, while the sounds of her packing were heard about the house.

There was nothing, except perhaps this very stillness, to suggest the turmoil that was going on inside him. But it was not the turmoil of a man in two minds, debating, regretting, reconsidering. It was the turmoil of a decisive man living with his decision. And he had made it, ironically enough, in much the same spirit in which he had fallen in love with Rose. It was one of those plunges over the edge that people who only knew his coolness and rationality were surprised at, but which were as much a part of his personality as his dapper dress, his taste for foreign cooking, his professional self-confidence. His crisp Gallic mind had surrendered the reins to the passionate side of his nature and, folding its arms, did not care to pick them up again. In that utter blackness of mood into which jealousy had led him, only the extreme would satisfy.

And it was because of this that, stirring at last, he went out to the hall and looked at Rose carrying her bags towards the door and could only say the bitter, unconscionable, self-destroying words: 'You're going to him?'

She gave no answer. And both of them, in different ways, felt that to this question no answer was needed.

# FORTY-ONE

Aunt Dolly had a lodger now, of course; but even if she had not, Rose felt it would be unfair on the old lady to go to her. She knew Dolly would take her in, of course – gather her in fact to her kindly bosom with no questions asked. But it was that very kindness that she could hardly bear to think of. As long as there was only pride and indignation in her hurt, she could keep going; but at the first touch of kindness she knew that all the pain of her loss would flood in and she would howl like a child.

But when she decided to ask refuge of Millie at the Arcadia, she knew the kindness would be forthcoming anyway. Yet she couldn't think what else to do. There was Elizabeth to consider. Waiting for her outside the school, surrounded by their bags, Rose realized dismally that she just didn't have the strength to do anything but lie to Elizabeth. How to tell her that she had left the man Elizabeth had begun to call Daddy and that their wonderful new life was at an end? Easier to tell the child for now that they were going for a stay with Aunt Millie.

How much Elizabeth guessed at, when she came out of school to find Rose waiting like that, was hard to say.

'Why isn't Daddy coming?' she said, when Rose told her where they were going. Rose said he had a lot of work to do. Elizabeth seemed to accept that; but as they were boarding the Saxburgh bus in the market square she said, with a curious look at Rose, 'You never told me we were going.'

'I forgot,' Rose said; and could only feel grateful, as to a tactful adult, when Elizabeth said no more.

There were no thoughts of the future in Rose's mind as the bus trundled them along the hummocky coast road to Saxburgh. Indeed the future hardly seemed to exist: there was only the past, a great hideous bulk which she had thought to escape but which was now pinning her down to this squirming, agonizing present.

Fog lay thicker across the shingle shore and flint walls of Saxburgh, and the Arcadia, overlooking the grey sea, looked ghostly and deserted. But when Rose knocked the door was snatched open at once. The Captain, the hotel's ancient and permanent resident, stood there. He was wearing a deerstalker hat and pyjama bottoms.

'I'm terribly sorry,' he said in a courtly way, 'the hotel is closed for the winter.'

Millie appeared, pushing him gently but firmly aside. 'Captain,' she said, 'please don't answer the door – that's our job, you know. Weren't you going up for your nap?'

'Hello, Millie,' Rose said when he had shuffled away. 'Any vacancies?'

'Only the one that's always here – whenever you want it,' Millie said. She looked down at their bags. 'Oh, my dear, whatever . . .?'

'Sorry, we've rather surprised you, haven't we?' Rose said with a fixed smile at Millie and a significant glance down at Elizabeth's head. 'We just thought it would be a nice change.'

Millie rallied. 'Yes – d'you know, just what I was thinking. I was saying to Frank the other day we ought to have Rose and Elizabeth over. Come in, come in . . .'

Millie took them through to the Watlyns' private parlour at the back of the house; and at her prompting, Elizabeth went in search of little Carrie. Rose waited until Elizabeth was safely out of the way, and then burst into prompt, straightforward, miserable tears.

'Oh, my dear,' Millie said, patting her hand, 'I hope this isn't what I think it is.'

'I'm afraid that's just what it is,' Rose said. 'Oh, Millie, I'm so sorry to put this on you – but that's exactly what it is . . .'

Sylvia walked down to The Rows to see Nell that evening in a cheerful frame of mind. Sea fog had rendered the midwinter darkness thicker still, and once away from the esplanade and into the old fishing quarter of Shipden the street lighting was erratic at best. More loving parents than Dr and Mrs Vickery would have been anxious for her going out like this, and anyone without Sylvia's peculiar compound of confidence and masochism would have felt some anxiety on their own account. But as far as Sylvia was concerned, if she were attacked it would be satisfyingly dramatic, and if she were not it would give her something authentic to talk about – how the danger of these unlit streets was exaggerated and how she had walked them a thousand times and so on.

This evening Sylvia had a glow about her. It was a glow of vindication, even high-minded pride. She actually felt, such were the layers she had built against self-knowledge, that she had done a hard and necessary and heroic thing today. She even felt gently sorry for Rose and James and their predicament, as an uninvolved onlooker.

Nell Henning never bothered to bolt her door, and it was Sylvia's habit to walk straight in. So she did this evening – and then stopped, pausing in the greasy kitchen. It was more noisy than usual in Nell's little parlour: there were shouts of wild laughter. Surely Nell wasn't, Sylvia hoped, entertaining one of her men friends. But no – the voices were only those of Nell herself and Mrs Scace.

About to sweep into the parlour, Sylvia heard something that made her stand quite still and listen.

'. . . God, what a cow, what a terrible daft cow she is,' came Nell Henning's drink-loosened voice. 'I'm sorry, dair, but she is. Poor ole stick wants to be a mantrapper – but who's going to come near her when she woon't shut her gob for five minutes? Imagine some poor chap trying it on with her. "Miss Vickery, would you care to dance?" "Now – first of all I must insist that you call me Sylvia because, you know, I don't agree with all this here formal business and I never have, it's just something I've always believed you know, and while we're on the subject blah blah blah . . ."'

Mrs Scace could be heard whooping and tittering with scandalized laughter. Moving like an automaton, Sylvia stepped forward to the door and peeped in. Even now, her egotism was such that she could not resist listening to something that had the recommendation of being about herself.

The parlour was strewn with empty beer bottles, some of which the Henning children had arranged for an impromptu game of skittles. On one side of the fire sat Mrs Scace with a bottle in her hand, her tiny legs up on a stool; on the other side Nell Henning, pink-faced and boozy and careless, was loudly holding forth.

'I'm sorry, dair,' Nell was saying, as Mrs Scace shrieked and hugged herself and wiped the tears from her button eyes, 'I can't help it, she do get on my tit so. Here – here, you imagine this every day.' Nell levered herself up and began parading up and down the room, her nose in the air. '"Oh! Oh, Nell, my dear, you don't want to do it that way! Oh, don't put that there! Oh, don't use butter for that, you want dripping instead! I know about these things, don't you know – I've had a lot of experience of these things as it happens . . .!"' Nell paused and made an exaggerated mime of peering into the corner, where she still kept her curtained bed. '"Oh! Nell, my dear, whatever are you doing in there with that man"'

'Stop!' squealed Mrs Scace. 'I shall wet 'em!'

Nell did not stop. '"Oh! Oh, my golly!"' she said, throwing up her hands in mock horror. '"Oh, Nell, what are you doing with that man? He's – he's getting on top of you! He's – oh, I don't know about that! That's the one thing in the world I don't know nothing about, my dear . . .!"'

With their laughter ringing in her ears, Sylvia ran from the cottage.

'No . . . no . . .'

She was screaming it out as she ran, blindly, about the courts and alleys of The Rows. She kept colliding with walls and posts in the darkness and fog, and soon her knuckles and her cheeks were grazed and bleeding. Like a panicked mouse she scurried round and round The Rows, hysterically screaming and crying, her hands clamped over her ears, as if that laughter still rang deafeningly inside her head and would never leave it.

# FORTY-TWO

'You know you can stay as long as you want,' Millie said. 'And you don't have to do this either. You're our guest, not a maid.'

They were changing the sheets in the Captain's room. The Captain took all sorts of things into bed with him – a bar of shaving soap, a starfish, currant buns – and so the sheets needed changing pretty often.

'No, I want to,' Rose said, tucking the clean sheet in on her side. 'It helps.'

'Does it?' Millie shook a pillow into a clean pillowcase. 'Does anything, my dear?'

'Well, it . . . it keeps me busy. Anyhow, I've got to earn my keep somehow.'

'Nonsense. Really, Rose, it *is* nonsense. If we were struggling I'd tell you, but with Frank's contract for the Kinema we're doing pretty well . . .' She sighed. 'Inappropriately enough.'

Rose shook her head. 'No, no. Well, even if you can manage with us for now – I've got to sort something out sooner or later.'

'Don't you mean you and James have got to sort something out?'

'I don't see how that can be,' Rose said, sitting down on the bedside chair. 'It's been a week now, and there's been no—'

'No communication from the other side,' Millie said drily. 'In other words, no one's made the first move.'

'True. But I'm afraid it isn't even that – that basic. If it were just a matter of that . . . But if there is any move, it'll just have to be to sort out the practical matters.'

367

'Oh, my dear,' Millie said, sitting on the bed, 'is that how it is?'

Rose, remembering James's chill, empty gaze as she left the house, just nodded, unable to speak.

'Well, then, in that case,' Millie said, trying to be brisk, 'you're entitled to financial support and so on.'

'I suppose,' Rose said. 'I'd rather get my own living somehow. I don't know whether Madame Carette would take me back . . .' Normally she would have been firm and clear-sighted about this, but now she no longer seemed to have the energy. It was all very well thinking she ought to pick herself up, but she simply hadn't the heart. It felt as if she had picked herself up once too often; and the wreck of the marriage that had seemed, finally, to offer a haven of happiness after the struggles of her younger years had left her numb, dry, and feeling strangely and horribly old.

'Elizabeth will have to know, of course,' Millie said.

'Yes. I've been thinking of that. And putting it off.'

'Rose – do you think you've put it off because – well, because there's a little hope lurking somewhere?'

'Oh, there's hope,' Rose said with a little laugh. 'But what it's for I don't know.'

'Still love him?'

'Yes. Yes, I still love him. I don't know, perhaps he even loves me; but we came to a place where love isn't really any use by itself.'

'Really?' Millie said. 'I'm very far from believing that it conquers all, but it's about as good a foundation as you can get.'

'Not without trust. That's the awful thing. I've never doubted James's love for me for a single moment, never had a single jealous or suspicious thought in regard to him. And yet my trust has gone too. If it goes on one side, it goes on the other. Because how can you trust what that person's thinking about you? You have no trust in – well, in their trust. And so it goes on. It's a cage.'

'There must be a way out of that cage.'

'Yes. Alone. We couldn't leave it together. That's the sadness of it.'

'Men are jealous creatures, I'm afraid,' Millie said. 'The ones who say they aren't are liars. And you don't have to do much to set them off.'

'Well, I'm not even sure that it was that business of going to Alec's house,' Rose said thoughtfully. 'Not that in itself. It was the trigger, perhaps. But perhaps it goes further back than that. I wonder if James ever quite believed I was his. Looking back at myself, I always seemed to carry this . . . this stupid woman-with-a-past air about me. As if I'd seen it all, drunk deep of the cup, experienced the grand passion and all the rest of it. Perhaps deep down I even believed that. And the absurd thing is I know now, seeing Alec again, that it wasn't so – that there really wasn't anything much to it at all. And all this time I was creating this image, unconsciously maybe, but still . . .'

'Now, Rose,' Millie said, 'don't you dare start blaming yourself.'

'Oh, I'm not,' Rose said truthfully. 'I was just thinking what a pity it is that we always seem to see things just that little bit too late.'

James, entering the lounge bar of the Victoria Hotel, supposed it was a little early in the evening to be drinking, but time weighed so heavily on him now. Everything he did seemed to finish too early, too quickly, leaving him staring in bemusement at the tardy hands of the clock and wondering what came next.

He sat down with a weak gin and leafed through the *Shipden and Saxburgh Post*. He wasn't reading: this was just pretending, like everything this past week. Even when he shaved his own face in the morning, it felt as if he were pretending, like a child playing mummies and daddies.

So much of life was sham: he seemed to see this with new perception. The furnishings of the Victoria's lounge bar, with their heavy fringed drapes and flock wallpaper and overstuffed upholstery and endless dangling, gleaming knick-knacks, were a parody of homeliness. Excessively, unconvincingly, they tried to say that sitting in here alone drinking was really just the same as being at home.

Home. The place was ghastly without Rose; Elizabeth too. He shunned it.

And yet the stone of stubborn renunciation remained in his heart. He had made no effort to find out where Rose had gone. This, he told himself, was because he knew damn well: to that man. If there was a part of himself that hesitated to find out because it feared being proved dreadfully wrong, he managed to keep it down. The jealousy had entered so far into his life that he had had to fix his pride to it, and James had perhaps an excessive amount of pride.

But he didn't have much else just now: everything seemed to have come to an arid, rocky end. All he could do was go through the motions of life. So when Ernie Crimmins came over nursing a large whisky and asked if he could join him, James just said yes even though he didn't want company. It didn't matter: it was all pretend.

'Best prescription, eh, doc?' Ernie said, raising his glass. 'That's what I always say.' He fumbled for his cigarettes, noticing that the one in his mouth was nearly smoked down. 'Still, there's always some who'll say it's no answer. Be damned to 'em, I say. If it makes you feel better, why not?'

'Why not indeed,' James said. He had a dismal consciousness of being, just now, the sort of man he disliked very much – the sort who morosely drowned his sorrows in bars and gave an impression of being pathetically misunderstood. But what the hell . . .

'See the Kinema's about ready to open?' Ernie said.

'Is it? No, I didn't know.'

Ernie sipped and made a face. 'Turned it into a nasty vulgar sort of place by all accounts. Not Shipden's style at all. Select, that's what we should be here – friendly, but select. Like Eastbourne. Not all spit-rock and picture palaces.' He worked his fresh cigarette convulsively round his mouth, as if physically chewing on some inner grievance. 'I could have made the place like that if I'd wanted. Only I prefer to keep the tone of the town, d'you see? I dunno. Done my best for this town, I have. It ain't been easy. First season after the war I had to get a whole summer's bookings for the Pier when there wasn't a complete dancing troupe left in the country, seem'ly. You couldn't get a light comedian who wasn't saucy because they'd all been entertaining the troops. The theatre was all out of repair and you could hardly put your foot on the boards because of the rot. But I managed to put on the best season we'd seen in years. Record takings. And what thanks do I get? None. Treated like a joke, more like.' Ernie finished his whisky, which plainly was not his first, and set the glass down with a bang. 'But along comes me laddo and it's, oh, see the conquering hero comes. You know what game he's up to now?'

'What?' James said, his body tensing.

'You'll never guess,' Ernie said, focusing on James with difficulty through his smeared spectacles. 'Only reckoning to take a lease on the old Assembly Rooms and start putting on shows there. He's found out they're already licensed for public entertainment on account of how there used to be recitals there, you know, Brahms and Liszt and what have you, in the old days. Yup – that's me laddo's latest game, if you please. What do you think of that?'

For a weird moment, James almost found himself ready to defend Alec Taverner because some neutral part of himself thought that Shipden's having another place of entertainment was not a bad thing at all. But Ernie was already carrying on.

'I'll tell you what that is, Doc. That's nothing more or less than a deliberate attempt to push me out. I can see it all. He's had my living in his sights ever since he came back to this town. He won't be happy till he sees me on the breadline.' Ernie snatched up his empty glass and banged it down for emphasis, snorting like a seedy dragon. 'That's his game. Nothing less.'

'There's surely room for both of you in Shipden,' James found himself saying.

'What?You're kidding.You must think I was born yesterday. It's a plan, I tell you. He's trying to take my place in this town. And just because he's got some money and the bloody chat he thinks he can do it without a fight.Well, he's got another think coming. He might be laughing at me now, but he'll be laughing on the other side of his face soon. I might not be some clever-clogs big-talker with a lot of fancy new ideas, but I've been in the business a lot longer than him.We'll see – that's all I've got to say, we'll see . . .'

Making an excuse, James put down his unfinished drink and left the lounge bar of the Victoria. He suddenly couldn't bear to be sitting there any longer. It was not so much the jaundiced grumblings of Ernie Crimmins that he couldn't stand as the fact that he could see himself reflected in those grubby spectacles.

# FORTY-THREE

It had taken Sylvia Vickery an hour to get ready to go out. Fifteen minutes had been spent pinning on her hat and checking her bag and pulling on her gloves. The forty-five minutes had been spent lingering about the hall and trying to pluck up courage to go out of the door.

She was frightened to go out: terrified of being seen. This was not simply because of the still vivid mark on her face, sustained during that panicked flight around the darkened Rows. It was because of what Shipden must think of her.

But she owed the Trueloves a visit, and even her mother and father had begun to notice that there was something amiss with her. She hadn't been out of the house lately – why ever not? She couldn't tell them, and so she had to take the plunge. Even though it needed forty-five minutes of sweating anguish before she could do it.

Walking with clipped, tight steps, her stole wrapped round the lower half of her face, her eyes lowered, Sylvia kept thinking of *A Tale of Two Cities*. She read a lot – though impatiently, flicking through the pages as if in search of something that was never there – and she knew the book well. And what lodged in her memory now was the fate of Miss Pross, who inadvertently fired the gun that killed Madame Defarge. The bang of the gun left Miss Pross deaf for the rest of her life. A silly melodramatic touch, Sylvia had thought, and not one that could be squared with medical fact.

But the way the mocking laughter of Nell Henning and Mrs Scace still echoed around her head, every waking moment, could not be squared with medical fact either. It had not faded in the least since that night. And as she ventured out into the streets of Shipden she seemed to hear it thrown back at her from every bay window and cobbled passage. Every pair of feet that she passed – she did not look up at the faces – seemed to pause, as if in momentary savouring of that same cruel merriment. Even a tabby cat that crossed her path appeared to meet her eyes with a smirk of knowledge.

But at least no one stopped to speak to her and taunt her – as they surely must do. Now that she knew what people thought of her, it seemed certain that they would stop dissembling and just come out with it. If she could only get down to the seafront, which would be deserted at this season, spend an hour or so walking there, and then go home, she would have satisfied her mother and father and then could hide again . . . As long as no one spoke to her . . .

'Sylvia!'

To her horror, Sylvia saw Alec Taverner jogging across Pound Street towards her.

Nell's employer. He must be laughing at her more than anyone else.

'Sylvia, how are you? You know, I can't thank you enough for recruiting Nell for me. Made all the difference. She rustles up a very nice steak-and-kidney pudding, and it's absolutely wonderful not having to hunt down an elusive clean pair of socks every morning!'

Sylvia, with difficulty, looked up into his face. He was smiling – as good as laughing. He knew all about her. She couldn't speak.

'Anyhow,' he went on, 'I just wanted to say how much it's appreciated. Speaking as someone who only has bad habits, I must say you seem to have a very nice habit of helping people out.'

'It isn't – it isn't anything,' Sylvia managed to say. She was going to have to run: she couldn't bear this mockery any longer.

'It is to me, I assure you,' Alec said. 'Well, now, can I expect you at the grand opening of the Kinema? Complimentary seats for you and your parents, best in the house. We've a rather good film with Mabel Normand for our first showing, called *Peck's Bad Girl*, and I think . . .'

Sylvia began shaking her head. It was partly the result of the trembling that had overtaken her and partly at the thought of going to the Kinema. Best seats in the house? Where everyone could see her? Where she would be – oh, God, no – the centre of attention?

'No thank you,' she got out, and found herself repeating it, in a muttered monotone like a child, as she fled from him. 'No thank you, no thank you . . .'

Alec gazed in puzzlement at Sylvia's retreating form. It was the beginning of a strange day for him.

It should have been a good one. They were just putting the finishing touches to the Kinema and he hoped to open at the weekend. As he walked down Pound Street in the morning he was feeling rather proud and excited about this, and when he saw Sylvia Vickery across the way he was glad as always to see a familiar female face, and ready to chat and flirt and talk nonsense a little.

And instead Sylvia was like that! There must have been something wrong – her eyes had looked huge and naked and somehow raw, as if they had had sand rubbed in them. He had noticed a mark on her cheek as well. But it was her behaviour that was extraordinary. Before this she had been almost thrustful in getting to know him. Had he offended? Alec wondered, and concluded that he couldn't possibly have; and once he had established in his mind that it was nothing to do with him, he lost interest. Still, the encounter left him with a strange unpleasant feeling, rather as if he had unwittingly put his hands on something unclean.

There were still some workmen at the Kinema – decorators, the upholsterer finishing off the seating in the gods – and

Alec strolled about talking to them for a while, looking round at his creation, imagining it filled to the balcony with people – toffee papers rustling, cigarette smoke curling upwards, and then the expectant hush as the lights went down. He was, for all his lightness and amorousness and changeability, a shrewd man when it came to dealing with the public in business. While living with his stepmother at her Lowestoft hotel before finally settling in Shipden he had made several suggestions about the running of the place and they had all turned out well. He had a knack of knowing what people wanted, and he understood the importance of appearances. At the Lowestoft hotel he had dissuaded his stepmother from serving the best butter: second best would do, as long as it was served in artistic little curls – people always thought it tasted good when it came like that. And he had paid a lot of attention to the décor of the Kinema, insisting on such things as spangles on the curtains that covered the screen. As long as the eye was sufficiently impressed, people wouldn't notice that the seats were rather close together or that the carpeting didn't reach beyond the aisles.

Appearances counted in the matter of staff too, which was partly why he had given the cashier's job to a pretty girl named Lois even though she had no experience of cash handling. He had asked her to come in today so that he could show her the ropes, and he spent a good part of the morning with her, going over the procedure of selling tickets, the different prices for circle and balcony and stalls and for matinées and evening performances, and testing her arithmetic with mock transactions.

She was a little nervous but a quick learner and he liked her. It was quite a tight squeeze for the two of them in the cash booth, and it seemed quite natural to him to begin feeling amorous and, at length, to slip a flirtatious arm around Lois's narrow waist.

To his surprise she at once drew away, as far as she could, and fixed him with bewitchingly pretty but solemn eyes.

'Please, Mr Taverner,' she said, 'don't do that. That isn't right.'

'Sorry,' he said grinning, holding up his hands. 'Forgot myself. It's the proximity, you know – bit too tantalizing.'

'I'm serious, Mr Taverner,' she said, looking distressed. 'I'm engaged to be married and I – I really can't work here if you do that.'

'Won't happen again,' he said lightly. 'Word of honour.'

But he felt curiously oppressed after this trivial experience. He could not shake it off.

Alec's usual remedy for low spirits was to begin something new – a new undertaking, a new love affair. But he found, as he took a walk down to the esplanade to clear his head from the smell of paint and varnish in the Kinema, that something new was not what he wanted. There came a time, he supposed, when you wanted something more than novelty.

There were few people about on that raw, murky December day, but one hardy young couple were down on the beach with a yapping, frisking dog and a little boy who, warmly wrapped from head to toe, was galloping along the dun sands and laughing in sheer exhilaration. The sound reached the watching Alec's ears with piercing clarity, a delightful bright free sound that also had, to him and today, a certain sadness in it.

The melancholy that stole over him was real, though he could only express it – indeed only experience it – in sentimental terms. 'What a bloody fool you are, old man,' he said to himself. 'And to think . . .!'

He walked back up to the town and dropped into a pub for a drink; but he did not stay long, for there were only a few commercial travellers standing about the bar, holding in their paunches and eyeing the barmaid with a mixture of bravado and furtive unease. Alec found himself thinking again of Rose, as he had so often of late. In fact he had not thought of her so frequently as he pretended to himself; but the regretful picture that now came to his mind's eye was genuine enough, and so too was his sense that he might have behaved differently at their last meeting. It was no wonder she hadn't believed him: the tone had been all wrong. He couldn't with honesty say that he had believed what he said himself, at the time; but now it seemed to him both desperately true and urgent.

Still no definite aim or plan of action attached to this feeling of lost opportunity: the feeling was sufficiently luxurious in itself to occupy him. It might have died away altogether if he had not, on his return to the Kinema, got talking to Frank Watlyn, who had come to give him the final accounts for the rebuilding work. Frank was an excellent fellow, but he had never in his life been able to keep a secret. And what Alec learnt from Frank's indiscretion changed everything.

# FORTY-FOUR

It had been a strange morning for James too. After breakfast, when having forgotten a handkerchief he went back up to the bedroom, he came upon Mrs Penn apparently sorting out and folding some of Rose's clothes and underwear.

'What are you doing?' he said, and found himself unusually sharp.

'There was a note from Mrs Blanchard, Doctor,' she said, 'asking me to send on some of her clothes.'

'Where to?'

'The Arcadia at Saxburgh.'

He stood gnawing his lip and looking down at the clothes, all of which it was impossible to imagine on any but Rose's graceful figure. They even seemed to suggest her when folded.

'You didn't tell me this.'

'The note was addressed to me, Doctor,' Mrs Penn said.

He had told Mrs Penn nothing except that Rose and Elizabeth had gone away for a while. He had supposed that the housekeeper knew the truth pretty well, but in her granite way Mrs Penn had given no sign, going about her work as normal. This, he saw now, had rather helped him in sustaining the fiction – to himself – that everything *was* normal. Rather than facing the fact of the breakdown of his marriage, he had been living in a kind of limbo, a hiatus of pretence. All this was horrible, but it was not real.

The sight of Rose's clothes being folded away brought home to him, with an impact like a blow to the stomach, that it was real. And there was a letter from his father to reinforce it: Mr

Blanchard asked after Rose and Elizabeth and expressed a hope that they would all come to stay with him in London in the New Year . . . Everything, in fact, began to shout the inescapable truth at James.

And here was a new facet to that truth, which he would have to come to terms with. Rose had gone to the Arcadia. She had gone to stay with Millie Watlyn. She hadn't gone to Alec at all.

*Well, of course she wouldn't, not after you said that to her as she was leaving. She wouldn't want to give you the satisfaction of being proved right straight away. It doesn't necessarily mean . . .*

He listened to this whining, depressingly familiar voice for a while. It was a voice that always got a hearing just lately, like some loud boastful child in a classroom run by a weak schoolmaster. Another voice tried quietly to make the point that he had always known perfectly well that she was not going to Alec and the reason for that was . . . But it was shouted down.

Well, one thing was for certain – this limbo would have to end. He and his wife had separated, and this was a practical fact to be addressed.

Somehow. He didn't know how. Just the thought of its being a practical fact, a thing that would continue – the shape of the future, in fact – brought a revival of that sensation like a blow in the stomach, leaving him aching and breathless.

He wandered downstairs and stood looking at Rose's piano, sheet music still open on the stand.

'Oh God,' he said aloud, 'I don't know what to do.'

There was a knock on the front door. He called to Mrs Penn that he would get it and as he went listlessly to the door it occurred to him that today was the day Rose taught her favourite piano pupil – the Harwood girl. Another practical thing to be addressed.

It was, indeed, Angelica. She looked at him in shy surprise. 'Good morning, Dr Blanchard.'

He didn't know how to begin. He had a strange and acute

feeling, faced with this girl who he knew adored Rose, that he was a monster, always had been a monster, and had only just been found out.

'Miss Harwood, I'm afraid—'

'Oh! I'm not Miss Harwood any more,' Angelica said, with a bright flush of happiness. 'I'm . . .' Shyly she waggled the fingers of her left hand. 'I'm Mrs Stapleton now.'

James remembered Rose telling him about Angelica's suitor. So, she had done it. Drearily he hoped she wouldn't regret it.

Then he looked again at her beaming young face and thought that that wasn't much of a hope to express. God, what did that say about him?

'Congratulations,' he said. 'Many congratulations, Miss – Mrs Stapleton.'

'I know, it's awfully hard to get used to, isn't it?' Angelica said in her gasping way. 'That's Edward in the car back there. I just wanted to come and – and say hello to Mrs Blanchard and also goodbye, I'm afraid, and perhaps introduce Edward to her if she's agreeable—'

'Mrs Stapleton – er – come inside, won't you?'

'Oh my gosh, there's nothing wrong, is there?'

'No – not really. Please come through . . .'

Angelica, through force of habit, went towards the piano stool, then stopped and with beautiful awkwardness stood twisting the fingers of her gloves and regarding him with solemn deer-like eyes.

'Er, the fact is, Mrs Stapleton, I know Rose would have wanted to see you enormously and – and to hear your news, but . . .' Even now he had been contemplating some easy fib, but at the last it wouldn't come. 'She isn't here, I'm afraid. Mrs Blanchard and I are – not together any more.'

'How do you mean?' Angelica said, an exquisite dimple of puzzlement between her brows.

How *do* I mean? thought James. That love died? If it were true on his side, then he was even more contemptible than he thought. And on Rose's side . . .?

'We've separated, Mrs Stapleton,' he said, the words like ashes in his mouth. 'Mrs Blanchard is not presently living here. She is, I believe, staying at the Arcadia Guest House in Saxburgh, not too far from here. If you wanted to see her there, I'm sure—'

'But that's no good,' protested Angelica plaintively. 'I wanted to come here and see her before we went away. This is where we – well, where she helped me choose. I was so looking forward to it . . . Oh, Dr Blanchard,' she said with the bitterest disappointment, 'whatever have you done?'

'I . . .' James coughed. 'It isn't really a question of that, Mrs Stapleton. It's just one of those things that—'

'Oh, nonsense,' Angelica said. Emotion, and something else perhaps, had given her confidence. 'It must have been something dreadful for you to have split up. That is what you're telling me, isn't it?'

'Yes,' James said, while some inner voice – from the back of the classroom, perhaps – murmured *No*.

'Well then, that's what I mean. You must have done something awful because Mrs Blanchard absolutely adores you.'

It was James's turn to feel the blood rise to his cheeks.

'I'm sorry, Mrs Stapleton, this really isn't something I can discuss. Now if—'

'I know she does,' Angelica said, with some composure, 'because of how she'd always talk about you. You see, Mrs Blanchard and I – we used to spend more time talking than working at my music, that was my fault I'm afraid, but I don't regret it at all because otherwise I don't know what would have happened to me. I certainly wouldn't have found the happiness I have now . . . And that was the very same happiness *she* found. I know it was, I may be rather dense but it was plain in every word she spoke.'

'Mrs Stapleton,' James said frowning, and unconsciously using his professional diagnostic voice, 'you perhaps know there was a – a prior claim on Mrs Blanchard. Unfortunately

382

that prior claim . . . came back.'

'Oh gosh, do you mean she's run off with another man?'

'No – no, that isn't—'

'Well, there you are then. I *knew* it couldn't be anything like that.'

'Really, I don't mean to be rude, Mrs Stapleton, but it is a private matter and with the greatest respect you can't know—'

'I know Mrs Blanchard,' Angelica said, hotly for her. 'I know Rose. I know how very much she loved you. I can remember her face when I walked into Madame Whatsname's and she told me she was getting married, I've never forgotten it – and all I can think is you must have been perfectly beastly to her for her to have left.'

'I don't see any point in this,' James said, averting his face. 'Now, as I say, if you'd care to call on her at Saxburgh, I'm sure she'd be glad to see you, so if—'

'I don't want to see her if she's unhappy. It would make me feel too awful, when I've just got married and everything. She deserves the happiness a lot more than me.' Angelica's lip trembled. 'I'm sorry if I was rude, Dr Blanchard. But I'm not really because I think what I said is true. I never used to trust my own judgement at all but I do now and that's because of Rose. So I know it's true and you ought to as well.'

When James looked round, she had gone.

He took morning surgery in a sort of daze. At one point old Mrs Coxon, describing the topography of her rheumatism in great detail, stopped and gave him a pinched look, as if she suspected he wasn't listening.

Of course he was listening, he wanted to shout, but didn't she realize that doctors were human too?

He came out of the consulting room to find Mrs Penn laying the table for his lunch. The laying of that single place hit him like another blow. He told her he would skip lunch and shrugging on his overcoat went out.

'How long will you be, Doctor, in case you're needed?'

'Not long. I'm just going for a walk.'

Usually walking helped him think more clearly: something about the exercise seemed to set the mind into the same firm, even rhythm, each thought leading logically to the next. But today, as he set out along the cliff paths of West Shipden, his brain seemed quite out of harmony with his body. It did not stride along on firm limbs of logic. It flitted, halted, lingered. It circled again and again about the same ideas, or rather images. The image of Alec Taverner was one. But the more he stared at that image the more diffuse it became, rather as a single word excessively concentrated on becomes unutterably strange and meaningless. Alec Taverner the father of Elizabeth . . . the lover of Rose . . . the war hero . . . the proprietor of the Kinema . . . Taverner was, in fact, whatever the mind chose to make him. Just as he himself was, to old Mrs Coxon, simply the doctor, exclusively concerned with her ailments.

So was Taverner – the Taverner who had provoked him to the wildest and most vehement jealousy and the most violently negative feelings he had ever experienced – just an invention of his own, a bogeyman?

Perhaps. It was one thing intellectually to grasp this – quite another to feel it. And that was what was different about this walk. The further he went – and he had left the sight of the church and the pier behind now and was striking out along the wooded coast westward – the more feelings took the place of thoughts. It was not his mind but his heart that seemed to be moving inexorably towards clarity.

The truth of the heart. Probably he would have mistrusted such a concept formerly. It seemed such a potential licence for sentimentalism, for base instincts and desires, even for savagery. Yet he saw now that there was such a thing and that pretending it did not exist was as dangerous as submitting the whole of your life to its direction.

You either trust or you don't, Rose had said. And in his mind he had rejected that with a thousand provisos: trust needed firm grounds, trust could be undermined, trust could not be freely given unless this and unless that . . . Missing the point. Trust had no provisos. It was a leap into darkness. It was courage.

Rose: that was the image above all others that shimmered before him as he trudged the winter-hard paths through the silent pines. Rose alone – her essence. Not Rose in the arms of Alec Taverner, not Rose as she was five years ago, not some other Rose from the one he knew.

The Rose he had lost.

*Had* he lost her – for ever? And if there were the slightest, tiniest possibility that he had not, what was he doing?

Well, he knew now what he was doing, and where these apparently tireless steps were taking him – westward towards a shingle shore.

# FORTY-FIVE

Millie was the soul of discretion, but somehow the Captain – the Arcadia's only paying guest at present – had got wind of why Rose was here.

Coming upon her in the kitchen, where she was polishing the silver, he laid a tremulous claw-like hand upon hers and said: 'Would you like me to horsewhip him, my dear?'

'Oh – thank you, Captain, but I don't think there'll be any need for that.'

'Sometimes it helps.' The Captain picked up a fork and, apparently with some general idea that it had to do with food, popped it into his mouth; then drew it out with a vaguely disappointed expression. 'If ever you need someone horsewhipped, my dear,' he said, tottering off, 'you let me know.'

'Oh – Captain – can I have that?' she called after him.

He looked in surprise at the fork he was still holding, then handed it to her gravely. 'Certainly, my dear. Take it as a keepsake. Consider it yours.'

She cleaned and polished the fork, making a long job of it because it was all she had left to do. The Arcadia in the dead of winter did not call for a great deal of maintenance, and even by absolutely snatching every job out of Millie's hands Rose was still left with more time than she knew what to do with. Elizabeth was going to school in Saxburgh for now – term was nearly over anyhow – and for most of the day Rose could only drift about the house, listening to the soft grating and sucking of the tide on the shingle beach.

Not a good thing, because it gave her time to brood, and inevitably to brood was to regret what had been and what might have been. The most intolerable situation could appear tolerable when you looked back at it from a position of bored and empty loneliness. You forgot the bad things and saw only what you had lost.

She was not likely, however, to forget what it was that had driven her out of the house in Hill Rise. James had not kept faith with her: James had flatly refused to believe she was true to him. She had to keep that firmly fixed in her mind whenever she found herself – as she was now – missing him so badly that it hurt her chest. James, if it was love he still felt for her, had withdrawn it from her: James had let go.

James had just walked past the kitchen window.

Rose experienced something like panic. Frank was at work and Millie had taken Carrie shopping in the town, and the Captain was liable to let anyone in if he got to the door first. For a moment she actually looked round for a hiding place.

And then she realized, with a kind of wretched shiver of realism, that they were a married couple and that, whatever happened, they had things to talk about.

She went to the front door and opened it just as James was lifting his hand to knock.

'Rose.'

'James.'

'I . . . I heard you were here.'

'Come in.'

'I'd like to talk to you.'

'Yes, of course.'

She took him into the public parlour. Their exchange thus far had been as unemotional as Morse code, but her heart felt as if it were in her throat. In the short glance that was all she had allowed herself, she had seen him looking fresh and glowing from the outside air and also, somehow, wonderfully well-defined, like a brilliant portrait. And then there was the scent he brought with him – a cold outdoors scent but also

388

the scent of him. It was the scent of his clothes, of his crisp coppery hair that went stiff and crackling when he used brushes on it, of his lean youth-like body, of his cologne: it was the scent she liked to inhale from his pillow when he rose before her in the morning and she shifted sleepily over to his side of the bed.

It was intolerable.

'James,' she said, going to the chimneypiece and needlessly tidying a jar of spills there, 'shall we get this over as quickly as possible? It's all – all very difficult I know but if we can just get it settled then—'

'Rose,' he said, 'please come back.'

Clumsily she knocked the jar of spills over; started to pick them up, then let them lie, putting a hand to her face, unable to look at him.

'You know I can't do that,' she said.

'I know you feel you can't,' he said. 'After what I – after the way I behaved. But there must be a way for us. Unless . . .'

'Unless what?'

'Well. Unless it's true. About Alec.'

She shrugged, tightly: even hearing that name made her want to scream. 'There you are, you see,' she said dully. 'That's just it. You had to ask that.'

'Well, is it? Look – I have to ask it because I want us to try again, I want you back and I want a new start and that's the only thing that's standing in the way—'

'No,' she said. 'That isn't the only thing, James. Never has been. The question you just felt you had to ask me – that's what's standing in the way.'

'I had to ask it,' he said, taking an impatient step forward, 'because I love you and – and yes, I'm wildly jealous of Alec Taverner, I admit it. It's been like a terrible compulsion . . . But all I need is to be sure that I don't have to be, and then . . .'

'And then things will be all right?'

He swallowed. 'Yes.'

She looked at him. It was so tempting, the easy capitulation: every fibre of her wanted to respond, to say it was all right and run to his arms. Yet even now her bleak inability to accept less than the complete truth prevented her.

'Rose,' he said. 'Please forgive me. Please give me another chance.'

'When I went to Alec's house,' she said, 'what do you believe I was doing there?'

He hesitated. 'Look,' he said. 'I don't know – I just want to forget that and start again. It's us I care about – you and me. I'll put all that out of my mind, I promise you—'

'But don't you see,' she said, her voice breaking, 'I don't want you to put it out of your mind. Unless you can hold it in there and live with it there's no point in even talking . . .'

'I don't care what went on. It's in the past. It's the future I care about – our future. Whatever you feel you can give me of yourself I'll – I'll take.'

Rose twitched as if stung.

'It would be nice to believe we have a future, James. But I can't believe it.'

'Try,' he said.

She shook her head. 'You either believe something or you don't.'

Something about him changed then, as if the hope with which he had been supporting himself suddenly gave way, a crudely fashioned and temporary crutch. He ran his hand through his hair and said in a lower voice, 'If I've failed you, I wish – I wish you'd let me make amends.'

All at once it was on her lips to say that they had failed each other. But to say that was to take the exchange on to entirely new ground, one on which reconciliation was a possibility. And some part of herself still stuck doggedly to the fact that he had not believed or trusted her about Alec, refusing to move on. It was a stubborn part of herself and, she realized in that moment, a larger part of herself than she had ever admitted. She had always thought of James as the stubborn one.

But the revelation coming at such a moment as this only threw her into a hardened, defensive attitude. To think of the destruction of love was agony; to see that you had contributed to its destruction was torture.

'You'd better go, James,' she said, beginning to pick up the spills again. 'This isn't doing either of us any good.'

'Rose . . . please . . .'

Afraid that he was about to reach out for her, afraid of herself, she said with a harshness she did not feel, 'James, there's such a thing as too late.'

She concentrated on picking up the spills. It was hard because her hands did not look or feel like her own. And her words, echoing in her ears, sounded foreign to her as well. Such a thing as too late . . . Was that what she believed?

Was it?

When she looked up, a tear was running down her cheek, and James was gone.

# FORTY-SIX

Alec was driving along the coast road towards Saxburgh in a very mixed frame of mind.

What Frank Watlyn had told him – that Rose had left her husband and was sheltering at the Arcadia – had acted on him with something of the effect of a vigorous tonic. He was far from exultant about it – being romantic, he thought all such things a crying pity – but the news coming on top of his odd, dissatisfied, and even lonely mood seemed to him prophetic, almost supernatural in its aptness. Alec was certainly an opportunist, but he saw this characteristic of his in terms of fortune, destiny, happy coincidence and the conjunction of the stars. If Rose was alone, desolate, and probably vulnerable at just the moment when he had come to a poignant appreciation of what might have been, then surely that was a sign from above; and in motoring over at once to see her and try his luck again, he was not taking a cynical advantage of circumstances but rather surrendering to kismet. It was simply meant to be . . . and if it turned out not to be, he hadn't lost anything.

That was the mood in which he had set off. But on the way out of Shipden something had occurred to give an unpleasant twist to it. He had caught sight of Lois, his new cash-girl, walking home, and had pulled up alongside and offered her a lift.

'No thank you, Mr Taverner,' she had said; and again, 'No thank you,' politely but firmly, when he had insisted. And she had carried on walking.

It was a small thing, but it rankled. Did she really not trust

393

him? Or, looking at it from the other side, was he really such a non-starter in the romance stakes? He hadn't been thought so before. He found that his image of himself, which had been nicely fixed since puberty and had never given him any trouble, had wobbled and blurred. Yes, it was a small thing, he told himself, but it was a bit of a pill all the same.

The December afternoon was darkening swiftly, and he had just switched on his headlights when the figure came into sight, walking slowly towards him along the side of the coast road out of Saxburgh. The figure lifted its head as the headlights came on, and Alec recognized James Blanchard.

Alec stopped the car and leant out. Again he had nothing in mind, nothing so clear-cut as malice or calculation. He had no urge to crow. The reason he said what he said to James, though the result of a complex and troubled mood, was in essence simple, and the key to much of Alec's behaviour: he said it because it made him feel better.

'Hello, old man. Been to see Rose?'

James Blanchard looked pale, tired, and almost spectral, the sockets of his eyes deep-shadowed and lightless and his jawbone standing out. His shoulders had a defeated slump. Looking dispassionately into the car, he barely nodded.

'Ah. Well, she'll have told you then. Look, I'm sorry about all this, Doctor, but the fact is Rose and I were a twosome a long time ago and it's one of those things that never dies and – well, it just can't be helped. I'll be good to her – you have my solemn promise. No hard feelings, eh?'

He raised a hand, and drove on.

When he glanced back, he could see the figure of James Blanchard trudging on. Something about the mechanical way the doctor was walking made Alec momentarily wonder if, after all, he had laid it on a bit thick.

But he cheered up and stopped worrying about it as the pantiled roofs of Saxburgh came in sight. Because there was another reason why he had said it: he confidently believed that quite soon, perhaps in an hour or so, it would be true.

# FORTY-SEVEN

Rose had thankfully little time to brood on her meeting with James, for soon after he left Millie and Carrie came back to the Arcadia bringing in Elizabeth from school.

The two little girls were lively and rather quarrelsome. It seemed that Elizabeth, after some lesson she had learnt today, had taken up a fixed position on the matter of what a baby horse was called.

'It's a foal – it is, isn't it, Mummy? It's a foal.'

'You're making it up,' Carrie said, obviously not for the first time.

'It is – it is a foal. Just because you don't know. You ask my daddy – he knows. You ask my daddy and he'll tell you. Mummy, when are we going to see Daddy?'

'Elizabeth,' Rose said, 'go and take off your coat. And those muddy shoes. You're making Auntie Millie's floor dirty.'

'But when though? When, Mummy?'

'Just do as you're told and – don't keep going on so,' Rose said, nearly losing control of her voice.

Millie, with a glance at Rose's face, spirited them into the kitchen. 'Come along. You can both have milk and biscuits if you sit up at the table nicely and behave yourselves . . .'

When she came back Rose was lighting the gas in the public parlour. Her hand shook so obviously that Millie, coming over to her, took hold of it and held it forcibly down by her side.

'Your nerves, my dear,' she said, 'are in a state.'

'Sorry. Just had a bad day.' Pressed by Millie, Rose sat down. 'James was here.'

'Aha . . .?'

Rose shrugged, her chin in her hands. 'He . . . he went away again.'

'Went, or was sent?'

'A bit of both, maybe.'

He was here, she thought, in this room, just a short while ago. This simple fact filled her with a dreadful aching. It was not sentimental, merely an accurate description of symptoms, to say that she felt as if part of her physical body had gone with him.

If he was here – what? What would they say that they hadn't already said? Probably nothing, she thought. But that aching, missing part of her would be put back.

*There's such a thing as too late.* Had she ever really believed that? Perhaps it had been an unacknowledged feeling in her bones back before she had met James: the idea that love was all over for her, a thing of the past, put away and done with. But James had proved her wrong. It had not been too late for a new beginning.

And now he had come to beg her forgiveness and had sought to prove, once again, that it was not too late. Could she not meet that belief with a belief of her own? She had *wanted* to believe – quite desperately. But perhaps what had stopped her was that old Rose – the figure she began dimly to see as a little self-pitying, a little self-dramatizing, making of her betrayal five years ago a fetish, and morbidly detecting a repetition of its pattern in every experience that fell short of perfection. Perhaps what had stopped her was the feeling that to believe was to surrender the safe halo of the eternal victim, and be like everyone else.

'What you want, my dear,' Millie said, 'is a good stiff drink. And I shall have one with you. Shan't be a moment.'

A drink would be good, indeed – but what Rose wanted, truly wanted, was for James to come back. She was angry at him, she loved him, she felt like hitting him, she didn't know what was to become of them; but above all this, she simply wanted him to come back.

And as she thought this, sadly holding and caressing the thought like a precious stone, there was the sound of a car in the drive of the Arcadia and, a few moments later, a hearty knock at the door.

Rose was on her feet and, a few moments later, looking into the eyes, first of Millie – which looked helplessly apologetic – and then of Alec Taverner. Which crinkled up in his old, wry, ingratiating grin as he stepped into the room, took off his driving gauntlets, shrugged and said, 'Rose – sorry. I just – I just had to come.'

Millie got smartly out of the room – which was just as well, as Rose's hands itched to grab everything within reach and hurl it at him. But what stopped her was his own swift astonishing progress towards her, arms out as for an embrace.

He very nearly touched her; and what must have stopped him was not the look of anger on her face but something she was hardly aware of until she saw him stop dead – a shrinking, uncontrollable distaste.

'I'm sorry, Rose, I didn't mean . . .' He hesitated, then stuffed his hands in his pockets and took a step back. She realized that this was the first time she had ever seen him really, genuinely put out.

'How did you know I was here?' she said.

'Frank told me. Or he let it slip. It wasn't his fault. Rose . . .' He seemed to be feeling his way back to his habitual confidence. 'I'm more sorry than I can say about what's happened – with you and your husband, I mean. It's a beastly thing – must be pretty fair hell for you. I just wanted to come and see – if you were all right, and whether there was anything I could do. I can't help feeling a little bit responsible—'

'You're not,' she said. 'It's nothing to do with you.'

'All the same, I wish—'

'It's nothing to do with you,' she repeated. 'You're not the centre of the picture, Alec, not this time. Get that into your head.'

It was odd that, now she scarcely cared what he thought or felt, now he really was less than nothing to her, she suddenly seemed able to get through to him. She saw his face pucker at her last remark and he said quickly, 'Look, Rose, that's a bit cool. I only wanted to help.'

'How?'

'Any way I can,' he said, brightening. 'I'm at your disposal.' He made another cautious step towards her and said, his voice low, 'You know I'd do anything for you, Rose. You know that, don't you? Anything. Say the word.'

She thought of saying, 'Leave Shipden, then,' but saw at once that that really wasn't relevant. As she had said, he wasn't the centre of the picture.

And then the fact of Alec standing here, in this room where she had seen James just an hour ago and in which she had so leapingly thought to see him again, was intolerable. Here he was once more – relentlessly thinking he was in with a chance – and there seemed no way of getting rid of him short of murder.

There was another way, though; it came to her and she said it, all at once.

'Well, thank you, Alec,' she said, 'but there isn't anything. We've made it up, you see: everything's all right. I'm going home this evening.'

To her surprise, he was smiling ruefully.

'Rose, you little fibber,' he said.

'No fib,' she said, breathing hard. 'Everything's all right, Alec; you'll just have to believe it.'

'Well, I *might*,' he said, amused, 'if I hadn't just seen your husband on the Saxburgh road. I think I know a fellow with his tail between his legs when I see one. If that's *all right* then I'm a Dutchman. Besides, when I spoke to him, he . . .' Alec hesitated fractionally. 'Well, same again.'

'You spoke to him? What did you say?'

'Oh, nothing much,' Alec said; but she had him, unusually, on the back foot and he lost a little conviction. 'It wasn't anything really—'

Rose darted forward and seized Alec by the lapels of his coat. Physically strong, she shook him with the force of a man in a brawl. 'God damn you, Alec, what did you say to him?' she yelled, and her voice was not shrill but deep and fierce and dangerous.

'My God, Rose, it can't be that important,' he said, amazed.

'It is.' She loosened her grip, but her eyes held him just as tightly. 'Alec, it is.'

He let out a slow breath. 'It's . . . it's the real thing, then, eh?' he said, with a note of genuine sadness. 'You and the doctor . . . James.'

She nodded.

'H'm.' He took her hands gently away from his coat with his own, but did not linger in his touch. 'Look here, Rose, I did come here in good faith. Or hope anyway. What I mean is – what I said to him – I suppose I said it because I wanted it to be true.'

She did not take her eyes from his; it was he who at last looked away.

'What was it you said, Alec?'

'Well, damn it, I said that you and I were – you know – together. Damn it, Rose,' he said as she gave a cry, 'I didn't know – I mean I thought it was all up with you and him and so . . . Well, all right.' He held up his hands. 'I hoped it was. And so I said it. I swear to you I didn't mean any harm.'

'You never do, do you?' she said, almost neutrally, while her mind fastened with panicked intensity on her last sight of James. But *what* last sight? She had turned from him, and when she looked up he had gone.

And then on the road he had met Alec, who had told him . . .

Fear whirled through her. She began to tremble violently and she had to wrap her arms around herself as she said,

'When? Where did you see him?'

'Like I told you, on the road out of Saxburgh. He was just
. . . walking. I don't know how far he'd have got by now – West
Shipden maybe—'

'You can do something for me after all,' she said fixing her
eyes on him. 'But there's nothing in it for you. Do you
understand that, Alec? I'm not asking you to do this out of
love for me, or in memory of what there was between us, or
anything like that. Because that's just trash and you can forget
it.' She felt great fury – it seemed she had never known its
like; but it was on behalf of herself and James. Alec must not
even claim credit for rousing this feeling in her. 'I'm asking
you because you owe it to me – to me and James. You've caused
such hurt already and now you've made it a hundred times
worse and you'll pay that debt, Alec. I demand it. Drive me to
Shipden. I've got to see James, now. And so have you. You've
got to tell him you lied. You've got to tell him that was a stupid,
idle boast that you made up off the top of your head. Just like
all the rest of it. Because there hasn't been anything between
us since you left all those years ago – has there? If you're
going to tell James the truth, you're going to have to face it
yourself first. Face it, Alec.'

'Bit hard that, Rose,' he said, faintly. He could not quite
meet her gaze. 'Bit hard.'

'I don't care if it is. It's true. My God, Alec, don't you
see? I've got to go after him – I love James and I can't let
him go . . .'

'The way you let me go? Five years back?'

She nodded. 'Yes. I let you go; but James is different. Jealous,
Alec?'

'Perhaps I am a little.' His lips went tight and for a moment
she saw a little boy who did not like to lose; and a little boy,
too, who was ashamed of himself. He opened his mouth to
speak again, then snapped it shut and picked up his driving
gauntlets. 'All right. Tie a scarf or something round your head:
it'll be cold. You know, I don't have to do this—'

'No. But you have to live with yourself, don't you?'

He sighed, and as if he could hardly bear her to see him do it, half-turned away as he nodded his head.

It seemed to take an age to crank Alec's car; but once she was running he put his foot down and they lurched at speed away from the Arcadia, down the steep cliff road and on to the narrow coastal route that ran through the pine woods between Saxburgh and Shipden. It would have been hard to make her voice heard over the roar of the engine, but Rose did not want to speak anyhow: her mind was occupied with the single, burningly intense thought of James, and it seemed to throw out her desperate anxiety before it as the beam of the headlights was thrown on to the tree-shadowed darkness of the country road. Only randomly, dimly, did she notice that Alec was rather a loose and erratic driver.

'Rose!'

He had shouted to her over the noise of the engine.

'What?'

'I hope everything will be all right,' he said, glancing over at her. 'I do mean that.'

She didn't much care at that moment whether he meant it or was spinning another line: she just wished he would keep his eyes on the road.

'It will be if you come clean,' she shouted back.

He ground at the gears, and the car, chassis rattling, bucketed on the hummocky surface of the road. Bracing herself as best she could, Rose saw that Alec drove much as he went about most things – with bravura, hoping for the best. But there was more to it than that. From his frown, from the set of his jaw, she could tell that what she had said at the Arcadia had got to him, at last.

'You'd better slow down a bit,' she said loudly, as the car lurched again. The shapes of trees seemed to flicker past them, as if the woods were in frantic flight. The headlights seemed to cut such a small and insecure path through the darkness, like the tappings of a blind man's stick.

'What?'

'The road's so dark – be careful!' She was desperate to get to James, but the hurtling of the car through the roaring darkness was alarming. She found she was breathing in short gasps.

'Oh, it's all right . . . It must be really worth fighting for,' he said, turning his face to her again in frowning enquiry. 'What you have with James. That's what gets me . . .'

*Me*. Always *me*. She would have said something of this to him, if she had not been so anxious for him to keep his eyes on the road.

'Look where you're going,' she cried, trying to find a grip on the dashboard.

'It's all right, I tell you. I know how to drive . . .'

Turning his eyes back to the road he saw, simultaneously with Rose, the figure of James in the headlights, walking towards them. He was walking along the side of the road, but Alec's careless handling had brought the car looping over to that side too, and they were on a collision course.

Rose saw James jerk back, throwing up his hands in front of his face as the car bonnet sped towards him. Then Alec, with a retching gasp, spun the steering wheel a hundred and twenty degrees and they were flung in a lurching arc to the right, missing James by inches and plunging hectically right across the road and into the trees at the side.

For age-long moments the world was a nightmarish kaleidoscope. Trees and branches, slices of dark and light, capered before Rose's eyes as the car bounced hideously, relentlessly on. She was aware of blood in her mouth as her jaws clashed together, and of Alec helplessly gripping at the wheel as he was flung about beside her. Then the car gave an almighty stomach-loosening lurch over a hummock, and, as it tipped, the passenger door came open and Rose found herself flying – it was literally flight – out of the car. Wind shrieked in her ears and she saw the shapes of trees like horizontal bars in front of her eyes. Then she hit the grass in a clumsy, bone-jarring roll. When the roll stopped she was lying on her back and hearing, as if from the end of a long tunnel, a thunderous smash.

Shakily, she got to her feet, somehow managing the manoeuvre in spite of the fact that her legs seemed to be hollow tubes, and turned herself dizzily about. Thirty feet away into the trees Alec's car, stationary and smoking, was crushed against the trunk of a fir, looking bizarrely and horribly as if it had tried to burrow into it. There was a searing smell and silence, except for a peculiarly obscene hissing sound of escaping petrol. And then the car began to burn – swiftly, it seemed, as a great candle being lit – the orange flames throwing the shapes of the surrounding trees into sudden unearthly relief and also illuminating the figure of James.

He was running towards the car, swiftly and silently. He did not stop when he got near it but, ducking his head, plunged in through the smoke and flames, until Rose could not see him.

She started screaming his name and staggering towards the burning car. But neither her throat nor her legs seemed to have any efficiency: the screams sounded to her own ears like a long hoarse whisper and she did not seem to be getting any nearer to the car.

She must have, though, because she was close enough to feel the heat of the flames on her face when a figure emerged from the smoke, a strange monstrous waddling figure that seemed to be dragging a great tail strenuously after it. It came nearer to Rose and took on the form of James – James grunting, heaving, blackened like a miner, pulling the motionless body of Alec clear with forearms tucked under Alec's armpits and, at last, with a kind of barking whoop of exhaustion, setting him down on the grass.

'James!'

Suddenly her voice found volume, her legs strength, and she lurched to hold him where he knelt beside Alec. 'Your coat – quickly . . .' It was smouldering, and she dragged it off his back and hurled it aside. She saw his hands dark red and blistered. 'My darling . . . Oh, God . . .'

'Are you all right?' he demanded, holding her with weak, stiff arms. 'Yes? You sure . . .?'

On the ground, Alec's chin went up and he coughed, wide-mouthed like a child; then he was sick on the grass. Bending low, James ran swift professional hands over his body, peeled back his eyelids, then dug a finger into his mouth to clear the last of the sickness.

Alec's hair and clothes were scorched, his hands were burnt, and his eyebrows were gone. That seemed to be the extent of it. Coughing, groaning, he sat up a little and looked down at himself, then up at James; then twisted his head to see the burning car.

'My God,' Alec said, 'my God. I don't believe it. Charmed life.' He coughed again. 'Need a smoke, I think . . . You all right, Doc? Rose? My God . . . I thought that was my lot . . . I'll tell you something, Doc,' he said, reaching out and gripping James's arm, 'you deserve a bloody medal.'

James sat back on his haunches, wiping his hands on his handkerchief.

'Are you going to present me with one?' he said hoarsely.

'Would if I could, old man,' Alec said with a weak laugh. He looked up at Rose. 'What I can give you is . . . the truth. Afraid I've been a bad boy. What I said to you earlier – about me and Rose. Not true. It was mischief, I'm afraid. Just like . . . the way I've been carrying on lately. Rose made it clear to me right from the word go that I wasn't wanted but I . . . I kept meddling.' He hung his head and coughed again. 'Not a pretty story. I'm sorry. Wish you'd left me in the car now?'

James looked at him, then at Rose.

'If it comes to medals,' he said, 'I think there's only one person who deserves one.'

# FORTY-EIGHT

Walking wounded, Alec made his way back to the Arcadia supported by Rose and James on each side.

Millie was as resilient as ever, but while she didn't mind the public parlour becoming an impromptu treatment room she would not let James do the treating. He had suffered some burns himself, and she made the three of them sit tight while she sent for the old Saxburgh doctor. He roused himself reluctantly from his lethargy, came and bandaged James and Alec's hands, told Alec to rest up, gave Rose a cursory examination, and seemed to think it all a great fuss about nothing.

He also gave Alec, however, a soporific painkiller which made him quickly drowsy; so Millie made up a room for him for the night and despatched him upstairs, shakily supported by the Captain, who, under the impression that Alec had been bombed by a Zeppelin, commiserated with him and told him that they would beat the Huns in the end.

'Thank you, Millie,' Rose said. 'I'm sorry about all this.'

Millie smiled. 'Makes a change to fill the vacancies,' she said. 'You know you're both welcome to stay the night, too, don't you?'

Rose and James glanced at each other.

'Well, think on it,' Millie said. 'Elizabeth, will you come and help me make us all a nice cup of tea?'

Elizabeth had clung to James ever since he had come to the Arcadia, and had even hung about, wincing in sympathy, while his hands were being bandaged; but now, at a smiling

405

nod from Rose, she left them alone in the parlour.

Flexing her bruised limbs, Rose looked at James sitting in the wing chair opposite her. He had cleaned his face up and did not look in pain, but her heart still ached to see the bandages on his hands.

'They'll soon clear up,' he said, observing her eyes.

'You've got such beautiful hands,' she said, and found herself weeping, quietly, almost composedly, and without pain.

When her eyes cleared and she looked up, James was sitting on the settee beside her.

'You were on your way back,' she said.

'Yes. I was coming back. What Alec said – I just didn't believe it, even then. Finally,' he added, shaking his head ruefully. 'So I turned round and came back. To have another go.'

He made it sound like a small and simple action, but she knew it was not. He had not just turned round on a dark road: he had made a vast leap, the leap of faith.

There was as great a momentousness in that as in his pulling Alec from the burning car.

'I was coming to find you,' she said. 'I thought – I was afraid—'

'No,' he said, making a hushing motion.

'I wanted you to come back,' she said, her face wet with tears. 'Oh, James, I wanted you to come back.'

'I'm here,' he said. He made an impatient gesture with his bandaged hands. 'I wish I could wipe away those tears.'

'You can,' she said.

She held her face up to him. He kissed the tears, his lips dry and soft.

'I suppose we should give Millie an answer,' he said.

'It's nice of her to offer,' Rose said, touching his face. 'But I'd rather go home.'

# Kitty Rainbow

## Wendy Robertson

When the soft-hearted bare-knuckle fighter Ishmael Slaughter rescues an abandoned baby from the swirling River Wear, he knows that if he takes her home his employer will give her short shrift – or worse. So it is to Janine Druce, a draper woman with a dubious reputation but a child of her own, that he takes tiny Kitty Rainbow.

Kitty grows up wild, coping with Janine's bouts of drunkenness and her son's silent strangeness. And she is as fierce in her affections as she is in her hatreds, saving her greatest love for Ishmael, the ageing boxer who provides the only link with her parentage, a scrap of cloth she was wrapped in when he found her. Kitty realises that she cannot live her life wondering who her mother was, and in Ishmael she has father enough. And, when she finds herself pregnant, deprived of the livelihood on which she and the old man depended, she must worry about the future, not the past. But the past has a way of catching the present unawares . . .

'An intense and moving story set against the bitter squalor of the hunger-ridden thirties' *Today*

'A rich fruit cake of well-drawn characters . . .' *Northern Echo*

'Fans of big family stories must read Wendy Robertson' *Peterborough Evening Telegraph*

'A lovely book' *Woman's Realm*

0 7472 5183 5

HEADLINE

# Cradle of Thorns

## Josephine Cox

Nell Reece has never known her mother and her father's burden of guilt about his wife has kept him cowed for years, working as a common labourer on his sister's farm. For all her aunt's spiteful attempts to break Nell's independent spirit, she has never succeeded. But now Nell, pregnant and alone, is forced to leave behind the men in her life, believing she might never be able to return.

With little but the clothes she wears and a tatty horse and cart, she travels across the Bedfordshire countryside of 1890; a journey fraught with hazards for a vulnerable young woman. When she encounters a scruffy urchin called Kit, a ten-year-old orphan who's lived his whole life on the street, she takes him under her wing. The pair become devoted friends, never knowing where their journey will take them, but each aware that the time will come when there must be a reckoning.

'A born storyteller' *Bedfordshire Times*

'Hailed quite rightly as a gifted writer in the tradition of Catherine Cookson' *Manchester Evening News*

'Pulls at the heartstrings' *Today*

'Driven and passionate, she stirs a pot spiced with incest, wife-beating . . . and murder' *The Sunday Times*

0 7472 4957 1

**HEADLINE**

If you enjoyed this book here is a selection of other bestselling titles from Headline

Headline books are available at your local bookshop or newsagent. Alternatively, books can be ordered direct from the publisher. Just tick the titles you want and fill in the form below. Prices and availability subject to change without notice.

Buy four books from the selection above and get free postage and packaging and delivery within 48 hours. Just send a cheque or postal order made payable to Bookpoint Ltd to the value of the total cover price of the four books. Alternatively, if you wish to buy fewer than four books the following postage and packaging applies:

UK and BFPO £4.30 for one book; £6.30 for two books; £8.30 for three books.

Overseas and Eire: £4.80 for one book; £7.10 for 2 or 3 books (surface mail)

Please enclose a cheque or postal order made payable to *Bookpoint Limited*, and send to: Headline Publishing Ltd, 39 Milton Park, Abingdon, OXON OX14 4TD, UK.
Email Address: orders@bookpoint.co.uk

If you would prefer to pay by credit card, our call team would be delighted to take your order by telephone. Our direct line 01235 400 414 (lines open 9.00 am–6.00 pm Monday to Saturday 24 hour message answering service). Alternatively you can send a fax on 01235 400 454.

Name .......................................................................................

Address .......................................................................................

.......................................................................................

.......................................................................................

If you would prefer to pay by credit card, please complete:
Please debit my Visa/Access/Diner's Card/American Express (delete as applicable) card number:

| | | | | | | | | | | | | | | | |
|---|---|---|---|---|---|---|---|---|---|---|---|---|---|---|---|

Signature ...................................................... Expiry Date ..............